Out on a Limb

HANNAH BONAM-YOUNG

Author's Note

& Content Warnings

Only five days after my first child was born, I posted the following caption on Instagram...

"The only thing I have ever thought I couldn't do with one hand was be a good mom. It might not be rational, but every time I heard some cliché comment about moms needing an 'extra set of hands,' it would make my stomach churn. Growing up, there were often times when adults wouldn't let me hold their babies out of fear, and at some point, I took that to heart. I have held on to this insecurity, and I didn't really address it until this week. Now, I'd like to say that ten fingers are overrated, because this kid and I have got a good thing going on so far."

I had been a mother for less than a week, and yet I felt as if I'd experienced every possible human emotion under the sun. I was physically and mentally recovering from a traumatic labour experience and difficult pregnancy. My nipples hurt, my body ached, and I was *convinced* my vagina would *never* be the same. And yet... I was *so, so* ridiculously happy.

Not just because of the tiny baby we'd brought home (who's pretty great), but because I was wrong to be afraid. Because *they* were wrong. I was absolutely capable of being a good mother.

I, like Win, was born with my limb difference. I have a less-developed right hand that is identical to Win's as described in this book. And while I've tried my best throughout my life to not let it hold me back, it has certainly created challenges. I've always found myself attempting to perform things in private that I'll be expected to do in public. Things as small as buttoning a new pair of pants or typing to take notes in class. I've spent hours upon hours thinking through daily obstacles, coming up with small adjustments, and planning out my days in agonising detail in order to avoid any awkwardness or failure. Then, I found out I was pregnant, and suddenly I felt totally and completely unprepared. I knew that nothing could prepare me for what came next, and I was terrified...

I wanted to write a book for anyone who's let fear of failure slow them down. Not just for those of us who choose to have kids, or those of us who are disabled, but for anyone who's been thrust into something new that took them so far out of their comfort zone they no longer recognised their past, afraid self. I wanted to write something about two people who love each other so much that they're able to change the negative thought patterns they've held on to and embrace their differences fully. Where love is shown to be validating, kind, considerate, joyful, patient, and gentle.

In this book, Win goes on a journey to motherhood via pregnancy. Because her pregnancy is entirely unexpected, I chose to include conversations between Win, her medical team, and her support system about the option of abortion. It's worth noting that this book is set in Canada, where rights to abortion are not currently under threat as they are elsewhere, and therefore, her options are less limited. Ultimately, Win chooses to keep her baby, but it felt necessary to include those discussions, given that the fundamental right to access safe, legal abortions is being challenged near constantly. Win's choice is not superior, nor is she pressured into it. Win's choice is just that. *Her choice.*

To end this note, I just want to say that I know that pregnancy in romance novels is a hot topic. It's not for everyone, and that's perfectly okay. But this book is a lot more than a one-night stand turned baby. It's about learning to let someone see the messy, needier parts of you. It's learning to be loved well as you are and accept help. It's about challenging expectations and overcoming obstacles. It's **disabled joy**. Which we all need to see more of, if you ask me.

I hope you love Bo and Win as much as I do.

All my love,

Hannah Bonam-Young

Content Warnings: Graphic sexual content, pregnancy and symptoms of pregnancy, brief discussion of abortion (pro-choice stance, not performed), ableism in reference to a limb difference, verbally abusive ex-partner (no reappearance), death of a parent (past, off page) depression and suicide (past, off page), cancer (past, not reoccurring), amputation (past, off page).

For Ben, for always being my right hand man.
I'm sorry you'll never win at rock, paper, scissors.
I love you.

CHAPTER 1

"Did you know this song might be about an orgy?" I ask the witch standing next to the punch bowl, pointing toward the speaker.

"What?" she shouts, using tar-black talons to pull her willowy silver wig away from her ear.

"The song—'Monster Mash.'" I point toward the speaker again.

"What about it?" she asks, louder.

"An orgy!" I yell just as the music comes to an abrupt stop—my friend and host of the evening, Sarah, hopping onto a dining chair to address her guests.

"No, thanks..." Witch woman sends daggers my way as she slowly turns around and walks, funnily enough, toward the archway decorated in bloodied weapons.

"You should be so lucky," I mutter under my breath as I fill my cup with an undisclosed neon-green substance, avoiding the floating candied eyeballs successfully.

Sarah, my lifelong best friend, is giving her yearly *thank you so much for coming to my Halloween party; it's the only thing I care about* speech while I'm debating about whether anyone is secretly keeping track of how many hot-dog-mummies I've eaten thus far.

Nah. And so I reach for another.

"Aye-aye Captain Winnifred!"

Fuck, I've been spotted. I drop the mummy into my drink and cover the top of my cup with my hand.

"You okay?" Caleb, Sarah's husband, asks, eyeing my cup with suspicion.

"Never been better," I chime sweetly. "It's another successful year," I say, admiring their home, decorated with professional precision.

Caleb does the same, and when his expression turns to subtle pride and admiration for his wife's work, I place a bet to the universe that the next three words out of his mouth will be...

"Anything Sarah wants," we say in unison. He smiles into the top of his beer with a hint of guilty shyness, but mostly resolve. Sarah and Caleb met in the ninth grade. He's been carrying her textbooks, literally and metaphorically, since.

I love Caleb. He's like a brother to me. A brother-in-law if Sarah and I were *actually* sisters like we used to boldly claim (see: lie) in school. Turns out, according to a DNA test a few years back, we're fourth cousins once removed. Sarah simply says we're cousins now, when given the chance.

"You know, my friend Robbie is here. I thought I might introduce you," Caleb says after a long sip of his beer.

Yeah, absolutely not.

I've been successfully avoiding the guys Caleb wants to set me up with since my date with his buddy from work. Winston cried while describing his—*very much alive*—mother and the "beautiful bond" they shared. He also brought me an orchid, which could have been a sweet gesture—I do love plants. Unfortunately, it was in a large ceramic bowl with rocks and bark, and it weighed a ton. I couldn't just put it on the ground, lest a server trip over it and meet an untimely death, so it had to sit on the table between us—blocking our view of one another. Then, after a dull dinner, I had to carry it home with me, clinging to it in the back of the taxi as I wrote a kind but firm *let's not do this again* text.

If anything, that date only solidified my desire to remain casual and stick to dating apps where I could properly vet the men for myself.

"Maybe later," I answer Caleb. "I'm just waiting to talk to our hostess." I tilt my chin toward Sarah, who's dressed as the Princess Buttercup to Caleb's Westley.

"Okay, fine. This one is different, though. He even has a dead mom," Caleb adds far too excitedly.

"Oh, bonus!" I say, matching his energy. "I love when their mom is dead. It makes things so much easier around the holidays."

Caleb laughs, turning to fill a cup with lime punch. "Here." He holds it out to me before taking my mummified drink and tossing it into the trash can. "Eat however much you want, Win."

I take the drink, leaning toward him. "That might be the sexiest thing you have ever said to me, Caleb."

Just then, someone slaps my ass. "Is he flirting with you again? God, I've told you both so many times—if you're going to have an affair, at least be discreet."

"Buttercup! So nice of you to join us," I say, smiling broadly.

"Love the costume... again." Sarah sighs, pointing with a limp wrist to my elaborate pirate get-up.

"Until I grow a hand, this will still be prime comedy." I jab her boob with my hook until she giggles, swatting me away.

"We have to go talk to a bunch of people, but do you want to sleep over tonight? I made up the spare bedroom and—"

"Yes, I will help clean up. I do it every year, babe," I interrupt. "Go! Entertain your masses."

Sarah jumbles the words *thank-you-you're-the-best* into one long sequence as she tugs Caleb away like an extremely willing puppy on a leash.

"Great costumes," an exceptionally drunk woman dressed as a red crayon slurs, walking toward me. The blue crayon next to her adds, "Think you might win the couples' contest," as they pass by.

Couples costume? Me? Single Winnie? Puh-lease.

They must have mistaken Caleb for a pirate and my betrothed. Westley was the Dread Pirate Roberts, after all. So it's not a far-off presumption. But my pirate style is a lot more of your classic wench-whore. My boobs are practically earrings at this height, and my fishnet stockings are ripped from years of re-wear, giving them the perfect *accidentally* slutty look. My waist is cinched with a wide pleather belt, and I've tied a red bandanna around my shoulder-length black hair. That's a new addition after my accompanying pirate's hat was lost during last year's debauchery. May she rest in peace.

I will keep wearing this costume until the joke gets old. That wasn't a lie. But it's also because—let's be real—I look hot in it.

Additionally, I'm too broke to buy something new. But let's not talk about that.

There's another layer of Sarah's genius. Lock down the cutest computer geek as early as possible, make them fall madly in love with you, and then wait for them to become filthy rich. Now Sarah's the fun friend full time. Party hostess, event planner, voracious reader, a childless housewife with a maid. She's currently trying to decide between themes for *my* thirtieth birthday party, which still isn't for another eighteen months.

"Pardon me?" a low, sardonic voice calls from behind me, making me turn.

Oh, *there* he is. The other pirate I've been unknowingly paired with. Though this one, I would certainly not make walk the plank.

My first thought? He's tall. Really tall. As if his body was stretched out with a rolling pin before being placed into whatever magical golden boy oven he was baked in. He's got that tousled, nineties-boy-band, middle-parted hair that's suddenly back in style. It's dark blond, which I can choose to forgive. He has a crooked smile that says *get out while you can* under a not-crooked but rugged nose and soft eyes. The juxtaposition of which is strikingly adorable.

"I'm so sorry," he says without any sincerity, "but one of us has to change."

"Oh my god," I say, flattening my skirt before resting my hands on my waist. "This is so embarrassing... What are the odds?"

"Right? I mean there's no way either of us is winning the singles costume contest this way and"—he leans in to whisper by bending over at the waist, and he's *still* taller than me—"I'm not wearing anything under this."

I fight the laugh, not wanting this bit to end. I so rarely get a new sparring partner. Never one this cute.

"Well, that's unfortunate. You should have planned better. I have a few costumes under this one."

The corner of his lip twitches, but he seems to resist giving me any reaction beyond that. Challenge accepted.

"Such as?" he asks, crossing his arms over his chest.

"A Viking," I answer.

"Now that you mention it, I do see a horn peeking out just a little." He motions to the side of my head with a bent finger.

"That's actually standard issue for all of Satan's spawn, but I could see how you got confused."

"Concerning. What else?"

"A sexy maid, of course," I say, batting my lashes.

"Well, that I have to see," he quips back far too quickly.

Here, I think, is where I win the laugh-off we're pretending not to have. Shock value always wins.

"But I must insist on keeping the pirate costume, I'm afraid. You see"—I let go of the hook's inner handle and pull it away in my left hand, revealing my smaller, less-developed right hand underneath—"I am in need of a hook." I wave at him mockingly, my tiny, curled fingers, shorter than the first knuckle, waggling as best as they can.

He doesn't break like I want him to. But he *does* grin mischievously. His eyes crackle with humour, pulling me in at a concerning speed. I'd be frustrated if his expression wasn't so damn intriguing. Something about his amusement signals that, perhaps, he's one step ahead of me.

"Oh, I see. Well, then... maybe we can come to some sort of compromise." He sticks out his foot between us.

You've got to be joking.

CHAPTER 2

He's got a prosthetic leg. It's covered, loosely, in a vinyl sticker made to look like wood, the kind you'd use to line your kitchen shelves, giving the illusion of a pirate's peg-leg underneath black trousers he has tied up at the knee with thin, corded leather rope.

"God dammit!" I yell. Which finally gets him to laugh. And it's a great one too. A hearty, deep, boisterous sound from the back of his throat that makes his jaw tense and his neck jump. Uninhibited. And, dare I say, sexy.

"I really felt like I was going to win this round," I say, my voice unsteady.

He hasn't stopped laughing—harder than I am, actually. I'm not used to that, and it's honestly refreshing. I've been told I laugh obnoxiously loud. Some have even gone so far as to compare me to a baby seal calling for its mother. *Some* meaning more than one person—in two separate instances—have expressed that exact sentiment.

"This is a couple's costume. The crayons were right," I say through breathless fits of joy.

He clutches his chest as if to steady himself, his laughter finally beginning to die down. Then I'm treated to the view of a boyish, tilted smile and sincere eyes sweeping over me from head to toe and back again.

I wonder if he likes what he sees. Actually, I'm *hoping* he likes what he sees. Because I certainly like what he's got going on. The longer he looks me up and down, the more I consider him approving of my appearance.

My black not-quite-straight but not-quite-curly shoulder-length hair. My thin eyebrows from merciless plucking in my teenage years. My sharp-edged nose, with a simple gold piercing on the left nostril, set between glacier blue eyes. My body is shoved and tucked into this costume to prop up my tits and shrink my waist, but that's mostly illusion.

I would describe my frame as fairly average. I enjoy long walks, swimming, and dancing, but I equally love rainy days plastered to the couch, pastries, and overly sweetened coffees. My arms and back are strong and sculpted from years of training in butterfly and breast strokes, but my hips and stomach hold the pleasure of a well-fed, comfortable woman. I don't try to force my body to be something or deprive it of pleasantries. It just *is*. And I like it, *enough*, as is.

But what does this seemingly perfect specimen before me look like on an average day? He strikes me as someone who grew up beautiful. The small tilt of arrogance of his chin combined with the naive sweetness in his smile that I wish wasn't so disarming. He's probably a foot taller than me, and I can't help but wonder how hard I'd have to yank on his pleated pirate blouse to bring his lips down to mine.

"I'm Bo." He extends his left hand—which my body hears as *would you like me to fuck you?* Because there's nothing more awkward than shaking with my right hand and *nothing* more attractive than a man who could have anticipated that.

I shake his hand enthusiastically. "Win."

"Is that short for something?" he asks, dropping his hand and sliding it into his trouser pocket.

"Winnifred, but no one really calls me that. What about you?" I make a point to emphasise the stretch of my neck, staring up at him as if he's some sort of fairy-tale giant. "Are you tall for something?"

He can't *stop* laughing now. I can't stop wanting to make him.

"What?" he asks, eyes lit with enjoyment.

"Seriously, what are you? Nine feet tall?"

"Six."

"Six *what* though?"

"Six-five."

"Wildly unnecessary for daily life. Do you play basketball?"

"Eh, used to." His smile falters only a touch—but I notice. I notice, too, that he—perhaps subconsciously—moves to rub his knee, just above where his prosthesis begins.

I wince. "Sorry," I offer plainly. "I was born with my hand. So I stupidly forget other people—"

"No worries," he interrupts me, smiling with his chin pushed out.

"I ruined that. But this was nice before then, wasn't it?"

He looks away, smirking yet visibly shy, his eyes shifting and his body softly swaying. "It can still be nice. I could even the score? Make fun of your hand, if you'd like?" he offers, clearly unserious.

"Yes, please do. That would actually help a lot," I say, calling his bluff.

He turns to face me, staring me down with crescent eyes and an ever-growing smile that has the blood rushing to the surface of my skin. I raise a brow in challenge when he appears to be calculating his next steps, his head tilting to the side.

"All right." Bo holds out his palm, then crooks two fingers, gesturing for me to move closer. "Let me see it then."

I narrow my eyes on him playfully as I present my smaller hand to him, placing it in his open palm that is about double the size of mine. I swallow on impact, the brushing of our skin shooting sparks up my veins.

"Shit..." he whispers under his breath, turning it over with a grip on my wrist that I *love*. "It's adorable," he says, studying it intently. Then he tuts and lets go, practically tossing it aside. "What am I supposed to say?"

"Right?" I agree, throwing both arms up in the air. "It's impossible to make fun of. It's too damn cute. It's official. I've ruined the evening."

"The best I had was a sarcastic 'nice hand, *Finding Nemo*,' but that's sort of endearing, isn't it?"

"He's an icon," I agree.

"I loved that little fish." He rubs the back of his neck, looking past the archway and hallway to our left. "Want to sit?"

I nod, leading the way to the tufted yellow two-seater couch in Sarah's den. The walls are covered in Sarah's many books and maps of various lakes up in Northern Ontario. It's a cottage-inspired room. Because rich people have themed parties *and* rooms.

"So how do you know Sarah and Caleb?" I ask, curling my legs under me to face him. This close to Bo, I can see that his eyes are hazel with the smallest smattering of green. He's got more stubble than I originally noticed, but that's because it's fairer than his hair. He also smells *very* good. Like cinnamon and something else that's musky and warm and delicious. Like someone who could build a campfire and bake me a birthday cake too.

I keep studying him unabashedly. I can't help it, so I don't resist. And, eventually, when my eyes leave his *surprisingly* attractive collection of costume rings below his black painted nails, I realise he's looking straight down my blouse. He's doing some unabashed admiring of his own.

I smile to myself, pride lifting my shoulders and, in turn, my chest. I give him a few more seconds of leering before I clear my throat delicately.

"Sorry." He shakes himself. "What did you say?" He blinks like a caught, guilty man.

"Shameless!" I cry out, laughing. "You *ogled* me."

He chuckles nervously. "I know, fuck, sorry. I've never—well, I've never forgotten to pretend I'm not checking someone out before." He cringes bashfully, the corner of his lips still upturned.

"This costume has an intended purpose." I shrug, fiddling with the hem of my skirt.

"I really am sorry. I'm not—"

"How do they look?" I ask, interrupting him.

He looks up to the ceiling as if he's searching for some deity to help him handle me. I like that a lot.

I watch as a slow smile forms, the corner of his bottom lip tucked between his teeth. "They, like every other part of you, look great," he says slowly. Now it's his turn to clear his throat when I'm left blushing with my eyes stuck on his face. "But... what *did* you ask?"

I fumble, forgetting everything I said. But when I look around the room, blinking until I focus on my surroundings, I remember whose house I'm in and, therefore, what I asked. "How do you know Sarah and Caleb?"

Bo shuffles back against the couch, his hand playing mindlessly with the loose, ruffled collar of his shirt, tugging it away from his neck. "Caleb and I met through a mutual friend about six years ago. We reconnected earlier this year for a work thing. He's a good guy. What about you?"

"I've known Sarah my whole life. Our moms were best friends in high school and they both got knocked up accidentally during their senior year. They raised us together as pseudo-siblings."

"Damn, so you've known Caleb since—"

"Grade nine, yeah," I interrupt. "We all went to the same high school. I've been third wheelin' ever since."

"Third wheeling," he repeats. "So, you're not..." His smile quirks to one side. "I was going to ask if you were here with anyone, but let me rephrase. Is there someone who would deck me for checking you out the way I just did?"

"Nope." I cover my smile with a curled pointer finger, tracing my knuckle along my lip before I gather my confidence once again. "No one. Here or in *any* room." That sounded a lot more suggestive than I intended, but it works in my favour when I notice his smile inching back up and his eyes darting to my lips for a second.

"Any room." He nods, chin tilted up. "Noted."

"What about you? Have a girlfriend I should know about?" I ask before swallowing.

He looks offended that I'd even suggest such a thing, his brows jolting upward. "No!"

"You'd not be the first unavailable guy to act totally available," I argue. My ex, for one, did that often.

"Fair." He settles down. "No, no girlfriend. Here or in *any* room," he taunts.

"Right." I get comfortable, leaning against the couch—pushing my breasts together, which Bo briefly makes note of. "Then... tell me about yourself. Who are you?"

"Why does that question always feel so intimidating?" He brushes his knuckles against his cheek, swiping his thumb along his jaw.

"Because human experience cannot be summed up in a few sentences," I offer, "but it's still polite to try."

He nods, side-eyeing me in a totally curious, stirring way that seems effortless to him despite the way it makes my heart pound. "Fair enough," he begins. "I'm twenty-nine. I'm a financial analyst." He puts up a hand, as if to stop me from interrupting—which I *was* going to. "I know, it's a riveting career choice, but I actually love it." He scratches his nose with the back of his thumb, looking sideways across the room. "I'm an only child," he adds. "My father lives in France, so I don't see him all that often. But he's, rather pathetically, my best friend. My mother passed away when I was young." He laughs dryly, as if maybe he's unsure of whether he's oversharing.

"Uh... I worked as a barista through university, and it made me agonisingly pretentious about coffee. When I was a teenager, I read a book about healthy brain habits, and now I do a sudoku puzzle every day because I'm paranoid about my brain rotting. My favourite animals are dogs, but I've never had one as a pet. Um, my favourite colour is purple?" he asks, as if he's unsure of where to stop.

"That was great, thank you," I say.

"Yeah? I pass?"

"Yes, very informative. Though I do have some follow-up questions."

"Don't you have to tell me about yourself first?" Bo asks, raising one brow.

"Oh, right, okay," I say, reaching for the cup that I placed on the table in front of us.

Bo waits for me to speak, his eyes intently focused as he leans farther against the back of the couch.

"I'm twenty-eight." I take a sip of my drink. "I work at a café, so I'm *also* a bit of a coffee snob. I work as a lifeguard seasonally, which I love. I'd spend my whole life outdoors if I could. My mother used to affectionately refer to me as her pet squirrel because of that *and* because I tend to hoard things. Currently, that's plants. My mom lives in Florida now with a string of boyfriends who are nice enough... I try to visit her once a year, but we aren't exactly close. I never met my dad. And..." I try to think of one last thing. "Oh, *my* favourite colour is green."

"Well, it's good to meet you, Fred."

"Please don't call me that," I say forcibly, half joking.

"What? Why not?" He looks comically offended.

"It's not a particularly sexy name," I say. "Winnifred is bad enough, but *Fred*? I sound like the creepy uncle you don't invite to Thanksgiving."

"Agree to disagree."

"Imagine crying out 'Fred' in the bedroom." His smirk grows, and I glare at him, deciding to make my point clear. "Oh, Fred." I moan. "Yes, Fred!" I cry, probably a bit too loudly, in fake passion. "It's awful." A few of the other party guests, confused and perhaps the tiniest bit offended, turn toward us. I salute them before they go back to their own conversations, my eyes held on Bo.

It's horribly cliché, but his smile is beaming—far brighter than the sun. I feel myself bloom with it, as if it's my own personal version of photosynthesis.

"Why are you looking at me like that?" I ask, feeling suddenly shy.

"You're funny," he says matter-of-factly, his expression remaining.

Huh.

I do my best to look around the room, pretending the other guests and their costumes are suddenly much more interesting to me. I'm hyperaware that I'm blushing at the compliment and wishing, desperately, that I could stop.

When I do finally look back, Bo's attention is focused on the back of the tufted couch. With his hand around the top of my seat, the tip of his thumb traces one of the fabric buttons in a small, circular motion over and over.

I shouldn't be affected by it, and I'll deny it if ever confronted, but there's something inherently sexual about the motion. I watch, feeling far too enraptured, as he circles the button tenderly. My throat tenses as my lips part, imagining his thumb working *me* over in a similar way. It's been months since a date went well enough that I allowed a man to touch me like that—not that it was all that great when he did. Still, judging by the rattling of stuttered breaths in my chest, I think I'd let Bo give it a try.

"So," Bo says, dragging my gaze from the button toward his face, "you're not here with anyone..."

"Is that a question?" I ask, regaining my voice with a noticeable rasp.

He rolls his eyes. I like that too.

"I suppose," he elongates the word, "the question is: why?"

"Oh, so we've gotten to the *what are your faults?* part of the evening?" I ask.

"I was thinking more along the lines of *how is someone like you single?* but *sure*," he says.

"Ah, well, thanks." Despite my sarcasm, I feel my face heat again and curse myself for it. Three blushes in one evening? It has to be a record. One that I hope to never beat. "Honestly, the answer isn't all that interesting. I'm just not looking for anything permanent. I've been told by Sarah that I'm independent to a fault."

What I don't say is that I grew up watching my mom bring home loser after loser, knowing damn well we'd all be better off without them. It only took her boyfriends a few weeks into dating before they started acting like they had some sort of authority over her—*our*—life. They usually started off small, like my mom's favourite brand of coffee being switched out for their preference. Then it slowly escalated. Our soap-opera evening marathons became *well, sweetie, the game is on. Why don't you go finish up your homework in your room?* Or *no, we're not having tacos tonight. Insert-boyfriend's-name-here doesn't like them.* Then, eventually, they'd leave, and we'd reset. Sarah, her mom, and I would enjoy the brief interim before Mom's next man came through, and then we'd look after Mom when that inevitably went to shit again. Because of this, I learned quickly that in order to preserve the life I wanted, I had to avoid inviting a man in.

But, like most hopeless-romantic idiots, I forgot my self-appointed golden rule in my early twenties and moved in with my boyfriend Jack—who wanted *everything* his way and didn't care how he had to act to have it. That, of course, also ended terribly. I've been picking up the pieces since. My self-esteem and life plans are still, mostly, in shambles.

"What about you?" I ask. "In search of a wife?"

"No." Bo laughs out, his eyes flicking up to the ceiling momentarily. "I am not."

"Well, that's certainly... compatible." I chew my bottom lip, hoping he catches my not-so-subtle suggestion.

He catches it, all right, and stares at me a little *too* long. To the point where I start to feel my heartbeat pulsating in my neck. I wanted this response, sure, but for some reason, from Bo, it feels a little overwhelming. Perhaps it's the way his eyes search my face like he's trying to place me. Like we've met before. Or maybe as if he can't believe we haven't.

Whatever this *look* is, I need it to stop. It's causing too much blood to rush to my head—making me warm and flustered and dizzy.

"I like your pirate's leg," I say in a truly horrific attempt to take the attention off me. "I-I meant—your costume. Not just your leg, obviously. The whole thing," I say, floundering.

"Oh, well, good. I was worried you only wanted me for my leg for a second," he teases.

I choose to ignore his flippant use of the words *wanted me* and take a sharp turn away from my blunder. "Has that happened to you yet?" I ask, reaching for my drink, praying it can cool me off. "I got a doozy of a message last week on Instagram. Reese24 told me his dick would look huge in my *baby-hand*."

"Oh my god." Bo's face distorts as he laughs in horror.

"Yep."

"That's so many layers of fucked-up."

"Truly."

"But..." Bo lifts two palms, mimicking a tilting scale.

"No," I say, punctuated by a shocked laugh. "No. Don't you dare."

"I *mean*," his eyes turn teasing as he shrugs, "he's right. It probably would."

"Oh my god."

"It would do a great deal for the ego. Reese24 may be onto something."

"Awful," I sputter through a laugh. "You're both awful." I curl my lips up to my nose like the room stinks as Bo sits back comfortably, his arm once again resting behind me.

We continue to make small talk for enough time that Sarah's playlist has now replayed 'Monster Mash' twice. Bo laughs at my theory around the song, unlike witch woman, and eventually decides he'll need to do his own research with a thoughtful analysis of the lyrics once he gets home. The party is starting to die down when our conversation does too. A slow fade to contented quiet and a third round of drinks fetched by me.

But, oddly enough, our lull in conversation isn't uncomfortable. I've been on plenty of dates where the banter stops flowing and it's easier to either call it quits or take things back to someone's apartment than it is to wait for the next quippy exchange to roll in. But tonight, there's no shortage of topics and no fear of some forced, humourless conversation.

These quiet reprieves feel more like intermissions. As if we're performing for each other. Taking turns being the entertainment and the entertained. Keeping each other laughing. Keeping each other guessing. It's *fun*, and part of me wishes we had more time before Sarah and Caleb decide to kick everyone out for the night. But *maybe* I could convince him to stay a little longer.

Given everything I've learned about Bo so far, I'll have to take the lead. He's so completely unaware of his own charm it's comical. He's shy, almost. I could see him asking for my number, but I doubt he'd be bold enough to ask me back to his place. Which, I've decided, is what I want to do.

"Is this a wig?"

I don't notice until I feel the back of Bo's finger brush my cheek, but he's holding a strand of my hair between his thumb and pointer finger, twiddling it mindlessly.

"No, that's all me." I gulp as his thumb grazes the underside of my chin.

He continues twisting my hair through his fingers, curling it around the backs of his knuckles as if it's a snake he's charmed. I fight the urge to crawl into his lap and purr.

"Sorry," he whispers, wetting his lips. I notice that he doesn't let go, however.

"I don't mind," I answer softly. What I *should* say is: keep touching me. Anywhere you'd like.

"It's beautiful," he tells me, looking at me with an unsteadying lack of humour. He releases my hair and leans back, taking a long breath that flares his nostrils. "I've had too much punch, probably."

"I really didn't mind." I lean in, trying to catch his gaze. Attempting to plea with him, silently, to ask for more. But it's no use.

He's so gorgeous, yet clearly oblivious of that fact. It's as endearing as it is frustrating.

So I decide enough is enough. I can take charge. I'm a modern woman, dammit. I can go after what I want, even if I don't exactly practise that concept in my daily life. I can do *this*.

"Bo, would you like to go upstairs with me?" I ask, my voice a touch louder than intended after forcing myself to speak with confidence.

His eyes widen in surprise, and his head tilts. "Upstairs?"

I didn't count on having to repeat myself. Or clarify. I feel like covering my face with a couch cushion, but *screw* it. I'm in it now. "Would you, maybe, like to go have sex with me? I have a room here," I explain, trying my best to keep my spine straight in order to not shrink into myself. The illusion of confidence is key.

"Here?" His brow twists in confusion.

"Yes?"

"Do—do you live here?"

"No, I just stay here a lot." I wait a few seconds, hoping he'll put me out of my misery, but he appears far off and a little stunned. Was I truly misinterpreting all of this? I've been off before, but never *this* much. This seemed like a sure thing.

He laughs nervously, his head hanging. "Uh, actually, um—"

Blame the neon punch, I tell myself. "Sorry. Forget I said anything." I will lie to myself in order to move past this. Bo is a virgin. Celibate due to his solemn lifelong vow. I've been the most tempting offer he's ever had, but he must stay strong. It's not me. It's not me! It's not—

"No," he says a little too forcefully. "Don't—don't forget it. Uh, sorry, it's just"—he shakes his head—"I haven't since..." His eyes fall to where his hand rests on his knee, right above where his prosthesis begins.

Ah.

I should think. I should *absolutely* think before I speak. But I don't. I rarely do, unfortunately. "Did something happen to your...?" I finish the sentence I never should have spoken by pointing to his lap.

Winnifred June McNulty, you cannot ask people if their junk is broken. What is wrong with you?

"Oh, no. Nothing. Top shape." He winces at his choice of words. Or perhaps just the conversation overall.

I have to fix this. I'm not this person—the one who pries and fumbles and makes someone feel uncomfortable about their body or its differences. I cannot be that person. That'd make me a *massive* hypocrite.

I approach gently, resting my hand on top of his. "Then I'm sure it's not all that different." I hesitate, waiting for him to make eye contact with me. "I'm willing to try, if you are. It could be a lot of fun."

He turns to face me, and his eyes are darkened, enlarged pupils and tight-knit brow. "Why was that so hot?" he asks, whispering, his voice near disbelief.

There it is, I think. A sliver of my pride returns.

"The moment you shook my hand with your left, I was ready to do this." I bite down on my smile. "I imagine it's something similar to that? Knowing I get the holdup, to some extent?"

His eyes dip down to my lips again as he nods, eyes entranced and glistening.

"So what will it be?" I ask, leaning close enough that I can count the exact number of freckles on his cheeks that spread across his nose like a bridge between them. "Because if I have to inquire again, I may attempt to drown myself in the punch bowl."

Without hesitation, Bo closes the distance between us and kisses me, tender and brief, with his hand across my jaw. His lips are plush and warm and damn near intoxicating. "Yes," he says, inhaling hungrily, his forehead pressed against mine. He laughs lowly, tucking a strand of my hair behind my ear before letting the same hand drag down my neck, shoulder, and arm. "C'mon," he says, taking my hand in his as he moves away to stand.

"Wait," I say, pulling him back. "I'm going to go upstairs first. I'll make sure no one else has gotten the same idea and is defiling the guest bedroom. You go to the kitchen and get us some water or something. It's the last door on the left."

"Okay." He nods eagerly, a few too many times for my liking. It reminds me of Caleb's puppy-dog willingness, causing a quick thrill of panic to course through me.

I can't handle one more guy being *too* nice in the bedroom. I need to know that all this chemistry between us won't fizzle out the moment we get upstairs.

"Bo, can you promise me something?" I ask.

His bottom lip pushes out as he nods again, less eagerly. "Sure?"

"I need you to promise me that we'll *both* enjoy tonight. I've had a string of lousy hookups this year, and if I have to fake another orgasm, I think I'll be legally required to become a nun or something." I bite my lip, anxious that I perhaps am asking too much from him, a near perfect stranger.

He doesn't bat an eye, but his boyish grin comes back in full, brutal force. "Win, if you walk out of that room sturdier than me, I won't be happy."

A leg joke? Be still my beating heart.

I cover my mouth as I gasp, a singular laugh breaking through. "You did *not*."

"I did," he says, relaxing back on the couch. He raises his hand back to my hair again, playing with it as his eyes fall yet again to my lips with equal measures of desire and amusement. "Now... go upstairs and wait for me."

CHAPTER 3

"That feels *so* good," I sigh out blissfully, letting my belt fall to the floor of the en suite bathroom. I open the drawer under the sink that Sarah keeps stocked with an obscene amount of toiletries and find everything I might need for a quick refresh.

I fetch floss, mouthwash, deodorant, and a few makeup wipes for a quick *downstairs* clean. It may throw off my pH balance, but that's Win of tomorrow's problem.

I hear a soft knock, followed by a creaking door opening, then shutting in the adjoining room.

"I'll be out in a minute!" I call, removing some of the dark eye makeup I smeared on before the party.

"This is their *guest* bedroom?" Bo asks from the other side of the door, clearly impressed.

"You're in finance, right? How much do you think this house is worth?" I ask before taking a shot of mouthwash and swishing it around my mouth, then trying to *quietly* spit it out.

He laughs but doesn't humour me with a guess.

I toss my head forward, using my forearm and the crook of my wrist alongside my left hand to gather all of my hair into a high pony. I take off the leather skirt and boots but leave my white blouse—with extra buttons undone—and fishnet tights on.

With a few centring breaths, I apply some lip gloss, smack my lips together, and attempt to gather every shred of confidence required to open the door to the bedroom.

Sarah's guest room is decorated in grey moody wallpaper and dark floors with a small chandelier in the centre of the room. I dimmed all the lights to a soft, flattering glow before making a mad dash to the bathroom. In the middle of the room, there's a queen-size bed covered in a crisp white linen duvet, taupe knitted blankets, and throw pillows.

Bo sits on the edge of the bed, facing the doorway that I've yet to move from. The moment he spots me, he automatically lowers his hand to his lap and adjusts his trousers. Which does *great* things for my ego.

"Damn," he says, his jaw working. He leans forward, chuckling to himself in an agonised, bittersweet manner before he looks up at me through hooded eyes. I'm struck by the illusion of power born from the eager look on Bo's face telling me that he'd ask *how high* if I simply said *jump*.

"I took off some of the… stuff," I say, holding on to the door frame for balance.

"I can see that." Bo wets his lips. His hands rub up and down his own thighs as if they're seeking out friction of any sort. "It's a good look." He clears his throat, sitting up slowly. "Great—you look… great." He smiles, but his eyes don't—they remain raptly focused on me.

I take five steps toward him on pointed toes, stopping between his parted knees. His hands find the back of my legs, just under my ass. They're tense as they roam over my skin covered in thinly netted tights. Even with him sitting down, my face is only slightly above his.

"I guess you were kidding about the sexy maid costume, then," he says, his hands roaming from the back of my knees to the crease below my ass, his thumbs playing with the strings crisscrossing my thighs like a harp.

"Disappointed?" I ask, leaning forward. The tip of my ponytail falls against the hollow of his cheek. Bo tilts his nose toward it, and his eyes close briefly as he breathes in.

"Only a little." He moves one hand from the back of my thigh to the nape of my neck and pulls me closer, tilting his jaw up to press his lips to mine.

"Maybe next year," I whisper just before our mouths collide.

Our kiss is exploratory at first. Gentle but intentional. It isn't until Bo's other hand reaches my waist that it grows heated—teeth tugging, hands pulling, mouths crashing. I climb into his lap, my knees straddling his hips, and moan unwittingly when he tilts up into me as he leans back—the feeling of him *just* between my thighs.

"I fucking love Halloween," he practically growls against my lips, smiling even still.

All I think is *off.*

Take my clothes *off.*

Let's get each other *off.*

Help me turn my brain *off*.

"I can't really do other people's buttons," I say, peppering kisses along his jaw toward his ear, my voice raspy. "I mean, I can do it but... slowly."

"Take all the time you need," he says, words parted by tender kisses on my neck that have my eyes drooping, weighed down by heady lust.

I move my left hand to the centre of his chest and find the first button of his shirt. I go down from there, one at a time, unbuttoning as best as I can.

Bo begins undoing my shirt. At first, I think he's teasing me with a slow, seductive unravelling. But then I realise he's matching my pace purposefully, clearly slower than he's capable of for my benefit. Which is *just* as sexy as if he was teasing me. Maybe even more so.

It is also, tragically, one of the larger romantic gestures of my life.

Once his shirt is open, I push it off his shoulders and down his arms, kissing feverishly as we go.

Once my shirt is off, I lean back and let my hands wander across his chest as my eyes drink him in. He's got freckles across the tops of his broad shoulders and chest, sprinkling down his biceps before fading to just a few spots on his forearms.

I trace them with my hand, like drawing out constellations in the night sky as I lean in to kiss him again. He stops me by ducking his head lower, sucking at the top of my breast that has spilled over the cup of my bra.

I whimper, pushing my tits out toward him. His eyes flick up to me, watching my reaction as he kisses across my chest. My breath turns short and shallow as he tugs my flesh between his teeth and grips my hips tighter.

I place my right hand on the back of his head, desperately trying to take hold of his hair and keep him in place. Then shame creeps in. I drop my smaller hand off his head and over his shoulder, hearing the words of my ex loud in my ear. *Don't. No, use your other hand.*

"I liked that," Bo says, mouth and nose pressed under my collarbone as he kisses his way up toward my neck. He places my hand back where it was amongst his hair. I try my best to thread my short fingers through it, gathering as much as I can between my thumb and the side of my palm to pull.

Bo groans in response, so I do it again as he sucks on my pulse point under my ear, his hair brushing softly against my chin.

"I love how you smell," I say, conscious of the panting breaths between us growing more urgent.

"You too. Like candied apples." He presses his nose into my hairline, his lips against the edge of my jaw. "It makes me want to…" He tenses, his mouth opening and his teeth lightly dragging across my chin. "God," he breaks the word into two syllables, laughing without humour.

"I want you," I say breathlessly.

"Will you lie down for me?" he asks, gentle tone spoken against my cheek. "I want to see all of you."

I nod demurely, moving off his lap and crawling toward the middle of the bed. Lying down, I soak in the feel of the luxurious linen on my bare arms and back. It's all so soft that it turns me on even more. The feeling of the sheets against my skin and the sound of feather-filled pillows envelops me.

Bo moves to the foot of the bed, standing only in his black trousers. I watch as he takes off three rings without removing his eyes from my body. The rings clatter to the floor around his feet, but he doesn't seem to care where they fall.

I rise onto my elbows, grinning in satisfaction at how Bo's hair is already sticking up on all ends. It only gets messier as he rakes his hands through it again.

He's losing his mind over *me*.

"Win," he says, my name an anguished plea, shaking his head. "Fucking *look* at you."

"Yes?" I ask, feigning innocence as my smirk only grows. I didn't even say he couldn't touch me or move closer, yet he's distressed. He's using all the self-control he has to make this last as long as we *both* want it to.

Admittedly, I love this feeling. The power I've harnessed while laid out on my back. The way my body can turn someone crazed. It's the most in control I ever feel, next to being in the lifeguard tower on the beach.

He points at my knees with both hands. "Open those for me, honey."

Honey? Hmm, I think I like it.

I dig my heels into the mattress, popping my knees up as I slide my legs apart.

"Like this?" I ask sweetly.

"Yes," Bo answers, teeth bared around his knuckles. "Just like that," he says slowly before flicking his hair out of his eyes.

I splay my fingers across the band of my tights around my waist and follow the side seam down to my hips. Then I trace a string cutting against the thickest part of my thigh. "Would you take these off?" I ask, toying with them.

Bo nods like a man possessed, bending over the bed to reach for my waist. He pulls the tights down in one strong, fluid motion until they're off and resting over his shoulder. I thought that was an accident, and he'd soon discard them to the floor, but he's keeping them close with a tight grip as he moves his opposite hand up the inside of my leg.

"Win," he says, nearly whimpering. "Who *are* you?"

I'm more turned on than I have been in *years*, and the guy hasn't even touched me yet. "Bo," I whisper longingly, my hands clinging to the blanket underneath me.

What I want to say is *stop caressing my leg and bring your hand, mouth, dick, or any part of you, closer.* "Come here please," I say instead, biting my bottom lip.

Bo walks around the bed, only giving up his hold of my tights when he sits to undress. Then he discards them to the floor.

I shuffle over to the right side of the bed as Bo undresses down to his boxer briefs. With his trousers and costume gone, I get a clearer view of his prosthetic leg. It looks more futuristic than I was expecting—metallic, with silver hinges and joints under a grey plastic socket.

Then I remember what he said downstairs about not having had sex since... since whatever happened. I want him to feel totally safe to choose what to do next, but this is uncharted territory for us both.

"You can take your prosthesis off or leave it on. Whatever you're most comfortable with," I offer, trying to keep my voice indifferent, making an effort to remain breathy so he doesn't think I'm any less turned on than I was just moments ago.

Bo nods with his back to me before using his arms to help twist himself onto the bed. He lifts and adjusts until his back is straight against the headboard and both legs are out in front of him.

I waste no time getting back to it, moving my mouth from his bicep to the top of his shoulder and across. Once I lift my leg over his lap, straddling him once again, we come alive. The glorious sensation of nothing separating us but two thin, matching black layers of cotton is exhilarating.

"Call me honey again," I say, grinding myself against his hardness.

"You liked that?" he muses, his voice cocky. "It sorta just slipped out."

I don't answer. Well, I do. Just not with words.

We fall back into kissing intuitively. Rough and greedy but co-ordinated—no bumping noses or awkward slips of tongue against teeth. Just two people winding themselves up higher and higher with the hope that we'll eventually fall, crash, and burn.

I continue writhing against him, grateful that he doesn't seem to be in too much of a rush. Dry humping is *so* underrated.

I'm starting to feel my body float away to that perfect edge when he reaches around my back and unclasps my bra. Two large hands find my tits immediately, playing with them until I'm gasping and moving for him like a puppet on his string. Bo drops his lips to my chest as I arch my back for him. He plucks my nipple between his thumb and finger before sucking it into his mouth and flicking it with his tongue.

"*Yes*," I hiss, my hips' rhythm picking up speed.

Moaning around me, Bo splays his fingers across my lower back, pressing me into him with his mouth passing between my breasts greedily.

"Lift up," he says, his voice forceful through his teeth, his hand placed at the base of my neck.

I go onto my knees without question, lifting off his lap. He smoothly guides himself down the mattress until he's flat on his back, his face perfectly positioned between my thighs.

"Good," he says, scratching my inner thigh with his stubble as he pulls my panties to the side with an unexpected roughness. "Now sit for me... *honey*." He throws in the *honey* at the end like he's trying to sweeten the deal. I needed no additional persuasion.

Before I even have time to lower myself fully, Bo's got both of his hands on my hips and he's dragging me onto his face. His fingers dig into my sides until it *almost* hurts.

"Relax," I breathe out as he burrows into me. But my smugness doesn't last long. I gasp when his mouth begins working against me. My knees tremble, then give out entirely until I'm *actually* sitting on his face and holding on to the headboard for dear life as he presses his tongue exactly where I want it.

"Yes, yes, yes," I whisper, my voice rough.

He reaches up with both hands, taking my hands from the headboard and placing them behind my back, holding them together in one strong, unrelenting fist. My body is *entirely* at his mercy, and I simply do not care.

He hums against me in response to every sound escaping my lips. A rewarding, prideful groan rumbles from the back of his throat each time I gasp, moan, or cry out.

I've had a fair number of men eat me out. But none have done it like *this*. Like they were truly *starved* for me. Like they enjoyed it just as much as I do.

Pleasure builds and builds and builds until I finally come undone, shuddering out one long, grateful whimper as I orgasm. Equal parts relief and pleasure cascade over me.

Bo gently releases my hands as he continues to lick me, sending shudders up my spine with each languid swipe. I wipe the sheen of sweat off my brow with my wrist, twitching as he works me over delicately with his tongue.

"I can't," I whisper, attempting to pull myself up and off him. Bo shakes his head between my thighs, groaning his displeasure at me trying to move. He attempts to hold me in place with a hand clasped around the back of my knee, but I break free.

He bites—not nibbles, but *bites*—the softest part of my inner thigh when I lift one leg to move off him. I yelp, laughing in surprise and sobering immediately, falling onto my ass next to the pillows.

"Sir!" I call out in shock. As in, *how dare you?*

I look over at him and find myself momentarily stunned. Bo's parted lips are sparkling wet and slightly swollen, and his eyes are satiated. "Oh, hell yeah," he breathes out a laugh, "I could definitely be into being called *sir.*"

I roll my eyes, though I can't help but smile.

Attempting to catch my breath, I lie next to him. He moves a piece of hair out of his face before bracing his weight on his forearm to suspend himself over me and kissing me leisurely. I get off on the taste of myself on his lips, and based on the way he keeps brushing his tongue against mine, he does too.

Not long after that, I'm tracing his hardness through his boxers. "May I?" I slide the tip of my thumb under the hem. "*Sir,*" I reward him with only a *hint* of sarcasm.

"Have at it, honey," he drawls, his voice arrogant as he falls onto his back with his hands braced behind his head.

CHAPTER 4

B o's dick is huge. I should have guessed, given the sheer height of him and the feel I got through his boxers. But I didn't have much time to think ahead.

"Have you considered porn?" I ask, marvelling.

"Are you just going to keep looking at it?" Bo asks, voice strained.

"You had your turn to ogle. This is mine," I argue.

"It's a bit vulnerable." He throws his hands out at his sides. "Just naked and lying here."

"I could tie you up," I offer. "That's helped me with some of my shyness in bed before." I look around. "I'd have to find some alternative to rope."

"I'm *not* shy," he says pointedly. "But now I'm definitely imagining *you* tied up." He reaches for me with a hand on the back of my neck, but I tilt away from him, still unsure of what to do with this *surprise*.

"Be quiet while I try to calculate how this is going to fit." I go onto my knees and sit next to his lap.

He sighs, placing a hand on his forehead, half covering his eyes.

"There's just so much I haven't done, you know?" I say.

"What?" he asks, laughing exasperatedly and running a hand through his hair.

"I wanted to travel, maybe have kids, learn how to make my own candles. I still haven't watched all nine seasons of *The Office*. I thought I had more time."

"Are you implying—"

"That this dick is going to murder me? Yes," I interrupt.

"Oh my god," he groans out.

"Do your hands get tired of holding it while you pee?"

"I'm gonna leave," he mumbles. "I'm going to leave," he says definitively when I press my forearm next to his lap for comparison.

"Sorry. Okay, sorry. Don't leave. I'll solve it."

"It's not a *Rubik's Cube*; it's my penis."

"Can you not say penis? It's not a particularly sexy word."

"Right, because the rest of this conversation since I got *naked* has been *so* very sexy."

"I see your point."

"Thank you," he replies, his voice indignant.

"Just... *real* quick... how—"

He mutters under his breath, reaching for the back of my head and tugging so hard that I immediately turn to putty in his hands. "No more questions." He runs his thumb across my mouth until I part my lips for him. Then he moves his thumb between my lips and pushes down against my tongue, prying my jaw open. "Better," he says on a sharp inhale.

Oh my god.

"Ready?" he asks, his eyes searching mine. I nod for him, curling my tongue around his thumb. His malevolent smile only grows fiercer before he pushes my head down onto his lap. He's got a tight hold around my ponytail and his other hand on my cheek.

Okay, so it *does* fit.

And Bo is *not* too sweet.

And I'm possibly going to have to consider the *one* part of the term *one-night stand*.

He moans shakily as I swallow him back. "So much quieter," he says teasingly, breathless even still. I glare up at him but, *strangely*, it doesn't have the same effect while his dick is hitting the back of my throat.

I continue working him over, pressing my tongue flat against him and tracing the veins along his shaft. When I hollow out my cheeks, his whole body tenses, and he pulls my hair far too tight until I whine.

"Shit, sorry," he says, letting my hair go nearly completely.

I release him from my mouth with a wet *pop,* continuing to stroke him with my hand. "Don't be." I grin like the devil as I lick from base to tip. "I can handle it."

What I mean is; I'm so tired of men treating me like I'm delicate because of my hand. I'm not breakable. I'm definitely not broken. Use me. Let me drive you to the point where you'd do *unspeakable* things. Let me have that power over you. I'm capable of it.

Minutes go by of rhythmic push and pull. With my mouth wrapped around him, Bo seems to be in heaven—calling out my name and whispering unsparing praises, as if he's willing to lay his life at my feet.

Bo's hand moves from its hold around my hair to my ass, kneading and gripping my flesh. I arch my back for him, pushing my bum into the air.

"Goddamn," he whispers, taking hold of my panties and tugging them downward. He helps me lift out of them, and once they're long lost to the ever-growing pile of clothes on the floor, Bo reaches between my legs, cupping me in a way that feels possessive and lit with desire. I thank him by humming around his dick while increasing my mouth's speed and intensity.

He shivers on a long exhale, hissing as I come up after gagging. Bo traces a finger around my wet entrance, and instantly, I feel myself flutter in anticipation.

"Stop," Bo says forcefully, pulling me off him with a hand on the back of my neck. He sits up, reaching toward me. "I need *you*." With two hands on my waist, he picks me up and drops me onto his lap. I giggle, my chest crashing against his.

"Impatient," I say, raising an eyebrow as I look between us to where his glistening, wet hardness is pressed against his abdomen.

"Maddening..." He laughs slowly, rolling his neck. "You are *maddening*."

I bite my lip, trying not to blush or smile as I lean toward the nightstand. My breasts catch Bo's attention while I reach into the bedside drawer. As he licks and nibbles around my nipples, I absentmindedly sweep my hand inside the box of condoms. Then I do it again. Finding... nothing.

No... No. No. No!

"Shit." I straighten, forcing Bo off my tits as I peer into a completely empty box.

"What?" he asks, his eyes drifting between my look of disbelief and the bedside drawer.

"Do you have a condom?" I ask.

He rubs his right shoulder with the opposite hand, making his bicep tense in front of his chest, which is *not* helping my focus whatsoever. "No. Shit, sorry. I, uh, didn't exactly see this happening."

"Damn it," I whine, going to my knees next to him on the bed. I can't think properly while I'm on his lap.

I *could* throw on some clothes and run across the hallway to Sarah and Caleb's room—but I vowed to never go back into their drawer after the *traumatic* sex toy collection discovery of 2019. I bite the small nail on my right thumb nervously, assessing our next best option.

With Bo's eyes held on me in concern, he does the unexpected. He brings my small hand away from my teeth and to his lips. Then he kisses each of my little fingers, one by one.

No one has *ever* done that.

I've never bothered to imagine that anyone would touch me there so intimately.

The whirling in my chest tells me I'm unsure of whether this level of vulnerability is okay. I don't stop him, though. I don't want to. I just stare in equal parts awe and confusion.

Bo grazes his teeth along my palm, then plants a few delicate kisses onto my wrist, his eyes holding mine the entire time. I'm a little stunned. And conscious of how my heart's rhythm has quickened and swelled into a forgotten affection I haven't felt in *years*. Possibly ever.

"Do we need to stop?" he asks, his voice low.

No, everything in me answers.

"I'm on the pill," I choke out.

He nods thoughtfully. "I've been tested since my last time. All clear," Bo says with an unmistakable desperation in his voice.

"Me too." I nuzzle against his neck as he winds his hands around my waist and pulls me back onto his lap. "I don't want to stop," I say as he places kisses across my collarbone.

"Neither do I," he answers.

Lulled with such adoring kisses, I eventually lower myself onto him completely bare. At first, we both remain perfectly still as I adjust to the stretch of him inside me. I feel him deeper than I thought possible, and while it's not exactly uncomfortable, it steals my breath away and causes a shudder to pass through me. A throbbing ache needing to be satiated.

We do something between fucking and making love. Something new and a little bewildering, unlike any casual sex I've ever experienced. It's not gentle, but it's not entirely hedonistic either.

We fit together perfectly. Me, with my legs wrapped around his back. Him, a pillar of strength sitting at the centre of the bed. Bo's hands travel up and down my spine, gripping the flesh of my hips, my ass, and my neck. My hands feast in his hair, trace his jaw, grip his shoulders.

We continue passionately kissing throughout. Biting when it's all too much—lips and shoulders and jaws. Breathless gasps and moans exchanged, breathed into the other's flushed skin and hair.

Eventually, we finish together, with his thumb on my clit and his teeth harsh against my jaw telling me—*demanding* me—to come. It's incredible.

And yet, when I come back from cleaning myself up in the bathroom, Bo is half dressed and searching in the dark for his carelessly discarded belongings.

"Here," I say, handing him one of the rings he so casually threw to the floor at the end of the bed.

"Thanks," he says, smiling shyly at the ground between us as he slips it on.

It's not that I expected him to stay afterward. We were both clear about what we were looking for. I, even more so. Nothing serious or permanent. Nothing long term. And I still feel that way.

But... I can't help the sinking feeling that starts in my chest and creeps its way down my spine at the thought of sleeping alone after sharing such a vulnerable time together. I can't help but wonder if it wasn't nearly as unique for him to experience such great sex. If I wasn't as good for him as he was for me.

I cover myself with a bed sheet and watch as he effortlessly buttons his shirt back up.

Once dressed, he stills. He pats his pants for phone, or keys, or wallet, and nods to himself. Eventually, he looks at me with hesitancy heavy across his features.

"Thank you," he says, reaching for my left hand. He bends over to kiss it, his eyes looking up at me. "I can't entirely explain what this meant to me," he swallows thickly, "but thank you, Win..."

I nod, unsure of what to say. Nervous that the word *stay* might escape my lips if I answer him. I lower to sit on the mattress as he grabs one last thing off the chair in the far corner of the room and walks toward the door without looking back.

After shutting off the lights, I fall against the pillows and begin convincing myself that this is definitely for the best. The last time I felt this sort of immediate connection with someone, the effortless back and forth, the rush of excitement followed by great sex, I landed myself in a horrible place.

Jack had been kind at first too. Sweet. Funny. Generous in bed. If he was entirely horrible, I wouldn't have given him the chance to crush me like he did. That's how men get you. A false sense of comfort, and then boom—ten months later you're telling people you have allergies to avoid explaining your red-rimmed eyes *again.*

And, like my mother, I'm far too soft hearted. Often too eager to see the best in people. Too attached to leave when I should. Too scared of being alone.

And I *do* struggle with the idea of being alone forever. But that's even more reason to keep it that way, I think. What's worse than a woman who can't enjoy her own company? Independence is a virtue, and one that is best learned without too many hard lessons.

My logic will always have to reconcile against my foolish, helpless heart. And I think logic will win in the end. I can make sure of that.

So I shut my eyes and will myself to sleep well. Determined to not lose sleep over any man. No matter how wonderful he may seem.

CHAPTER 5

Six Weeks Later

"Pregnant?" I ask through hysterical laughter. Doctor Salim stares at me with increasing concern as I spiral further. "No way. Nope! No-no-no. Check again. Run back the tapes. Recount the votes. Something is *wrong* here."

The doctor takes a deep breath in as she sits straighter, poised like the impressive woman she is. She at least pretends to look over the papers in her hand again—the folder she must have mistaken as mine. "Win, bloodwork does not lie. If your last period was October sixteenth, that'd make you about eight weeks along."

"Winnifred McNulty," I point to the top of the lab report, "is a more common name than you'd think." I swallow nervously. "The labs probably switched my results with someone else." That's it. That has to be it.

We're interrupted by the sound of a swift knock, followed by the arrival of a disembodied hand through the crack of the door—presumably attached to the nurse who made me pee in a cup. Another sheet of paper is handed over. Those are *not* my friends today.

"Your urine sample was also positive for pregnancy," the doctor says, adding another paper to my ever-growing folder. "Win." She sets the file on her desk and places one leg over the other before resting her tightly clasped hands above her knee. "I take it this is somewhat of a surprise?"

"I'm on the pill," I say, my voice far off. Perhaps my voice is somewhere with my body. My non-pregnant body. The one I had only minutes ago.

"No contraceptive is 100 percent effective against pregnancy."

"I also use condoms," I add.

"Every time?"

Shit, *right*. "Well, one time... no." Before Halloween, I had a perfect record. Then Bo. The guy I've tried to push out of my thoughts since.

"One time about five to six weeks ago?" Doctor Salim asks, her patience momentarily lapsing.

"About that, yes," I reply, snarkier than intended. "Shit, sorry," I whisper into my palms, covering my face. "I got knocked up by a pirate..." I say, my voice muffled by my hands.

"Sorry, what?" The doctor's tone alerts me to the very unusual thing I just said.

I peek through my fingers at her. "It was Halloween. He was dressed as a pirate."

"Oh." She sighs. "Were you intimate with anyone else that same month or shortly thereafter?"

"No, just him."

"The pirate?"

"Aye," I whimper softly.

She gives me a *this is not the time* look that I've only previously gotten from my mother. "Well, you have the good fortune of knowing exactly when conception was, which sets your due date at about..." She picks up a circular cardboard device from her desk and rotates between dates. "July twenty-fourth."

"Okay." I nod, my eyes finding a spot on the wall to steady me. A small piece of chipped paint becomes my focal point as the walls swell and tilt around me.

July twenty-fourth. That's a fairly inconspicuous day. What do I normally do on July twenty-fourth?

My summers are usually spent lifeguarding on the beach at the local campsite, Westcliff Point. Last year, I worked extra shifts at the café to pay for a trip to visit Mom in Florida at the end of the summer. We ate dinner outside every night while I was there to the sounds of whistling through palm leaves and aggressively vocal frogs. Her skin looked like leather, and my concern for her sunbathing habits grew. But nothing significant happened. Nothing this significant has *ever* happened.

I can't be a lifeguard when I'm nine months pregnant.

I can't visit my mom with a newborn.

What *can* someone do at nine months pregnant other than... wait?

"The good news is that at this stage of your pregnancy, you have every option available to you. We have some time to decide how to best move forward."

"Okay" is the only word I seem to have available to me.

"Is there someone you could call to help you process this news? A friend? The, er, father, perhaps?"

"Yeah," I murmur, pulling out my phone to text Sarah. Not that I'd call him now *if* I had it, but not having Bo's number suddenly feels humbling to say the least.

"Why don't we set up another appointment in a week's time? If you make your decision before then, just call and we can go from there. If not, we can discuss your options some more."

"Yeah, okay," I say, my eyes caught on the small scale in the corner of the room under a collection of pamphlets and advertisements with pictures of chubby babies on the front.

"I'm also going to schedule an ultrasound for a few weeks from now, since they book up fast. If you're no longer pregnant, we'll cancel it, of course. But that way, you can have your first-trimester scan as we recommend."

"Ultrasound, right." I imagine it, the little black and grey blob on a screen. The sound of a heartbeat, like the ones you hear on television. Except now it'd be the inhabitant of my womb on some tech's monitor. The probe pressed against *my* belly.

I lift my left hand from my lap and press it against the corduroy overalls covering my stomach. There's no discernible change in its shape, size, or hardness whatsoever. Yet everything has changed.

My phone chimes with a text. It's Sarah, letting me know she's already on her way. No hesitation and no questions asked. Just like our mothers taught us. *Go first; ask questions later*, they always said.

I think of our moms in that tiny apartment together almost thirty years ago. They were *so* young—so much younger than I am—when they had Sarah and me. We would all sit for hours on our old, crusty maroon couch, flipping through photo albums as they told us stories. Countless books filled with pictures of our moms dressed in horrific nineties fashion, their bellies growing in each photo under busy-patterned pastel sweaters. I think of the pale green colour they painted the nursery Sarah and I shared. The ceiling they lined with wallpaper cartoon ducks. The way they had to do all of it on their own and *still* made it special for us.

Unlike them, I'm at a stage of life where many of my friends have chosen to get pregnant. I've gone to three baby showers this year alone. And, secretly, I've hoped for a baby of my own. A *someday* wish. A *once-I-have-my-shit-together* dream.

But truthfully, I can't help but wonder... is *anyone* ever ready for a kid?

Even with that shred of comfort, I don't think I've ever felt as judged as I do right now. Not by Doctor Salim, of course, but by the world outside. I can almost sense it—the millions of invisible eyes set on me.

You can't go a day without hearing the choice of pregnancy being debated, broadcasted, and fought over in some way or another. Still, I never considered how it would feel to sit front and centre. It's as if I'll find reporters outside, trying to predict what I mean to do next. Protestors and politicians waiting in the wings to decipher whether I'm morally right or wrong. Too many opinions for this small corner office.

So I shove them all away as best I can.

Here, it's just Doctor Salim and me. The way it should be.

"So, symptoms you could expect before our next visit..." Doctor Salim begins listing off the most horrible-sounding possibilities.

Sore boobs, nausea, increased saliva, irritability, exhaustion. "But what you don't want to see is..." Even worse stuff. Bleeding, intense cramping, blurred vision, extreme bouts of depression. "... then you call me, okay?"

I nod, feeling entirely emptied out.

"If you're unsure of what the next step is, I suggest treating this like a viable pregnancy." She stands, reaching into the cabinet above her desk. "Prenatal vitamins once a day. We recommend no smoking, drinking, or recreational drug use. There's a pamphlet in the waiting room about which foods to avoid, as well." She smiles softly, handing me a vitamin bottle. "Though I will tell you I enjoyed sushi and an occasional glass of wine with my second pregnancy, and all was well. Moderation is key."

What is she talking about? Sushi? How delicate are babies that you can't have a goddamn maki roll?

"Okay," I say, standing as Doctor Salim holds the door open for me.

"I'll see you in a week but feel free to call before then," she reminds me.

I hug her. I'm sure it's not appropriate, but I do. Right now, she and I are the only people in the world who know this secret, and I feel as if we've formed some sort of bond.

Doctor Salim accepts the far-too-tight hug, patting my back before moving to shut the door behind us. We stand in the empty hallway as I watch her professional mask slip just a little, a weary, gentle compassion overtaking her features.

"I know this may not be any consolation, but my patients who plan for pregnancy feel overwhelmed too. All of this is a lot to process. But you're very capable, Win. Whatever you decide for *yourself* will be for the best. You have my full support for any choice."

I'm about to thank her again, and perhaps force her into another hug, when I hear my name called from the lobby, and the concern in Sarah's voice is obvious.

I turn around and instantly feel a tear fall at the sight of my friend. She looks half thrown-together in sweatpants and a messy bun put up in a claw-clip. She really did drop everything to come here right away.

"Thanks for coming," I say, possibly just to myself, as she jogs to me with her arms open at her sides. We collide in a hug.

"What's going on?" she asks quietly over my shoulder, her voice cautious—as if she's afraid to hear my answer. I immediately think of her mom, Marcie, who, in so many ways, was my mom too. How, nearer to the end of her life, every piece of news we got from her doctors felt like another blow.

"I'm okay," I reassure her. "Promise," I say, stepping back. "Can we talk in your car?" I wipe my tears on my sleeve.

"Of course, babe. Come on." Sarah drags me toward the exit, her hand wrapped tightly around my wrist. I thank the doctor silently over my shoulder as we make our way outside.

CHAPTER 6

"Y ou're moving in with us." Sarah's grip tightens even further around my forearm. She's taking the sudden, life-altering news as she normally does—by attempting to take control.
It's our way.

"Sar, you're being ridiculous. I have my own apartment. You and
Caleb don't even want your own kids." I sigh out through my nose,
chewing my lip. "Plus, I don't even know what I'm going to do
yet."

"You're going to keep it, Win. We *both* know that."

She's probably right.

The moment I left the office—before I'd even worked up the
courage to tell Sarah—I took a prenatal vitamin and added the
reminder to my phone, hitting *repeat* for the next nine months
without another thought.

But I could delete that reminder. Easily. I *could.*

"I should consider it, right? An abortion?" I ask.

"Have you?" Sarah asks, her tone free of judgement.

"Not yet."

We sit in silence, our eyes on each other absently.

I begin drafting a list in my head entitled *reasons to not have this baby*. And while Sarah shouldn't be such a snob, she *is* right. My apartment building is trash. There's been pretty much every kind of vermin imaginable, and when they manage to get rid of one, another always seems to show up.

My neighbours are loud and inconsiderate. The train passes at four every morning, so loudly that the walls shake. And there's mould growing under the kitchen sink that my absentee landlord claims is "healthy bacteria like yoghurt." But kids have grown up in worse. Sarah and I did. And we turned out fine... *ish*.

I also add my job to the baby-don't list. The café pays slightly above minimum wage, and I'm fairly certain that parental leave in Canada is about 50 percent of your normal income. I don't know if I could reasonably live off that. Money is tight as it is. If I did need to get a new apartment, it would probably mean paying more for rent, and then I'd have even less money to work with. On top of that, I'd have another mouth to feed, a second body to clothe, and diapers to buy.

But our moms always got by on next to nothing. And growing up without money builds character. I think. I hope.

Of course, there's the factor of the *other* parent. Bo, even from our brief evening together, didn't strike me as the type of guy to leave the mother of his child high and dry. But ultimately, I don't know him at all. And I didn't really intend to ever get to know him. That's sort of the whole point of what we did. Still, maybe he'd help? I'd have to tell him first. Which would mean having to see him again. Something he may not be interested in.

Something, which is another reason for concern, I *am* interested in.

I struggle to think of any reasons that I can't dismiss after a little thought. And, clearly, I know what side of the debate my heart is on when I'm desperate to not think of another reason against keeping the pregnancy.

Hesitantly, even inside the privacy of my own thoughts, I allow myself to say it. *I want to have this baby.* Deep down, in an I-know-it in-my-bones type of way, it feels right. So I think it again. And again. Testing my reaction to it each time. Waiting for a hint of panic or a rush of fear. But nothing comes. Just... resolve. A tiny kindling of excitement, actually.

I've always known I wanted a kid or two. It was the life partner I haven't been so sure about since Jack. Maybe this is the way to get the best of both worlds. An accidental baby for an intentionally independent life.

"I'm keeping it," I say out loud, hoping it feels right. Nodding, I repeat myself, a touch more certain. "I'm going to have the baby."

"You sure?" Sarah asks gently.

"Yes." I look at her, smiling for the first time since I got the news, though tears still sit lodged in the corners of my eyes.

"Win?" she asks, twisting her lips from a soft smile to unease. "I'm trying to find a delicate way to ask this, but... who's the dad?"

Ah, yes. The elephant in the room. Well, in the car. The elephant in the car. "I have a confession to make," I say, wincing.

She sits up straighter, putting two tight fists around the steering wheel, though the car's still parked. "Ooh, what did you do?" she whispers, her eyes lit with mischievous curiosity. "Is it an affair? Is he much, much older? A mafioso? Your childhood best friend? Oh, wait—that's me."

She reads too much, and it's addled her brain.

"It happened on Halloween," I confess.

"Oh my god." Her whole face comes alive. "You fucked someone at *my* party?" She gasps. "Your baby was conceived in my house?" She laughs, tilting her head back as if it's all too much. "How did you sneak a guy up there? Sneak him out? Is this how our mothers felt when we were in high school? You are in *so much* trouble, young lady!"

"The guest bedroom was out of condoms," I whine, throwing my head back against the passenger seat's headrest.

"See, you make fun of me, but *this* is why I take restocking so seriously."

"Maybe focus on the life-changing toiletries next time and not the six extra bottles of travel-sized shampoo in your drawer."

"Caleb and I like to mess around in there sometimes and pretend we're at a hotel—sue me. Wait, this means the baby daddy is another friend of ours. Who is it?" She leans forward, her intense eyes attempting to pierce through my soul.

"A friend of Caleb's that I hadn't met before. Bo?"

"Who the *fuck* is Bo? Caleb doesn't have friends I don't—oh my god," she gasps again. "You slept with an intruder!"

I glare at her. "Listen, he said he knew Caleb through a mutual friend and..." I feel guilty, knowing this is similar to how I've been identified in the past and not loving that fact, but it *is* the easiest identifiable feature. "He has a prosthetic leg."

"Wait," she laughs dryly, "Robbie?"

"No!" I cry out. "The friend Caleb *wanted* me to hook up with?"

"He's going to *love* this." Sarah beams. "I haven't even met the guy."

"I fucked a guy named *Robbie*?"

"You're having a *kid* with a guy named Robbie, babe."

"The *with* part is tentative."

"You're going to have to tell Robbie. You know that, right?"

"Stop calling him that."

"You know you're going to have to tell Bo, right?" Sarah says sternly.

"Yes," I grumble.

"Soon?"

"*Sure.*" I throw my hands up before crossing them in front of my chest.

We both fall back into our seats, letting out a long breath at the same time. I stare out the moonroof and watch the withered, empty branches of a tree above us blow in the wind. We're due for snow tomorrow, and yet my brain is stuck in July. *Next* July, that is.

"I'm due July twenty-fourth," I say diffidently.

"We have plenty of time," Sarah says, reaching across the centre console for my hand, tugging me toward her and lowering her head to my shoulder. I let my head fall on top of hers. Neither of us turns away from the view above us.

"I bet she'll arrive August first," Sarah says solemnly.

I admit, I had forgotten the exact day Sarah's mom, Marcie, passed until Sarah spoke. I miss her almost every day, so maybe that one day in particular has lost all its meaning.

"Mom would love that day to be good," she adds when I don't answer. "She'd have loved to have a granddaughter to spoil."

"I would love that too." I kiss the top of her head. "But we don't know if it's a girl."

"If it's a girl, you should name her Sarah."

"And if it's a boy?" I ask.

"Sa-rah-yan," she fumbles.

"Beautiful," I say.

"We'll call him Ryan for short."

"Can you go home and get knocked up too?" I whisper, half-serious.

"No, definitely not." She nuzzles into me.

"Rude," I huff.

"I'm not made to be a mom. We've been over this." She pats my cheek, then sits up, her kind eyes steadying me. "But I *am* going to be the best auntie ever."

It hits me all over again. A turning-over feeling in my gut, like the seconds before a tall wave hits. An anticipatory spike of awareness. "I'm having a baby, Sarah."

"Sure seems that way."

"There's a kid floating around in here." I point to my stomach. "A human being."

"We should download one of those apps to figure out what it's got going on."

"Huh?"

"You know, what size it is. Like if it's an apple seed or a papaya."

"It's probably really tiny at this point." The thought of that fills me with a nagging sense of dread. *How tiny? How fragile?* I try to push those thoughts away, but they linger quietly. The realisation that even if I choose to have this baby, it may not *stick* hits me like a freight train.

"I'll find out," Sarah says, pulling out her phone.

I blow out a breath, trilling my lips. "I was on the pill, for the record," I say, though Sarah's preoccupied and not entirely listening.

My knee starts bouncing as I think of all the things I've done in the past few weeks that a pregnant woman absolutely shouldn't. I had a drink at Sarah's last weekend, ate mystery meat from the food truck outside the grocery store, sat in my gym's sauna after a swim the other night, smoked a joint after a long shift a few days ago. I haven't even drunk water today. Actually, I might have left my water bottle on the bus, now that I'm thinking about it.

This *could* explain the intense brain fog I've been feeling for the past few weeks.

Sarah snorts sarcastically, as if to say, *uh-huh, sure.* "I've seen you forget to take your pill every time your phone is dead before nine p.m."

"I was getting better at it," I say defensively.

She turns toward me, purposefully looking between my stomach and face in a slow, sarcastic sequence. "*Clearly.*"

"You have to be nice to me now. I'm with child," I say, dramatically tilting my nose into the air.

"Hey!" Sarah points to her phone. "It's the size of a coffee bean," she says, her voice full of adoration, showing me her phone's screen. "You're going to have to drink less caffeine. You know that, right?"

"Yes," I answer snidely.

"I still don't want you living at your place. Will you please consider moving in?"

"Listen, Daddy Warbucks, I appreciate the offer, but my apartment is *fine.*"

"It was fumigated two months ago," Sarah argues.

"Which means the problem should be gone." I reach for the seat belt behind my shoulder, then buckle myself in.

"Just think about it." Sarah reaches for her seat belt and drops her phone into the cupholder between us. "Where to now?" she asks.

"Wherever. I took all day off work for this. I convinced myself I was dying when my period was late."

"Ah, yes. So much more likely than a baby." Then she stills. "Wait, how long have you been worrying about this? Why didn't you say anything?"

"Just a week. I didn't want you to stress."

Sarah frowns. She and I frequently argue about this. Ever since Marcie died nine years ago, I've felt even more responsible for her. I'm only three months older, but growing up, I definitely took on the older sister role of looking out for her.

Sure, now she's got more money than me and a loving husband to share the load with, but Sarah is *pure*. She is outgoing, a touch naive, and has a tendency to get herself into situations where people take advantage of her kindness. She's also been through a lot. Too much. I don't want her to ever worry. Especially not about me.

"Next time, let me." She turns the ignition and begins pulling out of her parking spot.

"Wait, so where are we going?" I ask.

She smiles, checking her blind spot as she changes lanes. "My place. Caleb is going to *flip*."

During the brief car ride to Sarah's house, I read pamphlets out loud until we're both sure that pregnancy and babies are completely terrifying and, in equal measure, magical.

I also, quietly, think of Bo.

I wonder where he is today and what his normal workday looks like. What he might look like out of pirate costume but not naked. In his line of work, suits might be required. That, I'd like to see.

I wonder whether he'll be horrified or glad to hear that he's going to be a father—or, more likely, somewhere fluctuating between the two.

I wonder if he'll show up for the baby, unlike my dad or Sarah's.

I wonder if I want him to, or if I'd rather do it all myself. Lessening the chance of disappointment, the blow of rejection for me or this kid down the line.

Once we arrive, I allow Sarah the honour of telling her husband my news. The *moment* Caleb walks into the kitchen to greet us, the words burst from her lips, immediately sending him into a state of shock.

"He's frozen." I turn to my best friend, who's giggling into her phone, taking photos of her dumbfounded husband. "You broke him," I say.

"No, *you* did." She laughs again. "He's just rebooting. He does this sometimes." Sarah slides her phone into her back pocket. "Caleb," she singsongs his name. "Come back to us, sweetie."

"Why is no one else freaking out?" he asks, lowering himself onto a kitchen stool.

"I think it just hasn't fully hit me yet." I shrug, throwing back some shredded cheese from a bag in their fridge.

"I had a premonition that this would happen someday." Sarah does this. She loves to claim that nothing in life catches her by surprise, due to her very much–unconfirmed psychic ability she proclaims to have. I find it oddly comforting.

"What—what do we do?" Caleb asks. "What are we going to do?" he asks, nearing hysterical.

"Well, *you* do nothing," I answer. "As incestuous as this may often feel, you're not the father."

"This is so strange. It's always just been the three of us." He pinches the bridge of his nose, his elbow propped up on the counter.

"Oh, darling..." Sarah says, her tone laced with fake amiability. "You will *always* be our first baby. We love you *so* much."

"Who's the dad?" Caleb asks, ignoring his wife and turning to me as I shut their fridge with an armful of an assortment of snacks.

"Tell him," Sarah says smugly, moving to stand beside Caleb.

I glare at her, dropping my haul onto their counter. "Bo," I answer plainly.

"Who the *hell* is—"

"Robbie," Sarah interrupts, bursting. "Robbie!"

"Oh... *shit*," Caleb says, grimacing.

Sarah and I turn toward each other with urgency, terror in both of our expressions.

"What? Why *shit*? Is he some sort of... delinquent?" Sarah asks, turning to face Caleb.

"No! He's just...Well, he's—"

"You wanted to introduce us, Caleb," I say, my rage piquing within every syllable. "What do you mean *oh shit*?"

"I thought you'd have fun together!" he says, holding up his hands, his voice reaching an unbelievably high pitch. "I didn't think *this* would happen!"

"Spit it out, man!" Sarah yells.

"He's Cora's ex."

Sarah gasps like she's in one of our favourite telenovelas.

"What?" I ask, deathly low.

Cora, Caleb's older sister, is the spawn of Satan. We've often joked that Caleb is such a good guy because there was no evil DNA left once she left the womb. Cora told Sarah she looked *tired* on her wedding day. She also asks me to remind her of my name *every* time we're at the same event, even though I've been an adjacent part of their family for the better part of fifteen years.

Other than her beguiling personality, all that I've heard about her in the last few years is that she was recently engaged to and *dumped* by a man named... *Robert.*

"Why is he using so many identities?" Sarah asks what I'm wondering out loud, her voice barely audible. "Why did you tell me about a *Robbie* and not a *Robert*?"

"Robert is Robbie *and* Bo," Caleb clarifies, as if we haven't put that together. "Cora insisted on calling him Robert. My dad started calling him Robbie, so I did too. I think he mostly goes by Bo these days."

"So *this* is Robert who left his fiancée out of the blue? That Robert?" Sarah asks, pacing in small circles.

Caleb grimaces but nods.

"Cool, cool, great. So what I'm *hearing* is that my baby daddy is known to fall in love with women who seemingly enjoy hunting children for sport"—I inhale sharply, my voice cutting out—"and *then* proceeds to drop them like they're hot garbage?"

"Well, I mean," Sarah says, crouching closer to me across the counter, "*some* women *are* hot garbage."

"That's my sister!" Caleb protests.

"You know who she is," Sarah fires back from behind gritted teeth.

"How did you not know?" I shout at her.

"I avoid Cora like the plague. You know that! I never even met the guy!"

"I feel like I'm going to be sick," I say, nausea climbing. But no one is listening. Sarah and Caleb are squared off with each other. Sarah is poking his chest as he backs away slowly.

"Why the *fuck* would you try to set Win up with Cora's ex?"

"It's not as bad as it sounds. Robbie is a good guy. He's—"

"This is why you have to run all of your decisions past your wife!"

"Wait..." I say, far too quietly for them to hear as I press my palm into the clammy skin on my forehead.

"I didn't think he'd even come to the party. But he and Win are very similar. Clearly I was right!"

"Oh, because they're both disabled? You prick."

No one else seems to notice that the room is spinning on a tilted axis. I walk over to the tap and try to splash cold water on my face.

"Obviously not *just* that!"

"So what? What would possess you to do this?"

I'm actually, very much, definitely going to be sick.

"Like I *said*; he's a good guy! It's only the Cora thing. It's not—"

Caleb and Sarah are interrupted by the sound of me barfing into their kitchen sink.

CHAPTER 7

When I left Sarah's place, Caleb was still on thin ice and had been forced to tell us everything he knew about Robert, Robbie, *and* Bo.

According to him, Bo and Cora met when they were both interning at some finance-gig. They didn't really get to know each other until they were battling it out for a permanent position a year later. Honestly, it sounded like the start of one of Sarah's romance novels, which only fuelled my annoyance further. I know I have zero claim over the guy, but I don't particularly enjoy him having an enemies-to-lovers meet cute with the Antichrist.

They dated for a few years, off and on. Caleb said it seemed to be very up and down until, out of nowhere, they announced their engagement. That was just under two years ago. They were seemingly in the middle of wedding planning when, a few months later, Cora told her family that Bo'd left her high and dry. Caleb apparently never inquired further. Because he's decidedly the *worst*.

Bo and Caleb reconnected by total coincidence at work this past spring. Caleb happened to have tons of information about the project that Bo had been hired to consult on that neither Sarah nor I wanted. They've been friends in a loose sense since—mostly meeting up at the gym, apparently, which Caleb was super vague about—and have never even talked about Cora, or the breakup.

Men are beyond strange.

Caleb had *very* little else to say. He had no clue about what happened to Bo's leg, for example. Caleb said when he last saw Bo with Cora, he didn't have a prosthesis. Then, when he started on the project for Caleb's company, he did. He thought it would be rude to ask, and I suppose he's right. But it means what happened to Bo was quite recent. Which, even though I barely know the guy, makes my heart ache. That's a big, dramatic change to undergo. And Bo's got no idea what further change is coming his way.

Could that be too much for one guy to handle? I'd understand that. I don't even like when my manager adds a new menu item at the café.

After climbing up the six flights of stairs to my apartment, I arrive at my front door slightly winded and still a touch nauseous. My neighbours down the hall are arguing *again*, and the lights in the hallway flicker like a horror movie, but my apartment is my own piece of heaven. Well... it's perhaps more like purgatory.

This apartment was the only place I could afford on my own after I left Jack, and at the time, anywhere would have suited me just fine. It was a not so perfect solution to a much bigger problem. Though I did think it would be more of a *temporary* solution. I definitely didn't think I'd be here four years later. Even still, I've made the most of it.

To cope with the brutal Canadian winters, I've secured more house plants than your average greenhouse. I consider them excellent investments. A hobby, decor, and air-purifiers all in one. Well, not in *one*. In dozens. I keep most of them in front of the large square window that sits behind the couch that doubles as my bed. Not that I'm sleeping on a couch—it's a pull-out.

Ha. *Pull-out*. Should've maybe tried that.

I throw my keys onto my dining table that is half-covered by towels under drying dishes and turn on the switch that works the lamp in the far corner of the room above my purple dresser. Sure, the apartment is one room plus a bathroom and less than 350 square feet. *And* the walls are all a little yellow from the smoker who lived here before me. And the carpeting under my couch is permanently stained with god only knows what. And I guess it would be nice to have windows that open to get some fresh air. But this place is mine. That counts for something.

It's the first thing I ever saved up for. The first lease I ever signed on my own. The first home that I ever lived in by myself. Had complete control over.

I grab a glass of water, chug it back, and then refill it before I open the bath playlist on my phone and connect to the speaker in my bathroom. I follow the sound of Carole King's voice, shaking off my clothes as I go. Leaving a trail behind me of handmade socks, a blue sweater, orange corduroy overalls, beige underwear, and an ill-fitting matching bra.

When in doubt, take a shower, my mother used to say. *When in trouble, take a bath,* Marcie would add. They were always speaking in tandem like that—little doses of life lessons piggy-backed on top of the other.

Oh, *fuck*. I'm going to have to tell my mom about the baby.

Nope. Not thinking about that yet. First, a bath.

Well, first, *several* things.

In fact, most things before I tell my mother.

I'm not ever really sure how to talk to my mom about what's happening in my life. Sometime after I turned eleven, I became more of a friend and confidant than a daughter. There was never enough space in the conversation for two sets of problems, and hers always seemed more important.

Truthfully, I think she was lonely. Other than Marcie, she didn't really have many friends or any family. Her parents wanted nothing to do with her the moment I came into the picture, and she's an only child. Plus, I think some people have loneliness sort of built in. It often seemed that there was not enough attention in the world that could fill that void inside her.

I worry that I only recognise that because I have it too.

And I heard what people said about her. The other parents. They'd call her brash, noisy, gaudy. They'd make jokes about locking up their husbands when she came around. But June McNulty has always been unapologetically herself. I've got to give her credit for that. And I do truly love her.

I could have done with fewer late-night wake-ups when she'd stumbled home from a bad date. Actually, I'd probably go back and request fewer debriefs after the *good* dates—that's just stuff no daughter should really ever hear about their mother. But I know she tried as best as she could. That was her way of communicating—sharing her life with me and probably hoping I'd return the favour. I just never felt like I could. I had Marcie to confide in. She'd give me room to let my thoughts percolate, to come to her when I needed to. And she'd listen without interrupting or jumping to conclusions.

Regardless, I always knew I was loved. Even if I wanted the love from my mother delivered differently.

I light a candle and wait for the tub to fill as I wash the day's dirt and grime off my face at the sink—seeking comfort in how my warm, wet palms feel on my cheeks. Allowing myself to take hearty deep breaths as my tea-tree face wash evaporates with the steam.

Lowering myself into the tub, I bring both hands to my stomach and stare at the area I typically avoid looking at for too long.

It's not that I dislike my body, or my stomach in particular. It's just that I find there's less risk of insecurity spiking the more I act as if I don't have a body at all.

I, like most women my age, have learned to hate myself *just* enough to appease others. If you're too fond of how you look, you're told you'll be unlikeable. Labelled as self-involved, egotistical, or stuck-up. But it's purposeful—pinning us against one another. Consumerism *demands* we remain unsatisfied with our appearance. If we all liked ourselves, dozens of industries would crumble like Babylon. We have to want a solution to whatever or however many problems plague us in order to keep those factories running. To keep money in men's pockets.

Acne? Wear more makeup that will only make matters worse.

Stretch marks? There's a cream for that and a more expensive one if need be.

Stained teeth? Not with these white strips! Just don't ask what's in them.

Too fat? Here's a diet plan so expensive you can't even afford food.

Too skinny? Wear this bra that pushes up your tits—because you *still* need massive tits.

What I realised, though probably far too young, is that some things can't be "fixed." There were no *ten quick ways to grow more fingers* magazine articles for me to read as a teen. No creams that would *blur* or *fix* or *correct* my hand. Just deep pockets, long sleeves, and strategic posing that kept my hand out of view. Hidden like all flaws should be.

And though it was positively mortifying at the time, I owe a lot to Marcie for calling me on the hiding. It was my fourteenth birthday party, and I had all my friends meet us at the local pool. We were taking photos together with my friend's disposable camera when Marcie came storming over from the set of lounge chairs she and my mother had claimed earlier in the day.

"Winnifred June McNulty, what are you doing?" she roared.

"Nothing," I answered with a *hefty* dose of attitude.

"Baby girl..." She laughed without humour. "The rest of these girls have their hands up in the air. Two arms and two hands. You can count, can't you? Where are yours?"

I glared over at Sarah, as if to say *come get your mother*, when Marcie reached between me and a friend and pulled my right arm up into the air, holding it there in a talon-like grip. "This is who you are, baby. And it's beautiful." She stepped back, admiring the row of us girls with a fondness that still sits lodged in my heart. "You can't change anything by hiding it. You'll just look back on memories and realise you tried to erase yourself. And how *sad* that would be."

It was the way she said *sad* that hit me. That I can still hear so clearly to this day. Sad like *pathetic*. Which, to a teenage girl, is a blow not long forgotten.

Until then, I hadn't realised I'd been doing it. Hiding proof of my hand, as if I could someday look back on my life and forget that I was different. After that, I tried, bit by bit, to stop erasing myself.

It was a lot of effort at first. A lot of catching myself in the act and readjusting. Then, slowly, over time, it got easier. To the point where I didn't have to remind myself not to hide anymore—at least on the outside.

The internal struggle was harder to kick. The awful game of comparison and shame spirals followed me through most of my adolescence and into early adulthood. I often stopped myself from trying because I was scared to fail. I was being told it was okay to struggle with simple tasks while also being fed news stories of those... overachievers.

The disabled elite, if you will.

The surfer with one arm, the mountain climber with no legs, a drummer with one hand.

And, deep down, I knew I should be proud of them. They were my community, and they were only working to erase stigma for the *rest* of us. But I didn't feel proud. I felt bitter. Jealous too. Angry that they weren't just *great surfer, record-breaking mountain climber*, and *successful drummer*. To me, they were a reminder that the world will always view me differently—put me in a different bracket—even if I landed myself on a pedestal.

I didn't want to achieve despite myself. I didn't want to *defy* anything. I just wanted to feel ordinary. To not overcompensate every day. I wanted to be bad at things and have people laugh at me because that's life. I didn't want pity.

And when I was great at something like swimming, I didn't want to feel praised for what I'd overcome. I wanted to just be *good*.

It fucks you up, competing against low expectations. Nothing feels like a win.

But, like most people, I aged out of my insecurities to some extent. I found my own rhythm. I figured out who I was outside of the hold-ups and resentment I held. I started to build my identity in things that grew confidence. Who I was instead of who I wasn't or couldn't ever be. I stopped hiding parts of myself away.

Then came Jack.

Which rocked my confidence like nothing else.

Jack had wanted to be the hero in my story. At first. He'd hold my smaller hand in public but would smile at me in this way as if to say, silently, *you don't have to thank me*. Truthfully, every *regular* boyfriend thing he did for me—the little, partially expected things like carrying bags or opening doors—was never for the purpose of being kind. It was always done with some ulterior motive. An *ugly* attitude that I hadn't wanted to acknowledge for fear of it all unravelling.

I was his good deed.

He loved me in spite of; never because.

Eventually, I think, it all grew a bit too tiresome. I was incapable in his eyes. Not *trying* hard enough. Then he chose to become the villain. And he was good at it—I'll give him that.

One night, late for his friend's engagement party, I was fiddling with the strap of my heels for, I suppose, a minute too long.

"Just fucking *try*, Win," Jack had yelled, exasperatedly throwing his body around. "People aren't going to spend their lives waiting on you hand and foot. Stop being so goddamn useless."

Suddenly, I was back to being that fourteen-year-old girl with her hand behind her back. Wishing, desperately, to change. To hide.

Attempting to become less of a burden, I plotted out my days in precise detail—ensuring I wouldn't have to ask him to do anything for me. But he would inevitably find something to yell about.

And even after I finally left him, I still found myself grateful for Jack in my lowest, most insecure moments in the year that followed. Thankful that I had learned at least *someone* would want me. That I was capable of being loved.

That scared me far worse than Jack's temper ever did. The power that I had given him to validate my desirability. The power I *could* give to someone else if I was foolish enough. So I decided I wouldn't give anyone that power ever again. Not until I love myself enough that someone's favour—or disfavour—won't turn the tide.

It's taken me almost four years to get back to a place of neutrality and vague acceptance of myself. Some days, like on Halloween, I think I'm beautiful. Inside and out. Other times, I hear Jack's voice in my head, the cruelty in his aloof, melancholic drawl, telling me how useless I am... and I believe it.

But I learned to not trust those thoughts once, and I can do it again. I'm going to *have* to do it again. Because what comes next is an entirely new challenge. One that will require all my confidence. The very best of me.

Tomorrow, I'll give myself permission to try and fail. I'll start planning and overthinking strategies for motherhood that are adaptable. I'll begin stockpiling baby clothes with easy fasteners, researching hands-free wraps and carriers, and plan on testing strollers and car seats.

But for today, I'll pretend that it won't be an issue at all. I'll let myself feel like anyone else who just found out they're pregnant unexpectedly. I'll feel giddy and terrified and nervous for all the usual reasons without adding further baggage on top. I can give myself today.

Doing just that, I sink farther into the bath and daydream. Eyes closed, with my hair flowing around me like ink in water. My ears under the surface blocking out the sounds from surrounding apartments, muffling Fleetwood Mac's "Songbird" until it's nothing but a softened lullaby.

I imagine a small, sweet newborn laid across my chest in here with me. I think of the many baths we'll take together. All the wonderful things we'll do together. The sleepless nights and the tantrums and the teething and all the other things parents worry about. But mostly, I think of the good. The bedtime stories and slow, sunbeam-filled mornings. The walks to the park where we pick dandelions or skip stones at the beach. The cuddles, the warmth, and the sanctity of loving someone more than myself.

And I tell myself, over and over and over again, that I *can* do this. Until, eventually, I feel like it's at least a little true.

CHAPTER 8

Nine Weeks Pregnant. Baby is the size of a grape.

I nhaling feels nearly impossible as I approach the end of the counter to pick up my order. Everything on the café's menu sounded disgusting. Just as most foods have for the last week. Even better, when the food *is* acceptable to my brain, I *still* throw it up later.

Doctor Salim calls it morning sickness, as if it doesn't happen every hour of the damn day. She did say it would most likely stop in the second trimester, and I pray she's right.

But today's nausea is not from the tiny baby growing inside me. No, *this* is the result of a week spent mulling over an imaginary conversation and still not being sure of what to say when Bo arrives. It's from not knowing how he'll respond *or* what my reaction to his response will be.

Granted, my emotions *have* been extremely up and down—again, to be expected—but this conversation is pit-in-your-stomach, sweating-when-it's-cold-out scary.

During this past week, I've begun attempting to calm myself with a peaceful visualisation entirely from my imagination. Me, on the beach in July. My belly *huge,* sticking out far past my bikini, and my brightly painted toes pressed into the sand, with a warm breeze blowing my hair off my face. I have both hands on my stomach, feeling the baby kicking up a storm as the seagulls fly overhead and the waves crash ashore.

I think, deep down, I'm reminding myself that either way, it will be okay. I'll still have me, the beach, and this baby come summertime, even if Bo reacts poorly. Even if he wants nothing to do with us. I'll still have my peace. I just might have to work a little harder for it.

I thank the barista, taking my London Fog to a small round table tucked away in the most private corner of the café. I sit facing the door and wait for the blond giant to arrive, fighting the urge to flee through the back exit or a bathroom window.

It was a little embarrassing to have to ask Bo to grab coffee, considering the last time we were together, he was getting dressed to leave *moments* after he'd been inside of me.

I'm sure he was under the same impression I was—that we'd never see or hear from each other again. There would be no follow-up, no dates, certainly no coffee meet-ups on a random Sunday morning two months later. But he agreed to meet me. So that's a start. Enthusiastically so, actually.

> ME: Hey Bo, this is Win.
> The other pirate from Hal-
> loween... I was wondering
> if you'd be free to grab cof-
> fee this weekend?

BO: Win, hey. You didn't
have to follow up your
name. I remember you, ob-
viously. And yeah, I'm up
for grabbing coffee. Do you
know Saints on Cosgrove
Ave? Sunday at ten?

The café door chimes, and in walks the unknowing father-to-be. And dammit, he's even more gorgeous when he's not dressed as a swashbuckler. He's got on a long beige sport coat and scarf with a green knitted sweater underneath. Black jeans with matching black boots. His beard is a little longer than it was on Halloween, and his hair is still just as unruly. He waves at me from the doorway as he kicks the snow off his boots, a broad smile overtaking his face. Then he points to the counter, silently asking, *do you want anything?*

I hold up my mug in response. He throws me a thumbs-up, turning toward the barista to order.

Poor guy has no idea his whole life is about to change.

I realise, suddenly, that I'm the Doctor Salim in this situation. I have to try to remain cool, factual, and compassionate. But *shit*, I don't know if I can be. I'm still reeling too. And I'm flustered around him. I've run into past hookups accidentally. The city isn't *so* big. But I've always been able to play it off. This, I certainly can't play off. There's nothing cool or casual about this.

Eventually, he makes his way over with a wide-mouthed mug and a plate filled with three different pastries. I grind my teeth, wondering if he'll wish he'd gotten them to-go.

"I thought we could share these," Bo says, setting the plate on the table between us. "And, uh, hi," he chimes warmly, lowering into the seat across from me, unwinding his brown scarf. "This was a pleasant surprise."

"Hi," I force out. My voice already has the *I'm so sorry* lilt to it. "Um, how are you?" I ask.

"I'm okay." Bo tilts his head and pushes his tongue against the corner of his mouth, eyeing me sceptically.

I can tell I look nervous, so it's not exactly surprising that he's already watching me with such concern. My lips are rubbing together against my will, and my eyes are twitching slightly, probably blinking a little too much. Plus, I can't seem to sit still.

I attempt to force a smile, but I can tell it's unconvincing when Bo's eyebrows knit together subtly.

He clears his throat with a fist in front of his mouth and continues. "Work has been busy. Um, it always picks up the closer we get to the holidays. Before we shut down for a little bit. But honestly, er, not much else is going on." He laughs half-heartedly, studying my expression some more.

"Right," I agree.

He takes a long sip of his coffee, his eyes darting to my bouncing knee at the side of the table. "Win, are you—"

"I'm pregnant," I interrupt loudly, all the breath leaving my lungs at the same time the words pass through my lips.

Bo pales instantly. His shoulders fall like he's forgotten how to support his own weight. "What?"

"I'm sorry," I whisper, "I couldn't hold that in any longer."

"You're..." He swallows, looking at the table between us. He raises his hands from his lap and places both palms flat on the table as he hunches over. "Did you say," he tilts up to look at me, his eyes wide and unblinking, "that... you're pregnant?"

"Yes. I-I did."

He nods. Then, again. Then so many times it seems like his neck might be broken. "Okay. All right. Okay. And I, uh, I gather you're telling *me* because..." He inhales a long, trembling breath, still nodding to himself.

"Yes. You are," I answer.

"Wow." He pinches the bridge of his nose, taking a deep breath. Then he rocks gently in his chair, his palm placed overtop his mouth with his fingers cradling his cheek. "Okay," he says into his hand. "Okay," he repeats, dropping it away.

"I know it's a lot." Wringing my hands in my lap, I look at the next table over and wonder how many times in my life I've sat next to life-altering conversations and remained blissfully unaware. "I'm sorry," I offer again.

"No, uh, I—" His breath shakes some more as he reaches for his coffee and takes another long sip. "Wow," he says, swallowing.

"Yeah," I agree. I look over to the end of the counter and notice a pitcher of water and glassware. "Would you like some water maybe?" I offer. Mostly, I just want to leave the table, even if only for a few seconds.

"Oh. Uh, yeah. Sure. Thanks."

I stand and pour two glasses, grateful for the momentary distance between myself and the bomb I just dropped. "Here," I say, placing it in front of him and taking my seat.

He chugs the whole thing in one go. "Shit, sorry. Um, how are you feeling? How are you? How—how are you?"

"I'm okay," I answer honestly. "I've been sick a lot. Nauseous. But I'm okay. We, er, *we're* okay." I place a hand on my belly under the table and out of view from him.

Meet your dad, kid.

"I really didn't see this coming." Bo's eyes finally stop bouncing around the room, and he holds them on me, confusion overtaking him. His whole face droops in concentration. I can practically see his brain replaying our evening together and the exact moment he gets to the missing condoms.

"Neither did I." I clear my throat. "I... I wasn't lying when I said I was on the pill."

"No, I didn't think that." His brows furrow as he quickly shakes his head.

"I wasn't trying to... you know... *get* knocked up or anything."

"Right."

"These things just happen, sometimes." I shrug, trying to act nonchalant where all I feel *is* chalant. *Very* chalant.

Bo rubs two palms down his face, dragging his skin in their path. "So... do we—do we get married?"

"What?" I jump back. "No! What? Why would we get married? We don't even know each other!"

He sits straighter, blowing out a breath. "Sorry, I'm not sure what came over me just then."

"The ghost of your great-grandfather, evidently," I say.

"But then, what do I do? How do I help? What can I—"

"Bo, I've decided to keep the baby," I interrupt. "I don't expect anything from you, but I will work with you here. However involved you want to be is fine by me, but you should know that I will expect you to stick around if you agree to be in their life. This isn't going to be a game of hide-and-go-seek father. You want the baby? You also have to be there for the kid, the teenager, and the adult too. Understand?"

That was the only part I rehearsed. It came out slightly different from how I planned, but I do feel a weight lifted having said what I came here to say. At least part of it. The rest, now, is up to him.

"Okay," he says, his lips slightly parted and his eyes distant once again.

For whatever reason, that perplexing expression on his face slows me. He's so forlorn—like something even heavier is weighing him down. Heavier than this, somehow. I want to inquire, but it might be none of my business. We're practically strangers, after all.

Still, sympathy for him builds. He's handling this relatively well, and from what I know so far, he seems like a good guy. Maybe I was a touch harsh. "You don't have to decide right now, obviously," I say gently, attempting to soften the blow.

He comes back from the far-off land, his stare focused and certain as he threads his fingers together in front of him on the table.

"No, I-I am *in*. However much I can be. However I can support you most, I'm in. Definitely."

"Oh," I whisper involuntarily. "Right," I concur.

"I'm sorry," he says on an exhale.

"It's no one's fault." I bite my lip, reconsidering. "Well, actually, it's definitely our fault. Both of us. A collective fault. I suck at taking my birth control on time, neither of us had condoms, and you probably could have pulled out."

"I didn't think—" He stops to take a *python* bite of some sort of chocolate pastry from his plate—chewing and nodding to himself. Then another bite, in which he finishes the whole thing. After, he reaches for another pastry and does the same. "I thought I couldn't," he says, mouth full.

"Couldn't what?" I ask. Have sex? He said it hadn't happened since he'd lost his leg. But *that* certainly happened. I already know that's why he wasn't carrying around condoms, if that's what he means.

He swallows the food down in a large gulp. "Win, there's something I think I should tell you..." Bo picks up another pastry, clearing the plate at a record-breaking speed.

I decide that he's a nervous eater once he throws the final pastry back whole and struggles with it until he swallows and takes a sip of coffee after to wash it down.

"Things in my life were not going according to plan a few years back, and I didn't..." He glances from side to side, appearing as if he'd rather crawl out of his skin than say whatever's next. It's now that I notice he barely fits in the café's chair, his frame overtaking it. For someone so physically large, he appears so small right now. He's shrunken in on himself, his face younger than before. When he finally stops fighting it, he rolls his neck and sits up straighter, his chest rising on a considerably long breath.

"I had cancer," he says abruptly. "Bone cancer. Stage three. I was diagnosed shortly after my twenty-eighth birthday and had my surgery last October. It was a—it *has* been a dark time for me. I didn't freeze my sperm before treatment. I didn't think I'd be around to use it, and I didn't think I'd want to. I had just gotten out of a relationship, and it all felt pretty hopeless."

"Oh," I say, startled. "I'm so sorry, I..." My voice fades away to nothing. What *is* there to say? Nothing useful. Nothing that could possibly capture how much I wish he hadn't had to go through that.

I attempt to slot *cancer* into the timeline I've begun crafting in my head, filled with mostly useless information from Caleb. I realise that this would be around the time of the sudden engagement and subsequent breakup with Cora.

I drag my eyes up from the corner of the table toward his face. "Bo, I am so—"

"I just... I didn't think this was possible," he interrupts, wiping a tear from the apex of his cheek. His *smile-risen* cheek. "Shit, sorry," he says, coughing. "I just..."

This is a *much* bigger conversation than I planned for. My heart breaks for the man across from me and yet feels put back together at once. Relieved by the promising, wonder-struck expression in his features.

I reach across the table, placing my hand against his elbow. When he feels my touch, he removes his hand from his face and moves to hold my hand instead, bringing my wrist to his mouth and pressing his lips to my pulse point.

It's not sexual at all. It's for the purpose of giving and receiving comfort. It's because neither of us knows what to say next.

"I'm going to be honest. I was *not* expecting happy tears," I say, half joking, trying my best to give him a reassuring smile as he drops our hands to the table between us.

Bo's laugh is bittersweet. "Neither was I." He clears his throat. "Sorry, I didn't mean to make this about me."

"I had my star-of-the-show moment at the doctor's office. *And* every day since," I say.

"You seem... calm?" he asks, sort of.

"Um, yeah. I think I am. I feel okay. When I'm not throwing up. I was really scared about telling you, actually, but other than that, I feel weirdly at peace about it all. I've always wanted a kid; I just didn't think it would be *this* unplanned."

He nods, studying me as if he's memorising my words. It's too much. Almost. Him staring as if I hold the answer to this predicament of ours. "Plus, as far as baby daddies go, mine has pretty good DNA," I say, putting the attention back on him as I remove my hand from his and place it back onto my lap.

"Minus the cancer," he says meekly, his eyes holding on me like an apology is being whispered between us.

Then it dawns on me. The reason for his far-off look earlier—his uncertainty about being able to commit to *every* future stage. "Are you still sick?" I ask cautiously, my heart in my throat.

"No. I'm not. I get tested every few months, and it's been clear for over a year now. But—" He breathes in through his teeth, shuffling in his chair. "There's always the chance it could come back somewhere else."

Nausea rises *again*.

"I'm sorry," he says with a tilted, uneasy frown. "I know that a guarantee would be nice."

"No, Bo... Don't." I shake my head that's hanging between us. "There's no guarantee for any of us. We just have to do the best with the time we've got," I say, tilting up to look at him.

His nose twitches, along with his lips, an unexpected grin appearing. "We're speaking in clichés now, huh?" he teases.

I scoff, despite my own smile growing. "Shut up," I whisper, laughing. "Sorry. There's no finding-out-your-surprise-baby-dad-dy-had-cancer how-to guide. I don't know what to do here. I thought I'd be the one with all the juicy news today."

"No, I appreciate it," he says with no sincerity, "try adding something like *there's a reason for everything.*"

I roll my eyes.

"Ooh! Or *you're so brave*—I always liked that one."

"You know, actually, this was all an elaborate ruse. I'm not pregnant. I'll be on my way." I cross my arms, leaning back in my chair and smirking.

"No?" he asks. "Wow, you are *full* of surprises."

"I was just bored, you know? Figured maybe I could get a free cup of coffee out of it. But it's not worth it. You're far too annoying."

He licks his lips. The mischievous gleam in his eye tells me he's thinking of his next quip. I wait impatiently, remembering how fun this rapport between us is. Then he blinks and shakes himself, wiping the expression from his face entirely.

"When did you find out?" he asks softly.

Oh, right. I suppose we've got more important things to discuss.

"Last week. The baby is due July twenty-fourth." I look at the emptied plate between us, covered in sugar dust and crumbs. "And I have an ultrasound booked for next Friday."

"Friday?" he asks, pulling out his phone. "What time?"

"Yeah. Four."

"Where?" He looks up, thumbs poised to type.

"The clinic on West Ninth—it's a blue building."

He types that into his phone, nodding, then tucks it into his front pocket. "Want me to pick you up?"

"You... you're coming?" I ask.

"Obviously."

"No, uh, I'll meet you there."

"So..." He smiles weakly, taking a breath that seems to calm him some. "What happens now?"

"Can you get us more snacks?" I point to the graveyard of pastries. "I'm hungry."

The abruptness in which he stands and walks over to the counter to order makes me shake my head, a small smile forming.

A dangerous feeling erupts in my chest. A goofy, body-possessing type of affection for this man. I shove it down and blame the hormones, some primal part of my DNA telling me to stick close to the man I procreated with.

At least, given that we'll have to spend—you know—*forever* in proximity, he's not entirely intolerable.

CHAPTER 9

Ten Weeks Pregnant. Baby is the size of a strawberry.

"Happy tears?" Sarah asks, flipping a chair onto a table for me to sweep under. She's been stopping by the café at the end of my shift for years. Returning like a stray cat, knowing the leftover pastries must go *somewhere*. But she usually ends up cleaning alongside me. I like to tease her that she's cosplaying as a woman who has to pay her own bills. She jokes back, disturbingly, about how she earns her lifestyle in the bedroom.

"Happy tears, Sar." I flash my eyes at her, hand resting at the top of my broom. "Truly the *last* thing I was expecting."

"But that's good, right?" She lifts the opposite chair, placing it upside down on the table.

"It felt good in the moment but—"

"But you went home and started overthinking," Sarah interrupts me. I glare at her. She sighs, her eyes mustering *some* amount of patience, but her expression tired. "Win, sometimes good things are just good things. Bo was happy about the kid. Let's celebrate that."

I make a sceptical whining sound from the back of my throat. "I thought Jack was sweet at first. He did all the right things too."

I notice it each time. The little flicker Sarah's eyes do when I bring up Jack. She performs a quick surveillance of my face to determine how upset I am just at the mention of his name. My *own* mention, mind you.

"Bo is not Jack," she says carefully.

"You haven't even met Bo," I point out.

"Caleb vouches for him, and I trust my man," she says, reaching for another chair to stack for me.

I stop sweeping, thinking about how wrong I've been before. How well some men hide their ugly side and how quickly they can turn. "I need to get to know him more, right? Like, he wants to be involved and come to all the appointments and stuff. But we're basically strangers. What if he wants to be in the delivery room? He'll see *everything*," I say, grimacing.

"Bo seeing *everything*"—Sarah gestures wildly with an open palm toward my hips—"is how you got into this situation." She takes the broom from me, as I've apparently lost the ability to speak and sweep at the same time. "I think you'll be fine."

I shudder. "There's a difference between a dimmed bedroom after a few drinks and a handsome stranger standing between my stirrup-parted legs and looking into the eye of the storm."

"Did you just refer to your *vagina* as the eye of the storm?"

"In that delivery room? Yes. That is what it will be."

"He doesn't have to be there if you don't want him to. But for the record," she pauses, putting a firm hand on my shoulder, "I love you, but I will *not* be there."

"Sarah, you faint at nosebleeds. I won't let you *near* me while I'm in labour."

"Even just thinking about it makes me ill," she whispers, her attention lost over my shoulder.

"Yes, thank you." I stare at her blankly. "That's very helpful."

She rolls her eyes, then follows me to the next table, sweeping around the counter next to it as I wipe the table down. "The ultrasound is Friday afternoon, right? If he's free afterward, you should invite him to our place. We'll do a game night. If we all team up, we can see how he reacts to losing. That's like a fundamental test of stability."

"He's probably travelling this weekend for the holidays. His dad lives in France."

"See? You do know stuff about him!" She sweeps up the mess into a dustpan. "Just invite him. If he's busy, he's busy. But I doubt he'll say no to an extra bit of time with his sexy baby mama." She shimmies her shoulders at me, waggling her brows. "Maybe he'll try to knock you up again."

"There will be absolutely *none* of that."

"What are you worried about? Twins? That's not how it works."

"We have to..." I say, trying to formulate words as Sarah dances against me suggestively. "We have to remain entirely professional. We're colleagues now."

She stops dancing, mid-pelvic thrust. "*Colleagues?*"

"Fine, not colleagues. But you get my point. We have to still like each other in nine months. Hell, we have to like each other for the next eighteen years. *Minimum.*"

Sarah nods, standing slowly and folding her arms across her chest. "But," she says tentatively, "would it be so bad if maybe you were like co-parents with benefits? Obviously, you have chemistry. And the sex was good."

"I never said the sex was good."

She points to my face, barely stopping short of poking me with the tip of her acrylic nail. "But *that* does. Every time Bo has come up, you blush a little. You're betrayed by those sweet, supple cheeks of yours yet again."

"Don't say weird shit like *supple cheeks* while you're this close to me." I swat her hand away. "Fine," I give in, "the sex was good." *Possibly the best ever.* Though I don't add that aloud. "But it would still complicate things," I argue.

"Or make things fun? From where I'm standing, Bo is a hottie with nice clothes, baby-news happy tears, a great sense of humour, a good job, and a house of his own. All *your* words; not mine." She stands straighter and sticks her nose up, acting like a sit-com character from the fifties. "Oh golly, what trouble! I sure do hope you don't fall in love with a man such as this!"

I resist the urge to flick her nose right out of the air. "You're incorrigible."

"And you're not thinking of all your options here, babe." She hops up onto the counter and brushes off her hands. "Just, don't close yourself off to getting to know him in more ways than one," Sarah says, surprisingly earnest. "You deserve good things. Let's see if he's a good thing. That's *all* I'm saying."

"He is a good thing, Sar. For the kid." I lift to sit next to her on the counter. "He's going to stick around, and that's all I need from him."

"Okay, I hear you." She lets a few seconds of weighted silence pass, but I know she's not done. Sarah rarely backs down. "But..." *There it is.* "Stop me when I'm close to the size of his dick." She places her palms together in front of her and slowly starts separating them. Her mouth continues to fall farther open as her hands drift farther apart.

"Yep. *There,*" I say with a satisfied smile.

"Seriously?" Sarah whispers, eyes playful.

"Seriously," I answer, feeling awfully proud of myself for something that is certainly not an achievement. At least not *my* achievement.

"No wonder you got pregnant. The guy had a direct line of sight to your ovaries! A clean shot!"

"I'm buying you an anatomy book for Christmas."

"I blame our health class teacher," Sarah sighs.

"Do *not* bring Mrs. Forestein into this. She tried her best." I look around the café, cleaned and prepped for the morning shift to take over. Still, I find myself not wanting to leave just yet. We do this sometimes, linger long past closed. Going home can be hard, admittedly. It's a touch lonely there.

"I'll invite him Friday." I attempt—and fail—to gracefully lower myself off the counter and nearly roll an ankle. "But don't pull anything. No shenanigans."

"It will be purely an investigative mission on the behalf of my future niece," Sarah says, hands clasped over her heart.

"Or nephew," I add, reaching out my hand to help her down.

"Hey, uh..." Sarah gets uncharacteristically timid, looking at our hands pressed together. "Have you considered whether they'll have a little hand too?"

"The baby?" I ask. "Oh, uh, no. I *think* it's random. Not genetic."

"Right, but, like, the theory was that it's because of your mom's uterus, right? Like your hand was pushed up against the side of it? Her uterus was a weird shape or something?"

"That's what Mom always said, but... who knows?"

"So, like, are uteruses-eses genetic?" she fumbles.

"I don't know," I say, zoning out over her shoulder. "I'm not sure."

Sarah's smile is small but reassuring as she leans into view. "You'd have *wicked* secret handshakes."

I take a deep breath, bringing myself back into the room. It is that simple, I suppose. Nothing to worry about, because we won't know until we know, and even if that is the case, it's not a *bad* thing... right? "We would," I agree.

"Let's get you home." Sarah throws her arm around my shoulders and guides me toward the back door.

CHAPTER 10

I had to leave work early to make it to the ultrasound on time. Thankfully, the café's owner, Lisa, is unquestionably high most days and doesn't particularly care about any of her staff's personal lives, interests, or—quite often—names. She didn't bother to ask what the nature of my appointment was when she sent me on my way.

I've been working at the café long enough that I've earned that level of trust. Enough to bail on the end of my shift, at least. I'm not technically a supervisor, but I've picked up a few extra tasks here and there when asked.

I make the schedule, mostly so I can control who closes the night before I open. I also train the new employees when Lisa's not around. But I don't want the title of assistant manager, though she's offered it to me a few times. That title comes with expectations of sticking around. It was never supposed to be a permanent position. I've had one foot out the door since I started. Not that I've done anything to get *two* feet out.

Snow has just started falling when I get off the bus and begin walking toward the big blue medical building across the street. Walking through the front doors, I spot Bo in the lobby. He's standing under a directional sign, looking down at his phone. I make a quick note that the ultrasound office is on the second floor before looking at him as I make my way over.

He's wearing a brown suede coat and blue jeans. Much more casual than his outfit from last week at the café, but still more put-together than me in my black yoga pants and a teal sweater I knit last winter zipped under my knee-length puffy purple jacket and far-too-long scarf that I've nearly suffocated myself under.

Have I mentioned I hate winter?

"Well, fancy meeting you here," I chime, unwinding the scarf from around my neck.

When Bo looks up, he's already smiling. "Hey, *you*." He slips his phone into his back pocket. "We've got to stop *bump-ing* into each other like this," he says, awfully proud of himself.

"Really? Bumping?" I raise a brow.

He shrugs, his cheeky grin far too wide for his face. His *stupidly* handsome face.

"Ready?" I ask, tilting my chin toward the stairs.

He nods, immediately following me as I start walking toward the second floor. "Oh, wait," Bo says urgently, reaching for my hand. He tugs me closer by my wrist, and I huff in a breath at the surprise of being pulled to an abrupt stop.

"Sorry. Before I forget." He pulls his phone back out of his pocket and holds it up in front of us, turning his camera around so he and I fill up the small screen. "Three, two..." *Click.*

I smile automatically when presented with my own reflection, but I'm still questioning why we just took a photo together in the middle of the lobby when Bo places his phone into his pocket and starts walking toward the stairs as if nothing odd happened at all.

"What was that?" I ask, my tone half amusement and half confusion.

Bo pouts disingenuously, as if to say *oh, you poor thing.* "A cell phone, honey."

"Yes, thank you. I'm familiar. But why did you take our photo?" *And you probably shouldn't call me honey. It does things to my stomach. Like what I'd expect a cartwheel in space to feel like.*

"I'm documenting! We're about to meet our kid. I don't want to forget anything."

"Okay." I smile, despite my eyes narrowing in on this strange, strange man. "Fair enough." I charge up the steps, making it to the first landing before dread sets over me, realising Bo's half a staircase behind, walking at his own, necessary pace.

I fight the urge to apologise and draw *more* attention to our difference in speed, and instead decide to act as if I'm fascinated by the shitty mural on the landing until Bo's once again next to me. Then I walk slower, matching his pace until we reach the ultrasound office.

I give my name and identification to the receptionist before we're seated in a waiting room alongside a *very* pregnant woman and her partner. The room has bright blue walls and awful fluorescent lighting. Decals of butterflies and forest animals half-cling to the walls, and there's a small selection of magazines in the corner, which the far-more-pregnant lady is rifling through.

She looks… *smug*. Rubbing her belly like it's a fortune teller's crystal ball. Smiling with a pointed-up nose as if she, and she alone, is keeping the human species from extinction.

"First one?" she asks, her voice like spun sugar as she points toward my stomach. She snaps that finger back into place, raising her shoulders with giddy amazement.

I nod, wearing a polite, thin-lipped smile.

"Your first is *so* special. Oh, but you must be *really* scared," she pouts insincerely.

No shit.

"Poor thing," she coos, frowning.

Did I answer her that time? I check with Bo, who's suddenly fascinated by the nonexistent lint on his jeans, picking at his knee. His subtle side-eye matched with his tilted smirk tells me he's also hearing how ridiculous fertile-Myrtle is being. Though, based on her tone, she might prefer *Mother Mary* as her nickname.

"This is probably *our* last scan." She places a hand with a diamond ring so large on her stomach that I worry about the load-bearing weight of her placenta. "We're thirty-nine weeks." She places her *other* hand on her husband's shoulder. He's beaming at her with pride, his eyes glued to her. He looks distinctly like Ned Flanders, with a bushy moustache and a *golly-gosh* way about him.

"We'll be having this baby any day now," Ned chimes to Myrtle, loud enough for the room to hear.

"Wow, and you're not even showing." I point to his stomach, wearing a shit-eating grin that *could* be mistaken as friendly.

"Oh boy, she's funny." Myrtle points to me, looking at Bo. "Hopefully that's genetic."

"Funny wife, happy life—that's what I always say," Ned adds from beside her.

Bo gives me the smallest, briefest glance that asks about a hundred things. I agree, silently, to all of them.

"Oh, I wouldn't know. We only just met in the lobby. I wanted to see what all the fuss was about, and she allowed me to follow her up," Bo delivers, deadpan.

"I'm Guinevere, by the way." I present my hand to shake. "Sorry, forgot to introduce myself before."

"Lance," he replies, looking at the couple across from us. "You are?"

"Melissa..." she answers, oddly shy all of a sudden.

"Ted." *Close enough.*

"Good to meet you both." Bo bows his head across the aisle. "And you," he says, winking at me, out of our new friends' view, as to not blow our cover.

"So... you're not the father?" Ted (née: Ned) asks.

"Whose father?" Bo replies, dumbfounded.

"*Her* baby." Ted looks at me, his lips parted and pointing away from one another. Poor man could not be more confused.

"Oh! Gwen's baby?" Bo points to me with his thumb.

I fight a laugh so hard my nose twitches.

"Yes," Ted clarifies, growing more bewildered by the second. Bless him. Melissa only looks annoyed, glaring at her cuticles.

"No, he isn't," I confirm, my voice wavering. "But," I turn to Bo, "if you *are* available, the job can be yours."

"Oh, wow." Bo places a hand across his heart, holding eye contact with me. It takes everything in me not to crack a smile. "I would be *honoured*..."

Melissa clears her throat, capturing our attention. "You know, if you didn't want to talk, you could have just said so. You don't have to be rude."

Ted, seemingly oblivious, is still enraptured by our little performance. "So you don't know who the dad is?"

"It's a bit of a *Mamma Mia* situation, I'm afraid," I answer.

"Here we go again," Bo mutters under his breath as Melissa pulls Ted toward her and begins whispering into his ear. Once finished telling her husband to *stop* interacting with us, Melissa reaches next to her and opens a *People* Magazine from the early 2000s with an aggressive flourish.

Bo and I avoid eye contact, but I feel his shoulders shaking next to mine as he suppresses his laughter to no more than a few broken breaths. I've only ever been that stupid in public with Sarah, knowing that she'd always have my back. I suppose it can be taken as a good sign that being stupid alongside Bo came so easily.

Though I do feel a *little* bad for Ted. Sweet, simple Ted.

"McNulty?" The tech calls from around the corner, appearing only once I look toward the incoming voice.

"Yep!" I push to stand and notice my legs suddenly feel a lot weaker than when I walked up the stairs. Honestly, I'm grateful to Melissa, Ted, *and* Bo for the welcomed distraction up until this point. I was beyond nervous at work all day and barely slept last night.

It's not that I think something terrible has happened to the baby. It's been pretty smooth sailing symptoms-wise, though I'm still nauseous every day. Doctor Salim promises that having to keep a sick bag in my purse and crackers next to the bed is a good sign the baby is growing strong.

The fear, I think, is coming from how real this all suddenly seems. As if every step closer to the patient's table at the end of this hallway is a recommitment to choosing *this* path forward. A reminder that I've made this *very* big decision with *very* little logic and a whole lot of instinct. Keeping *the* baby felt hypothetical to some degree. Once we're in that room, I'm keeping *my* baby. *Our* baby.

Bo's walking faster than my legs will let me go, ahead of me, next to the technician. He turns over his shoulder and gives me a sweet, encouraging wink and smile before turning back around.

I can't help but wonder if he feels *this* too. The seriousness of this moment. The immense pressure. The looming feeling, as if gravity has been sucked out of this building and we're floating down this hallway. Barrelling, really, toward this new reality.

Probably not.

Though when I find myself lying on the table in the middle of the room, hiking my shirt up to expose my still unchanged belly, I look to *him* for comfort on my left. And Bo provides it, reaching out a hand for me to hold.

"It's okay," he tells me. His voice reminds me of the way parents comfort their children before the plane takes off. A tone of *people have done this before; there's no reason to worry,* but a tiny hint of concern of their own lying underneath, as if to say, *then again, plane crashes do happen.*

"Promise," he says, his brows furrowing as he nods—his expression more concentrated and steady. I must look as scared as I feel for him to have to throw a word like *promise* around.

The tech is talking, a *lot,* to my right. And I'm only picking up about half of it. I keep my eyes on Bo. Watching him listen to her intently and nod along keeps me from spiralling even further. He's present, at least. He'll leave with whatever information we might need.

The tech's hand on my right shoulder makes me turn toward her and the machine she's standing in front of. "I'm going to apply the gel now—it'll be cold. We'll make sure to wipe it all off once finished." She shows me a bottle of gel, and I nod, smiling weakly.

I tighten my hold on Bo's hand. He squeezes back rhythmically, as if he's attempting to match my heartbeat. I find myself briefly wishing I had brought Sarah along too. That way, I wouldn't be clinging to this guy for dear life.

Cold gel lands on my stomach, and I feel pressure as the tech lowers the probe and presses down more forcefully than I was expecting. She's really digging around down there. After a few achingly long seconds, I start to worry that maybe she can't find the baby. That maybe there *is* no more baby.

Dread creeps up my spine like ice water as a million and one worst-case scenarios take my brain hostage. I feel a chill in the room that wasn't there before, a cool breeze washing over my skin, raising each hair, goose bumps forming across my skin. Every nerve ending sends a signal that it is *absolutely* time to panic. But then Bo's gasp pulls me back from the ledge.

I look at him as he, wide-eyed and slack-jawed, stares at the screen behind me that I'm too afraid to face. He exhales shakily, joy overtaking his features. He leans forward, whispering something I don't quite make out that I'm not even sure he intended to say. Then he stills when the probe moves again, angling against my stomach.

I watch as Bo's small wonderment bursts into a full-fledged, beaming smile that he attempts to subdue by biting his lip and shaking his head.

"Winnifred?" the tech says from behind me. "Did you want to see as well?"

I turn slowly, bracing for impact with squinted eyes and puckered lips.

But there, on the black and white screen, is a small, perfect, bean-like *thing*.

My baby.

Not *the* baby. But *my* baby.

And it's not nearly as terrifying as I thought it would be—knowing it's mine. It's actually really fucking unreal. An honour. An amazing, incredible, spectacular, sublime *thing*.

I watch as the baby moves in tiny, fluttering rotations. Relief warms my skin and senses like standing under a sunbeam on an otherwise cloudy day, my heart swelling with joy to the point where I feel it might give out.

The tech smiles softly as she presses the probe against me further, trying to get a better view on the screen. "They're certainly active," she says. "You're going to have your hands full with this one."

"Hmm," I murmur my agreement. *Hands are kinda the issue here, lady.*

The baby moves on the screen again. A little twitch-like jump that reminds me of a flea. And I forget the world.

Do it again, I shout internally, imagining my veins and the blood pumping through them as radio transmitters, hoping foolishly that the baby can hear me somehow.

Bo laughs, deep and low, as the kid does another flip away from the probe's view. "Seems like they want some privacy," he says.

"Oh my *gosh*, Mom and Dad-*uh*. Leave me alone," I say like a moody teenager.

"You guys are *so* annoying," Bo adds in his own similar whine.

We're already so obnoxious. I love it. Probably more than I should.

The tech types as she continues clicking around the image, making notes and taking measurements. Her concentrated face could be just that: concentration. But it could equally be concern. Maybe there's something not quite right only someone with a trained eye could notice.

"They're okay?" The two words fall out before I think to ask them.

"All seems well to me," she answers, turning to face me instead of the screen. "Do you want to hear the heartbeat?"

"Yes, please," Bo and I answer in unison.

With a few buttons pressed and knobs twisted, a quiet sound begins. Turned louder, the baby's heartbeat fills the room, reverberating against the walls in a perfect rhythm. The most life-altering, exquisite sound.

It's all I can hear. Above my panted breaths. Above Bo's seemingly subconscious happy murmurs of amazement. Above *everything*. The city outside, the voice of anxiety in my head, the subtle creaking of my ribs tightening under the weight of all this change.

Ba-dum, ba-dum, ba-dum. Like a steady train.

Ba-dum, ba-dum, ba-dum. Not a mistake.

Ba-dum, ba-dum, ba-dum. A *happy* accident.

"Wow," I breathe out, tears blotting along my lower lashes.

"Heart rate is one-sixty-seven," the tech says, typing.

"Is that good?" Bo asks softly, as if to not disturb the moment.

"Yes, that's right where we want it."

He huffs a sigh of relief. Then his warm lips are pressed on the back of my hand. I turn away from the screen toward him, hit with a rush of surprise at that form of contact. Which may be absurd, considering all we've done.

"Thank you for letting me be here," he says. Or maybe he mouths it, I'm not sure. All I can hear is that steady beating heart.

"Can you record this?" I ask hoarsely, emotion tightening my throat.

Bo lets go of my hand to pull out his phone, then, after a moment, holds it up slightly, the voice recorder on his phone blinking red.

A few moments later, the nurse turns the volume down slowly and shuts off her machines. "We'll print off some photos for you. You can expect to hear from your doctor within the next few days—" The tech stops herself. "Well, actually, given that it's only two days before Christmas, you most likely won't. But," she leans close to whisper, "I can tell you there's absolutely nothing to worry about. Just between us." She winks.

"Thank you," I say.

"I'll give you two a minute," she says, handing me a warm towel. "For the gunk." She points to my stomach as she walks around the bed and leaves.

"That was amazing," Bo says as I wipe off my stomach. "They're a lot less human-looking than I was expecting, though."

"Like a little jelly bean," I say, smiling fondly.

"And it was moving a lot," he says in disbelief. "Like, it's free to just move about in there. It's wild."

"They seem to be making themself at home, yes." I sit up, lowering my shirt. "Wow..." I say again, because *wow*.

"Yeah..." Bo says on a long breath, a crooked smile in full, bold agreement.

"A baby," I say, flashing my eyes at him.

"A baby," he repeats, shaking his head.

"Insane."

Bo sighs, dragging a hand down his face. "Pretty fucking cool," he says, then looks up at me. We share a small, giddy smile before I hop off the table and we make our way out toward the reception-ist's desk.

After the tech hands us an envelope with two identical ultra-sound photos, we walk downstairs to the lobby in companionable silence. Arriving at the main floor, I notice the snow is coming down harder, illuminated only by the streetlamps outside.

"Yikes," I say, looking out toward the no-doubt blistering cold, winding my scarf around my neck.

"Can I give you a ride?" Bo asks, buttoning up his coat. But then he stops and watches me intently for a moment. "Actually, I'm going to insist. I'm giving you a ride."

I roll my eyes with affection. "Yes, that would be nice. Thank you." Then I remember Sarah's suggestion. "Actually... do you have plans tonight?"

He finishes doing up his coat, shoving both hands into his pockets. "No." He raises a brow, lifting the corner of his mouth alongside it. "What were you thinking?"

"Want to come to Caleb and Sarah's with me? We're doing a game night."

He nods enthusiastically. "Yeah, sure. I'd love that. My car is around the corner." Bo opens the front door, and we step out into the storm. He leads me by a floating hand above my waist toward his car as the wind whistles around us. The passenger door is opened for me and closed behind me. Then I'm regaining my senses and attempting to warm my hands with my breath as he opens his door briefly before throwing himself inside.

His car is *really* nice. I don't know a lot about cars, but with a monitor screen the size of a tablet in the centre console and leather-wrapped seats with buttons for seat warmers, I imagine it cost a pretty penny.

"Great ride," I say like a total dunce.

His lip twitches as he pushes a button and the car erupts with beeps and lights and a subtle *vroom* of the engine. "Thanks."

"You remember how to get to Sarah's?"

"Think so. Pretty sure everything about that house is carved into my memory." He pulls off the side street, windshield wipers working overtime.

At first, I think he means it because of how nice their home is, or something alluding to Sarah and Caleb's obvious wealth. But then I realise the way in which he said it. As if the home was infamous. Referring, subtly, to the *last* time we were both at Sarah and Caleb's. I feel my cheeks warm with a blush and thank the moon for not shining too brightly.

"I'm glad you asked me to come. Honestly, I haven't been sure about how to do *this*, but I think spending some non-appointment time together would be good. To get to know each other. We're sort of..." His voice trails off as he looks over his shoulder, changing lanes.

"Stuck together?" I offer.

"I was going to say something like working toward a mutual goal, but that sounded too unattached."

"I called us colleagues the other day, and Sarah was aghast."

"Aghast, huh?" he teases.

"Flabbergasted, if you will."

"But there is no proper term for this," he says in a way of agreement.

"Co-parents, I guess."

"But *parents* feels like a title reserved for when a kid is physically present," Bo says. "No offence." He speaks to my belly.

"Let's aim for friends?" I suggest.

"Friends that are having a baby together."

"Yes. Friends with foetuses."

"A totally new type of benefit." He laughs. "But yes. Friends is good."

"Great," I concur.

"I'm going to friend the shit out of you, Freddie McNulty."

"So aggressive," I say, giggling.

"A trait of mine you should probably know. I'm wildly competitive. Even in a mutually beneficial task. So prepare to be friended. Hard."

"You've already made it weird." I sit straighter, crossing my arms. "And you should know, I'm also very competitive. Which, I'm sad to say, is why you'll never win. I'm going to be your best friend so fast that your head will spin. As for you? You'll be a mere acquaintance to me."

"You're on," Bo fires back.

"And don't call me Freddie," I say, crossing my arms.

"Sure thing, *Frederick*."

CHAPTER 11

"What in the *ever-loving fuck* is going on?" Sarah asks, whisper-yelling, as she reaches for more tortilla chips from her pantry.

Sarah and I have teamed up for every round of *Catan* since Bo and I arrived three hours ago, and yet we're still not coming close to either of us winning. Bo is absurdly good at board games, and Caleb is certainly not helping by giving the guy every trade he asks for.

"If I knew, we wouldn't be getting our asses kicked by the Jolly Green Giant out there. I blame Caleb," I answer, pulling salsa out of the fridge.

"Bo's so eerily calm while trading. It's like he *knows* what you're going to do. It's... strangely hot?" Sarah says, taking the jar from me, her face twisted into concern.

"Oh thank goodness. I thought it was just me," I whisper. "Like, he keeps doing this smug little chin-scratch thing when he builds a new settlement and—" I cut myself off. "Oh my god, what am I saying? What is he doing to us?"

"Babe?" Caleb says from the archway as he enters the kitchen. "Hey, d'ya need some help?"

"Yes, we need help," Sarah seethes. "Help understanding why you'd give that man six ore for one *fucking* sheep."

"Honestly?" Caleb asks. "I don't know. It's like he just charmed them out of my hand."

"We need to get it together and form a united front. He is *destroying* us." Sarah sighs, reaching in front of me for a chip bowl from the cabinet. "Maybe we should just stop playing board games and go into full interrogation mode. Who is this guy? What went down with the she-devil? Why did he call off the engagement? What are his intentions with Winnie? Caleb, you'll be the good cop. *Obviously.*"

I'm about to protest when footfalls sound from the hallway.

"Everyone in here?" Bo questions, entering the kitchen in leisurely stride with a hand in his jeans pocket. He glances around, taking in our faces with a perplexed smile. "Did something happen?"

"Nope! Totally fine," Sarah replies in a pitch several octaves above normal.

"They're a little mad you're winning at everything," Caleb says. The little rat.

"I did try to warn you," Bo says, pointing to me, grinning *far* too wide. "I'm competitive." He shrugs one shoulder.

"This isn't normal competitive," I argue, pointing back at him.

Bo moves closer to me, his eyes held on my extended finger as he keeps walking, only stopping when the tip of my finger presses into the hardness of his ribs. I ignore the overturning sensation in my stomach as he arrogantly smiles down at where we touch.

"You're not flipping the Monopoly board because you lost or faking dice rolls. This is some sort of sexy Jedi-mind-trick shit." I jab him in the ribs *hard* before turning toward the kitchen's barstools and dropping onto one with the tiniest of tantrums.

"Me? Sexy?" Bo clutches his chest, amusement lighting up his features.

"You pulled that word out of context."

"We don't know how you're doing it, but *when* we figure it out, you're done," Sarah says, stepping to my side and throwing her arm around my shoulders.

"Maybe we just play a new game? Cards?" Caleb suggests, his mouth full of chips and salsa.

Three, two, one...

"Strip poker?" Sarah says, crossing the kitchen toward her husband, smiling ear to ear.

"*Sarah*," Caleb sighs out quietly, letting his head hang. "No," he says, dejected. *No,* he mouths again when she pouts at him, twisting her body from side to side, quietly pleading.

"I'm always up for a little strip poker," Bo says, smirking at my friend.

"Oh god," Caleb says to no one in particular, his expression filled with horror. "There's two of them now."

"No one is getting naked," I say, at first to Caleb, then to the two troublemakers. "The last time I was naked in this home, I left with a very expensive, lifelong party favour. So, no thanks."

Bo's laugh escapes through tightly closed lips. "Fair enough." He reaches across the counter for a chip, tosses it into the air, and catches it in his mouth.

"Ooh! Speaking of that party favour..." Sarah walks to the other side of the kitchen and into her butler's pantry, disappearing out of view. "I got you two a present," she says, returning with a basket that covers half her torso. It's wrapped in clear cellophane with a big red ribbon on the top.

"Sarah," I whine as she places the present on the opposite end of the island. "Christmas is in two days. You really shouldn't have."

Sarah turns her attention to Bo, straightening her back with false wounded pride. "Win hates presents. Because we have money, and she doesn't, and that makes her uncomfortable. Even though I have told her many times that it's my way of showing love, she continually tries to deny me. How do *you* feel about presents, Bo? And please answer carefully—this *will* determine whether I like you or not."

"I love them," Bo says abruptly, taking a few strides over to the counter, eyeing the gift cautiously. "Thank you."

Sarah makes a proud *hmph* sound in the back of her throat.

"*Judas*," I whisper, glaring at Bo.

"Are you really not going to open this present with me?" he asks, toying with the ribbon—mimicking pulling it off. A sudden, striking image of him toying with my panties thrashes around my brain, then leaves just as quickly as it came.

"I worked *so* hard on it," Sarah adds in the same mocking voice.

These two are a dangerous and annoying combination.

"Fine," I say, hopping off the barstool and moving to stand next to Bo.

I tug indelicately on the ribbon and gesture for Bo to do the rest once it's off. He unwraps the cling-wrap, revealing the green woven basket underneath filled to the brim with items, some wrapped and others not, and one white card-sized box with writing on it sitting on top.

Twenty Questions to Fall in Love, I read.

I turn my gaze toward Sarah, who's spilling over with mischievous glee.

Really? I ask her silently, my right eye twitching in her direction.

"I saw a video about this game online. The title is... *evocative,* but really, it's just twenty questions to get to know someone well, quickly. I thought that may be helpful," she says that word sharply toward me, "since you two have a lot of catching up to do in the getting-to-know-each-other-while-*clothed* department."

I fight the urge to mock her in a childlike whine and repeat her last few words out loud.

"That's very thoughtful, thank you," Bo says, as if he's schooling me to do the same. I'm about to roll my eyes when he continues with, "we were just talking about having to get to know each other more on the way here. So this is great."

"Yes," I give in, *only a little.* "Thanks."

Bo picks up the card box, flipping it over in his hand.

I nod, smiling politely, and reach for another gift to pull out.

"And to think," Caleb whispers dramatically, circling the counter to stand next to me. "If you did one question every day, you could be in love in less than three weeks."

I smack him over the head with the *really* nice bath pillow Sarah picked out.

"Thank you, *Sarah,* for the gift," I say pointedly, glaring at him.

"I also made sure to stock condoms in the guest bedroom in your honour. Extra-large ones too," she says, winking at Bo.

He sputters a cough, which I find *deeply* rewarding.

"I'm sorry," I mumble into the space between our shoulders, pulling my lips in to stop a grin.

"No you're not," he replies for my ears only, reaching into the basket alongside me as I pull out something soft and white.

"Aww," Caleb coos at the onesie in my hand.

"That's *small,*" Bo stares, blinking slowly.

"Babies tend to be," I reply, rubbing the soft cotton against my cheek.

"Bo, how big were you when you were born?" Sarah asks, eyeing his tall frame.

"Oh, uh, I don't know actually." He shrugs, pulling out some chocolates that he points at enthusiastically. "Fucking *love* these."

"Ask your mother. I'm worried about my girl's parts," Sarah says.

Caleb groans, catching Sarah's attention from across the counter.

"What?" Sarah asks, looking between the men.

"My mom passed away when I was really young," Bo says without emotion, pulling out a sleeve of crackers. "Ooh these are my favourite." He rips them open with vigour and takes a loud bite, nodding as he chews, as if he's listening to his favourite song.

Who has a favourite cracker?

"Sorry." Sarah winces.

"No big deal." Bo smiles at her, swallowing. "Thanks again for all of this. And for letting me crash game night." He turns to Caleb. "You too, man."

"You're welcome," Caleb says as Sarah walks around the island toward him, placing her arm around his back. "We like to keep in touch with *every* couple that conceives a baby in our home."

"Yes, it's a tradition of ours," Sarah adds.

"I didn't realise this was such a common occurrence. Is there a support group? An online forum?" Bo asks.

"Yes, they meet here Tuesdays at eleven," Sarah replies. "Light refreshments are served."

"Wonderful. Count us in," Bo says, pulling out the last item. "Whoa," he chuckles, "I *don't* think this is for me."

I turn my attention to the box in his hand and immediately swat it away. The second the box hits the kitchen floor, I kick it instinctively. Hard enough that it soars across the room, through the kitchen's entrance, and down the hallway. Bo stays, slightly red-faced, looking at his feet and biting his lip.

"Sarah Abilene Linwood," I say, grinding my jaw. *You promised no funny business,* I say telepathically, flaring my eyes at her.

She clasps both hands in front of her mouth, but it does nothing to quell her laughter. "Okay, in my defence, I started this as a present just for you, and I *may* have forgotten *that* was in there."

Caleb eyes me impishly as he slinks off his stool and creeps toward the hallway. I glare at him as he tiptoes backward, looking like a cartoon villain.

I don't have the energy to attempt to get to the box first, so I ignore the giggles being shared between my *previous* best friend and the traitorous father-to-be and begin sorting our gift into two neat piles. Items for Bo on the right, items for me on the left.

"The Clit-Stim 9000..." Caleb strolls back into the kitchen, slapping the box against his palm. "Do we have this one?" he asks his wife, who's at least looking a *touch* guilty under her thin-lipped smile.

"They had to make *nine* versions?" Bo asks.

"It must have been made by a man," I say, dropping a book titled *First-Time Dad* onto his pile with a not-so-subtle *thud*, "if it took them nine tries to figure out how to properly please a woman."

Bo's tongue pushes against the side of his cheek as he nods, an arrogant gleam in his eye returning. "Not all men need nine chances, if I remember correctly." He moves the chocolates that I had allocated to his pile back to mine, leaning closer. "Some of us only needed one," he whispers.

He then absolutely destroys the tension he began pulling like a corset around my throat by biting down on his cracker in a purposefully aggressive manner, spinning on his heel toward Caleb, and throwing a hand up.

"Toss it," Bo commands.

Caleb throws the box, and Bo catches it, palming it in one hand. "Here," he says, placing it next to my pile.

"My hero," I say dryly.

"You can keep all of it," Bo says, looking at our piles. "Well, maybe I'll keep the book and the"—he holds up the black T-shirt with white writing on it, wearing a lopsided smirk—"*Call me Daddy* shirt." He waggles his eyebrows suggestively.

"Sarah is a pervert," I say.

"I heard that!" She swipes a cracker from Bo's open tray as she walks by.

I glare at her as she and Caleb begin uncorking a bottle of wine together. "Keep your half," I say to Bo. "I distributed it fairly."

"But *this*," he points between us, "isn't particularly fair either. From where I'm standing, you're doing all the work. I'm like the kid who asks to see the group project the day before the presentation."

I admire his pile thoughtfully. "Okay, fine. I want this, and you take *this*." I take some ginger candies—which, in hindsight, were probably meant for my nausea anyway—and hand him the pack of twenty questions. "You can be in charge of asking those. A little piece of responsibility."

"Great." He smiles.

I walk over to the sink and fetch an empty cup to fill, feeling a little flushed.

"You okay?" Sarah asks.

"Yeah, just getting that my-stomach-is-turning-upside-down feeling." I turn off the tap and bring the glass to my lips.

"What feeling?" Bo steps nearer, his eyes narrowed on me in concern.

"Nausea," I say, trying to sip slowly. "It can come out of nowhere sometimes." Clammy skin, rushing blood, quickening heartbeat. Everything begins smelling weird all of a sudden, and my tongue feels too big for my mouth. All the usual signs that point toward needing to get to a bathroom *quickly*. "I'll be right back. Are you okay?" I ask Bo.

Bo looks taken aback at my question, his head jarring backward. "Yes, of course. I'm fine. Go, I'll—"

I don't let him finish before I'm running to the main floor's powder room, fighting the vomit forcing its way up my throat from escaping too soon.

CHAPTER 12

A soft knock is drowned out by the sound of the toilet flushing.

"You okay in there, champ?" Sarah asks from the other side of the door.

I groan, letting my forehead hit the cool tiled wall next to the toilet seat.

"Do you need anything? Water?" she asks.

"Yeah," I say, reaching for the toilet paper to wipe my mouth, my throat dry. "Water, please."

"Okay, Bo's coming in."

What? No! He can't see me like—

"Hey," Bo says, his voice full of sympathy as he opens, then immediately shuts, the door.

I whine internally as I imagine what I must look like, tucked in an upright foetal position against the wall. Sarah's aversion to anything bloody or gross is turning out to be extremely inconvenient. She could have at least sent Caleb in instead.

"I have water and some of those ginger candies. Sarah said they might help." He hands me the glass of water, then twists open the paper candy wrapper. "Do you want one?"

I nod, avoiding eye contact, and present my palm to Bo. He drops the golden candy into it, then tosses the wrapper into the garbage next to the toilet.

"So this is an everyday thing, huh?" he asks, opening a drawer under the sink.

"A few times a day lately."

"Shit, Win. I'm sorry," he says. I look toward him when I hear the sink turn on. He's holding a washcloth under the water, letting it soak. Seconds later, he turns off the tap and wrings it out twice before folding it into a neat rectangle.

With a firm grip on the corner of the bathroom's vanity, Bo supports his weight as he lowers to one knee. "Here," he says, delicately pushing my hair aside and placing the cool cloth on the back of my neck.

I have to admit, it feels amazing. Though Bo's *far*-too-big body is *far* too near in Sarah's *far*-too-small half bath. I can't tell if the nausea is residual or a sign of more to come, or if it's overwhelm due to Bo's looming proximity.

"Can you open the door?" I ask, letting myself look into his eyes as I take the washcloth from him and bring it to my cheek. They're such nice eyes. Gentle. "I think I need some... space."

"Yeah, of course." He twists to stand with a groan. "Let me know when you're ready to go. Sarah gathered up all your things, and I'll be just out there if you need anything else, okay?"

"Yeah, thanks," I say as he bows his head and shuts the door.

I press the cool cloth to my forehead, letting it also fall against my closed eyelids and the bridge of my nose. *Another* fun symptom.

Whenever I throw up, my head starts aching. Eventually, a pressure headache forms behind my eyes, making my vision blurry and every sound all too intense.

My next appointment with Doctor Salim is in five weeks. I've set that as a benchmark for how long I'll tolerate feeling like a walking vomit factory. If it goes beyond that, I may simply let the illness take me. I'll go to the seaside like all the sick or slightly insane women used to, and I'll *will* myself to either be done with it or enjoy an early grave.

Or, perhaps, I'll ask Doctor Salim to prescribe that medicine she suggested.

One of those two things.

When my stomach finally rests and my glass of water is empty, I slowly stand, wash my hands, and rinse out my mouth. Leaving the bathroom, I offer polite murmured goodbyes to Sarah and Caleb as Bo carries all my things out to his car.

The crisp winter air helps slightly, and I don't even attempt to put my coat on before getting into the passenger seat, enjoying the cool air on my clammy, hot skin.

"Are you warm enough?" Bo asks, shutting his door behind him, a cluster of snow falling and melting instantly inside his car.

"Balancing out," I answer, resting my cheek on the headrest.

"Okay. Mess with the dials however you'd like," he says, opening the GPS on his screen. I give him my address, and then we're off.

At some point in the twenty-ish-minute drive between my house and Sarah's, I fall asleep.

I'm woken up by the sound of gravel under tires in the back parking lot of my building. I lift my forehead away from the window and attempt to subtly wipe the drool off my chin. Bo pulls into a visitor's spot as I blink awake like a startled creature.

The tiny nap and cool air did help, though. I feel a *lot* better.

"Sorry, uh, I fell asleep."

"Yeah, I figured that out halfway through my drawn-out tale of my own public puking incident in middle school." He smiles at me, his hand on the gearshift between us. "Probably for the best," he says, putting the car in park.

"Ah, well, next time." I unbuckle and look at the back seat with all my items. "Thanks for the ride," I say, beginning the mental calculation of how I'll balance the gift basket, my purse, and the plant Sarah begged me to take and revive. I'm a pro at this point—you'd be amazed what you can do with one-and-a-half hands and a bull-like stubbornness.

"I'll walk you in," Bo says, already turning off the car. I don't bother to argue, though I probably should. I haven't cleaned my apartment other than some dishes and laundry in a few weeks between the exhaustion and the not-so-morning *morning* sickness. Work pretty much takes up all my energy, and by the time I'm home, I just fall asleep. I can barely muster up the desire to bathe.

We make our way through the freezing night air toward the back entrance—a grey metal door with cracked glass on one side that hasn't been repaired since I moved in. I start shrinking internally, thinking about the state of my building's hallways and lobby. The smoke-filled scent, the peeling flooring, the flickering lights, the... *shit.*

The broken elevator.

"Thank you." I attempt to take my basket from him but fail when having to balance it with my purse, phone, and keys in one hand. *Okay, just re-shuffle.* I put my phone into my purse and use the keyring to hook my keys around my small hand's thumb. There, now I have a free hand for the basket. Easy enough. "Okay, I'll be on my way." I take the basket and curl it against my left hip. "Have a good night!" I say, a little *too* peppy.

Bo's tongue darts out as he narrows his eyes *ever* so slightly on me, then the lobby around us. "There's no elevator here, huh?"

I wince. "Technically? There is. But it hasn't worked in four years. So, no, sorry."

"Which floor?" Bo asks, looking toward the stairs.

"Sixth," I answer meekly.

A small inhale flares his nostrils. "That's going to be quite the challenge." He laughs without humour, scratching his eyebrow before placing that same hand on his hip.

I look over at the metal bench near the abandoned elevator and tilt my head for Bo to follow behind. Sitting, I lower the basket and plant to the floor and cross one foot in front of the other, shifting nervously in my seat.

"I've been so tired since I found out about the baby, but I've been meaning to look for a new place," I say, looking at the floor. "This building kind of sucks, honestly. It's not like I'd want to do six flights of stairs super pregnant either. I might end up giving birth on them if I do."

Bo laughs quietly, more of a breath than anything.

"And, obviously, your ability to get inside of wherever I live is a necessity now too," I say, gently sitting up to look at him.

He slowly tilts his head up toward me. His eyes are hesitant but appreciative, I think.

"I know we haven't figured out a lot of our plan, or anything else really... but you should be able to come visit whenever you want and—"

"Not just visit, Win. I want..." He shakes his head, taking in a long breath. "I'm not sure how to say this without it sounding demanding, but I'd like to have the baby at my place too. Overnights or weekends. I'd like to be as involved in their daily life as you are."

Well, the nausea is back.

A powerful maternal possessiveness falls over me. I know that I'll need help with the baby, but no part of me has considered Bo to be anything *but* help until now. This, what he's asking for, is so much more than that. I breathe through the influx of emotions rising up, waiting to calm down before I formulate a response. Logically, I know that what he's asking is fair. That this baby is as much his as it is mine. But, perhaps a touch selfishly, I haven't imagined any scenario where I'm not the *main* parent and Bo is the additional. The second, supporting parent not all of us got to have.

"I don't know when that would be possible," I stutter. "I'm hoping to breastfeed. For the first few months, the baby couldn't be away from me for more than a few hours."

"Maybe, er, well, could we do both? Bottles and breastfeed?" he asks, shyly. "I suppose I can only do *one* of those things." He chuckles anxiously.

"I've heard that it can be confusing for babies to switch, and it can mess with the mom's milk supply and..." I take a deep, sharp inhale. "Okay, let's put a pause on this. We don't have to figure it all out right now. I was just going to say that I'll focus on getting a new place. Something accessible and nicer if I can cover the rent. This apartment was the only affordable one left in the city four years ago, so I doubt I'll find something *much* better, but I'll try. We'll aim for accessible and see where we land."

"How much do you make at the café? If—if you don't mind me asking."

"A little over twenty grand a year, after taxes. Then, usually, about six thousand in the summer from lifeguarding."

Bo rests both of his elbows on his knees, then curls his arms to support either side of his neck, appearing deep in thought. His eyebrows are pressed together, creating a deep crease in the centre of his forehead, and his jaw is tight, his back teeth shifting against themselves.

"We *will* talk about all of this, Bo. I promise. It'll be fair. To both of us. I don't want to exclude—"

"Move in with me," he says, interrupting, his eyes holding on me with a hesitant yet somehow certain stare. "I have a spare room and an office that we could turn into a nursery. My house is small, but it's nice. If you move in, you can save money for a new place while pregnant, and we can get through the newborn stage together. I'd hate for you to be on your own for every long, sleepless night. I don't want to mess with your routine or the baby's feeding schedule so... yeah. What do you think?"

"I think you're a stranger," I say, taken aback, the words falling out of me.

"Not for long, right? What better way *is* there to get to know someone?" He clears his throat. "And, I mean, strangers move in together all the time and call themselves roommates."

"What if we hate it? What if I'm a nightmare to live with? Or *you* are?"

"Then... you can move in with Sarah and Caleb, maybe. Or, hell, you can have my house and I'll find a hotel or something."

"I don't know. It seems like we're already way in over our heads, and then we'd be roommates too?"

"Think about it for as long as you need to, but I think it makes sense." Bo swallows, his eyes darting down to my stomach and holding for a lingering, heavy pause. "I can't do much else right now," he says lowly. "I can't help in any other way, but I *can* give you a place to live that will work for all three of us. If you moved in next month, we could agree to a year. Six months of pregnancy, six months of baby. Then we can reassess. You could save a lot of money during that time. It might even be enough to put a down payment on something. Or maybe you'll want to stay a bit longer, or leave earlier... I don't know. What I do know is that I want to help however I can, and *this* seems like a way for me to do that."

I think about the last time I moved in with a guy. Jack said all the right things too. How we were *starting the rest of our lives together.*

That we would save so much money by splitting everything. *What do we have to lose?* he asked me, dark eyes wide with excitement he never normally showed, his black hair sticking up on all ends. Sometimes it was like Jack was so filled with life it was firing out of him like bolts of electricity. He could charge me up just as easily as he'd burn me out. It was up to him each day which option it was going to be.

We had only lived together for a few weeks when Jack shouted at me for the first time. We'd gotten into arguments before, but nothing like that. I burned our dinner, and three hours later, he was still berating me for wasting *his* food and smoking up *his* house. It was like that from then on. Even though I was covering most of the bills, it was *his* place, his food, furniture, routine. I was infringing. A trespasser in my own space.

"I'd want to pay rent. At least a little bit," I say, my eyes shifting from side to side as I think. "And I'd also like to have something in writing. Something legally binding that says we are committing to at least a year, and that if something happens where one of us has to leave before then, we will help with that person's costs of moving or finding something new." I mean me. There's no way this guy would move into a hotel before kicking me out of his home.

"Sure, whatever you'd be most comfortable with."

"And I'd like to be able to have friends over. Sarah and Caleb. I'd want to feel like it was my space too."

Bo's eyebrows push together again, his head tilting. "Of course, Win." He stares at me a little too long. "It would be just as much your home as mine. You could paint the entire thing neon green for all I care." He laughs. "Okay, well, maybe run it past me first. But you could."

"I'm going to sleep on it," I say, moving to pick up my gift basket. I offer him a tight-lipped smile as I stand. "I appreciate the offer, though. Thank you."

"We're in this together, Win."

"I know," I agree reflexively. I don't truly know whether I believe it. Right now nothing feels certain at all. Not a single thing.

"Let me know when you get in safe." He points to the stairs.

"Between here and the sixth floor?" I ask dryly.

"Yes." He leans back farther on the bench. "Because I'll be sitting *right* here until you let me know," he says stubbornly.

I roll my eyes, shuffling the basket against my hip. "Fine." I make my way across the lobby and onto the bottom step before I turn to ask, "Do you have your own washer and dryer?"

His smile is slow forming but entirely optimistic. "I do."

I nod. "And how do you feel about plants?"

"Love them," he fires back without hesitation.

"Okay," I say, turning back around and bracing myself for the climb ahead.

"Okay," he repeats, the optimism in his voice echoing around the lobby. "I have a good feeling about this, Fred!"

"Uh-huh!" I highly doubt I'll be calling him my roommate anytime soon, but it doesn't hurt to think it over.

CHAPTER 13

Fifteen Weeks Pregnant. Baby is the size of an apple.

"**M**oving day!" Sarah shouts excitedly the second I open my door. Caleb stands behind her, alongside two men I don't know, both tall and muscular, with shoulders that barely fit through the doorway. They smile and nod politely as they enter my home.

"Who are they?" I ask quietly as Sarah pushes past me. She drops a shallow produce box in front of my window and turns toward me. She's wearing bike shorts and a cute, oversized sweater with the word *Velaris* written across it. I think that's from a favourite book of hers, but if I ask, we'll never get out of here on time.

"Michael and Levi," she says, her voice uneven. Caleb sets into motion behind us, directing the two men toward my purple dresser. They pick it up effortlessly and exit before I can even admire their... *capabilities.*

"Did you hire movers?" I ask her, clearly annoyed. I explicitly told her not to.

"No!" She has the audacity to sound offended. "They're friends of ours."

This is exactly why Sarah enjoys playing strip poker so much—she's a terrible liar. Hence why I had to pull her naked, drunk ass away from so many parties as a teenager while Caleb was at home studying.

I level her with a scowl. "I told you not to hire movers, Sar. If I could afford it—"

"Let me stop you right there, preggo. You can't be making trips up and down six flights of stairs all day. Plus, Caleb and I are not exactly in fighting shape, so what were we supposed to do here? Suffer? I've spent a few hundred bucks on *way* less necessary shit."

"I'm perfectly capable of going up and down stairs," I argue.

She rolls her eyes, beginning to untangle the leaves of my pothos plant. "Puked yet today?" she asks, her ponytail swinging violently as she turns to me with a *do we want to go there?* blank stare.

I open my mouth to argue but stop myself with a deep breath. Honestly, I *have* been really dreading today and the multiple trips up and down the stairs. Packing up over the last few weeks has been tiresome enough. So has going through all my things, making donation runs, and getting supplies. Sarah has been here most days, and I really shouldn't be so ungrateful. She's already done so much to help me get out of here before the end of the month. It's just, I wish I could have hired the movers myself and left Sarah and Caleb out of it. I hate feeling like a burden.

"Fine, just, don't let them touch my plants."

"That's like half of the shit you own," Caleb says, wrapping his arm around my shoulders. "Happy moving day." He pats my arm. "Can't say I'm not happy to never have to see this place again."

"Snobs," I tease, reaching out a hand for Sarah. She steps closer, until the three of us are wrapped around one another like the tangled plants on the windowsill. "Thank you, guys," I mumble into Sarah's shoulder. "I love you both, and I really *do* appreciate your help. I'm sorry I'm crap at accepting it."

"We love you too," they answer in unison.

"Now teach us how to carry your plants safely so you don't end up murdering our nice new mover friends," Sarah adds.

The rest of the morning goes smoothly. Michael and Levi take my small selection of furniture down piece by piece—with help from Caleb on the monster that was my pull-out couch. She now lives on the curb until a new home is found, since Bo's spare room comes equipped with a queen-sized bed.

Sarah, Caleb, and I do two trips with my plants while the rest of my boxes are taken down. Everything I own is packed up in just over two hours. Caleb pays the guys and waits with the truck as Sarah and I make our way upstairs for one final look-through.

"Fuck these stairs," Sarah says, opening the top of her water bottle on the landing to the fourth floor. "Fuck these stairs so much," she says breathlessly, bending at the waist.

"Last time," I say, standing straighter to pull a candy out of my fanny pack. It's stocked with saltine crackers, ginger candies, heartburn tablets, and gum—all little nausea hacks I've discovered over the past six weeks. None of which are helping right now. Other than today, I have been starting to feel better.

Eventually, we collapse onto the floor next to my door, on the peeling beige-brown linoleum used for the few square feet of the entrance and kitchenette. I take small sips from Sarah's water bottle and try to focus on my breathing, but it's no use. I suppose it's only right to throw up here one last time.

Once I finish up in the bathroom, I check under the sink and all around it for any leftover stuff. I, of course, find another bobby pin and tuck that away in my pocket, but everything else is gone. Sold, donated, or on the truck outside.

"It's really happening, huh?" Sarah says, patting the floor next to her as I near.

"It is," I say, sliding down the wall to sit.

"How are you feeling?"

"Better now," I answer, throwing a stick of gum into my mouth.

"I meant about moving in with Bo."

"Oh..." Right, *that*.

"Still worried?" she asks.

"Yeah," I sigh out. "Hard not to be."

"At least you'll be closer to our place. I looked it up. It's only an eighteen-minute walk."

I nod absentmindedly, chewing like I have a vendetta against my gum.

"You can move in with us any time if you need to. But I do think this is a good thing. Maybe it'll be awkward for a bit, but it'll be easy to get to know each other. And once the baby arrives, you're going to need another set of hands."

I wince.

"Sorry... you know what I mean."

I nod, offering her a relaxed smile.

When it became obvious, five weeks ago, that I couldn't remain at this apartment any longer, I considered taking Sarah up on her offer to move in. But ultimately, I decided I couldn't. Sarah and Caleb have very consciously chosen not to have kids. I never would have shaken the feeling that I was ruining their child-free existence. I'd have felt so guilty.

"I could do it on my own," I argue, my pride beckoning to be consoled.

Sarah flicks my nose. "Of course you *could*. But the point is you don't have to. Our moms had each other, right? Just think of Bo as the Marcie to your June."

"It's more complicated than that."

"Because you slept with *your* Marcie? Because you want to again?" Sarah asks, her voice suggestive.

Yes, but not only that. "It's just the hormones."

"The ones you had on Halloween or the baby-growing ones?"

"Both."

"Give yourself more credit than that." Sarah leans against me, shoulder to shoulder. "But I get why you don't want to complicate things more now."

"It's not just that I slept with him. It's also the Jack-effect. I've only ever lived with one guy before."

"That won't happen again, Win. I promise," Sarah says sternly, taking another sip of water.

"I know it sounds ridiculous because Bo has been nothing but kind and supportive and I'm literally moving in with the guy as if

I don't have a care in the world, but I can't help but feel like the *moment* I let myself settle in, he'll turn on me like Jack did."

"Want to play worst-case scenario?" Sarah asks.

It's what Marcie would offer to play with us when we were worried about shit growing up. Which, in hindsight, was mostly stuff not worth worrying over. I nod, taking a deep breath.

"So you move in with Bo, and things go well. *Until* one night, he snaps. Changes like Jekyll and Hyde. Like Jack." She says his name with total disdain. "What would you do?"

"Leave. Immediately. Walk or taxi over to your house."

"Then what?"

"Um..." I try to play it out in my mind like her mother taught us. Pretend it's actually happening and get into the nooks and back corners of my imagination to build a realistic scenario. "Caleb would probably go over and get the stuff I'd need right away. You and I would go back for the rest when Bo was out or something."

"And then?"

"My kid wouldn't have a dad. Or they'd have a dad that I was scared of. Then I'd have to be worried forever. Anxious about them having visits, nervous during drop-offs and pickups. If it escalated, I'd have to get a lawyer and pay to go to court. I could lose my case because Bo has more money and could afford a better lawyer. I could end up being the one in trouble, somehow. Being the one who asks *him* for visits."

"Okay," she says softly, rubbing my back in slow circles. "That's the worst-case scenario, right? Finished?"

I nod, wiping a single hot tear off my cheek.

"Good, *now*—does that seem likely?" she asks, her voice sincere.

"No," I answer plainly. "No... it doesn't."

"What do you think is *actually* going to happen?"

"That's the thing. I don't know. I don't see Bo being a problem, but I don't know him well enough to know what it will *actually* be like. When we hang out, we banter, and it's fun and easy—but that's as far as I know."

"So it's a wait and see."

"It just keeps coming back to getting to know each other more."

"Right, which is why I think moving in with him *is* a good choice. He wants to be involved, and I think trusting him until he gives you a reason not to is healthy."

I imagine Bo the last time we saw each other in person—the night he proposed this idea. His navy cable-knit sweater under his unbuttoned suede coat, blue jeans with bright green socks poking out underneath. Not threatening whatsoever, which is impressive, considering his height.

I also think of the texts we've exchanged since then. The way I can't seem to stop my smile with each flash of his name across my screen, knowing something funny or sweet is about to appear. The daily check-ins and the thank-yous and the apologies for how sick I've been. The anecdotes he's learning from his first-time dad book.

I've convinced myself little by little over each day in the last few weeks that this is a good idea, but I think I'll have to be comfortable in the unsureness to some extent. Most likely, there will always be a lingering amount of distrust, given what I went through. Self-preservation lives in doubt, after all.

Sarah clasps her hand around my knee, appearing deep in thought herself. "But it's not just you in *any* of that, Win. In the worst case or the best possible outcome, I'm right here. You've got me and Caleb. Whether you want us or not."

"I used to have your back. Remember that?" I pick at my leggings, frustrated with myself.

"Yeah, I know. I still feel it." She leans against me, and I stop pinching the fabric around my knee. "It's just your turn right now. That's all it is. Turns."

I'm about to tell her we really should be getting out of here before my landlord shows up for inspection when an echoing voice comes from down the hall. "Sarah?" Caleb shouts from the stairwell, his voice full of comical amounts of distress. "No one is answering their phone. Are you guys okay?"

I pull out my phone at the same time Sarah does, and we grimace at each other. Between us, there are a dozen missed calls and texts. "Forgive me," she whispers. "Sorry! Win's having a meltdown, and I'm looking after her! Be down in a minute!"

Caleb appears at the doorway, red-faced and sweating. "Please don't stop on my account." He laughs, falling to the floor in front of us. "I'll just lay here and *die*."

"It's probably a good thing you two have chosen not to procreate. How dramatic would *that* child be?"

"Hopefully Bo's DNA levels *you* out," Caleb says, peeking at me with one eye open. I throw my gum wrapper at his face.

We sit for a while in silence. I take in the emptied apartment that suddenly feels *so* much smaller while Caleb catnaps on the floor as Sarah rubs his shoulder.

In the four years I've been here, everything has been for the purpose of getting by. A job to pay the bills, waiting for summer to come to feel a little more like myself, not pushing myself to *do* more or *be* more because I've been afraid. I haven't made any real progress here. I've settled into a stagnant, passable life—safe but perhaps *too* safe. Smaller than the life I'd like to live moving forward. Maybe this is the fresh start I needed to get my ass into gear.

Maybe a little discomfort will do me some good.

CHAPTER 14

Following behind Caleb in the moving van, Sarah and I pull onto a quiet street lightly dusted with snow and lined with mismatched, picturesque older homes. The sun is out today, and it's glistening against the ice-covered black roof of house number fourteen. Bo's house.

We planned for me to come visit a few weeks ago, but between Bo taking on a new project at work, my general level of exhaustion, and a few winter storms, we just ran out of time.

It's *stupid* cute. A Tudor-style bungalow with a high gabled roof on the right side and dark brown timbering over top of the white stone exterior.

"You didn't tell me he lived in Snow White's cottage," Sarah says, parking in front of the house. Caleb is parked in the driveway to the right of the home and is already unlatching the back of the truck before we step out to meet him.

"I wonder if the seven dwarves will come help us," Caleb says, turning to face us as we come up behind him.

"I just made that joke," Sarah chimes, sickeningly sweet, swatting her husband's ass. "Wait, is Bo not here?" she asks, looking between the driveway and the front door.

"He's at a work conference all weekend—it's a once-a-year thing. He should be back tomorrow. He thought it would be nice for me to have some time to settle in by myself."

Sarah hands me a box of plants, passed to her by Caleb, who's standing in the back of the moving van. "Perfect. That means we can snoop." She wiggles her eyebrows, mischievous grin in full force.

I take the box and make my way across the gravel driveway to the front door. I put in the code Bo texted earlier, and the door beeps and unlocks itself. A small entryway with gorgeous, mosaic blue tiling under a black welcome mat greets me. Against the lime-washed white wall is a row of coat hooks with a dark wooden shoe bench beneath.

There's a narrow door straight ahead of me, a closet presumably, and a rounded archway to the left that leads into the living room. With a heavy-framed window facing the front of the property and a hollowed mantel of a nonfunctional fireplace, the living room certainly does *feel* cottage-like. Those and the wooden beams across the high ceilings work to add a cosiness to the otherwise undecorated room.

Bo doesn't seem to have many personal items. There are a few books on the coffee table and a set of wall sconces on either side of the mantel, but other than that, the walls are bare. A simple grey sofa sits in the centre of the room, standard to most single men I've ever encountered, alongside a matching wingback chair in the corner next to the window. I wonder if I can steal the spot next to it for my plant stand. They'd get great sun there.

Moving farther into the home, I step into the adjoining room that is designed to be a dining room. Currently, the only pieces of furniture in here are a desk, tucked into the far corner and topped with a monitor and piles of loose sheets of paper, and a walnut media unit housing an *impressive* vinyl collection. There must be hundreds of records organised into the slots below the speakers and turntable that sit on top of the unit.

Until now, I haven't considered that the man I made a baby with could have terrible taste in music. Or, even worse, could be one of those people who doesn't like music at all. That should absolutely be a determining factor when considering who to mix DNA with. So when I spot a Nat King Cole record next to Fleetwood Mac's *Greatest Hits*, I thank Bo silently for being someone with taste, for the sake of our child.

To the right of the media unit, through another wide archway, is Bo's kitchen, which appears to be the most updated room in the house. Under long rectangular windows overlooking the large snow-covered backyard is a wall of dark-grey bottom cabinets with white marble-top counters, separated by a stainless-steel gas oven. Between those cabinets and where I stand is an island with no overhang for sitting. In the centre of the island is a deep, matte-black sink. The cabinets on the far wall form an L-shape, stopping just before a narrower archway leads to a brightly lit hallway. Between the cabinets and the archway is an equally beautiful stainless-steel fridge with an ice dispenser.

That's right. A fucking ice dispenser! I am *that bitch* now.

"Okay, so it's a very cute but very *blank* canvas," Sarah says, coming up behind me and placing a box on the kitchen counter. "With your plants and a little sprucing, this place will be absolutely perfect." She throws her arm around me, jumping once with giddy excitement. "What are you thinking? Why are you looking so sad?"

"The idea of having a constant supply of ice is making me a bit emotional," I say, raising a slow finger to point at the fridge.

"Your priorities are, as always, impeccable," she says, pushing past me toward the hallway. "Let's see what your bedroom looks like."

I follow her down the hall, caressing the fridge longingly as I pass by.

"He left all the doors open so you could look around. That's thoughtful," Sarah says over her shoulder, disappearing into the farthest bedroom.

I peek in the first door on the left to see a decently sized square-shaped bedroom with the same white lime-washed walls and dark flooring as the rest of the home. There's a simple walnut-coloured bedframe pushed into the far corner under a blind-covered window and not much else, other than a glass dome ceiling light. My new bedroom, I presume.

Next door is a smaller bedroom with light-grey walls, a long vertical window that overlooks the backyard, and a small built-in closet to the left. It's also completely empty apart from some ethernet cables tangled in the far corner, a wi-fi router, and a half-filled box labelled *Donate*.

Realising that this is the room intended to be the baby's nursery, I lean against the doorframe and admire it a little more carefully, noting the way the afternoon sun creates a small rainbow on the wall closest to the closet. I wonder what Bo would think of painting the room yellow. I think it would take that little cluster of afternoon light and make it feel even brighter.

When I turn around to wander towards the next room, Caleb is standing silently behind me. His eyes are locked over his shoulder, then he slowly turns his attention toward me. We share a shy, hopeful smile.

"Baby's room?" he asks simply.

I nod.

"Do you like it?"

"Yeah," I say, tears threatening to spring loose.

"It's a great room."

"You think?" I ask, my voice wobbling. I laugh at myself, wiping a single tear away. "Oh my god, these fucking hormones," I complain. "It's nice though, right?"

"Hey," Caleb says, outstretching one arm. I walk to him, letting my head rest on his chest. He pats my shoulder a few times, then grabs hold of it and shakes me against him, laughing in a mocking yet gentle manner. "This is good, Win. This is a great place, and that's a perfect room. Don't be sad. Don't cry."

"I'm not sad. It's just a big change, you know?" I say, standing on my own and stepping back. "I think it's just a bit jarring to see the room my baby will be sleeping in. That's all."

"I get that. But—"

Sarah appears in the hallway, windswept, as if she's been running, distracting Caleb mid-sentence. "I found condoms. Brand new in plastic-wrapped packaging," she announces in the tone of a news reporter.

Well, *that* was a sobering entrance. I look at her blankly, taking in her unblinking eyes and crazed expression. "In my room?" I ask, confused.

"No, obviously not. There's literally just a bed and mattress in your room. In Bo's." She darts back inside the door to our left.

"Sarah, no! Get out of there." I follow her in. "Stop snoop—" I cannot continue chastising her once I find myself in the centre of Bo's bedroom. Unlike the rest of his home, this room is curated to him exactly. It's filled to the brim with art and belongings.

One wall is painted dark green behind a slotted pine headboard. The bed is covered in greyish beige bedding and has a rustic wooden bench at the foot of it. Under both the bed and the bench is a large natural-woven rug that stops before two nightstands with open shelving and shallow drawers at the top.

On the right nightstand, there's a collection of what, at first glance, someone could mistake for *dirty* magazines. But they're actually—

"Comic books," Sarah says, snickering.

"I've seen what you read on your Kindle. You're in no place to judge."

She raises a finger to make a counterargument, then lowers it, nodding to herself in a sad sort of acceptance.

"Do you think he'd let me borrow this?" Caleb asks, emerging from Bo's closet wearing a knight's armour chest piece and helmet.

"Both of you, stop. We shouldn't be in here or touching his stuff."

"Do you think he role plays in bed?" Sarah asks, practically skipping over to her husband before brushing her hand over the metal on his chest. "That could be kind of hot," she says to me over her shoulder, smirking.

"Milady," Caleb says, bending to kiss her. She giggles as their lips meet.

"Oh my god, seriously? Now you're defiling his things!"

"Seems only fair," Caleb says, taking off the helmet and holding it to his hip. "We haven't been able to mess around in our guest bedroom since we found out that it has some sort of magic baby-making energy."

"That's not how it works," I sigh out under my breath. "Please, just—put everything back."

"Win, I think your baby daddy might be a huge nerd," Sarah says, walking back toward me as Caleb skulks away.

I look over her shoulder at the framed sepia art print on the wall next to the closet door. It's a pencil sketch patent of the Star Trek Enterprise. "Well, that's what I'm here for, right? To get to know the guy." *Definitely a nerd.*

"Exactly... Which is why I looked in his drawers."

"Oh my god," I mutter, pinching the bridge of my nose. "Not the same thing."

"Tell me, Winnifred June, why does a man buy condoms?"

I pull up my shirt and point to the smallest of baby bumps that's started to take shape. It looks more like a bloated stomach after a large burrito between my squishy, soft hips. "Maybe to avoid this?"

"No, but he hasn't *used* them. The box is still wrapped in plastic."

"Sarah, what is your point here? We have an entire truck to unpack, and I really don't think we should be in his room *or* discussing the man's sex life." I glance over my shoulder as a thud comes from the closet where Caleb is. "Stop doing whatever you're doing in there!" I shout at him.

"He's not having sex with anyone else," Sarah says, grinning like a feline.

Caleb is laughing in the closet, and I swear I hear the sound of a lightsaber opening.

"Or Bo had *so* much sex he ran out and had to buy more," I argue. Her face falls instantly. She's so betrayed by the very notion of Bo having sex with someone else that I *almost* feel guilty for suggesting it. "Sar, I know your heart is in the right place, but Bo and I are not a couple from one of your books. If he was planning on having sex with *me*, then he wouldn't need those, would he?"

"This logic has backfired. I'll admit it."

"And I'm not planning on having sex with him, which is another factor you seem to keep forgetting."

Just then, Caleb comes out of Bo's closet holding something in his hands, chuckling darkly. "Think he's a mountain climber, or...?"

My throat tenses and dries at the sight of silky black rope. Caleb throws it over his shoulders like a shitty feather boa.

Sarah snort-laughs, flipping through a comic book at the side of the bed.

"Put that back *now* and go wait at the truck," I seethe. "And *you*." I point to Sarah, but then draw a blank. "Just... come see the bathroom with me, I guess. Neither of you are allowed to come back in here, understood?"

They both roll their eyes. Caleb stomps back into the closet, and Sarah pouts as she slots the comic book back into the stack. I make them leave the room before doing a last check that nothing is out of place. I shut the door behind us and follow Sarah into the bathroom across the hall.

It's certainly a tight fit with both of us in here, because the large glass shower stall takes up most of the room. Black hexagonal floor tiles clash beautifully with white walls that turn to tile inside the shower with a built-in tiled bench. There's a small vanity with a little storage underneath the sink and a mirrored medicine cabinet above.

"You'll have to come take baths at my place, I guess," Sarah says, sitting on the closed toilet seat.

I have to admit, I wasn't expecting to be so devastated by the lack of a tub, but the reality is hitting hard. Baths are where I unwind, process, and decompress. And over the past month, it's where I've also found comfort for my tired, aching body.

"Maybe," I pout, turning the sink's faucet on and off again.

"Or get a tub installed? He's got the money, clearly. The room is big enough."

I laugh under my breath. "Yes, I'll start making a list of demands." I stand straighter, putting on an impression of my worst self. "Thank you, Bo, for letting me move in here because I've failed to become a successful adult on my own accord and got knocked up by you. How would you feel about a full bathroom renovation? And perhaps, while you're at it, could you build me a tower to sleep in?"

Sarah smiles up at me. "Fair enough," she says, moving to stand at my side. We look at our reflections in the mirror, and both sigh wistfully.

"Plus, the shower may be a necessity," I say, noting the multiple grab bars installed. "I'll miss baths, but I don't *need* baths."

"Agree to disagree," Sarah says, fiddling with her hair as she admires her reflection with pouted lips and raised brows. I do the same, fluffing my bangs so they fall better. "We used to do this every day," she says soulfully, making eye contact in the mirror.

"Hmm?"

"Get ready together, sharing a mirror. I miss it sometimes. I miss that old apartment a lot."

I miss it too. I miss Marcie and my mom together, dancing in the kitchen and giggling like schoolgirls into their glasses of pinot grigio. I miss the chaos of four women trying to share one bathroom and one vehicle. I miss feeling young and carefree and naive. I wasted so much of that time wishing I was older. Waiting impatiently to get out and live my own life. But that never really happened. I just got older. And now look at me. Nothing to show for it.

"You stole all of my makeup," I argue, avoiding the sinking nostalgia in my chest.

"Yeah, but I always braided your hair in exchange," she quips, fiddling with a strand of my hair. Then she rubs her lips together, her eyes locking on my shoulder as she twists my hair, her mind far off. "I, uh, talked to June last night, actually."

"*Oh.*" It's not a complete surprise that my mother would call Sarah, since I haven't returned her calls in over a month, but it *is* surprising that she waited until now to tell me they spoke. Usually, I get a text message from Sarah setting me straight right away. Telling me to knock it off and quit making her the middleman.

"She's worried about you. Says you've gone quiet on her."

"Right."

"I know it's hard, Win. I know what she's like. But you've got to tell her. She misses you, and I don't think she'll react terribly. She'd be a hypocrite if she did."

"I know. I-I'm going to. It's just been really busy since finding out. And processing all of these changes. And then packing up and moving. But I promise I will. I'll call her tonight."

"Okay," Sarah says, dropping the now tightly braided strand of hair next to my ear. "Good."

We smile softly at each other, facing the mirror.

"We should probably go help Caleb," she says, her mouth twitching into a grin.

I laugh, grimacing. "Oh, *shit*, right. I totally forgot about him out there."

Then we sprint to the front yard.

CHAPTER 15

After hours of unloading, unpacking, and shuffling furniture around my bedroom, we decided to call it a day. Sarah and Caleb took off after I had pizza delivered, leaving me with an entire box to myself in an eerily quiet house.

It took me a few tries, but eventually, I got the record player going. Now Frank Sinatra is singing about riding high in April as I load my sheets into the dryer, singing along loud enough that the house no longer feels so sparse. With no neighbours sharing a wall to worry about, I belt out the lyrics with flair. Laughing toward the ceiling when dear old Frank refers to himself as having once been a pirate. Because *that* is exactly what landed me here.

And, dammit, I'm going to pick myself back up and get back in the race too. Just as Mr. Sinatra suggests.

I glide around the house, smoothly waltzing with a hand on the top of my wannabe baby bump and stopping along the way for *many* ice chip breaks. When my sheets finish in the dryer just as the last track on the B-side fades out, I make my bed and crawl into it.

Pulling out my phone, I immediately check my texts from Bo. He asks how I'm settling in, provides instructions for the faucet in the shower—which was apparently installed backward and can be temperamental—and lets me know he'll be back tomorrow before lunch. I quickly respond before pulling up my texts with my mom. I type out a few apologies before I decide to just call her instead.

It rings only once before she picks up.

"She lives," my mother declares as a form of greeting.

"Hey, Mom. Sorry. Things have been really busy lately. I've missed you."

"Sarah said that too. She didn't say much else, though. Keeping your secrets, as always. I assume that's why you're calling? She didn't want to play middleman?"

"No! Well, yes, she did tell me you called. But things really have been busy. And yes—there *is* something I need to tell you." I look up to the ceiling, willing the words to come. Or, alternatively, willing the well-timed beginning of an alien invasion or apocalyptic event. "I'm pregnant," I say.

Two words. That's it. Simple. Out there now. No taking it back.

The line goes quiet. Painfully quiet.

"Mom?"

"I'm here."

"Did—did you hear me?"

"Hear what? Sorry, my show is on."

"*La Reina del Sur*? Mom, it's on Netflix—just pause it." Some traditions, like Sunday night telenovelas, never die. That's probably what Sarah is doing in bed right now too. That was always their thing, and sometimes Marcie and I were invited to join. Only if we didn't ask too many questions like: Wasn't he dead? Who is that? When did she have time for an affair between the murdering sprees? Isn't that her *stepfather*?

She grumbles, her chair squeaking as she reaches for the remote. "Fine, fine, fine. Just, you caught me during a juicy bit. Teresa just called—"

"I'm pregnant," I interrupt.

"You?" she says abruptly, accompanied by a stunned laugh.

I don't know why her surprise offends me, but it does. "Yes, *me*."

She makes a sound like sputtering. It's half amusement, partial shock. "Well... who's the guy?"

Of course. No *how are you feeling?* Or *how far along?* Or—okay, I suppose the next question might be *who's the guy*, but the first two matter more. "His name is Bo. He's a friend of mine. We got caught up at a party, and... you know the rest." Not a *complete* fabrication. My mom doesn't need to know I fucked the guy the same day I met him. Some things don't need to be shared with the woman who began preaching abstinence-above-all to me when I was ten.

"Birth control zero; McNulty women two," I joke flatly.

"And? Is he a *loser* or a decent man?"

I look around the nice bedroom in *his* house while sitting on my *new* bed that he provided and nod to myself. "A decent man. We've, uh, we've actually moved in together."

I hear a whimper down the phone. A happy sort of relief mixed with a contented sigh. "Oh, that's wonderful, Winnie. Truly, truly wonderful."

I probably should have mentioned the context in which we are moving in together, but why bother now? I'm not going to set myself up for a more difficult conversation if I don't have to. "I'm sorry I didn't call earlier; it's been a whirlwind. I've been really sick, and—"

"What's he like?"

"Yikes," I respond before I can help it.

"What?" she snips back.

"*Mom,*" I try to sound less agitated than I feel. "I was just telling you I've been throwing my guts up every day, and you interrupt to ask me about him. Bo is fine. He's great. But *your daughter* could use some maternal advice."

"Sorry, you're right. I was so sick with you too, chickie. It's awful, but someday soon, it'll all be worth it."

"Any tips?"

"The only thing that worked for me was consuming my weight in root beer and salted pretzels daily. Doctors would probably warn you against that method these days."

"Think that's how I got my hand?"

"Winnifred June!"

I giggle into the phone. My mom does too, but she's fighting it as she always attempts to.

"I'm due July twenty-fourth," I tell her once our giggles soften.

"Oh, wow. So... you're a *few* months along." There's an un-mistakable twinge of hurt in her voice that I obviously put there. I hate that she's upset, but I also can't say I wish I had called earlier. If I hadn't waited, if I'd told her *before* deciding to move in with Bo, this conversation would be a lecture and a series of disappointment-filled platitudes.

I thought you'd have learned from my mistakes. I raised you better than this. How exactly are you going to provide for this baby on your own while working at a café? What man will want you now?

And, sure, I'm using Bo as an unknowing safety net by allowing my mom to think we're together romantically. But what neither of them don't know won't hurt them.

"I'm fifteen weeks along, as of yesterday." I pause, feeling a tinge of guilt. "It really has been busy. I promise."

"Well, thanks for telling me now, I guess."

"I *am* sorry, Mom. I think I got in my head about telling you. I wasn't ready for it to feel real yet."

"Does it feel real now?" she asks.

"No," I answer honestly.

She sighs, some compassion returning to her humming tone. "I felt that way too. Up until they put a teeny, screaming *you* in my arms, it all felt a bit made up."

"Then it felt wonderful? The biggest blessing of your life? A gift from the heavens?" I ask, my voice theatrical.

"Sure did. Then scary. Then wonderful some more. Then scary again. You sort of repeat that until... forever. And if you're *really* lucky, one day, that baby calls you on a random Sunday evening in February and tells you that you're going to be a grandma."

"Surprise," I singsong weakly.

"Guess it's my turn to visit *you* this summer, huh?"

"I'd like that, please."

"I take it your schedule is a bit freed up," she laughs out.

"August may be best—to make sure the kid shows up before you arrive. Wouldn't want you here for my due date in case the baby gets stage fright." *And I don't want you anywhere near that hospital room,* I think to myself.

"Well, let me check with Duncan about when a good time for me to come up would be."

"Did you get a new psychic? What happened to Maureen?"

"No, *sweetie,* Duncan is my beau. We're going on four months. We've talked about him before. Oh!" She laughs in delight. "I have a *beau,* and you have a *Bo.*"

Duncan? I don't *think* I've heard of him before. But I can't say that to Mom without risking another feud like the *Travis* incident of last July. My mother takes great offence at my lack of interest when it comes to her love life and my inability to keep track of the men coming and going.

I know it makes me a hypocrite, because I couldn't care less when friends of mine sleep around or are serial monogamists, but I *hate* it for my mom. Always have. I want more than for her to pour all of herself into a man for a few weeks or months at a time and then feel emptied out when they stop showing up.

"Duncan, right. Of course. Is he a pilot or just very astute at knowing when travel is appropriate?" I ask, a tad bitchy, I'll admit.

"Well, I can't just take off on him, Winnie." She laughs at my *obvious* absurdity.

"No? Not for a few days to visit your only daughter and grand-child?"

HANNAH BONAM-YOUNG

"I said I'll check, Win. Quit sassing your mother."

I inhale and exhale slowly, shaking myself. "Yeah, okay. Just, let me know, all right?"

"Will do..." She smacks her lips, searching for another topic—and evidently, comes up dry. "Well, I'll let you go, then."

"Okay, Mom." I could ask her to keep talking. I *could* tell her how terrifying this all feels. How much I wish I could both fast-forward *and* rewind time. How much I'd really like one of her long, tight hugs. But I don't. "I love you," I say instead.

"Love you too, sweet girl. I hope you get plenty of rest. Tell that grandbaby to ease up on you."

"Will do. Bye."

I hang up and press the phone to my chin, rolling onto my back and staring up at the ceiling. I replay the phone call and feel relieved, knowing that with my mother—the *queen* of unpredictable emotions—it could have gone far worse. And *hey*, at least now she knows. I can take that off my eternally long list of to-dos before the baby's arrival. A list I should, now that I'm thinking about it, actually write down.

I'm about to count the day as a win overall, roll over, and pass out on my *very* comfortable new mattress when I realise I forgot to check whether the door was locked. And while the bed beckons for me to stay and cocoon inside it, I don't particularly enjoy the idea of being bludgeoned in my sleep or having the house burglarised on night one. So, whining even still, I drag myself out of bed and stumble toward the front door in the dark.

I notice the deadbolt is in place from a distance, but I still go into the entryway to check the handle. I accidentally step on a pile of mail on the floor that must have been delivered through the front door's slot.

Robert Durand, I read off the top envelope. No time like the present to find out the surname of my baby daddy, I guess... What on *earth* am I doing?

Amongst the collection of flyers and nondescript envelopes is a comic book, still half bent from delivery. I pick it all up with every intention of dropping the pile on the counter and going back to bed. But when I place the mail down, the shiny, floppy comic stares up at me with bright fonts and colours too interesting to ignore. I decide some late-night reading won't hurt and bring the comic to my bedroom.

I get back into bed, fluffing my pillows before I lie against them. *The Annihilator Issue 392,* it reads. I wonder if Bo has all three hundred and ninety-one previous editions somewhere. I guess, unlike Caleb, I never ventured into his closet to see what was in there. He could have a lot of stuff I don't know about. Like more rope, for example.

Nope. That's a dangerous thing to imagine. Decidedly *not* following that train of thought.

And sure, I don't know who this Annihilator guy is—or why he's so butthurt that the king of hell has been overthrown by this scantily clad Serinthina badass. But damn, this shit is entertaining from the jump.

There is a large bit of mutual pining going on between these two "enemies," and I am eating it up. I've also gathered that there's some sort of immortal deity that they *both* fear, which can only be destroyed if they work together—begrudgingly, of course. I don't know much else, however, given that I haven't read the previous issues. Half of these terms, names, and places mean nothing to me. Still... I sort of love it. On the last page, amidst some excellent banter post battle, Serinthina heavily alludes that these two got down and dirty on the Ice Planet *Borgue*. I blame the horny pregnancy hormones for the speed at which I pick up my phone to google which issue that could have been in.

Then I'm spending a little over three dollars to download issue one hundred and eighty-one onto my phone. All for the sake of getting to know Bo and his interests better, of course.

Not at *all* to see the horny aliens fuck.

CHAPTER 16

I stayed up half the night reading old issues of *The Annihilator* and paid for it this morning when my eyes had to fight to open at the sound of my alarm. I don't have work today, but I should spend a few hours this morning unpacking and settling in before Bo arrives home. It's one thing to have boxes or plants piled up in my bedroom, but I don't want them in the kitchen or living room, taking up too much space and getting in his way.

And just as I load my last mug from the final kitchen box into the dishwasher, the front door beeps and hums as it unlocks, announcing Bo's return.

"Hello," he calls out, shutting the door behind him.

"Hey," I reply, filling the dishwasher with detergent, grinning to myself. "I'm in the kitchen," I add.

When I shut the dishwasher and turn around, Bo's leaned against the archway, his coat folded over his arm and a canvas duffel bag in his grasp. "Hey, roomie," he says, his smile wide and downright contagious.

"Welcome home," I say, bowing into a stupid little curtsy that I immediately regret. "You have a great place."

Bo's eyes fall over my shoulder, admiring the plants I've hung in front of the kitchen window. "I like the plants," he says. "Out there too." He points to the living room with a thumb over his shoulder.

"Not too many?" I ask, grimacing.

He shrugs, as if to appear indifferent, but a quick twitch of his lips gives him away. "Not at all," he forces out, his pitch wavering.

"Oh god... it's too many."

"It's certainly more than I was expecting, but I like them. Promise."

"I did try to warn you," I say, grabbing a cup of ice. "Also, this was a great surprise."

"A fridge?" he asks, switching his bag between hands.

I huff out a laugh. "No, dingus. The ice maker."

"Did you just call me a *dingus?*"

"If the dingus-shoe fits." What the fuck am I saying? I shouldn't try to be funny or flirt on next to no sleep. Not that I'm attempting to flirt. That would be foolish of me... right? Right.

I look at his luggage, then back at his face, focusing on the dark circles under his eyes. "Sorry. Uh, I'll let you get settled. Did you want some coffee, maybe? If I make some?"

He hums. "Yes, I'd love one. Thank you. Do you need the bathroom before I take a shower?"

"Nope, go ahead."

Twenty minutes later, I finish making Bo a *red eye*, with the help of his very fancy espresso machine. And as if he smelled it, he promptly appears from the bathroom, wearing grey basketball shorts, a beige hoodie, and *glasses.* Black thin-framed glasses that his damp-darkened hair dips below on the right side.

I damn near swallow my tongue.

As if we needed to add glasses to this powder keg of hormones I used to call my body.

"Order up," I say, presenting him with his coffee in a clear glass mug.

"You're the best, thank you." He takes a long sip, his head falling back as he moans. "Espresso too?"

"You looked tired," I reply shyly while he hums his appreciation again.

"Seriously, you are the best."

"What's your plan for the day?" I ask, pulling some carrot sticks out of the fridge to snack on and dropping them into a bowl.

"I have today off since I was sort of working all weekend. What about you?"

I cover my mouth to avoid spewing bits of carrot at him as I speak. "The café is closed on Mondays. I was thinking about going for a walk to the beach before I hang out with Sarah later. Did you know you only live a ten-minute walk from one of the prettiest beaches with the most e-coli contaminated water in Southern Ontario?" I ask.

"The fish come out with an extra eye, but *man,* the view is beautiful," Bo replies, turning around to leave the kitchen.

"Also, I have a confession," I say, following him toward the living room, carrying a glass of water and a bowl of carrot sticks in the crook of my wrist. He lowers onto the armchair in the corner, gently moving a leaf of my fern away from his neck and tucking it behind the chair before he settles back into the seat. I take the couch. "I stole your mail."

"Theft on day one? Way to come out swinging," he says, smirking. "I respect it."

"*The Annihilator*," I say, flaring my hands for dramatic effect. "A *surprisingly* great read."

Bo's smirk turns into a full-fledged, lopsided grin, his eyes dancing around my face. "You *actually* read it?"

"I did, and then I fell down a rabbit hole and read about a dozen others before passing out last night. Had to download a reading app on my phone to do it. I committed."

"They're all in my room. You could've saved yourself the money."

"Ah, well, I-I didn't want to invade your space. More than I have already..." I say, wincing.

He scowls playfully. "You're not invading anything." He takes a long sip of his coffee, and I find great satisfaction in watching him sway from side to side as he drinks it—as if he's never tasted anything so delicious. "But I suppose if you *didn't* venture into my room yet, I should warn you that I'm a bit of a—"

"Massive nerd?" I interrupt.

"Okay, ouch," he laughs out.

"Sarah snooped around your room. Caleb and I followed. I tried to get them out, but they were like kids in a toy store. I'm sorry."

"I left my door open on purpose, Win. I knew you'd probably go in there. I hid all the shit I didn't want you to see."

"Such as?" I ask, my nosiness beating out any shred of politeness for time.

"Okay, fine, I only hid *one* thing."

"Curious..."

"I'm allowed *one* secret," he says, smiling into his mug.

Interesting. Whatever it is, it must be juicier than the rope, since he didn't bother to hide that. *Don't say anything about rope, Win. Change the subject before you do.* "You know, at first, I was surprised about your nerdom, but then once I started putting the pieces together? It all sort of made sense," I say, crossing my legs under me, leaning against the back of the couch.

"I have to know what *that* means."

"Well, you love math. You're far too pretty to be as humble as you are, which means you were either not as hot as a teenager, *or* you just weren't in with the cool crowd. I'm guessing you were like Caleb—a late bloomer with a bunch of geeky interests that kept the ladies from knocking down your door."

"Well, it worked for him," Bo says, one eyebrow raised as he takes a long, thoughtful sip. "Sarah's great."

"Well, am I right?"

"Annoyingly, yes. I was a band geek *and* a nerd in high school. A winning combination." He shakes his head, smiling at his lap. "I have to admit, I thought it'd be a *bit* longer before you read me like a book. I believed I had an air of mystery about me."

"You did. Until I saw the dork cave."

"Dork cave... okay..." He chews his cheek, mischievousness in his eyes. "So you're saying that if, on Halloween, we had come back here instead of Sarah's guest room, and you'd seen the *very few* collectibles I own, things may have ended differently?"

"I didn't say that." I lean back, confidently crossing my arms.

"So what does that make you? A nerd-chaser?"

"Just horny, I guess."

He laughs, his throat bobbing. "Well, I'm glad our plan of getting to know each other is already working."

"I remain a mystery, however." I wiggle my brows.

"We'll work on that," he says, his eyes flicking down to my sweater. "Starting with—did you seriously go to Harvard?"

I thrifted this sweater so long ago I forgot what it even said across the front. "No, heh, *not* Harvard. I went to Lakehead for Outdoor Recreation, Parks, and Tourism, with a concentration in nature-based therapeutic recreation. I have a bachelor's degree in how to take people canoeing for their mental health, essentially."

"Don't do that," Bo says sternly.

"What?" I blink at double speed.

"Dismiss yourself like that. That sounds really fucking cool and important to me. Don't trivialise what you accomplished."

"Oh, uh, well... thanks."

"What did you want to do after your degree?"

"The dream was to open a summer camp for kids with disabilities. A place built to show them how to adapt the equipment, give them the time and patience to learn that they hadn't gotten anywhere else. But obviously, that didn't happen."

"Why?"

"Why what?"

"Why didn't that happen? It seems to make so much sense."

"Oh," I stutter, reaching for my water to take a sip. "I guess, uh, life just *happened* instead."

Bo waits for me to go on, gently holding eye contact. I start to feel a tightness in my chest, spreading up my throat. But this is what we're here to do, right? Get to know each other? I'll give him the condensed version. He doesn't need to know *everything*.

"There was this guy... Jack."

"Hate him already," Bo says, one corner of his mouth raising.

"Yeah, well, good instincts." I laugh nervously. "We met in my second-year biology course. He was doing an undergrad in kinesiology. We seemed to have a lot in common, shared a lot of the same friend group, the usual stuff. Eventually, after a few too many beers around a campfire one night, we sort of fell into dating. We finished school together, but he decided to go for his master's degree."

I shuffle in my seat, looking everywhere *except* at Bo's face. "He asked me to move in with him, and I said yes. Our relationship up until then was mostly fine. But there were definitely some red flags I was choosing to ignore. Anyway... he was going to be a student full time again, and someone had to pay the rent. So I got an office job to get us by and sort of wasted those two years after graduation paying his way. Stupidly, I thought we were a team and that it'd be my turn to go after what I wanted next but... well, you know. When things ended, I moved back here, pretty desperate to get away from it all. I had to start fresh and couldn't really afford to dream bigger than the café and lifeguarding in the summers. Then time sort of moved on... but I *didn't*, I guess."

"He sounds like a jerk, Win. I'm sorry."

"Long time ago now," I say, shrugging.

There's a lingering silence. I resist the urge to look back toward him as much as I can, feeling his eyes burning into me. After what feels like *far* too long, I decide to give in, mostly to set him at ease with a smile. But when I do eventually turn toward him, I don't smile. I *can't*.

Not when Bo's looking at me like he heard far more than I was willing to say. Like he's seeing every invisible scar I've tried to cover up.

"He wasn't nice to you." He states it like fact. Simple. Sad. *True.*

I shake my head *no*. Just subtle enough that a part of me can pretend I didn't answer him at all.

Bo's jaw works, his eyes falling briefly before he shakes his head. "I'm sorry."

I inhale a shaky breath, biting the inside of my cheek. "Like I said, it was a long time ago."

He nods, then scratches the side of his nose with a bent knuckle.

Change the subject, everything inside of me shouts.

"Did, uh, did you go to university?"

Bo licks his lips, nodding, his usual lightness missing. "Yeah, Waterloo for Accounting and Financial Management."

"Sounds like a party," I tease. He rolls his eyes playfully, though his smile is still absent. It seems his thoughts are held elsewhere.

I wonder... if maybe... they're held on *her*. "Did you have a Jack too?" I ask.

Bo breathes into his hand as he wipes his mouth. "How much has Caleb told you?" he asks, eyeing me like he's got my number.

I tsk, hissing in through my teeth. "Busted," I say quietly through a nervous, soundless laugh. "Caleb hasn't said much, though." Nothing helpful, at least. "I don't think he and Cora are particularly close."

"Listen, things were complicated with Cora. I don't want to imply that—"

"You should probably know that Sarah and I refer to her as the spawn of Satan," I interrupt. "Frequently and in front of Caleb. She's been nothing but nasty to Sarah. So if you're trying to be diplomatic for my sake, don't bother."

"You shouldn't call her that," Bo says gently, leaning forward in his seat, his hands clasped between his knees, wringing. "I mean... sorry. You can call her whatever you want. I just..." His voice trails off.

I feel a twinge of guilt and unease pull my lips askew. "Sorry," I offer simply. So he's *not* over his ex, then. The sudden pang of sadness thrumming around my chest is unexpected. It's not jealousy, I don't think. Or at least, not entirely. It's more complicated than that. It's wondering if during one of the more meaningful sexual experiences of my life, certainly the most pleasurable, my partner was thinking of someone else. *Wishing* for someone else. If I was just... there. Available. Overly willing, throwing myself at him until he gave in. It's the crushing weight of questioning whether he wishes I was her. Them having a baby. Them sharing a home. It makes me feel like a trespasser. Inferior.

"I shouldn't have called her that. *We* shouldn't call her that. You're right."

I can tell Bo's choosing his words carefully as he sets his emptied mug down on the coffee table. "It shouldn't upset me. It wasn't exactly a good relationship. She, uh, Cora... things between us were not great."

Things are already awkward; I may as well get some answers. "Caleb *did* mention that you two were engaged." The moment I say it, Bo's hands are all over his face—anxiously rubbing at his chin and cheeks and forehead.

"Yeah," he says, his nose scrunching up. "*Technically*, yes."

"Technically?" I ask when he looks up at me.

"Okay. We're doing this," he says, under his breath. "Day one, pulling out the big guns." He laughs half-heartedly.

"I'm sorry," I say, shaking myself. "We don't have to..."

"Did you want to take that walk to the beach? Together? I always find it easier to walk and talk about heavier shit, you know?"

I *do* know. That's what I went to school for, at some level.

"Yeah, sure." I nod and stand from the couch. "Give me a few minutes to change."

A little while later, we're both dressed in warmer layers and halfway to the water. We've walked mostly in silence so far, making fleeting comments about cute dogs as they pass us by or how lovely the weather feels after an otherwise moody winter.

When we arrive at the beach, it's empty. The sand is nearer to mud in colour, wet and partially covered with half-frozen puddles in its valleys. The rocky shore is hidden under snow that's already begun melting under today's golden sun. The lake's ice is thin enough to see through and cracking all over. The sky is a hazy blue with soft, wispy clouds, as if a painter dried their brush against the horizon.

A perfect late-winter day.

A hopeful, spring-is-closer-than-you-think type of day.

I feel it all thawing my weary bones. The sunshine, the birds singing, the breeze that isn't frigid enough to hurt my skin. A sign of all the good to come when winter ends. When I can spend my days outside, feeling more like myself.

It isn't until we stop at the shoreline that Bo seems to begin collecting his thoughts once again. This time, I wait patiently for him to offer me whatever he wants. I shouldn't have pried, considering there's a lot I'm not quite ready to tell him about my last relationship, so I won't again.

I collect a few stones from the shore and silently offer them to him with an open palm. He takes one, smiles politely, and tosses it. We both watch as it skates across a patch of ice before sliding into the water. I throw one too. It lands directly in a patch of the lake with no ice at all. I watch the ripples form and fade to nothing.

"I got diagnosed a few months after Cora and I called things off for the third time," Bo says, his voice wayward but strong. "She, uh, she and I were on different wavelengths for most of the relationship. We kept, I kept, trying to fight the inevitable that we just didn't work. We started dating at twenty-three, and it was simpler when we were just two people focused on our careers who were working in the same field and trying to get ahead. But eventually, we were left constantly trying to figure out how we slotted into each other's lives outside of work, reconciling that we weren't a very good fit." He licks his lips, looking at the water with a furrowed brow and stoic concentration.

"God, it's pretty fucking pathetic to say out loud... but I think, maybe, she just never loved me as much as I loved her?" He says it like a question, looking down at me as if I might have the answer. I don't. Can't.

I think I've maybe already said too much, actually. Reducing Cora to this caricature villain instead of someone Bo shared *years* of his life with. Despite how she's treated Sarah or me, I don't know Cora all that well. Clearly, Bo does. And clearly, he *loved* her.

"Admittedly, there were a lot of reasons I shouldn't have called her the day I found out I was sick, but... I did. I was *really* fucking scared and... lonely. I'd *never* felt so alone." He laughs without humour, a hand splayed along his jaw as he grinds his back teeth.

I pick up a few more stones and offer one to him. He gives me a curt nod before he takes one and tosses it so far that I have to squint to see it land.

"I had friends I could've called, I guess. But I wasn't sure if any of them would know how to help. I needed company. I needed tough love, which Cora always had in spades." I hand him another stone, and he tosses it. This time it's a shallower, weaker throw. He shoves his hands deep into his pockets, widening his stance slightly as his chest falls on a long breath.

"I wanted to call my dad, but I was worried about burdening him. He lost his wife decades before my diagnosis, and he'd still never really moved on. I didn't have it in me to tell him that he could be losing his only son too. Cora was there when I didn't know who else to call, and I'm always going to be grateful she showed up for me."

"I'm glad she was there for you too," I say softly. And I mean it. Though it creates an ache in my chest. Perhaps it's guilt. Could be jealousy. Or, more accurately, both.

"A month into treatment, Cora sort of announced to me that we'd be getting married. I know it makes me sound like an idiot, but I kinda just went along with it. Everything in my life felt unstable and untethered, and suddenly, there was this woman I love telling me she was choosing to stick it out with me. I wanted that stability."

I feel a thrum of energy pass through me from head to toe. It hits my chest with a gentle but noticeable blow. *Love.* In the *present* tense. Bo *loves* Cora.

"But when the chemo wasn't working and the cancer was progressing, amputation became the only option. And... the odds were looking bleak regardless." We naturally fall back into walking at a relaxed pace toward the pier with a small lighthouse and empty docks where locals keep their boats during warmer months.

"At that point, I think it got to be too much for her. She stopped coming to appointments. Stopped coming over entirely. Eventually, she stopped answering my calls too. I got the message that she needed to step away from it all, and we haven't talked since. Not a lot of closure, I know. But... part of me feels like that's for the best, honestly. She was there for me when I needed her, and I think she did me a favour... in the long run."

"I don't think she did you a favour by leaving you when you needed her most. That's a pretty cowardly thing to do. She should've at least told you to your face that she couldn't handle it. Let you have that... proper end."

Bo shrugs. "She'd already ended things before, though. I was the one who tried to fix it every time—why we kept getting back together. Maybe she knew that was how it had to play out. She had to hurt me so I'd let her go. And I doubt many people would stick around when the worst-case scenario seemed inevitable."

I would, I think. Then immediately berate myself for placing myself morally above Cora, even inside my own thoughts. Ultimately, I don't know what I'd do in that situation. I doubt I'd have left him, though. I don't really understand how anyone could do such a thing. Even imagining what that would have felt like has me near tears, has me wanting to reach out for his hand or tuck him against my chest and brush my hand over his hair. Protect him from it, shield him, as if I could change the past.

"When did you tell your dad?" I ask.

"About six hours before the surgery..." he says, then trills his lips, looking away from me sheepishly.

I groan. "*Yikes.*"

"Yeah... not my best work."

"How did he take it?"

"Um, not great," Bo says in a higher pitch than usual, some humour returning to his features. "He reverted to his native tongue to call me every name in the book, then got the first flight out. He stayed with me for three months after the surgery. I couldn't have gone home without his help. I don't know what I would've done, actually."

"He sounds like a great dad," I say as Bo reaches down and pockets something from the sandy shore. "And I knew he lived in France, but I didn't realise he *was* French."

"Yeah, my mom was from here, and Dad is from a small town outside of Paris. They met playing in the same orchestra in Toronto and got married ten days after meeting."

"You're kidding." I snort.

"Nope, just ten days at nineteen years old. They didn't have me until ten years later."

"That's... that's *wild*," I say.

"My dad says the moment he saw my mom, he just knew. He took one look at her and watched the rest of his life play out." Bo stops, a sweet, longing look in his eye as he smiles softly at me. I imagine he's probably thinking of Cora and what could have been.

"You must miss her," I say, meaning his mother—but the possibility that it could have meant either Cora or his mother isn't lost on me. Sometimes the people who haunt us are still alive. I understand that too.

"Yeah," Bo agrees, turning back toward the path. "But I was really young when she passed."

"I'm sorry," I offer, matching his pace. "Do you remember much of her?"

"No," he says plainly. "But Dad had a lot of stories and photos. He kept everything of hers—like her vinyl collection. Most of the records at the house were hers." He stops, putting an arm out to block my next step.

I look toward the path ahead, expecting a skunk or something more nefarious to appear out of the bushes. But nothing does.

"Did you hear that?" he asks me urgently, his voice low. He spins, looking around us frantically.

"No?" I whisper-yell, leaning away from his floundering limbs. "What—"

"*Shit*, where is it?"

"What?" I ask, louder.

"I heard a goose."

I stop abruptly, my shoes scraping against the stone-covered path. I stare up at him in disbelief, my lips parting into a grin that I have to stifle before it becomes a laugh. "We're at a beach in Canada, Bo. You're gonna hear geese," I say, continuing to whisper for *whatever* absurd reason.

"They hate me." Bo turns his head toward a sound over the water to our left, his shoulders up to his ears.

"They hate you..."

"They go for my leg *every* time. I don't know if it's because it's shiny and they like that, or if geese are just little ableist fucks, but they're always trying to attack me."

I try to hold the laugh in. I really do. But I fail. Miserably. I burst. "Sorry, *what*?"

Bo bends to pick up a rock the size of his palm and waits to strike.

"You cannot use that," I say, taking the rock from him and chucking it aside. Our fingers brush briefly, though by the way my heart thuds, you'd think the guy had pinned me to the nearest tree and ripped off my tights. *Fucking hormones.* "No geese murder today, my guy. I'm pretty sure it's Canada's most sacred law, and I'm not bringing the baby to visit you in prison."

He hushes me, turning back toward the water and then in a full circle, like a bodyguard on watch.

I laugh at him, harder this time.

"Stop!" he whines, his own laughter breaking free. "It's not funny!"

I shake my head, forging back toward Bo's house. "C'mon," I call, a few paces ahead of him. "I'll protect you from any possible geese assailants."

"I will throw you to them," he says. "If it comes to it."

"Only if you can catch me first."

CHAPTER 17

When we got home from our beach walk, Bo took a call in his room while I got ready to go out. He was still on the phone when I left with Sarah, on a mission to get new art for my room and some lunch. And of course, because it's thrifting, I found what I was looking for *and* many things I hadn't known I needed.

Including a very cute rainbow stacking puzzle for the baby and a few bits and pieces for the living room's mantel. Some framed watercolour art, a few pottery candle holders, some pretty candles *for* those holders, and one small turquoise shell frame that perfectly fits our ultrasound photo. That, I put front and centre above the vacant fireplace.

Bo didn't seem to mind the new additions. When I placed the final item and stepped back to admire the mantel, I turned to find him standing behind me. He was leaned up on the wall, as he seems to be often, and smiling fondly. Not at me, but at that little photo in its new spot.

I figured it would be good to have the photo out somewhere. A reminder of *why* we're doing this.

Afterward, I took the pile of comic books Bo had left out for me to my room and read for a few hours. And now, I'm about six comic books deep out of eight, and my stomach has informed me that it is time for dinner. Thus, began my spiral.

Sure, dinner *sounds* simple enough, but it is far from it. This is our first dinner under the same roof, and it seems to me that we'd be setting some sort of precedent with how tonight plays out. I have no idea what Bo does for meals. I've only ever seen the guy eat baked goods, crackers, or chips.

Does he only eat beige and brown food? Is he offended by vegetables? Does he like spicy food? What allergies does he have? Will I accidentally kill him if I use eggs, soy, nuts, or shellfish?

And is it presumptuous to cook for us both? *Or* would it be rude to just cook for myself? When does he normally eat dinner? Is it already too late? Too early? I haven't left my room since four, so there *is* the possibility that he's already eaten by now. Though I don't smell anything wafting from the kitchen, and my sense of smell since getting pregnant is *no* joke. I'm like a bloodhound these days. People could use me to solve crimes. Decade old unsolved cold cases.

If Bo *did* eat without me, would I be offended? I don't mind if we do our own thing, but we should probably establish what our routine will be, right?

Then, there's also the matter of how we *get* the food *prior* to cooking. Do we grocery shop together? Separately? What's most economical? Will our system change when I'm on parental leave and my income is slashed in half?

"Win?" Bo calls through my door, knocking twice in quick succession.

"Hmm? Yeah?" I say, trying to present myself as calm. It's unconvincing.

"Are you hungry? I made soup," he replies, opening the door a crack and taking a step inside.

I pull my hair off my neck and swallow, feeling a hot flush across my chest and neck. This is all too much. There's too much we haven't discussed. Expectations I don't know about and will inevitably fail. Jack *hated* when I didn't have dinner ready when he got home. He was strange like that... performing long-winded monologues about how *society* was set to work against women while continuously making me feel like I had to fulfil certain roles and expectations in our home. Everything about Jack was some sort of performance.

Is that what this is? Bo making soup? Is this some sort of... act?

"You okay?" Bo asks, his eyes bouncing around my face, his hand tight around the top of my door.

I release my lip from between my teeth as my knee begins bouncing. "Do you have any allergies?" I ask.

"No." Bo walks farther into the room, presses his shoulder against the wall next to my dresser, and crosses his arms. "What about you?"

"No. Do you normally cook or order in? What time do you eat? About now?"

"I like to cook, but I'm not any sort of chef. I normally eat around six since I finish work at five. Are you okay? You seem a little—"

"I feel like I'm unravelling, maybe... a tiny bit. I appreciate you cooking, obviously, but I just don't know what the expectations are moving forward. I guess it's been a while since I lived with someone..."

Bo nods thoughtfully, his eyes holding on the lamp on the bedside table. "This seems like the same spiral I was having about an hour ago." He points to the bed, and I nod, shuffling over so he can sit next to me. "I don't want to overstep," Bo says, resting his elbows on his knees and clasping his hands between his open legs. "If you want to share this space like roommates—buy our own food, cook for ourselves, share some basic necessities, split costs down the middle—that's cool with me. But I think a different arrangement would make more sense."

"Different?" I ask.

"Less separate, I guess. I think I worked out a solution for the bills and money side of things. As far as the household chores go, cooking or whatever else, I think we should take turns."

"So, like, every other night, I'll cook dinner?"

"But sometimes you close at the café, right? So why don't I cook, since my schedule stays the same?"

"Then what do I do?"

"Clean up after dinner?"

"And what about the rest of the house? Do you keep things super clean? Do you have some sort of routine I should know about? A task you hate that I could do?"

"After my surgery, I hired a company to send someone to clean once a week, so it's more just that we have to tidy up after ourselves."

I add that to the list of expenses and wonder how much this home, Bo's lifestyle, costs to maintain. Does he shop at the type of grocery stores with butcher counters and organic produce or the kind where you can buy lawn furniture alongside your milk? That may be a determining factor in how we proceed. Can I even afford *half* of his life?

"So what about money? Splitting everything in half seems right to me, but I don't know what your bills are."

"My suggestion is a bit more complicated than that."

I raise a brow, waiting for him to continue.

Bo rises off the bed slightly, taking his phone out of his back pocket. "I know you said you wanted to pay half, and I don't want to dismiss that, but I think this solution is something we can both agree on." He holds out his phone between us, showing me a pie chart with a list of numbers below it that mean absolutely nothing to me.

I stare at it for a few long seconds before I give up. "What am I looking at here?"

He moves closer, our thighs touching, as he enthusiastically shows me around the screen. "Okay, this is our total yearly household income." He circles the entire pie chart with his finger. "And this is the percentage of that income that I make." He points to the much larger portion of the chart, coloured purple. His knee nudges mine, and I have to reset to focus on what he's saying. I'm glad my math teachers weren't as distractingly handsome as Bo. I'd have never gotten my diploma.

"This system splits everything proportionally. I put in our expected monthly expenses, including two additional savings accounts I've set up that we'll both contribute to. One is for housing and moving costs you have in the future, whatever you decide to do. The second is for the baby—furniture, diapers, clothes, whatever else. I then multiplied the total of our expenses by each of our percentages to see how much each of us should contribute overall."

I nod, looking at the screen when I spot my name below the chart, highlighted in green. "So this number, six hundred and seventy-four, that's mine?"

"Yeah," Bo answers.

"That's *way* too low for housing, food, bills, and everything else. There's no way."

"The percentages do not lie."

"You obviously fudged the numbers!"

Bo laughs softly. "I swear I didn't. I can go over the math with you, but the only expenses I left off were my car's costs—because I wasn't sure if you'd want to use it or not. But I could total that in too if you want to."

"What do I do with all the extra money I make from the café? I should definitely contribute more, given how much I'll have left over."

"Well, I didn't include your phone bill. Plus spending money, I guess. Another savings account. Invest some if you'd like." He shrugs, as if to show his complete indifference. "And when you're on parental leave, we'll readjust the percentages of our income so it's all still fair."

I snatch the phone from him, scrolling until I see *his* number below mine. "Robert! Three thousand, nine hundred and ninety-two?" I sigh, glaring at him. "This is *not* even close to even."

Bo's eyebrows shoot up, widening his eyes. "Robert?" he asks, smirking. "I'm *Robert* now?"

"Well, *Bo* seems rather informal, considering you're now my sugar daddy apparently!" I say, exasperated.

Bo rolls his eyes.

"I'm serious. I want this to feel fair." I've been taken advantage of before. I know how it feels. How quickly you can begin to resent someone for everything they *don't* do.

"It's exactly fair, Fred. These numbers are proportional. It's equity, not equality. Trust me. If it was solely up to me, your number would be a lot lower. *Zero.* Your income is about 15 percent of the household's total, right? The expenses of having you live here only rose by an additional six hundred and thirty dollars, which your portion is covering. Now *that* doesn't seem fair, considering you're also growing my kid. This is me compromising."

I whine, looking at the vast difference between our two numbers. I only make *15* percent of the household's income. I'm not *great* at math, evidently, but that must put Bo's income somewhere above one hundred thousand a year. I didn't expect that to feel *quite* so mortifying. How little I have to offer.

"Bo, are you sure? Absolutely sure? This feels like too much."

"Yes," he nods desperately. "Entirely, definitely, absolutely, and whatever other adverb you'd like, sure." His simple boyish grin levels me some. The way he tilts his head to catch my eyes, the way he nods as if he's trying to get me to do the same. The way this all seems so... unimportant to him. As if he truly could not care less.

"I'm a mooch," I say, sighing as we hold eye contact, our faces as close as our shoulders' widths and height difference allow us to be.

"You're not a *mooch*. You're an asset." He bumps his shoulder against mine, wrangling a smile out of me.

"An asset?" I ask, blinking up at him.

"Of course. You've definitely upped the house's value by adding decor and giving this boring room a makeover. Not to mention you're increasing the number of household members by 50 percent. Plus, you're good for morale," he teases with a wink.

"Morale, huh?"

"Yes. Your contribution to the *vibe* is worth at least a few hundred bucks."

"Right." I sigh, wrapping a hand around my grumbling stomach. Bo's eyes follow my hand's path and hold there, eyeing my belly with warm affection.

"Look, I know we don't really know each other that well yet, and you don't have reason to trust me with this, but I promise—this *is* fair. I can go over it with you some more, on my computer maybe, but regardless, this is as much money from you as I'm comfortable accepting. I'm very good at my job and typically honourable, but I *did* consider fudging the numbers when I saw your amount. I'd like to make things as easy as I can for you, Win. If I had it my way, you'd quit your job, put your feet up, and relax for the next few months."

"You want a kept woman," I tease.

"I certainly want to keep you." He blanches as soon as the words leave his mouth. "I mean, I want to keep you happy. Here and happy and—"

"Okay," I interrupt. "Fine. I agree with your arrangement, but if anything changes... if at *any* point you start resenting me or—"

"That's impossible."

"All right, but... if."

His shoulders fall on a long exhale. "Thank you."

"I don't know why you're thanking *me*. I'm rich now. I have an ice machine and an extra thousand bucks a month to play with."

He laughs, his face pointed up at the ceiling. "Okay, big spender, now that we got that sorted... soup?" He stands, offering me his hand to follow.

I place my smaller hand in his and *don't* miss how his eyes crease on either side when he wraps his full hand around it, covering it completely.

Not a chef, my ass. When I'm done with my third helping of Bo's butternut squash soup—that he made from *scratch*, I might add—I begin cleaning up.

I know it sounds ridiculous, because there is a dishwasher, but I decided to do the dishes by hand. I think part of me feels like it's only right to do it the old-fashioned way, considering Bo just made soup like a pioneer woman.

Halfway through washing our dishes, a scratchy guitar solo starts playing in the adjoining room, the music slowly being turned up.

"This okay?" Bo says, popping his head around the corner.

"Yeah!" I shout over the music, nodding along. "Who is this?"

"Rush—they were one of my mom's favourite bands."

"Your mom had good taste," I say, smiling over my shoulder as I scrub my soup bowl clean.

Bo's eyes hold on my hands with one raised, quizzical brow, but he doesn't say anything. And I appreciate that. I despise being micromanaged. Even if what I'm doing *is* nonsensical. Little doses of control are what I need right now.

I put the bowl onto the drying rack and grab a glass from the counter. I smile to myself as I shove my little hand into the water glass with a sponge. It's basically the best feature of having an underdeveloped hand. If it had an infomercial, it'd say I have a built-in scrubbing brush. Or, if I was a toy, it would say I'm karate-chop ready at all times.

"When you're finished up, I thought maybe we could do one of those question cards Sarah got us," Bo says, scratching the back of his neck. "You know, if you're not too tired."

"Sure!" I chime, smiling over my shoulder.

We're killing this, I think to myself. Day one, and we've already communicated the shit out of our arrangement, opened up about our exes, and established a routine. I can't help but smile as I keep cleaning, humming along to the music until I'm finished up.

Drying off my hands, I take a quick detour to my room to throw on some sweatpants. My body hasn't changed all that much so far, but I certainly notice how tight my jeans have started to feel in the evenings.

Once cosy, I find Bo in the living room, sitting pensively with a sudoku puzzle book in hand. The turntable paused itself once the needle reached the end of the record, leaving nothing but a quiet electrical hum of the speakers.

"Did you want me to turn the record over?" I ask, approaching the end of the couch.

"Oh, hey, sorry." Bo gently tosses his book and pencil onto the coffee table. "Didn't hear you come in... and no, that's okay."

"You don't have to stop on my account," I say, sitting on the opposite end of the couch from him.

"I already did one. I was just killing time."

"I'm so full of soup, I could die happy."

"How've you been feeling the last few days?"

"Before moving day, a lot better. I think the trips up and down stairs did me in, but I've been feeling great since too. No nausea."

"Maybe it's on its way out. That's what the doctor said, right? Second trimester, it might just go away?" Bo relaxes into the couch, his arms spread on either side of him along the back. I turn sideways to face him, tucking my feet under me.

"Hopefully." I look at him expectantly, spotting the cards behind him. "Shall we?" I ask.

Bo reaches for the arm of the cushion, where the unwrapped white box of twenty questions sits. Opening the box, he pulls out the instructions and reads them over. "There's a suggested order. Do we care?"

"Nah, chaos mode. Shuffle and deal."

He smirks, nodding as he begins shuffling the cards.

And I *know* it's ridiculous. But the way Bo shuffles is *very* sexy. His massive hands dwarf the cards, the ease with which he trills the cards with his thumb, sliding them together. Maybe strip poker *could* be fun.

No... no, Win.

"All right," he says, lifting a card from the top of the pile. "Ready?"

"As I'll ever be," I say, tugging my shirt away from my neck before clasping my hands in my lap.

"Would you like to be famous? If so, in what way?" Bo reads. "I'll go?" he asks.

"Sure."

"I wouldn't want to be famous. I don't hold a lot of weight to my opinions, and I think these days, famous people are expected to have a stance on everything. Twenty years ago, celebrities were *just* celebrities. Now, they're visiting the United Nations and talking about nature conservation as if there aren't more qualified people to do that."

"But aren't they just using their platform and position to help? They have the public's attention. Why not use it?"

"Well, there's nothing wrong with trying to help... and I get that they hold a lot of public influence, so they probably should. I just don't think I'd want that sort of attention on *me*. I'd rather just be mega-rich but not famous so I could give my money to the proper channels. To people who know how to use it for the most good. I'd like to stay *behind* the curtain."

I nod slowly, my eyes fixed on my lap as I reconsider my answer.

"Unless..." Bo says, dragging my attention back to his face. "I could be Andy Serkis."

"Who on earth is Andy Serkis?"

"Exactly," Bo says, grin tilted. "He's an actor mostly known for performance capture roles for computer generated films. He was Gollum in *Lord of the Rings* and Snoke in *Star Wars*. And he's been in a bunch of Marvel movies as well. He has all of these dream roles, but I bet he can go for a walk with his family and not be disturbed because no one really knows what he looks like."

"They'd have to drag you off those sets," I say.

"I'd still be there. I'd live in the walls. Or I'd have stolen everything that wasn't nailed down."

"Oh wow. Imagine the state of your bedroom with all *those* collectibles."

"See? It could be worse." Bo exhales gently, his smile holding. "What about you?"

"I think I'd like to be famous but like more of the creative, lesser-known side of things. Like a director or a screenwriter or something where I get to go to all the events and meet cool people but mostly get to focus on the work and not the publicity of *being* famous. Like you said—it's way too much public perception."

"I could see you being a director," Bo says.

"Yeah? How so?"

"You have an air of authority about you."

I snort. "Me?"

"Yeah, *you*," Bo says, narrowing his eyes playfully. "You're steady... like you have a calm under pressure way about you that I admire."

"Calm..." I say incredulously. "*Me*? Did you happen to miss my spiral about *dinner* a few hours ago?"

"But that's the thing. You communicated it all and we got on the same page. Now we're a better team. That's what a good director does."

"Oh, and you'd know that. From *all* your experience on set."

"Exactly."

"That's it, then?" I say, looking over at the deck as Bo tucks it away inside the box. "We finished the first question?"

"Yep." He places the cards down on the coffee table. "Guess in nineteen more questions, we'll be in love." He waggles his eyebrows suggestively before checking his watch. "Want to watch a movie or something?" he asks. "I could grab my laptop."

"Sure," I say. "You can introduce me to this Andy fella."

"Well, which one of his movies haven't you seen?"

I stare back at him blankly.

"Which one haven't you seen, Win?" Bo asks, concerned. I scrunch my face, looking up at the ceiling. "Have... have you not seen *Lord of the Rings*?" he asks, his voice slow and near cracking.

I shake my head, a small whisper of a laugh escaping me when his face quickly switches from pure horror to shock to amusement. Bo checks his watch, then looks back at me, then the coffee table, as if he's calculating something. Then he looks back to his watch again. It's strangely endearing how much this information has rocked him.

"Okay, if we start now, we can make it through the extended edition of *Fellowship of the Ring* before midnight."

"Midnight?" I ask wearily. "How long *is* it?"

"It's probably better that you don't know." He stands abruptly, moves to circle the couch, then stills. "I *cannot* believe I'm having a baby with a *Lord of the Rings* virgin." he says, near whispering. "This is amazing..." He takes off jogging toward his bedroom.

"I swear you were less excited to have sex with me than you are right now!" I call after him.

"Honestly? Maybe!" he shouts back from down the hall.

I made it two hours into the movie before I rested my head on Bo's shoulder and drifted to sleep.

CHAPTER 18

Sixteen Weeks Pregnant. Baby is the size of an avocado.

This past week, Bo and I have fallen into a familiar pattern. I've had morning shifts all week, so I get up early, brew a pot of coffee so Bo has some when he wakes up, and head off to work. I go for a swim at the gym after work and arrive home just as Bo's starting to prepare dinner. We eat together on the couch and tell each other about our days—not that I could explain to you in detail what Bo does for a living. He usually loses me once the word *data* is thrown around.

Still, I find that he's so excited to tell me every part of his day that if I nod enthusiastically and smile along, it doesn't matter if I truly understand. And I do like the way his face lights up when he talks about work. It inspires me to think of what I'd like to do after the baby. A camp might be the very big future dream, but maybe there's a step between that might fulfil me more.

After dinner, I clean up, soundtracked by whichever record Bo selects from his mom's collection. Yesterday we listened to "The Best of Etta James" and the night before was U2's "Joshua Tree." Joanna, like her son, was a woman of eclectic taste. I've spent a lot of time thinking about Bo's mom while listening and doing the dishes, actually.

I wonder whether she somehow knows about the baby, like I'm hoping Marcie does. I like to think that they're both in heaven, the ether, the afterlife—*whatever* you want to call it—proudly watching us fumble our way into parenthood.

Then, once I'm done with my daydreaming and tidying-up, we pull a question from the deck. The questions are a great tool to take little peeks at the inside workings of Bo's brilliant, albeit strange, mind. What I find most interesting, so far, is that Bo seems to be someone who's entirely indifferent or extremely opinionated and *rarely* in between.

You bring forty-six houseplants into the guy's home, and he barely bats an eye. But you defend orange juice with pulp in it, and he's ready to go to war.

Yesterday's question—*what is your most controversial take?*—turned a normally agreeable Bo argumentative in mere minutes. I was mostly joking when I suggested that juice with pulp was superior if not equal to juice without. I was not expecting the guy to fly off the handle, but, *oh,* was it entertaining to watch.

I genuinely *loved* watching him wildly push his hair out of his face and repeatedly fix his glasses as he paced the room. He was near hysterical, ranting about how disgusting pulp is and how, and I quote, any *self-respecting human* wouldn't subject themselves to *bits* in their juice.

His controversial take was that movie theatre popcorn is overrated and doesn't taste all that different from the microwavable kind when you consider costs.

We barely survived our first fight.

But as exciting as our new routine has been, it's on hold tonight. Bo has friends coming over, and I've yet to decide if I'll make an appearance or hide away in my room all evening.

He checked that having them here was fine with me at least a dozen times, and I assured him repeatedly that it was. Still, I'm nervous to meet them. If I *should* meet them. Maybe it would be best to just let them have their night and not get in the way. But equally, it could be rude to avoid them. How *does* one introduce oneself in this particular scenario?

Hi! I'm Win. I'm pregnant with your friend's baby. He took pity on me, and now I'm also his roommate. Yes, we've seen each other naked. And no, I haven't quite decided whether I want to again or if that could mess everything up. But also, it's hard to know what to do because these fucking hormones are making me so horny that I have to recharge my vibrator every night, and he sometimes wears glasses that make me feel like I could chew rocks and spit out diamonds. Also, do you happen to know, is he still in love with his ex? Does he talk about her? I'm not getting a good read on that whole situation, and I'm not sure how to bring it up. Anyway, hope you guys have a fun night!

That could probably use some edits.

They're coming over to play board games. Or *a* game, rather. Bo muttered the title under his breath while busying himself around the kitchen. His boyish smirk told me he was intentionally evasive each time I asked, so I gave up trying and decided to hide out in my room.

It was rather adorable watching him fret about preparing the house for his friends' arrival. The bowls of snacks on the counter, the foldable table that he's placed in the middle of the dining room, the black tablecloth overtop that he fixed several times.

The more I get to see Bo in his natural habitat, the more I realise that he cares *a lot* about other people's comfort.

And it's not only in big ways, like preparing his home for guests. It's the way he speaks with his clients on the phone. He meets every concern they have with gentle assuredness, patience, and confidence. Never with an air of arrogance or superiority because he's got a skill set not many people have. He truly wants the best for them.

Then, there's all he does for me. Like knocking on my door every night before bed with a fresh glass of ice water and a new comic book to read. Or the giant body pillow I found in my room after work yesterday with a note that said *for the world's best baby mama.*

When I asked him about it, he said his father-to-be book said that at around this stage of pregnancy, I'd start having trouble sleeping. The truth is, since being here, I've been sleeping like the dead every night. Still, it was a very sweet gesture.

Bo is clearly the type of guy who takes people under his wing. A natural caretaker type. It makes me glad to know that my kid will have a dad who goes above and beyond for the people he cares about.

"Win?" Bo says from the other side of my door with a soft knock.

"Yep?" I reply, dropping my crochet hook onto the bed beside me.

Bo slowly opens the door, steps inside, and closes it behind him. He looks like he's about to ask me something when his attention falls to the bed next to me. "Wait. Do you knit?"

"Crochet," I answer.

"What?" He elongates the word to several syllables. "That's so cool... I didn't know that!"

"I'm fairly certain crocheting isn't considered a *cool* hobby by most," I reply dryly.

"What are you making?" he asks, ignoring me.

"Oh, well, I thought I'd make a baby blanket. I'm doing a line of stitching every week of the pregnancy. I caught up with the weeks when I didn't know about the baby with this nice mauve colour," I say, holding up what I have so far. "Then, after that, I'm going to add a colour that sort of represents the week I've had."

Bo nods, studying the blanket as I drop it back to the bed. "What was this week's colour?"

"I chose grey," I answer.

His face falls.

"A nice grey," I assure him. "Grey like the stones we threw at the beach. I thought I'd remember our first day living together that way."

Bo inhales, his shoulder rising back to a normal posture. "That's going to be a very big blanket."

"Yeah," I huff. "I should probably do one of those normal pregnancy books that other people do instead," I say with a shrug of my shoulders.

"No, the blanket is more original. I could do the typical baby book thing. If you'd like?"

"Yeah, maybe." I smile up at him. "Did, uh, did you need something?"

"Oh, right." He laughs just once, rubbing his forehead, his other hand propped on his hip. "Yeah, actually. The guys are all here, and we haven't started yet, but I thought maybe... Maybe I could introduce you? It's okay if you're not up for it. I just know they'd all love to put a face to the name."

He talks about you! Of course he does—you're having his baby and living in his house.

"Sure, yeah," I say, standing.

Bo leads us out into the hall. We're halfway through the kitchen when he turns around, bends down, and whispers, "And... try to go easy on him."

"Easy on—" I stop, looking at the makeshift table set up in the dining room, the men around it I've yet to meet, and, most shockingly, *one* familiar face. "Caleb?"

Caleb, looking guilty as all hell and shrunken down to about two feet tall, has the nerve to *wave* at me. "Hey, Win," he says, his voice dejected.

"Uh, hey? What... what are you doing here?"

Caleb looks around the table, to Bo, then back to me before jumping out of his seat. "Excuse us, gentlemen." He charges toward me, grabbing hold of my elbow and using it to pull me back down the hall.

"Listen, Win, I—"

"Caleb." I choke out his name through a budding laugh. "What are—"

"I will tell you everything, but you need to *promise* me first that you will not tell my wife."

I cross my fingers behind my back and nod twice. *Puh-lease*, as if I'd *ever* promise such a thing.

"I'm so serious right now. We have been friends for *fifteen years*, Winnifred McNulty. I have never asked you for anything, but I am now. Please, god, *please,* do not tell my wife I play Dungeons and Dragons. She will *never* drop it. I will be ridiculed until my dying day."

"Caleb!" I shove his shoulder with my small hand. "Where does Sarah think you are right now?"

"The gym."

"Oh my god! The lying! The deceit!" I gasp. "Did you *pretend* you'd never been to Bo's house before when I moved in?" I ask in a breathy whisper-yell. "What else have you lied about?"

"I *technically* didn't say I hadn't been here before. This is the only lie, I swear. I just want this *one* thing. Let me have peace, Win."

"Caleb," I scoff. "Do you seriously expect me to *lie* to my best friend about her husband's whereabouts?"

"Not lie. Just... omit the truth."

"Caleb!"

"Look, I *know*, okay? I don't want to lie to her either, but..." Caleb wipes a hand across his brow, then places it on his hip. "Remember when I brought home that *Star Wars* Lego set last summer? The Death Star one? Which *is* for adults, by the way..."

He sighs, his head hanging between us. "Sarah only referred to me as *Darth Loser* for a month. A *month*."

I snicker. "Okay, but I do think she meant that affectionately. Plus—"

"Or when I suggested we all go to the renaissance fair when we were, what... eighteen? She *still* sends me advertisements for those with laughing emojis. She's subscribed me to several newsletters. It's been ten years."

Okay, one of those newsletter subscriptions was *definitely* me, but...

"Or the time—"

"Yes, yes, I get it. I see your point."

"I love my wife more than anyone. You know that. I also know that mocking is her way of showing love. It's one of my favourite things about her when I'm *not* on the receiving end of it. But I'd like to avoid it if I can. I'd like to maintain *some* level of cool."

I nod, my lips quivering as I resist a laugh. This is just *too* much.

"*Win*." Caleb says my name like a plea.

A small laugh breaks through.

"Win!"

"Okay, I'm sorry! I just, I don't think she'd be mean about this. When you put on the knight's armour in Bo's closet, she seemed kind of into it, actually."

Caleb mutters something under his breath.

"Come again?"

He repeats himself, still not enunciating clearly.

I roll my eyes. "Dude, what?"

"I'm not a knight, okay? I'm the... I'm the bard."

"Bard? Like a poet-musician guy?"

Caleb blinks, his eyebrows crawling up his forehead. "Yes, actually. I'm surprised you know that."

"So what? You—you sing? What *is* this game?"

"Sort of. I have magical powers that I harness with... song."

I cover my mouth, but not in time.

"Win!"

"I'm sorry! It's funny! You *have* to hear how fucking funny that sounds."

"See? *This* is why—"

"Yeah, okay! I understand. *I* won't make fun of you. But I *do* have to go meet the other guys now, okay? It's bad enough that you're keeping them waiting. They—they," my laughter interrupts me, "they might need your magical singing powers."

Caleb, resigned and exhausted, throws his arms up in the air and stomps down the hall. I follow shortly behind, already pulling out my phone to text Sarah.

ME: Come to Bo's now!
Caleb is here. Lying NERDS.

It's not my best text, but it'll have to do, because I ran out of hallway between me and the group of guys in the dining room. Their conversation comes to an abrupt end when I walk in. Bo looks between Caleb and me, shaking his head and wearing a shit-eating grin.

"Hi, everyone," I say, approaching the edge of the table cautiously, admiring the map laid out in the middle and the men around it.

Next to a sulking Caleb is an older gentleman who reminds me of a sturdy English bulldog in his stout posture, jowled face, and keenness in his expression. At the head of the table is Bo, who's lining up game pieces with a concentrated expression, and to my left, across from Caleb and the older man, are three more guys.

The one closest to Bo has dark brown skin, a kind but apprehensive smile, short black hair, and a lean frame. The other two seem to be a couple—based on the proximity of their chairs and the hand the man closest to me has placed on the other man's thigh. They're both broad and muscular. One of them has golden tanned skin and long brown hair, and the other has a pale complexion and a clean-shaven head.

"I'm Win," I say, raising my left hand to wave. "I won't get in your way, but I just wanted to say—"

"Well, aren't you stunning?" the older man says in a thick Scottish accent. He stands, wearing a beaming grin, then makes his way around the back of Caleb's chair toward me. "Bo said you were, lass, but I dinna believe him."

I giggle, putting out a hand to shake as he extends his own.

"I'm Hamish, but you can call—"

"All right, that's enough," Bo says, standing straighter and crossing his arms, towering over the table. "C'mon, man..." He chuckles breathlessly. "I distinctly remember telling you to be cool."

The stout man presses his lips together in a cheeky, mischievous grin. "Sorry," he says in a *not*-Scottish but entirely Canadian accent. "I like to test out my characters on new people. Did I have you fooled?"

"Totally," I laugh out, my face briefly turning toward Bo with a bemused grin.

"Walter," he says, reaching out for my hand, dragging my attention back to him.

I shake his hand. "Lovely to meet you, Walter."

"You too." He winks at me, his face adorably jolly. "And you seem to know the man who returned to the table looking like you kneed him in the crown jewels, but have you met..." Walter gestures to the opposite side of the table with an open palm.

"Adamir," the shyer one next to Bo says, extending his hand across the table and knocking down a few game pieces in his path. Bo immediately begins fixing them.

"Hi, Adamir," I say in a reassuring tone. "Great to meet you."

"Jeremiah, but you can call me Jer," the buff one next to Adamir says, extending his hand. "And this is my husband, Kevin."

"Good to meet you both," I say, shaking both of their hands. A small apology in my eyes each time, knowing they most likely feel the sensation of curled fingers tickling their palms as our hands part. At least handshakes are typically a *one*-time thing.

"I do have to say that you are *glowing*," Kevin says, his hand curled under his chin. "Let me ask you—we have a bet going. When you *met* Bo, were you in a particularly dark room? Or are you just a very kind, charitable soul?"

Bo laughs from the end of the table, crossing his hands over his chest, a tilt of pride to his chin.

"It was a *very* well-lit room," I say with a quick wink to Bo. "Too bad I didn't get to know him first, though."

They all get a kick out of that one.

"I like her," Walter says, jabbing his elbow into Bo as he returns to his seat.

"Me too, oddly enough," Bo says, his eyes tracing me from head to toe. The way he says it is so sincere and raw, you'd think that he'd choose to have me here rather than be forced by our circumstance. I feel the sentiment lock itself away in the hollow of my chest, like kindling being placed into a wood-burning stove.

Preparing to say my farewell, I take another glance around the room. I can't help but notice how odd of a group this is and long to know what brought them all together. What pieces of Bo they know of, and whether they'd be willing to share them with me. "So, how did you all meet?" I ask no one in particular.

"I met Bo in a support group. Matching cancers, I'm afraid," Walter tuts. "But both of us are still kicking—though some kick better than others these days. I've still got both legs." Walter barely gets the joke out before he begins laughing—a wheezing, happy one that I really enjoy.

Bo bites his lip, shaking his head with a slowly unfurling smile.

"He's been waiting to tell that joke," Bo says, watching me with an attentive focus as he bends across the table and places dice in front of Caleb. He's enjoying me meeting his people, I realise. He's deciding whether I fit. *Do* I fit?

"Bo and I met at Waterloo," Adamir says, putting up two fingers to signal his turn to speak like he's currently in class. "Bo was the TA in my freshman year economics course."

Professor Bo? I could be into it. Yep—I checked with downstairs management. I am.

"Bo and I work together," Jeremiah says simply.

"Jer is my boss," Bo adds, placing a token on the table. "He's trying to be humble, but he's the head guy in charge."

"Right, well, sure. But here I'm just your coworker, friend, and," he picks up an imaginary sword from his belt, "*warrior*," he says dramatically, slashing his sword down.

"Damn, I want on *his* team!" I say, laughing.

"Aw, she sounds like me when we started," Kevin chimes from next to me. "I'm here because Bo needed another member and my husband volun*told* me to come. No complaints, though. I like to be dramatic when given the chance."

"When did this start?" I ask, my eyebrow raised at Caleb.

"I believe the text was..." Jer interjects before Caleb gets the chance to answer. "*Hey, Jer, I have cancer*—shrug emoji. *Going to need some time off. Maybe forever*—question mark emoji. *Before you ask, because everyone keeps asking, if you want to help, you can play DND with me. I've always wanted to play. Need at least five guys, and I already have three. Maybe Kev could be in too? Anyway*—fingers crossed emoji—*I'll hopefully be back to work soon.*"

I, slack jawed and only *slightly* amused, gape at Bo.

He looks at me, smug, and shrugs. "I did what I had to."

"You cancer-guilted your friends into playing Dungeons and Dragons?"

"He definitely did," Walter says. "And I *had* cancer."

"I just wanted to play," Adamir says quietly.

"And you?" I ask Caleb.

"I only joined in September," he mumbles. "I told you. I didn't know anything else... Not before you told Sarah everything about Bo," he says pointedly. I may have deserved that, but I still glare back at him.

"We had another friend from our support group who had been playing with us," Bo explains, his expression holding as he scratches his cheek. "He passed in June."

I look between Walter and Bo, who share a sad but gentle look of reassurance. "I'm sorry," I offer around the table.

Walter pats Bo's back with a gentle series of slaps. "We're getting through it. And," he says, turning his attention to Caleb, "we're lucky to have Caleb to fill his shoes."

I nod, looking around at the men once again, unsure of when to step away. Adamir is stacking his dice in front of him as Kevin and Jer make lovey-eyes at each other, whispering. Bo sets one final piece down and nods to himself, as if the table is complete. Caleb mouths *did you tell her?* and I sharply turn away from him.

"Well, it was good to meet you all. I'm going to—"

The doorbell rings, cutting me off.

"Pizza must be early," Bo says, then circles around the table and passes by me, toward the front room.

"It's not the pizza, is it?" Kevin whispers to me, a giddy smile overtaking his face. He *does* love the drama. I like Kevin, I decide.

I shake my head—wearing a thinly veiled smile of my own.

"Caleb?" Sarah calls out from behind me, storming in. "Caleb Andrew Linwell, this is *not* a kickboxing class."

"That's my cue," I say to Kevin, pointing over my shoulder toward my bedroom. "Lovely to meet you all! Kick dragon ass! Escape the dungeons and whatnot!" I shout, jogging to my bedroom before Caleb's death glare strikes me down.

You know, with his musical magic and all.

CHAPTER 19

I'll say it. I'm not ashamed. Dungeons and Dragons is pretty fucking cool.

The moment Sarah was done giving Caleb the hefty public lecture he deserved for lying to her for months, she came to my room and dragged me back out to sit with her and watch. Sarah is not the type to leave an audience hanging, and based on all the giggling, *oohs*, and *ahhs* I could hear from down the hall—the men around the table were eating her *up*.

For the first ten minutes, I sat and crocheted while Sarah picked at her fingernails and sneaked pictures of Caleb, giggling to herself when it was his turn to speak.

But then, and I couldn't pinpoint the exact moment if I tried, our attention was captured. Bo was crafting a story so elaborate that Sarah and I simply gawked, passing a bowl of popcorn back and forth, while the men around the table played out a battle in which they took down a raven-feathered shapeshifter and his small army of thieves, defending a local inn.

"My husband's a goddamn hero," Sarah whispered to me, her lips parted in awe.

They were *very* convincing.

For me, it was the way Bo commanded the table that had me blushing and flustered. The ease with which he'd adapt to whatever the players decided to roleplay—the simple way he instructed and let them guide the story. And then, when he *was* the voice of the raven-feathered villain? Game. Over.

The haunted *evil* that washed over his features? The bass-deep tone to his lowered, gravel-like voice? I'd have gotten pregnant again, if such a thing was possible.

"What does this say about us?" I whispered back to Sarah when I caught her fanning herself.

"Let's not think about it too hard," she said, blowing a kiss to Caleb—who was clearly no longer sleeping on the couch.

Three hours passed before Bo called the time, and the men all left character and returned to the *real* world. Sarah and I began shouting our complaints, as we used to at the television when our telenovelas ended on a cliff-hanger.

"What about the swamp woman? Is *she* the dead princess? Does she have the sword of enlightenment? What happens next?" Sarah asks, eyes filled with desperation.

"I think we have an audience from here on out, lads," Walter says, placing his dice in a small wooden box.

I yawn, stretching my arms over my head, and Bo tilts his chin up, winking at me—as if my yawn was a nonverbal cue to get everyone out. I hadn't intended it to be, but I appreciate the concern.

"Walter, are you still okay to host next month?" Bo asks, making quick work of packing the table.

"Oh, well," Caleb interjects, "maybe I could? Now that..." His voice trails off as he side-eyes his wife.

"Now that you're not scared of your wife finding out?" Jer laughs out.

Caleb sighs. Poor guy can't catch a break.

"Ooh! Please, can we?" Sarah asks, jumping up and down next to Caleb, shaking his chest. "I could bring out some of the Halloween decorations! We could have ale and themed snacks."

"Fine by me," Walter says, admiring my best friend fondly.

Caleb smiles, kissing his wife on the forehead. He moves to turn away from her, but Sarah grips his shirt and tugs him right back, pressing her lips to his. Then they make it weird. Sarah gasps into his mouth as Caleb's hands wander a little too low on her back.

"Okay, okay, okay," I say, stepping forward and pushing their shoulders apart. "That's enough of that."

"You know, Win," Caleb says smugly, fixing his collar, "I think you were right." He eyes Sarah's ass as she walks over to talk to Bo, her limbs flailing as she recalls the battle. "Sarah *is* into this."

"What have I done?" I ask myself, too quiet for anyone else to hear.

Eventually, everyone makes their way outside. They commune every step of the way until Bo's talking to them on the front step, probably freezing as he says another *last* goodbye.

"Those two aren't going to make it out of the driveway," Bo says, shutting the door. I peek out the window to see Caleb and Sarah practically dry humping on the hood of Caleb's car.

"This is what I get for snitching, I guess. If the neighbours complain, I'll take responsibility." I lower into the armchair, and Bo seems to recorrect his path toward his dining room once he notices. He sits on the arm of the couch and begins rubbing his thigh, wincing slightly as he wraps both hands around where his prosthesis begins.

"You okay?" I ask.

"Oh, yeah, fine. It's just a little tight right now. The volume of my stump changes throughout the day. I can change the sock I wear underneath to help, but I didn't get a chance. Might as well wait for bed now."

I haven't seen Bo without his prosthesis on yet. I've wondered, since a quick google search told me that it was good to go without it when possible, to let everything breathe. Especially since he mentioned in passing once that his new prosthesis, resized to fit and suit him better, was coming at the end of March. He called it a belated birthday present.

"You never have to wear it for my benefit, you know. If it's uncomfortable..."

"No? It won't freak you out to see me hobbling around the house?" The corner of his lip rises, but his eyes give him away. A hint of hesitation, a twitch of concern.

"Not at all," I answer. "Of course not," I add, firmly.

He nods, but he doesn't move to take it off. "So..." Bo says in that familiar tone of *let's talk about something else*. "Sarah seemed to get on board with DND fast."

"I bet she's going to say some *real* unhinged shit in bed tonight," I say, grimacing.

Bo huffs a laugh, turning sideways to fall backward onto the couch with a grunt, spreading all four limbs across it. I instantly envision myself lying on top of him, the way his body could cocoon around mine so easily, and have to blink to erase it from my mind. "I'd pay *good* money to hear some Dungeon and Dragons themed dirty talk," he says with a crooked smile.

"Sarah reads some filthy books—it'll be creative, if haunting."

"She did seem to get a kick out of him saving that barkeep," Bo says, flashing his eyes.

"Oh yeah, she called him a hero."

Bo laughs, his throat bobbing. "There was a side-quest in October where Caleb had to flirt with a witch to get her to—" He stops himself, shaking his head. "Never mind."

"No, no, no... You *have* to tell me." My smile bursts wide. "Please, I need to know."

"You have to swear to me you won't tell him I told you or tell Sarah, because there's a decorum to these things—I can't be caught talking shit."

"I promise!" I mean it this time.

"He said..." Bo's laugh is near uncontrollable, shaking his entire upper body, his hands bouncing as they rest above his abdomen. He tries to complete his sentence a few times, but his voice fails each time as laughter overtakes him.

"Spit it out, man!"

"He looked me dead in the fucking eyes and said the words, 'not even King Arthur could pull me out of you.'"

"No!" I squeal, my hand shooting up to my mouth.

"Not even King Arthur himself..." Bo says, his face turning red as he struggles to catch his breath.

We both burst into fits of laughter so overwhelming that I truly can't catch my breath, clutching my stomach and sputtering for relief. The imagery of Bo roleplaying as a witch to be seduced is funny enough, but *that* line is possibly my new favourite quote. I've yet to get a tattoo, but I might consider it. In fact, I might request it as my epitaph. After all, it'll *kill* me not to tell Sarah.

I'll resist.

"Oh my god," I say, my voice weak as I wipe away tears.

"I didn't know what to do!" Bo says, waving his hand out to his side as he lies back down. "I rolled for it, and the witch *was* seduced. So I guess it worked?"

"Caleb gave it his all. I'll give him that." I try to take a deep inhale, but the laugh roils back up, taking my breath from me yet again.

"I thought Adamir was going to pass out. Poor thing."

"I really like your friends," I say on another long breath, steadying myself. "They seem great. An odd assortment, which I love."

"Even Walter?" Bo asks. When he sits up to see me, he does a slight double take. His eyes hold on my face with a sincere appreciation that catches me off guard and has me swallowing air. I put two palms on my cheeks, feeling their warmth. *Ah,* that's what he's noticed. I'm blushing.

"Especially Walter," I answer before clearing my throat. "Or should I call him *Hamish*?"

"You do that sometimes," Bo says, touching his cheek with a quick double-tap of his finger.

"Blush?" I look away, because often it gets worse when speaking about it. Or when beautiful men point it out. Both things. "Yeah... most people do," I say, my voice softened.

"Maybe when they're embarrassed. But you blush a lot... like when you're happy too."

"It's annoying," I say, pulling my hair off my neck to cool down.

"I like it," Bo says simply. I turn my face back toward him. "It feels like checking a box. It's the only way to know for sure my joke landed, or well, you know..." He swallows, his eyes fluttering closed with a rapid series of blinks.

"Know what?" I ask, tilting my head.

Bo scratches a hand through his hair, then bends forward as he rubs the back of his neck. He looks off to the side, his face disgruntled, as if he can't believe the words about to come out of his mouth. "You, uh, you blushed on Halloween."

I did a *lot* of things on Halloween. My eyes narrow, my smile creeping up sideways.

"When you... *came*," he adds, his jaw tight and eyes *definitely* on my neck, where there's no doubt a lingering pink hue.

Oh.

"Sorry." His eyebrows pinch together, creating a deep line down the centre of his forehead. "I don't know why I said that."

I'd tell him not to worry about it, as flippantly as I can, but my throat is quite possibly swelling up. All I can feel is the pounding of my pulse in my neck.

"We should go to bed," Bo says, his eyes raking over me while he leans farther away from me, as if he's resisting. Telling himself *no*.

I quirk an eyebrow, wondering if he knows he, perhaps subconsciously, propositioned me.

"Oh, no—not *together*. Sorry, not—" He drops his face into his hands, then runs them both through his hair, making it stick up funny. "Sorry," he laughs out. "See? This is why you had to take the lead."

Was it because of his awkwardness? I'd started to tell myself it was because he wasn't all that interested. Still, either way, it's *not* a good idea. I swallow the lump in my throat. "We, uh, haven't really talked about *that*."

Bo stares blankly back at me, his bottom lip pouted ever so slightly.

Shit, I'm really going to have to say this all out loud. Deep breath. In and out.

"I don't think it would be wise of us to have any sort of physical relationship from here on out." There, simple enough.

"No?" Bo says reactively.

No?

Fucking *No?*

What the fuck does *No?* mean? Does he disagree? What arrangement did he foresee us having?

"It's already complicated..." I say slowly.

"Right."

"And sex would just complicate things more, I think."

"*Right.*" He wets his lips, nodding even still.

"My main concern is that sex could lead to *more* between us, and then if *more* was to end badly... that could make co-parenting or living together impossible."

"Right," Bo says, *again.*

"Right," I echo him curtly.

"Sorry," he says, shaking himself. "I'm catching up."

"Well, where were you?" I ask before thinking.

He looks up to the ceiling, his hands rubbing together mindlessly between his parted knees. Once he seems to collect his thoughts, he holds eye contact with me a little too strongly for my comfort. Everywhere his eyes land on my body begins to burn. So soon enough, *all* of me is warm.

"Honestly," he says, his eyes hesitant but still locked with mine. "I'm not sure. I hadn't really thought about having rules, I guess. This is all so new, and well, if I'm being honest—"

"Rules are good, though, right?" I interrupt. If I was a betting woman, I would guess that at the end of that sentence, there's an *I'm not entirely over my ex,* which, if *I'm* being honest, I cannot bear to hear. "It's good we talked. Boundaries and whatever else... Designed to keep us safe." I'm unstoppable now, talking a mile a minute, making next to no sense. "This way, our focus remains on being the best team possible for the kid. We can keep things simple in an already complicated situation. That's the goal, yeah? Successfully co-parenting."

"That's the goal," Bo agrees, pressing his lips together, nodding tightly. "Of course."

"So it's settled, then. *Platonic* friends with foetuses." I lean back in the chair, sniffling just once. I watch as Bo brings a hand to the side of his face, his mouth leaning into it as he scratches beside his ear, smiling to himself like he's got a secret.

"What?" I ask. "What's that look?"

"Nothing," he says, dropping his hand. "I heard you. Understood," he says, voice pitching.

"Bo..." I say far too softly. Translating to him, I hope, as *don't lie to me.*

He traces his bottom lip with his thumb, then stares up at the ceiling. "If our goal is platonic... could you do me a favour?"

"Sure?" I ask, obvious confusion overtaking my voice.

"Could you keep it down? At night?"

"Huh?" I ask, seconds before my heart drops with realisation—nearly forcing it into my stomach. I immediately feel flushed, my face now burning red for all the *usual* reasons.

He notices, his lips twitching up just a little. "Old house, thin walls. Beautiful moaning coming from down the hall that makes me want to pull my hair out."

This is *not* happening. I *forbid* this from happening.

He doesn't look away, his eyes narrowing on me as I stare off over his shoulder, willing myself to teleport into the fucking sun.

This is *actually, truly, definitely* happening.

I must have been a prolific asshole in a previous life to deserve this. An oil tycoon. A corrupt dictator of a small nation. A mosquito carrying malaria. Whoever first decided to install fluorescent lighting in a changing room.

I nod, my mouth stuck open and my jaw locked into place. "Okay," I whimper involuntarily. "Of course," I say, standing on wobbly legs.

I'm leaving. Fleeing.

He can see the kid on their eighteenth birthday, if I somehow manage to survive this level of mortification. I refuse to acknowledge Bo as I pass him by and enter the front hall, slipping on my boots before reaching for my jacket.

"Win," Bo laughs out my name, coming in after me.

"Nope," I say sharply, reaching for the door handle.

He places his hand on top of mine, stopping me from my escape.

I do *not* look up at him. The big nerd with supersonic hearing and a stupidly cute face and giant warm hands. Fuck him. I *hate* him.

How much did he hear?

"Win..." Bo says, his tone laced with enjoyment that I *deeply* resent.

"Please let me go out into the cold to die." I drop my forehead against the door.

"I can't let you do that, honey."

"Do *not* call me that," I snap.

"Sorry," Bo recoils, removing his hand from on top of mine and taking a step back.

I lift my forehead and let it fall against the door again, my face turned toward him slightly. "How much did you hear?" *Meaning,* did you happen to hear the one time I accidentally let your name slip out? Or, perhaps, the second time it did when I realised how *close* just saying your name got me to the finish line?

Bo braces his forearm across the top of the archway and leans into it, closing the space between us half an inch. But I feel him *everywhere.* "Enough to know *you* think about Halloween too."

Shit, fuck, shit.

"Okay, well..." I try to formulate a defence, despite the need to shrivel up and die. "It was the last time I had sex. What else am I going to think about?"

"Your best time," he offers, his voice taunting. "Unless..." He drops his arm and bends at the waist, smug in his approach. "That *also* happens to be that night."

"You wish," I spit.

Bo sighs, his eyes falling to the floor as he straightens, standing and wiping a hand down his face. "I think you're right, though," he says, his voice far off. "About the rules... moving forward. I think that's the right thing to do."

But...

I wait. A thin tight rope under my feet leading to his.

No *but* follows.

I shouldn't be disappointed, right? It's ridiculous to be disappointed. These are *my* rules. I've only just shared them.

"Okay..." I reply, pressing my ear against the front door, giving him a few more inches of my face, though I can't bring myself to look at him for long.

"I'm sorry," he says. "I shouldn't have said anything."

"And keep hearing me? No..."

Bo looks at me sympathetically, a crooked smile and a long, thoughtful breath that raises his chest. "C'mere." He reaches out for my arm, tugging me toward him and away from the door. He wraps one arm around my shoulders, holding on to the top of my arm, and rests the other on the back of my head, pressing me to him. I grumble my annoyance, remaining stiff all over with my arms locked at my sides.

But I can't help but breathe him in. That cinnamon, musky scent. The one that's so distinctly him. Sweet and warm and inviting. And proving to me, once again, why we need these rules.

"We're going to figure this out, Win," he says, dropping his chin to the top of my head. "Rules, plans, boundaries... It'll sort itself out." Bo sighs, curling me closer. "I *am* sorry I teased you, though. I shouldn't have done that. Whatever you need to be comfortable from here on out, I'll do."

"What I need is thicker walls," I mumble against his chest.

"I'll call a contractor," he says, loosening his arms and stepping backward.

I still can't bring myself to look at him, so I study the floor between us, the grooves of the dark, wooden floors.

"I'm sorry too," I say meekly. "That you heard me. That's not... It's the pregnancy hormones—they're making me..." My voice wanders off, and I shake myself. "I'm sorry."

"Would it make you feel better or worse to know that I enjoyed it?"

Better. "Worse."

"Well, then I hated it." Bo reaches out, tilting up my face with his bent knuckle under my jaw and his thumb pressed to my chin. Slowly, I drag my eyes up to see him. "I truly am sorry I made you feel embarrassed. You have nothing to be ashamed of. I'm glad we're on the same page now. Keeping myself away from your bedroom was nearly impossible, but now, with these rules, I—"

I interrupt him, removing his hand from my quivering chin by stepping backward, my ass hitting the wall of the entranceway, next to our coats hung on the wall. "Just..." *Stop talking*, I beg with my eyes. That's *not* helping. I breathe in slowly, allowing my eyes to softly close as I do.

Then it's worse.

The second my eyes are closed, my imagination is overrun with images of Bo bursting into my bedroom and pinning my hands above my head, tossing my vibrator across the room, and using his mouth in its place. His teeth tugging at my flesh, his lips kissing across the swell of my belly, his tongue lapping at my breast. I can practically hear those perfect whimpering noises he made as he came undone beneath me.

Pressing my knees together, I open my eyes with a newfound stubbornness. I try to remind myself of the reality here. What I know versus what I *wish* could be.

I know that Bo is a good guy.

I *know*, unfortunately, that Bo is great in bed.

But I *also* know that Bo is at least a little hung up on his ex.

And I know my heart wouldn't be able to take having sex with him again. It'd be *far* too easy to fall for him now, with all these increasing layers of circumstance and proximity between us. And I don't think he's ready for what that could lead to. I don't think he wants that with me. I think he wants *her,* even still. He's, perhaps, loyal to a fault. Which is only more upsetting. Even his bad traits are good ones.

I cannot confuse being *here* with being wanted.

I cannot convince myself that he'd want me *more* than his ex.

I cannot let myself fall for a man whose heart belongs to someone else.

"Bring a girl home," I say with a false indifference. "A loud one, preferably. Get even, and we can forget about the whole thing."

His face falls, then hardens into a scowl. It's an expression I've yet to see from him. I don't like it. It doesn't suit him at all. "That would make you feel better? Me having sex with someone else down the hall?" he asks harshly.

"Yeah, sure. Why not?" I reply, unfittingly blasé.

He brings a hand to his face, sighing out as he pinches the bridge of his nose. "It's late. We should get some sleep."

I nod, folding my arms across my chest. I will my legs to move, but they refuse.

"I *am* sorry, Win. I didn't mean to—"

"We're fine," I interrupt, standing straighter. "Tricky topic, but it's settled now. Friends, right?"

Bo begins slowly walking backward until the backs of his legs hit the back of the couch. He lowers against it, looking rather defeated as he nods his agreement. "Friends... Always that." Bo smiles softly, his eyes filled with equal parts discomfort and reassurance. It upsets me. Seeing that he's trying to set me at ease.

And for the first time, I find myself wishing a man was *more* of a jerk.

"Okay, well, good night," I say, brushing past him toward our bedrooms. Once in the hallway, I press the heel of my palm into my forehead, wincing on impact.

As soon as my hand reaches my bedroom's door handle, I still.

Desperately torn between what I want and what I know, I linger. Hoping that *maybe* he'll bring me that nightly glass of ice water and slip into bed next to me, harmless in his approach. Wondering, desperately, if he feels this too. This tension, like a force, like a tether, so tightly wound between us. All these strings attached that were never supposed to be there.

I remind myself of them. One by one, plucking at each string, each reason, like an instrument in my mind. Telling myself, as I have for years, that logic needs to conquer my reckless heart.

So I go to bed. Alone.

Quiet as a mouse.

CHAPTER 20

This will help. It always does.

Every dazzling second of fractured, flickering blue-hued shadows projected onto the pool's floor. The *whoosh* of the water between strokes as I lift my head above the surface for quick gasps of air. The smell of chlorine, and the sensation of my feet pushing against tile as I roll forward into my next lap.

I repeatedly keep telling myself *this will help* while exhaustively becoming more and more tense.

I've been pent-up since last night. After tossing and turning for hours, I decided the only solution was to spend an early morning at the pool, exerting some of this tension as best I can. Pushing my body to its limits in cathartic release.

While I've always felt most at peace inside a natural body of water, swimming anywhere can bring me relief.

But not today, it seems.

This is lap seventeen. I've yet to determine how many it'll take to feel like myself again, but the number keeps increasing with every turn. I'll be swimming until I forget the very *loud* memory of my conversation with Bo last night. The mortification of living down the hall from someone who knows you touched yourself thinking about them and has *heard* you doing it.

And, simultaneously, I'll be here until I muster the considerable amount of self-control I need to hear that Bo *enjoyed* hearing me and still not make the reckless, short-sighted decision to sleep with him again.

I lift my left arm up and over my body, carving a stream into the water ahead of me at full speed, then switch to my right.

Left, right.

I haven't had sex since Halloween. But... has he?

Left, right.

He's not *actually* going to bring another girl home, right?

Left, right.

What if he calls my bluff?

Left, right.

When I reach the edge of the pool, I pull myself up and over and catch my breath as I tug off my goggles, bringing two palms to cover my eyes. *Fuck.* This is definitely *not* working.

All I can see is Bo's face, his arm leisurely draped across the top of the archway, his frame towering over me. His lips repeating *keeping myself away from your bedroom was nearly impossible* over and over and over until I want to scream, *so why did you?*

I could ask Sarah to spend the night at hers... Give myself a day or two to cool off. But am I seriously going to have to do that every time I find Bo attractive? I'm an adult, for fuck's sake. We've slept together. It's not exactly surprising that those *urges* didn't go away the moment the complications multiplied.

But something has to give.

And I'm increasingly aware that it might be my self-restraint.

"Win?" a deep, friendly voice calls out, echoing around the pool.

I twist to look behind me, looking up to the lifeguard tower to find a familiar face. "Cam?" I call up to him, smiling broadly.

I trained Cam three years ago at Westcliff Point, and he's been back every summer since as a lifeguard. I've only ever bumped into my *summer people* outside of summer months a handful of times, and it always throws me off a bit. But Cam is a sweetheart. Though the timing of running into him could be better.

"I thought that was you," he says, his dimples appearing as he flicks his copper hair away from his face.

"Hi!" I say, lifting my legs to rotate and stand. I look down at my swimsuit, wondering if he'll be able to notice my little baby bump. It's a toss-up, considering how tight the one-piece suit is, but even if he suspects, I doubt he'll ask. "How've you been?" I ask.

"Good, good, keeping busy. Lifeguarding here and teaching private swim. How about you?"

"Pretty good," I answer as he starts to descend the ladder. "At the café. *Still*."

Cam stops a few feet shy of me, tugging on the lanyard around his neck. "It's so funny I bumped into you... I was just thinking about you the other day."

Okay... maybe I *should* tell him I'm knocked up.

"I just started teaching this kid, Henry. He has a hand just like yours. I was telling him all about my friend who's the best swimmer I know, and he nearly lost his mind with excitement."

I pout, and an adoring whine escapes from my chest. "*Really?*" I ask, elongating the word.

"Yeah. He's so sweet. A really fun kid to teach. I was chatting with his parents after his first lesson, and they mentioned they're trying to find a summer camp for him. I immediately thought of you and that idea you told Casey and me about at last year's bonfire. Your camp?" He brushes his hair away from his face again and adjusts the whistle on his neck as his eyes glaze over in thought. "What did you call it? Camp..."

Camp Cando. A bit on the nose, *sure*, but it *is* for kids. "It was just an idea..." I shrug one shoulder while simultaneously wrapping my arm across my stomach, holding on to my elbow. "I don't even remember. I think I'd just drunk too much." Six beers. But I *do* remember. It felt incredible to talk about it again. That was the only time I've talked about my camp in the past few years, other than when I told Bo.

"That's a shame. These parents would love something like that."

I smile despite the ache in my chest nagging to be heard. "How's he doing? With the swimming?"

"Fine. But, actually, while I have you here, can I pick your brain?"

I nod eagerly.

"He's got most of the technique down, but he really overcompensates with his right hand—the bigger one—and it steers him a little off course. I've tried the usual stuff, but he seems to still get off balance. What would you suggest?"

"What position?"

"Nearly all of them, but it's worse with breaststroke."

"It's hard to say without seeing him swim. When's he here?"

"Tuesday evenings."

"I'm off on Tuesday next week. I could come by if you'd like."

"Seriously?" Cam asks, bending his knees, crouching down so our faces line up—his totally bursting with joy. I nod, caught off guard, as he picks me up and spins me around in the air. "That'd be amazing." He drops me, one hand stuck on my shoulder, and steadies me as I regain my balance.

"Any time?" I laugh out.

"Can I text you the details? I don't think I have your phone number."

"Oh, sure." I wait as he pulls out his phone, then I put my number into it. Saving myself as *Winnie the One-Handed Wonder*—because it just felt right.

And suddenly, I'm not in such a bad mood.

"He's going to be so excited to meet you. And," he smiles down at my contact information on his phone, tapping the screen, "the name suits you. I *did* talk about you as if you were a superhero."

"Well, let's hope Henry isn't disappointed."

"Aw, well, who could be?" He winks before glancing around the pool. "Shit, I am *very* lucky no one decided to drown just now. I, uh, should probably get back up there." He points a thumb over his shoulder.

"Right, yeah, I'm going to try a few more laps. Clear my head."

"You should really think about that camp, Win." Cam says, sauntering backward slowly. "I think it could be a very cool thing!"

And I *do* think about it.

I think about it so much that I'm no longer thinking about last night or what could have been. In fact, by the time I'm showered, dressed, and on the bus ride home—I can't think about anything else. My thoughts, ideas, and questions pile on top of one another. And suddenly, I have an entirely new conversation I'd like to have with Bo.

Finance Bo, that is.

Not to be mistaken with a Finance *Bro.*

God, no.

When I get home, Bo's on a client call at his desk, swivelling in his chair as he taps the end of a pencil to the far corner of his eyebrow. His long limbs are all spread out as he leans back, nearly capsizing.

I approach his desk, buzzing with energy, dropping my things onto the couch on my way toward him.

He tilts his head curiously at me, agreeing to whatever the other person on the phone is saying with a series of murmured *mm-hmms.* "What?" he mouths silently, his giddy smile matching my own.

"I have an idea," I whisper, hovering above him. "But... I need your help."

He checks his watch and nods at me, holding out one finger.

When I linger for what feels like *too* long, I begin biting at my thumb nail anxiously. Bo checks his watch again, apologising with an eye roll directed at the phone and a *wrap it up* motion with a finger pointed at the sky.

The immediate realisation that I'm standing over the guy while he's working strikes and fills me with embarrassment. I'm acting as if I'm entitled to his time. I'm very much *not* entitled to his time. Especially when *his* time pays the vast majority of *my* bills.

"Sorry, never mind. It can wait," I say, waving my hands and stepping back onto my heel.

He stops me with a firm grasp around my forearm, dropping the pencil onto the floor as he does.

I had only just gotten those thoughts out of my head...

"Hey, Odette? I'm so sorry to interrupt, but my colleague, Fred, just reminded me of a meeting that's already started without me. So I'll have to let you go." He nods, his eyes stuck on his computer screen and his hand still clasped around me.

I take a second to appreciate the veins in his hands. The sheer size of them causes envy on the best of days, but the strength and definition of them isn't lost on me either. I know it's ironic, to have some sort of hand fetish. But in my defence, I never even considered hands as anything other than limbs prior to Bo.

And I *could* shrug free of his hold, but I don't.

"Yep. Yes, of course. I'll check in then. Best of luck with the move. Okay, yes, bye-bye." Bo drops his phone on the desk with a careless thud and turns to me, eager-eyed and excitable, before he releases my arm. "What's happening? What's this idea?"

I grab a folding chair still left out from the DND game last night and drag it over to his desk. "I want you to help me with money."

"Seriously?" He grips the arms of the chair as he kicks a leg out. "Hell yeah!"

I laugh, a *little* offended. "I'm not *that* bad with money, am I?"

"No. Sorry, just—I'm glad you'd come to me for help. I like that."

Do *not* blush. "I want to figure out how to get a business loan. How to make a savings plan and how to really get the ball rolling on my camp. I don't care if it'll take me ten years or even more—I just want to start the process now. Tell me what I need to do."

His smile is warm and slow and thoughtful, creasing lines next to his eyes and eyebrows rising up his forehead. His tongue darts out to lick his lips as he nods. "Fuck yeah. Let's do some math."

I check in with him at the first hour mark, ensuring that he doesn't have *actual* clients or responsibilities he should be tending to instead. Then, when his phone rings for the second time as I fetch us snacks from the kitchen, I make sure he doesn't have to answer it. Both times, he dismisses me politely, focusing intently on the spreadsheet he's crafting.

Three and a half hours later, I have a file labelled *WinniFRED McNulty* on his desktop, a new monthly budget, a pile of sticky notes with things I need to do before contacting banks, and two different timelines for loan applications—depending on how aggressively I'm willing to save.

It's a start.

It's a *very* good start.

"This is exciting, Win." Bo shuts his laptop, making his monitor turn off as well.

"I seriously cannot thank you enough," I say. "This feels like the first time anyone's taken this idea seriously."

"Don't thank me. You deserve better than that. Not only is this a phenomenal idea, but it's also an excellent business plan—whoever decides to invest will be better off for it."

"So, in your professional opinion, does it feel... doable?" I ask, my hesitant optimism obvious.

"Yes, absolutely. But don't you mean Camp Can-doable?" Bo laughs from the back of his throat, standing from his chair and stretching. He seems to always wear a knitted sweater and dark jeans or trousers when he's working. He's always dressed sharply, even though I've never seen him pick up a video call. I have the urge to press my face against each of the sweaters that he seems to have stock in and test them for their softness.

"Really?" I sigh out, huffing out a weak laugh as I follow him toward the kitchen.

"Hey, I have a god-given *right* to make dad jokes now," he says, his head in the fridge.

"Why do I have the feeling you always have?"

He shuts the fridge, his lips pushed out to the side as he looks at me, an idea sparked behind his curious, hazel eyes. "Do you have lunch plans today? With Sarah?"

"Nope," I pop the *p*. "Why?"

"There's nothing in here I want. Want to grab lunch with me?"

"Ooh, can we get burgers? I've been really craving ketchup."

"Just the ketchup?" Bo asks over his shoulder, walking down the hall toward his bedroom.

"Yes. In a cup, preferably," I answer as he comes back into view holding a small box of cards.

"Bringing these, since we skipped last night." He stops still. "Did you say in a cup?"

"Hey!" I say defensively, clasping two protective hands over my tummy. "They'll hear you! Don't mock them."

Bo bends at the waist, a lopsided grin in full effect. "Kid, tell your mom you want ice cream or pineapple juice, or hell, pickles. Ketchup is a *weird* choice." He stands straight and brushes past me, heading toward the front of the house. I follow, playing up my offence, my mouth open and a hand clasped over my chest.

"How rude!" I exclaim, tugging on my winter boots. Bo holds up my jacket for me, and I slip my arms inside. "The first time you talk to them, and you decide to food-shame them?"

"It's not the first time," Bo says, grabbing his keys from the wall and throwing open the front door.

It's not until I buckle myself into his passenger seat that he's near enough for me to respond. "What do you mean? When else have you talked to them?"

"When you fell asleep watching *Lord of the Rings.* I had to tell all my fun facts and trivia to *someone.* Plus, once the movie ended, I needed to explain to them why they might feel a little... jostled."

I stare at him absently.

"How do you think you got to your bed?" he asks, his eyes narrowed.

"I assumed I just half sleepwalked."

"No, you were out cold," Bo says, turning the car on.

"You carried me to bed?" I ask.

"Yeah," he says, putting his arm behind my headrest to look over his shoulder as he backs out of the driveway. "Sorry, is that weird? I did try to wake you."

"No." I swallow, admiring the sharp line of his jaw as he keeps his eyes locked on the street behind us. "That's fine."

A few minutes pass as we drive in silence, other than the radio commercials. We both sing along to one jingle in sequence, starting and stopping at the same time without acknowledging each other.

"We've passed like *every* burger chain," I point out ten minutes into our drive.

"*Please*. You think I'd take the mother of my child to a McDonald's for a celebratory lunch?" He tuts. "C'mon, have more faith in me than that."

"Celebratory?" I ask. "What are we celebrating?"

"Your new plan. The kid you're growing. You, in general."

I blush immediately.

Bo notices, then glances away, his jaw working as his eyes narrow on the road ahead.

At the exact moment I ask, "Should we talk about last night?" Bo says, "I'm sorry for last night."

"It's all good," I say with full confidence. "Tensions are going to run a little high, given the circumstances. I think we're doing a great job and should probably expect there to be some... awkwardness. We'll keep focusing on getting to know one another as friends."

"Still, I should have never said—"

"I think I'd feel better if we just pretended you... didn't."

"Okay," he says, nodding, his hands tightening around the wheel. "Is it cool if I just apologise one more time?" He winces, turning toward me briefly with a sweet shyness in his eyes.

"One last time," I say.

"I'm sorry," he says compulsively, as if he's been holding it back for far longer than a few seconds. "From now on, we will pretend the baby was an immaculate conception, and you'll be my sexless pal Fred, if that's what you want."

I hear a high pitch ringing in my ear. The sound of my libido *screaming* for mercy, if I'm not mistaken. "That's probably for the best." Bo changes gears between us, and the back of his knuckles brush the side of my thigh accidentally. Still, I can't help but grind my teeth as I look out the window.

"Want to bust out a question before we get to the restaurant?" he asks, reaching into the inside lining of his jacket and pulling the deck of cards out of the inner pocket. He holds them out to me, his eyes flicking between the road ahead and my face.

"Sure," I say, taking the cards.

CHAPTER 21

The universe is laughing at us.

"Hey, I saw that," Bo says, his face twisting between me and the car in front of us. "No switching cards. What did it say?"

"Trust me," I say, dropping the deck to my lap.

"We're going to do them all eventually, right?"

"Yeah but—"

"No card-switching," he says, signalling as he changes lanes. "New rule."

"Fine." I take the card back from the bottom of the deck and turn it over, holding it against my bouncing knee. "What has been your most significant sexual experience? What did it teach you?"

Bo doesn't laugh, though I can tell he'd like to. "Good Q..." he says dryly.

"Solid. Not at all what we're trying to avoid."

"Perfect timing, really."

"I can take this one," I say, flicking the corner of the card against my knee repeatedly. The quicker we answer that, the quicker we can move past it. And hopefully get somewhere for food. "I mean... there's nothing *quite* as significant as the time I got pregnant," I joke weakly.

What I don't say is that I'd also never experienced sex like *that*. The intimacy shared with someone I hardly knew. How much trust I had in him, despite that unfamiliarity. The moment he kissed my hand plays on my mind far more often than I'd care to admit. How desirable it made me feel. That he wanted me not despite my differences but, equally, for them. But I can't say that; it's far too intimate. Far too true.

"And I learned to take my birth control on time, that's for sure," I add.

"Would you?" Bo asks, his attention facing forward.

"Would I what?"

"If you could go back, would you have taken your birth control on time? Prevented this?" He asks it with zero judgement, his tone genuinely curious.

"Oh, I, um..." I bite my thumb nail as I consider my answer. As unexpected as this all was, as unrecognisable as my life is now, I doubt I would change a thing. I'd been directionless for so long. Keeping my head down, living the day to day with no real plans for the future. But now, I have my head up. Longing for what's to come, as new and rewardingly terrifying as it may be. Planning for a life that isn't entirely my own anymore woke me up.

"If that's too intense of a question you don't—"

"No," I interrupt. "I wouldn't have consciously decided to get pregnant. That wouldn't be fair to you. But if I had the choice to go back, I wouldn't. I needed this." It's a simple admission, but completely true. I *needed* this.

A deeper part of me realises, too, that I needed Bo. Someone who, from the moment I stuck out my hand, has understood me at a fundamental level that many people cannot. Someone kind, compassionate, hard-working who *believes* in me.

That's enough, I think. To have a friend who believes in me. He doesn't owe me any more than that.

"Me either," Bo says decidedly, even though I didn't ask. "I wouldn't go back."

His voice washes over me like warm, silky water passing down my spine. Relaxing every muscle. Dismissing a worry that I'd kept hidden, even from myself. "You'd choose this?" I ask, feeling the start of tears sting my nose. I want to say, *me? You'd choose me?*

"Yeah, I think I would. I know the timing isn't exactly ideal, but if you lined up every other person in the world who I could've had a baby with, I'd choose you again. You're going to be a fantastic mom, Win."

I'd choose you again.

Every other person in the world.

I know he doesn't mean for *him*, but for the kid. But the sentiment is still nice. That he thinks I'm going to be that good of a mother, when I so often doubt that I'll be any sort of mom at all.

"*Blegh!*" I say, wiping a tear from my cheek that fell before Bo had even finished speaking. "Don't be so nice to me. I'm starving, and this baby is obsessed with making me a sentimental, emotional mess. I'm weakened."

"Want to ask another question?" he asks, smiling to himself as he exits the highway. "We've got about five more minutes."

"Whoa, whoa, whoa," I say, sniffling. "I see you. You didn't answer."

He licks his lips, looking bashfully at the road ahead. "Same answer. Us."

I had *so* many more words than him when I answered. But his answer carries more weight, somehow. I ignore the way my heart twists. I have to. "Same reason?" I ask. "The baby?"

"Kind of... The baby is a big factor, *obviously*. But, also, what it meant for me." I watch his chest rise and fall on a heavy breath.

"What *did* it mean?" I ask, so quiet I'm not sure he can hear me.

His jaw works, his eyes flicking over to my face with a nervous smile that twitches away. "I mentioned that since my surgery, I hadn't been with anyone. I think I had started to convince myself that maybe I wouldn't again. That no one would want me like *that* anymore."

"But you're *you*," I say, foolishly interrupting.

Bo's chin tilts up with a cocky smile. "I'd love to hear you expand on that."

"Shut up," I say, my cheeks warming.

He loosens his hand around the top of the steering wheel and swipes it across the leather. "You made me feel *really* wanted," he says *so* earnestly that it lands in my chest, reverberating like an echo in an abandoned tunnel. "You..." He laughs anxiously. "Fuck, why is it so hard to describe?"

I recognise it. What he's trying to say but can't find the words for. Because I felt it too. So *why* did he leave?

"Seen?" I ask, making two fists in my lap.

He nods. "Understood," he adds. "Like… I don't know." He laughs softly, looking up to the left. "Like maybe I'm fine as I am. As is."

"When you kissed my hand… that's how it felt. No one had done that before," I whisper.

Bo looks at me briefly, his face shrouded in disappointment. As if he'd wished he hadn't been the first. Which strikes me as incredibly selfless. I, on the other hand, enjoyed hearing that I was the only one who'd given him that acceptance. Perhaps, if I give him the full truth of what that night meant to me, it'll redeem me some. He deserves to hear it, regardless.

"It was the very first time anyone had paid attention to *that* part of me during sex. None of my hookups or my ex included all of me in their lust. I felt wholly desired with you, Bo. Not just the best bits."

Silently, we pull into a parking lot behind the restaurant.

"You deserve to have that in *every* experience," he says adamantly, parking the car and twisting his upper body to face me head-on. I feel my throat tighten at the intensity in his eye, and I grow lightheaded. "Thank you for giving that to me, when no one had given it to you."

The strange thing is, I don't think I did anything at all. Being with Bo was one of the easiest things I think I've *ever* done. Which, in a life filled with daily, mundane challenges, feels rather significant.

"I think we handled that question *very* maturely," I say, lifting my chin and attempting to catch his eye.

Bo nods, his usual relaxed and happy demeanour returning slowly, starting in his eyes and then pulling up his lips. "Yeah, me too."

"I'm *starving*," I whisper, tilting my head toward the restaurant.

"Yeah, me too," Bo says, his stoic eyes held on *me*.

There should be Olympic medals for this level of restraint, I think, opening my door.

CHAPTER 22

We're seated at a back booth in a restaurant bustling with the local demographic. A.k.a. wealthy people who also appear to exist in classy athleisure. A lot of Lululemon and L.L. Bean. Basically, who I want to be when I grow up and have more expendable income.

It's a red-brick interior, with art hanging from a wooden rail around the restaurant that seems to be done by local artists, all for sale. There are mismatched chandeliers throughout, repurposed from old baskets, it would seem. It's very cute.

"No menu?" I ask, glancing around the table.

"You can order anything you want. Even ketchup in a cup if you'd like."

"What? What sort of restaurant lets you have a free-for-all?" I ask, admiring the expensive-looking stroller at the table next to us. I always feel a little shame for longing after such nice things, but I still do. I think it's a consequence of growing up with hand-me-downs and thrift store finds. Sometimes, I just want to blow money on things for me. Especially the magenta, teal blue, and green anorak that a woman at another table is zipping up as her family prepares to leave.

"Your eyes are everywhere right now," Bo says, grinning. "What are you looking at?"

"Oh, just... coveting."

Bo snorts. "How biblical."

"Maybe this is why I've never had money. The powers that be know I'd blow it all. But it's justified if I spend *some* of my new disposable income on stuff for the baby, right? Like that stroller? Because that's truly beautiful." I tilt my eyes to the left, signalling for where Bo should look.

"You know, we always say *the baby*, and I keep wondering if we should name them. Like a nickname, maybe, until we find out the sex and give them a permanent one."

"I'd like to give them a fairly gender-neutral first name, I think. And I think I'd like to be surprised too?"

"Haven't we had enough surprises?" Bo asks, his head tilting with a crooked smile.

My stomach rumbles, pulling my focus. "So how do we order if there's no menu? Do we wait here or go up to the counter?" I ask.

"He'll be out in a minute," Bo says flippantly. "So we're not finding out, then?"

"If that's okay."

"Of course. Whatever you want."

"Are there any names you've always liked?" I ask.

Bo tilts his head, appearing deep in thought with his bottom lip pouted. "No, but there are definitely names I *don't* like."

"Oh, same. No exes or school bullies. No cringey television show characters. No shitty coworkers or mean customer service reps."

"That last one was very specific," Bo says, pouring two cups of water from the bottle left on the table.

"Brittany from Staples knows what she did."

"Family names?" he asks. "What was Sarah's mom's name? She was special to you, right?"

"Marcie, and yes, she was. But I'd have to be careful there. My mom always felt a bit jealous of how close Marcie and I were. They were best friends, but I think my mom might feel left out if I was to use Marcie as a name."

"What's your mom's name?" Bo asks, then winces. I feel it too, the discomfort of being so involved with someone and not knowing a whole lot about them. "Maybe one of these evenings we should write out a family tree or something."

"Her name is June."

"That's a beautiful name."

"It's my middle name," I say, glancing around for our waiter. "What's yours?"

"I have two. Robert Hugo August Durand."

I go entirely still. "August?" I ask.

"Yeah, it's the month my parents met."

August.

Yes, my heart sounds. *That's right.*

Marcie passed away in August. Sarah made a comment about the baby arriving then to make the month less sad. And my mother and I have a month in our name. So it's possibly the perfect name. It would honour each of us. Bo, his parents, me, and mine.

"I *love* August," I say.

"August," Bo repeats, pressing his lips together as he nods, a smile overtaking his face. "Did we..." Bo sits straighter, his expression *beyond* smug. "Did we just name our kid?"

"August," I whisper to myself, testing it aloud again.

"It should be illegal to be so good at this shit," Bo says confidently. "August... It feels right, doesn't it?"

"It does," I agree, smiling. It can't be *that* easy, right?

"There they are!" a familiar, boisterous voice calls from the kitchen door across the restaurant. I immediately look up to find Kevin bouncing over to us.

"Kevin?" I ask Bo, smiling widely as I stand to greet him.

"It's his place. Get ready to eat everything you can."

Kevin wraps me in a big bear hug before setting me down. "I've heard we're on a mission for ketchup, my dear."

"When did you—" I start to ask Bo, but then my stomach rumbles again.

"Actually, I think the baby changed its mind. I just want cheese. All of it."

"Probably avoid the soft cheeses, though," Bo says, holding up a finger before using it to scratch his ear. "You know, anything unpasteurised." I stare at him funny. "It was in the baby book... no soft cheeses."

Kevin turns to me, eerily calm. "If you want me to, I can have him removed."

"He's probably right. He's much better at pregnancy than I am."

"Well, all the *safe* cheeses will be yours. Are we thinking of a cheese board? Cheese on pizza? Cheesy sandwich? Pasta covered in cheese?"

"Oh, definitely pasta."

"Tomato sauce? That good enough to satisfy the ketchup craving too?"

"Yes!" I sway from side to side. "It's not too much trouble, right?"

"Not at all," he says, pulling out my chair. "You two lovebirds talk amongst yourselves. I'll be back with that and..." Kevin points to Bo.

"I'll have whatever she's having," Bo answers.

"Got it."

"He called us lovebirds," I whisper when Kevin disappears out of view.

"Did he?"

I nod, watching the woman next to us pick up her baby out of the aforementioned stroller and tuck them close to her chest. She bounces while shushing the baby, holding them against her with one hand as she forks her salad with her other.

I try to visualise whether I'll be able to do such a thing, my hand subconsciously rising to my shoulder.

"You okay?" Bo asks, his voice soft and low.

I shake myself, lowering my hand. "Sorry... I'm fine."

Bo looks toward the same table, the small baby in the woman's arms, and back to me. He purses his lips and nods, letting his head hang between us. "I'm worried that our kid will be really into sports, running or soccer or something, and I won't be able to keep up."

I detach from my haze and snap back to focus. "What? No. Bo, you're working on a prosthesis that hardly fits, and you're *still* doing great. Soon you'll have one that works much better, and you'll be able to run or do whatever you want. Plus, you kick with your right foot, not your left. Even if we come against barriers, we'll figure it out."

"I'm worried they'll be embarrassed, though. That their dad is different."

"No, they'll be *our* kid. They'll have empathy and kindness and—" I stop myself, noticing Bo's proud smile.

"Go on..." he says teasingly.

No, I don't think I will.

"You were saying?" he asks, a cheeky smile tipped into his glass of water.

"Were you tricking me into talking to myself just now?"

He nods, his shoulders lowering as he places his elbows on the table and hunches forward. "Maybe..."

"How did—how could you tell? I—"

"You frowned when she picked up her fork the second time," he interrupts.

I look away, feeling *far* too perceived for my liking. And yet a piece of me is grateful for it. It's so much easier to communicate insecurities when you don't need to communicate them at all. Isn't that all we ever want? To be seen and heard? Validated, even when we're not able to ask for it.

"Well, it's different for me. It's not the same."

"How so?"

"Think of all the expressions there are *just* for moms. 'She's going to have her hands full!' Or 'you're going to need an extra set of hands!'" I tuck my hair behind my ear. "It's intimidating. There are a lot of things I can barely do for myself, let alone for someone else. I mean, you've seen me with buttons."

"We're going to find solutions though, right? We'll make it work. Like you said, we'll figure it out together."

"Yeah, I know," I agree, though I can hear how unconvincing I am.

"As capable as you think I am, it's far less than how capable I think you are," he says, argumentatively. "Maybe what we lack in limbs, we make up for in enthusiasm and wits. Who else do you know that could go swimming, launch a business plan, and name a baby all before lunch?"

It's a *late* lunch, though, to be fair. "We did most of those things together, so I can hardly take credit."

"And that's what we're going to keep doing. Working together. That's the whole point of this." He gestures between us. "Isn't it? Being a good team?"

"Yeah," I agree, a little more convincingly.

"Win, Bo, and Gus are gonna take over the world," he says in an obscenely dramatic, theatrical voice.

"Gus? Seriously? They've been named for less than ten minutes, and they already have a dorky nickname?"

"What would you prefer? *Aug*? That's not a name. It sounds like the sound someone would make after stubbing their toe."

I roll my eyes, smiling toward my lap.

"Yeah, that's right," Bo says arrogantly. "Admit it. You love it."

I sigh out. I don't know if I love it, or if I just love that *he* does. "I do. It's cute."

"Damn right."

"If our food doesn't arrive soon, I'm going to eat my *other* hand," I say, unfolding my napkin.

"Don't be ridiculous," Bo says exaggeratedly. "You can eat mine. It's far bigger."

CHAPTER 23

Seventeen Weeks Pregnant. Baby is the size of a pear.

"Okay, buddy!" I say, kneeling in the shallow end of the pool. "Now I want you to ball your hand up in a fist." I help Henry fold up his bigger hand. "Perfect! Now we're going to swim as normal, okay? I just want to try something."

Henry nods, presenting me two thumbs with both fists before he falls onto his tummy and starts swimming toward the far end of the pool. Cam hovers by the side of the pool, waiting for him there and shouting words of encouragement.

Henry's smaller hand is a lot like mine but with a slightly less-developed thumb. It's on the opposite side of his body, too, so it takes some trial and error to find the right method for him.

But we do.

Forty minutes into his one hour of private swim, he's swimming straight and maybe even *faster* than he was before.

Because of me.

"You did an awesome job today, Henry!" I say, kneeling next to the pool as he shakes water out of his floppy hair like a puppy, giggling.

"I was so fast!"

"You were!" I say, smiling up at Cam over his shoulder as he approaches.

"And I'm not bumping into the rope anymore. I went like an arrow! Straight!"

"Like an arrow, exactly." I squish my face together, smiling so hard I can't help it. "Great job, buddy."

"Thank you, Winnie!" He throws his arms around my neck. "I'm gonna be a swimmer like you," he says quietly before letting go.

I stand up, watching Henry walk toward the glass door where his parents are waiting for him. I wave to Cam and turn to walk toward the women's changing rooms, but he stops me.

"Hey, wait. Come meet his parents. They're going to want to thank you."

"Oh, no, I don't—"

"Win, c'mon." Cam brings his hand up in the air, waving me toward them, in view of Henry's parents. It'd be rude not to now.

I follow behind, wrapping a towel around me as I do. They're bustling with excited conversation by the time I make my way over, and Henry is bursting with pride as his mom wraps him in a towel and a hug.

"Hi," I say, waving shyly.

"Tonya, James—this is Win."

"Win is the best swimmer of all time!" Henry shouts.

His parents laugh. "We saw that," Tonya says, smiling at me. "Thanks so much for coming. We could see how much confidence it gave him from all the way out here."

"And Cam says you're opening a camp?" James asks.

"Oh, well, not really. It's more of a dream at the moment. We're starting to make plans. Next step is finding investors, and then we have to find property. It's a big uphill climb, but...someday," I say.

They immediately look disappointed.

"I'm sorry. I'd love to have Henry at *any* camp. Maybe in a few years, huh, buddy?"

Henry nods, hitting me with a beaming smile with missing teeth and a wrinkled nose.

His dad, James, clears his throat. "I, uh, I don't normally do this, but..." He pulls out his wallet and hands me a business card. "If you're looking for investors, please get in touch." I take the card hesitantly. "We've seen what you can do in an hour, and I'm impressed. Other kids should get that chance."

"Oh, I—" I almost dismiss myself. I nearly tell them every way in which I'm unqualified, unprofessional, incapable. I even, almost, hand back the business card. But I don't. I stop myself.

Maybe it's because of the hope on their faces and the smile still stuck on Henry's.

Maybe it's because of Bo, telling me how capable I am. How *possible* this is.

Mostly, I think, it's because of me. Because of how much stronger I feel lately.

I let myself feel proud of everything I did with Henry today, the years of schooling that prepared me for this, the life I've lived with my hand and the experiences I've gathered just by having it. And I hold my head high.

"Thank you," I say. "I'll definitely be in touch. Thank you," I add again—because I can't resist. "It was great to meet you, buddy. You're going to do great with Mr. Cam, here."

"Thanks again," Tonya says as they usher Henry toward the changing rooms.

Cam shuts the door and then smiles at me with *I told you so* eyes.

I look at the business card in my hand and take a deep inhale. *James Burrough, President of Burrough Financial Holdings.*

"Win, I think you're getting your camp."

"I mean, he could easily change his mind. I still have to make a proposal and find—" I stop myself *again. Sometimes... things are just good things.* I could spend my whole life waiting for the other shoe to drop, or I could begin training myself to expect the best. Embrace gratitude and drop the scepticism. "This... this is very cool, isn't it? The chances of running into you here, meeting Henry and his parents... It's..."

"Very cool," Cam says, starting to lead the way to the changing rooms. "You said 'we' before. Do you have a business partner or *someone* else?"

"Did I?"

"Yeah. You said, 'we're starting to make plans,' when Tonya asked just now."

"Oh, I..." I consider what Bo and I are to each other and decide to simplify it as best I can. "My roommate and me. He's in finance and is helping me out."

"Oh, okay," Cam says, his smile crooked and his eyes narrowed in on me. *Uh-oh.* I know that look. "Would you maybe want to grab a drink, then? A late dinner?"

Yep, *there* it is.

I grimace, putting a hand on Cam's shoulder and patting him just once before removing it. "So, funny story about my roommate. Actually..."

"Got it," Cam says, laughing under his breath. "It's complicated, I take it?"

"Beyond complicated."

"Want to grab a very platonic drink and talk about it, then?"

I laugh, looking up to the ceiling. "So, actually, I can't drink either."

"Oh," Cam says, his eyes dropping down to my stomach.

"Yep..."

"The roommate's?"

"Yeah," I breathe out.

"That *is* complicated." He winces, smiling even still.

"It is," I say.

"So no Westcliff this year?" he asks.

I shake my head, frowning. "Not this year."

"Ah, well, we'll miss you."

"I'll miss it too."

"You know, if you wanted to, I bet Henry's parents would rather have you teaching him. I've got a pretty full schedule already, and you could take over his lessons. It's two hundred bucks a week after the pool rental."

"Two hundred?" I nearly yell. "For an hour?"

"I'm telling you..." Cam says, reaching down to grab his towel and flipping it over his shoulder. "James has got *camp* money."

"I'd love that," I say. "Are you sure?"

"Just remember me when it's time to hire for that camp of yours," Cam says with a wink.

"Absolutely," I say, smiling back at him.

"I'll text you the details, then," he says. "See you around, Win."

"Thank you," I shout after him when he disappears from view.

CHAPTER 24

Nineteen Weeks Pregnant. Baby is the size of a mango.

"If you could teleport right now, where would you go?" Bo asks me before filling his face with another spoonful of ice cream.

We ran out of questions from the deck a week ago, having fallen into the same routine for the past month of living together. Every evening, we eat dinner, tidy up to the sounds of another record, then ask a question. On the calmer days, when the music is jazz or soft-rock, Bo completes his sudoku puzzle on the couch. Other times, when the music calls for it, he plays air guitar or drums and throws his body around the kitchen for my amusement as I finish cleaning up.

Since we ran out, Bo's just been making up the questions on the spot.

The *twenty questions to fall in love* certainly did what it says on the box.

I'm pretty hopelessly in love with Bo at this point. Platonically, of course. *Mostly*. The primal, baby daddy hormones sometimes disagree about the platonic part. Usually when he gives me foot rubs while we watch movies, or when his eyes dip down to my

cleavage when they probably shouldn't, or when he... you know...
breathes near me.

Even still, we've been on our best behaviour.

"Ooh, good one," I say, taking the communal spoon from him as
he holds the carton out for me. "Somewhere warm and on a beach,
for sure. But not somewhere cheap to fly to—since I could just do
that myself. Maybe Greece? Yeah, Greece."

"I was going to say Greece too," Bo says, taking the spoon back
from me. "I want to see the Temple of Poseidon."

"Sure," I laugh out. "We'll go together."

"Excellent," he says, his mouth full of ice cream.

"Oh, Doctor Salim called, by the way. The ultrasound is in two
weeks."

"How are you feeling about it?" Bo asks.

"Uh, I'm a little nervous. Excited to see Gus, though."

"What day?"

I tsk, trying to remember. "Uh, not sure. It was a Friday." I lift
up, moving to grab my phone. "I think the tenth?"

"My dad will be here then," Bo says, swallowing another helping
before handing me back the carton. "If that's still okay?"

"Bo, I have *sworn* to you that it's more than okay. Multiple times.
I'm excited to meet your dad."

"Just checking," he says, raising his palms up defensively. "I'll
have that day off, though. So maybe we can drop Dad off somewhere and pick him up after the appointment."

"No, don't miss out on time with your dad."

"Are you crazy? As if I'd miss an ultrasound. This is when they look like a baby, right? Not a little bean anymore?"

"Yeah, think so." I take the final scoop of ice cream, finishing off the carton and setting it on the coffee table. "And how are *you* feeling about turning thirty, old man?" I say, draping my feet across his lap. He, rolling his eyes at both his new nickname *and* my silent demand, begins rubbing my feet.

"Honestly? Fine. I was thinking about it the other night, and I'm just grateful to still be here, and for all that's to come. My birthday last year was pretty terrible. During the dark times." He laughs dryly.

Bo has recently taken to referring to last year as the *dark times*. I've picked up little bits and pieces of information here and there without needing to pry all that much. After he was given the all-clear to live alone, three months post-surgery, his dad went back to France. And he *was* alone a lot, from what it sounds like. Other than DND with his friends once a month, he didn't really see anyone.

"Another year older and wiser..." I say, rolling my neck as he presses his thumb into the centre of my foot.

"And more handsome," he adds.

I snort. "Of *course.*"

Bo squeezes his hand around my heel, builds pressure, then releases. I let out a not-so-subtle moan, but I'm far too blissed out to care.

"There?" he asks teasingly.

"I need to get new shoes for work."

"You *need* to tell them you're pregnant," Bo says.

"They'll treat me differently..."

"You mean, like, give you a stool to sit on? Or maybe longer breaks? Heaven forbid."

"Watch it. I could easily kick you right now." I fall back against the couch, letting my eyes close as Bo wraps his giant hands around my swollen ankles and massages those too.

"Permission to bring down the mood?"

"Always," I answer. And I mean it. I'm so desperate to know everything Bo's got stored away that I'd let him say just about anything. I think he could unwrap the very worst parts of himself, and I'd still sit here, hanging on every word.

"I keep thinking that, as of my birthday, I'll be older than my mom ever was. I *hate* that."

I sit up slowly, peering up at him. His eyes are held absently on the mantel across the room, his hands busy working my ankles over. I consider whether I should move my feet off his lap, but it seems to me that this is keeping his hands occupied while his thoughts wander. Like he was throwing stones at the beach all those weeks ago.

Maybe Bo requires physical distractions in order to open up.

"That must feel really strange. I'm sorry," I offer gently.

"It's bizarre to live more life than the person who gave me mine..." he says, his voice far off.

"Is that a quote?"

"No," Bo shrugs one shoulder, his brows inching together. "Just something that's been rattling around my mind."

You're brilliant, I want to say. "We've never talked about how your mom passed. Would you want to?" I ask instead.

"Not now, if that's okay." He smiles wistfully, turning toward me as he pats my ankle, signalling that he's done.

I shift off him, sitting up and crossing my legs in front of me. I rest my cheek against my hand, supported by the back of the couch. "Of course. Whatever you need."

He looks at me sideways, appreciation in his eyes—mixed with a request. For a change of subject, I think.

"Are you excited to see your dad?"

"Yeah, I am. I can't wait for him to meet you."

My expression squeezes tight as I tuck my face into my palm, and my heart squeezes too. "Oh, well, I hope he likes me."

Bo shakes his head, scratching his chin. "He'll *love* you."

Now it's *too* tight, the burst of joy in my chest. I have to rub my palm over it, attempting to loosen it. I'm not sure exactly when such lovely sentiments from Bo began to feel slightly painful, but that's where we're at these days. It's a longing sensation. A reminder of the limitations and parameters we have to abide by. Still, it's better than blushing.

The song playing from the dining room fades, and then the turntable clicks into place, signalling that it's time to flip the record.

"Want me to?" I ask, pointing over my shoulder toward it.

"Nah, I'll grab it," Bo says, sitting up and adjusting his pants, pulling at the fabric bunched around the top of his prosthesis's socket. Lately, he's been going without his prosthesis around the house. Usually when he's freshly showered or has just woken up. I like it when he does. It feels like his trust is being extended.

"Fred?" Bo says, pulling my focus toward him.

I watch as he places a new record down on the turntable and lines up the needle. He turns a dial, and the music starts, an orchestration of string instruments. He turns to face me, his eyes sparkling but his lips tightly sealed. Then he holds out a hand. "Come dance with me."

My stomach nearly leaves me behind, flying across the room. All the more reason to say no, probably. "I don't really dance."

"What, why? Two left feet?" he asks, smiling wickedly. "Still more than I got."

I make a point to roll my eyes exaggeratedly.

"C'mon... *Please*?"

I'm screwed.

The scary truth of the matter is that Bo could get me to say yes to just about any request by adding a *please* that sweet and sincere at the end of it.

"I don't know what to do," I say, approaching just as Frank Sinatra begins singing "Strangers in the Night."

"Then I'll lead," he says, taking my smaller hand in his and pulling me closer. "For once," he mumbles. I reach up to shove his shoulder before resting my cheek against his chest next to my free hand.

"Like this?" I ask.

"Perfect," he says, curling his other arm around my back.

We rock from side to side, rotating slowly in mindless circles as the song plays on.

"This isn't so bad," I whisper.

I feel Bo's chest rise on a deep breath against my cheek.

When the song builds to the pinnacle chorus, drums picking up tempo and horns blaring, Bo tightens his grip around my little hand and pushes me away from him, spinning me in circles out in front of him as I yelp and giggle in surprise.

"You're a natural," he says, pulling me back to him, his hand falling dangerously low on my back.

"Do *not* do that again," I laugh out, falling back against him.

There's something so intimate about being held with zero expectations or reason beyond *wanting* to. Something so natural about Bo and me moving our bodies in sequence, in no rush to step away. Something so inherently safe about being in his arms.

Bo may slip up and check me out every once in a while, with his eyes held on me and his jaw taught, but he hasn't once tried anything since we agreed to remain platonic. He's too respectful for that. And I'm sure my eyes have done *far* worse damage to him over the past few weeks.

So when he presses me even closer, dips his chin to the top of my head, and curls his arms around me in more of an embrace than a dance, I let him, with zero hesitation, as I relax into the warm, solid comfort of his hold.

"One more?" he asks, his voice broken.

I nod against him.

One more song fades and blurs into five, or maybe even more. I've lost track. Eventually, when the turntable clicks, signalling the need to flip the record over, neither of us moves. If anything, Bo holds me tighter against him.

"You okay?" I whisper into his chest after a few moments of silence.

"I'm just trying to come up with the right words," he says, leaning his cheek against the top of my head, his nose on my hairline with deep, steady breaths. "To thank you for everything."

The way he says *everything* is like he really means *every single thing*.

Tears sting my nose instantly. "I should be thanking you," I say. "For letting me crash here, for being so kind to me, for—" I almost say *loving me* before I catch myself. "For being such a good friend."

"Win, I don't think you understand. I spent my birthday last year alone on my couch, drinking and miserable. I was so lonely. I felt like half a person. I—" He chokes up and clears his throat. "I felt hopeless." He sniffles, and I fight the urge to pull away to look at his face. To wipe his tears, if there are any. "But then *you* came along."

"If things were so bad, why go to some silly Halloween party?" *How did I get so lucky?*

"Have you ever been so low you stop caring so much? I think I hit rock bottom. I figured nothing else was working, so why not do something scary on a night where I could be someone else for a little bit? A costume to make light of it all."

The second I go to look up at him, he pulls me back and tightens his hold. He squeezes me to his chest like a favourite stuffed animal or blanket, tucking me under his chin. I splay my fingers out on his back and press into him, communicating back to him the same intensity. Clinging to him just the same.

"I'm sorry things were so bad," I say softly, his sweater against the corner of my mouth.

I wish I knew you then, I think to myself.

I'd have found him there, in that dark period. Sat with him in it. Until very recently, I was there too. Perhaps that's all Bo and I are. Two people leaving behind the worst, looking forward to the good to come. But is he ready to leave *everything* behind?

Because I think I might be.

"I'm not sorry," Bo says, surprisingly steady. "Not anymore."

He lets me go and steps backward. Even with red-rimmed, sullen eyes, he *still* smiles down at me. And out of the many, many smiles he's given me, this one is different. There's something unmistakeably hesitant about it, but mostly, it's the hopefulness amidst it all that strikes me.

Yes, I tell him silently with my own melancholy smile. I feel it too. And yes, it's absolutely terrifying. Let's pretend we don't. Not yet. Not tonight. Not until we're both certain.

"I'd do it all over again to be at that party," he says. "To meet you. To get Gus."

I damn near disintegrate, my face crumpling as I shake my head. Because how can I hear him say that and not fall in love with him at this exact moment? How can I tell myself he's not purely *good* when he says things like that?

"Bo..." I say, looking at our feet.

"I would," he says adamantly, nodding as if he wants me to do the same. "Wouldn't you?"

"If we hadn't met... if this hadn't happened," I say, placing a hand on my small bump, "I think I'd have been stuck playing it safe forever."

A tear falls from his eye, and without hesitation, I reach up to brush it away with my thumb, cradling his cheek in my hand.

"You'd have gotten yourself out eventually, Win." He presses the corner of his mouth to my wrist, releasing a trembling breath against it. "You can do anything," he whispers against my pulse point. And the way he says *anything* is as if he really means *any possible thing.*

And I believe him.

I truly do.

I feel my own tears come, slow and steady. To hide my face, I press myself back into his chest, and he meets me immediately, wrapping himself around me like a shield.

And we dance some more.

To the sound of nothing but each other's withering restraint.

Accepting that *this* is the best thing that could have happened to us. To get us out of our own personal dark spots. To give us purpose. To find each other.

Because even though we aren't *together*, I can no longer imagine a version of my life without Bo in it. Bo is simply lovely. Plain and true and all-encompassing.

So why am I still so scared?

Angry with myself, I wiggle free from his hold. I laugh weakly as he pretends to fight me, holding tighter as he sways me side to side.

"No, don't," he says, his hand going from shoulder to elbow. "Another record?"

I pat his shoulder at least a dozen times as I shake my head, unsure of what else to do to keep the overwhelming feelings and truths and fears from spilling out. His eyes follow the movement of my head as I shake it one last time, and he sighs, releasing me.

I walk toward the bathroom to shower without looking back, my head hung low and emotions caught heavy in my throat.

Leaving Bo still standing there.

Halfway through my shower, music starts playing again, and I fall against the tile, letting the water wash over me as I imagine Bo's body around me in here too.

And, I realise, I'm *completely* fucked.

CHAPTER 25

"I *fucking* knew it!" Sarah says, whispering inches from my face, her finger wagging.

"Whatever happened to hello?" I ask, looking around the hallway she dragged me into the moment Bo and I stepped through her front door for DND night.

"You want hello? Fine. Hi! How are you? When did you two start sleeping together?" Sarah shakes my shoulders, her smile open and wide.

"What? We are *not*," I say, shrugging her off. "Step back, weirdo!" I whisper-yell.

She opens the door to Caleb's office and shoves me through it. "Tell me everything."

"Literally nothing has happened, Sarah," I say, taking a few steps to get my balance after being pushed. "Would you calm down? Fucking hell."

"There was a *look*. I saw it." She points to her eyes in a fury.

"What look?" I ask, falling across the two-seater couch across from Caleb's desk in front of a dark oak–panelled wall.

"You two walked in, and Bo looked toward the table where we set everything up. Then he checked in with you. A tilt of his head and a sweet little smile, then you nodded. He was getting permission to walk over there. That's the look of a man on someone's leash. Pussy-whipped!"

"You did *not* just say pussy-whipped. Please, please, please tell me you didn't," I say, covering my face.

"So you do not deny," Sarah says, dropping into Caleb's chair and throwing her feet up onto the desk in the centre of the room.

"I *do* deny. The most we've done since Halloween is hug." *Dancing is hugging, just extended, right?* It doesn't count.

Sarah's eyes narrow on me in suspicion. "You do give great hugs," she whispers. "But not *that* good."

"Bo's thoughtful. He was just making sure I was cool before he ditched me to see his friends. Simple as that."

"So you're telling me that I haven't seen you in forty years"—*it's been twelve days*—"because you've been held up in your house with him *not* boinking?"

I choose to let her use of the word *boinking* slide. "We've been hanging out," I say defensively. "We go for walks to the water to talk. We hang out on the couch and watch nerdy movies that Bo likes. I'm also still working *and* growing a human. So yes, that's all we've been doing. Sorry to disappoint."

"How much talking do y'all need to do until you figure it out?"

I level her with a fierce glare. "We had to get to know each other, right? That was the whole fucking point of moving in together."

"And?" Sarah asks.

"And what?"

"Do you know each other?" She throws her arms up, apparently exasperated.

"Yes."

"And?"

"And *what*?" I snap, crossing my arms in front of my chest tightly.

"Is he a good guy?"

"Yes, obviously."

"And?"

"Oh my god, what now?"

"Do you feel safe with him?"

"Yes."

"So?"

"So *what*?" I yell.

"Are you in love with him?"

"Yes!"

Wait, *what*?

"No!" I say, panic-stricken. "No, no, no—" But it's too late. Sarah is up from her seat, slapping the desk with both palms like a drum.

"Vindication!" she shouts, her hands like claws pointed at the ceiling.

"Shut up," I whisper, rubbing my forehead. "Please," I beg pathetically. "Don't."

"I was right," she says, sitting back down. "Winnifred McNulty is in *love*."

"Sarah, I love him, but I'm not *in* love with him."

"Bullshit," she spits, shaking her head.

"I mean it," I say, my voice involuntarily pitching higher. "I mean it," I repeat, steadier.

Sarah narrows her eyes on me, swiping her tongue across her teeth under closed lips. "Okay, then. Let's play worst-case scenario."

"Why?" I sigh out.

"Humour me," she says, pushing the wheeled desk chair around the room until she's directly across from me, our knees almost touching. She's ridiculous but entertaining. I'll give her that. "Worst-case scenario—a year from now. Baby is happy and healthy. Just think about *you*. Tell me; no hesitation."

"Um..." I *immediately* hesitate.

"No!" She flicks the side of my head, and I swat her away. "Just speak!"

Fuck.

"This is stupid," I say, tightening my arms across my chest.

"You're being a child. Grow up and face your feelings. You love Bo. You're *in* love with Bo. Admit it."

"No!"

"Why?" she yells.

"I was *hurt*, Sarah. I was hurt so badly, and you don't even know the half of it." The moment the words leave me, all the breath in my lungs goes with them.

"So *tell* me, Win. Fucking tell me so we can work through it. I've been asking for *years* what happened. Or tell someone. Anyone. A professional, preferably. Or, Bo, maybe—since he *should* know."

"He made me feel small" is all I manage to say, tears threatening to pour. "Jack made me feel small and stupid and incapable, and I *never* want to feel that way again. I gave him my self-esteem on a goddamn silver platter, and like a fucking idiot, I was surprised when he took it and ate me whole."

"Jack is a fuckwad who will burn every bridge he ever builds. You are *not* any of those things, Win."

"Yeah, I know that *now*. It took me all these years since Jack to remember who I am and what I'm not. I don't... I don't want to forget again."

"You won't."

"I might! Because I keep forgetting a lot of things, apparently! Like, for example, the fact that Bo is most likely *still* in love with your sister-in-law. That night we spent together *meant* something to us both, but that's just it. It was a *night*. He was with Cora for *years*. And even though she broke his heart and left him during the worst possible time of his life, he still cares for her. Still. That loyalty. That... type of connection... I can't expect him to feel more for me after just a few months of being thrust into this situation together. I can't live with the thought that he might wish I was her. That I was just the available option."

Sarah sighs, her eyes held on me as her chest falls. "Win..."

"No, it's fine. I've got it handled."

"Win... you've *got* to talk to him."

"I can't," I whisper, my voice breaking. "I can't do it again. I can't talk to him. I can't put my heart on another platter and expect a different result."

"Just, tell me this. What *is* your worst-case scenario?" she asks, her eyes heavy and lips pouted in concentration. "A year from now, you wake up and…" she adds, waving me on.

That's the scary thing. At first, I wanted to answer that it was letting Bo *in,* just to be proven right. A type of right I'd never want to be. That he'd be careless with my heart and my feelings, and that a year from now, I'd wake up and realise I'd done it again—fallen for the wrong type of man. But that's no longer it.

The *worst*-case scenario is not having found out what being with Bo *could* be like.

"Seeing Bo in love with someone else. That he'll have a beautiful girlfriend who loves my kid too, and they'll take them for walks on the beach, and dance in his dining room, and—and I'll be somewhere else. Alone. Missing him. Missing what *could* have been. Realising that he was ready to move on… and I wasn't his first choice."

"Do you really think Bo would let it play out that way if he knew? Because, from where I'm standing, that man looks at you like you hung the moon. More than that. The sun too. I've never seen *anyone* look at another person like that."

"I don't think he'd intend to hurt me," I whisper, mostly to myself. "But we don't know if he feels the same. I don't know if it's just… attraction."

"It's not lust in his eyes, Win. It's so much more than that."

"What if it's just hormones? What if it's just some primal, lizard part of my brain telling me to stay close to the man I procreated with? What if I pop this baby out, and suddenly, he's some intolerable toad?"

"Do you *seriously* think that, Win? That women are just skin suits operated by poor instinct and hormones?" She rolls her eyes, sitting straighter—in a man's wide-spread posture. "Women are *too emotional*," Sarah says in a deeper voice. "They can't be in charge when their bodies make them go crazy once a month."

"*No*," I say pointedly, glaring at her.

"And why are we acting like *his* emotions should dictate yours? I'm asking what *you* feel. Not him."

"Right. Yeah," I respond weakly.

"So say it. Say it out loud. Be honest with yourself *and* me."

I take a deep breath in, straightening my shoulders. Still, my voice comes out soft and timid. "I love Bo."

"Even if he's in love with someone else?"

"Yes," I say, pathetic as it may be.

"Even if he's not ready to love you back the same?"

I nod, staring up at the ceiling as I place my hands on my neck. "But isn't that *beyond* stupid?"

"Love *is* stupid, Win," she says softly. "So what are you going to do about it?"

I crumple into myself with a pathetic whine. "Do you *really* think he looks at me like that? You'd truly bet—"

"I do, Win. I do, and I love it so much." Sarah reaches out, untangling my arms folded tight against my chest. She grips both of my hands and holds them. "You deserve this!" she says, shaking me a little until I smile for her, as forced as it may feel. "And I know this is also a *pregnant* thing, but you're glowing. You seem so much lighter. When you two stepped in here together, it wasn't like it was a few months ago. Then, it was like two people with chemistry and a sexy secret. Now, you look like the real deal."

"I'm scared," I whisper, crinkling my nose as we hold eye contact lightly.

"I know," Sarah says, brushing her thumb over the back of my hand. "But I think if you ask him, he'll be gentle with your heart."

I nod, inhaling deeply.

"I also think you're not that girl with the silver platter anymore. You've grown past that version of yourself. And I think assholes like Jack would take anyone as kind as you and try to twist them into something ugly. That's what people like him do. It isn't your fault you tried to see the best in him. Or that you didn't want to be alone. You've gotta forgive yourself for that."

I roll my eyes up, feeling a tear slip out. "Fucking hell," I whimper, half laughing.

"Too much?" Sarah asks, laughing softly at me.

I shake my head, lifting off the couch and throwing my arms around her shoulders. "I love you," I say.

"I love you," she repeats back to me. "And that's never going to change."

When I sit again, neither of us moves or speaks. We just let the moment linger, encouraging smiles reflected back at one another. "I'm gonna try," I say, sniffling. "I'm not sure when, because doing it sober will be a challenge and a half. But I'm going to tell him how I feel. Eventually. Soon, if I can."

"And I'll be there to say I told you so when that man tries to get you knocked up all over again."

I roll my eyes, but I can't help but grin, all the while imagining what could be. The *best*-case scenario, for once.

The version of life where Bo and I walk hand in hand into something new for us both. Slow, assured, and delicate with one another. Where maybe we *would* do this on purpose. Maybe a *few* times—if we're any good at the parenting side of things.

And I can see it, clear as any memory. We'd build our kid a tree-house in the spring and drink wine on unhurried summer evenings on the back porch. Our limbs intertwined as we sit on a swinging bench, watching them play. A life where we'd make love as many times as we find each other with teeth and force and passion. Years and years spent still getting to know one another, unlearning and relearning each other as the decades go by. Uncovering the intricate layers and deepest spots until every darkened corner is found. The mess and the chaos and the beauty of a life well lived—a life shared.

I'd like it very much.

So much it scares me even more.

But not enough to not try.

"Maybe you could tell Bo how you feel on his birthday? Tie a bow around your tits and let him unwrap you. You must be *dying* to fog up those glasses of his." *And she's back.*

"I need your help with that, actually." Sarah gapes. "No," I say sharply, silencing her. "Not *that*. A party. I'm going to ask Bo's dad to keep him busy during the day so I can set up and have a few of Bo's friends over. He deserves something to celebrate him. Will you help me?"

"Obviously! Bo's one of us now. I can't be caught slacking on a birthday."

I smile up at her before looking around the room absently, then to the door on a steadying inhale. "Should we get back out there?"

"Nah, let them miss us." She smiles mischievously. "Oh, I forgot in all the chaos... Did you want to take a bath while you're here? I picked up your favourite stuff, just in case."

"I could kiss you right now," I say to her, reaching to gently pat her cheek.

"I'll take that as a yes," she says, pushing off her knees to stand. "And save the kissing for Bo." She snickers, walking toward the door.

CHAPTER 26

Twenty Weeks Pregnant. Baby is the size of a banana.

I'm frozen, standing on the front step. I've been here for enough time that a child riding their bike outside has now passed behind me twice.

It is deceptively nice for March—a fool's spring, if you will. Fellow Canadians will ditch the heavy winter jackets and boots and inevitably fall into a deep, dark depression when the snow returns someday next week. Every year, we're shocked by such a thing—as if the collective memory develops amnesia. But I like that about us humans. How willfully blind we can be to the gloomy realities ahead.

In reality, we aren't safe until April. Or maybe even until after my birthday, in May.

Still, at least I'm not *literally* frozen on the front step—dreading meeting Bo's dad.

While I was at work today, Bo picked his dad up from the airport. He's staying with us for four days before he goes back to France, enough time to see his son ring in his thirtieth birthday. Bo, on the night we met, called his father, Robert, his best friend. He's also his only living family member. So zero pressure to impress the guy. Nope, none whatsoever.

He's going to love you.

Damn, I sure hope so.

When the little girl on her bike passes a third time, eyeing me suspiciously, I decide enough is enough.

"Hello?" I call out, stepping inside the front entryway.

I hear music coming from the dining room and the electric whirl of some sort of machine from the kitchen. A stand mixer, I think. Do we even own one of those? God, I should probably offer to cook some time.

I shrug off my jacket and shoes and follow the sounds of laughter coming from the kitchen.

"Hi, just me," I say, turning the corner. In the kitchen is the most gorgeous man I've ever seen... and his son.

Holy mother of—No, actually. *Holy father of Bo.*

"Hey!" Bo says, circling the counter to stand next to me, smiling brightly as always. "Win, this is my dad, Robert. Dad, this is Win." Bo pronounces *Robert* with a French accent, and I nearly swoon. There's not enough oxygen in this room. He should have prepared me. I should have requested family photos.

"It is *so* good to meet you, Winnifred," Robert says in a thick accent, lifting his flour- and dough-covered hands in the air. "I'd shake your hand, but I've been kneading bread."

"Dad went to make himself a sandwich and saw we were out of bread," Bo says, bending to speak into my ear. "I *did* offer to go to the store."

Robert has all of Bo's similarities in height, natural charm, and build, but his hair and beard are peppered black and grey and trimmed shorter. They also have different eyes in shape and colour—Bo's wide hazel eyes to Robert's smaller deep brown. The deep lines and creases around Robert's lips and eyes speak to a man, like his son, who loves to laugh. If *this* is a sneak preview of what Bo will look like in thirty-ish years, then I better get to work locking that shit *down.*

Too bad Bo doesn't have the accent.

Though... I wonder if he'd speak French in bed if I asked nicely. *Oh my god, Win. Focus! It's your turn to speak!*

"It's good to meet you too," I squeak, swallowing. "Bo's told me so many wonderful things. And please, call me Win or Fred."

I don't miss Bo's crooked smirk when I offer his father the nickname that, until very recently, I was not fond of. I don't miss, either, the warm affection in Robert's eyes as they land on my stomach.

Robert picks up the ball of dough, passing it back and forth between his hands, an eyebrow quirked toward his son, the same lopsided smile under his moustache that I know well. "He also speaks of you very, *very* well..."

Bo clears his throat. "How was work?" he asks, walking behind me toward the dining room.

I peek my head around the corner to watch as he pulls his work chair away from his desk and brings it over to me. "Oh, uh, fine." I say as he gestures for me to sit. My feet were *killing* me, but this might be a tad over the top. "The to-go guy came back," I say, giving in and sitting.

"That's the third time this week!" Bo says excitedly.

Robert looks between us blankly.

"There's a man who comes into the café and orders everything to go but always stays for hours and works." As soon as I say it out loud, I realise how mundane that story really is. When I told Bo about him, he sort of picked it up and ran with it. We created a whole backstory for the stranger. Bo theorised that he's secretly in love with one of our other patrons and is waiting for the right time, and I agreed.

Little close to home, actually, now that I think about it.

But regardless, Bo is good at that. Taking something little and making it feel grand and important. Just like he's done with every step of the pregnancy. Every answer to our nightly questions. Everything is worth celebrating to Bo. Worth getting excited about.

"But yeah, good day." I turn to look at Robert. "How was your flight?"

He nods several times, covering a glass bowl with a tea towel. "Good, good, fine. The food on the plane was terrible, but it was a smooth journey."

"I see where Bo gets his cooking skills," I say, pointing to the bowl.

Robert smiles proudly, his face pointed down to his feet. "Ah, well."

"I'm not half as good," Bo says, throwing a chocolate chip into his mouth, cradling the jar from the pantry against his chest.

"I don't know. I'm still thinking about that soup you made on day one," I reply.

"The butternut squash?" he asks, and I nod. "Why didn't you say so? I'd have made it again."

"Oh, well... you already cook for me every day. I'm not going to start making requests."

"I'll make it this week," he says, throwing another chocolate chip into the air and catching it between his teeth. I clap for him as he curtsies back at me, his hand still gripped around the jar.

Robert laughs under his breath, glancing quickly between us. I realise immediately that I've probably interrupted their time together and should make myself scarce.

"I'll give you two some space," I say, pushing off the chair's armrests to stand.

"*No,*" Robert says, halting me, his eyebrows pressed together in obvious offence. "No, no, no. Sit, please. Please," he repeats, opening the fridge. "This is what Robbie and I do. We talk and cook. You must stay and provide us with some fresh material," he says, pulling out the egg carton and milk. "How does quiche sound?"

I settle back into the chair. Bo's hand falls to my shoulder, patting gently before he walks toward a cabinet and pulls out a cutting board and places it on the counter next to his dad and ditches his jar of chocolate chips.

"Quiche sounds delicious," I say, smiling at both men and crossing my legs under me, settling back against the chair.

The quiche *was* delicious. I had three servings, and I could have had more if my stomach would allow it. It took about an hour to prepare after Bo convinced his dad to use the crust we had in the freezer instead of making it from scratch. All the while, I got a front-row seat to their family's dynamic.

They're surprisingly affectionate for father and son. A lot of hands across shoulders to pass by one another, a few quick pats of Robert's hand against Bo's cheek to encourage him or tease him in equal measure.

Robert is less timid than Bo is. He has a booming, throaty voice and isn't afraid to talk with his hands. Or his whole body, for that matter. But he's still got a gentle presence about him too, like Bo. The way they interact makes me even more excited to have a kid to throw into their dynamic. It would be *very* funny to add a third character to their routine.

After dinner, the men choose a record together and begin cleaning up, insisting I rest some more. I fetch a bottle of nail polish from my room and set myself up on the floor in front of the coffee table as Edith Piaf plays from the adjoining room.

Robert joins me soon after, kicked out of the kitchen by his son, balancing a glass of wine as he dances into the room, his body walking in time with the dramatic French singer.

"She was my wife's favourite," he says, pointing to the other room. "That's how I knew Joanna was the one. Excellent taste. In men too, *obviously*," Robert says, his voice echoed by the wineglass he's speaking into.

I laugh, folding a piece of paper towel to put my hand over top of. "Bo told me that you and Joanna fell in love very fast. Ten days, right?"

"Yes. Ten days is all it took to go from strangers to married." He takes a long sip, his eyes held on mine and teasing just like his son's. "Seems you're both taking a *slower* pace."

I bite my lip, looking back down at my nail polish on the table, opening it.

"Yes, ignore the old man's silly comments. Very wise."

I smile, shaking my head as I dip the applicator into the mauve polish, pinching it between my thumb and the side of my palm in my right hand.

"Was this from an accident? Or sickness like Bo?" he asks, pointing at my right hand.

"Oh, no. From birth."

"It's funny. Bo didn't mention it. Even though he speaks of you *a lot*."

I raise a brow at him, shaking my head at his blatancy. "I'm sure it would've come up." But I sort of *love* that it didn't.

"*Dieu, j'adore cette chanson!*" Robert exclaims, jumping from his seat. "*Monte le son, mon fils!*"

I dropped French after grade ten, but I'm fairly certain Robert just said he loves the song and asked Bo to turn it up. Or that he loves cats and asked Bo for a slice of pie. One of those two things. Based on the fact that Bo appears from the kitchen and moves to turn the volume up, I think I got it right the first time.

Bo flips a tea towel over his shoulder before leaning against the archway to the kitchen, smirking at Robert performing with *gusto*.

Robert dances over to Bo, clasping a hand around his shoulder as the song builds toward the chorus. Then both men sing, or rather *shout*, the chorus together. Robert somehow manages to not spill any of his wine as he shakes both arms up in the air above his head, using his whole body as an instrument.

I laugh, bobbing my head along to the music, as they start performing some sort of terrible can-can routine side by side.

"You must imagine it with all four legs, you see!" Robert shouts to me over the song. "And also the feathers and jewels and whatever else," he adds, gesturing to his torso.

Bo kicks him hard with his prosthetic foot, and Robert gapes at his son, wincing as he laughs.

"Seems like it kicks just fine," Bo says, shrugging away from him and going back to the kitchen as he smiles to himself.

I twist the lid of my nail polish closed and begin blowing on my nails. Robert lingers next to the record player, tracing one finger along his wife's collection, pulling out a few and inspecting them as he goes.

Once the music ends, Robert and Bo join me in the living room. After a few stories about the jazz band he's playing with back in Paris and a handful of suggestive comments alluding to the relationship between Bo and me—or lack thereof—Robert excuses himself for bed. Claiming he's evaded his jetlag long enough.

Which is exactly the moment I spot the extra pillow and blankets laid out on the corner chair and realise Robert has Bo's room for the next few days. Until now, I haven't thought of our sleeping arrangements for the visit, but there's no way Bo should be on the couch. He won't fit.

"You're not seriously considering sleeping on the couch, right?"

"Don't act like you haven't discovered the magical sleeping powers of this couch."

"For a nap, maybe, but it's not at all big enough for you to sleep on. You'll mess up your back."

"I did find myself wishing I could detach both bottom halves of my legs." He laughs, bringing his glass of water to his lips.

"Seriously, though, you'll be miserable."

"I'll go to the store after our appointment tomorrow and pick up an air mattress."

"I can take the couch tonight," I offer.

"What? No way."

I roll my eyes at his immediate dismissal. "Why not?"

"I don't know," he says, dripping with sarcasm, "maybe because I'm not making my pregnant—" He stops and tenses, then with a quick shake of his head, starts again. It was less than a second for the whole series of movements, but I noticed it all in agonising detail. What *was* he going to say? *My* what? "I'm not going to make a pregnant woman sleep on the couch," he says firmly.

C'mon, Win. Three seconds of bravery. An innocent enough offer. You can do this.

"Well, we could share my bed…" I say, forcing my voice to sound indifferent. But then Bo studies me far too intently. His brows knitted together and his head tilted. And I feel myself struggling to not take it back or chase it with some overwrought disclaimer.

"We *could*," Bo says, nodding, his eyes still narrowed on me. "Are you sure? You wouldn't mind?"

I *think* I can find the kindness in my heart to share a bed with you, sure.

"Yeah, why not?"

"Totally sure?"

"Yep," I say, clearing my throat.

"At least until tomorrow, when I go to the store."

I shrug one shoulder. "Sounds good... I'm going to take a shower before bed. Um... feel free to set up your stuff in my room. I'll sleep tucked against the wall—I like it better that way." I have to consciously stop my feet from running to the bathroom Road Runner style once I'm done speaking.

CHAPTER 27

I brush my teeth twice and do a far longer skin care routine than I usually do in order to buy myself some extra time to calm down. The only thing that gets me out of the bathroom is the concerning thought that the longer I spend in here post-shower, the higher the chance that Bo thinks I'm avoiding sharing a bed with him.

Which I am, but not for the reasons he may think.

I knock on my bedroom door hesitantly, even after scurrying across the hall in nothing but a towel.

I hear a mumbled "uh-huh" from the other side of the door, and so I walk right in, summoning as much confidence as I can.

My bedroom is lit dimly by the lamp on the nightstand, casting the room in a soft, glowing hue. Bo is laid out on the bed next to the nightstand, resting above his pale grey comforter. One hand is holding his sudoku puzzle book and the other is in his hair, scratching above his ear. A pencil is between his teeth, causing his lips to form a straight, thin line. He's wearing a dark purple T-shirt, black basketball shorts, and his glasses. *Fuck me*, those glasses. I notice that his prosthesis is leaned up against the wall, next to my dresser and the mess-heap of clothes I forgot to pick up this afternoon.

I hope he didn't judge me too harshly for that.

"Sup," he says, his voice exaggerated as he brings the pencil out of his mouth, jots something down, then places it back between his teeth. He's yet to look up to greet me, and I smile to myself, seeing him in my room so comfortable. As if it's completely natural for him to be here.

But I *do* enjoy what happens the moment he does look up to find me, probably wondering why I'm so quiet as I slink into the room. The pencil drops out of Bo's mouth and clatters to the floor as he stares, slack-jawed, and his eyes practically double in size. Shaking himself, he shuts his lips tight, unable to keep his eyes still, switching between the towel wrapped around my body and the one on top of my head. "Do you need me to...?" He points to the door, *vaguely* looking over my shoulder, as if he's in some sort of self-imposed dissociation.

"No, you're good," I say, straightening my shoulders. "Just, uh, close your eyes for a second." Once he does, I drop my towel and pull out the only *remotely* sexy pyjamas I own. It's just a black slip dress, but it's the closest thing to lingerie in a drawer otherwise occupied by ripped, baggy T-shirts and biker shorts.

It's not that I *think* something might happen if I wear this "nightgown." Without a conversation first, I highly doubt Bo's going to suddenly make any sort of move on me after such clear boundaries have been established and upheld. And I'm certainly not going to. I'm already using all my courage just to share a room with him. It's more of a little reminder...

Hey, I have a body. You like it, right?

When I turn back around, Bo's eyes are clenched shut and he's repeatedly stabbing his forehead with the rubber-eraser end of the pencil that he fetched off the ground.

He likes it, all right.

"All clear," I say, pushing my lips together in order to not laugh at his tortured expression the second he opens his eyes and takes in the nightgown. The look across his face, before he corrects it, is the tiniest, most wonderful reminder of the desirability I felt all those months ago. All I can do is hope he wants my heart just as much as he seems to want my body.

Bo clears his throat, forcing his attention back to the book in his hand, tapping the corner of it with his pencil in a quick, unsteady rhythm.

I attempt to get into bed as delicately as I can, climbing over the shallow baseboard and up toward my pillow. I lie on my left side, facing Bo, propped up on the ridiculous number of pillows I now sleep on to avoid heartburn in the night.

Pulling my duvet over my bottom half, I stretch my neck to see his puzzle. "Four..." I point to an empty spot. "Right?"

"Oh, uh, yeah," Bo says distractedly. "Thanks," he adds, filling in the square.

When I move away, his eyes follow me, dropping down to admire the hollow space between my breasts. He bites his lip and shuffles up the mattress, sitting straighter against the headboard.

"Will the light bother you?" he asks, his voice a little hoarse. "I can turn it off."

"All good," I say, pulling out my phone.

"I'm almost done."

It's not until I catch myself yawning for the third time that I decide to look up from my phone. Bo's sudoku book is closed on his lap, and he's wearing a quiet, lazy smile as he looks down at my phone.

I've been looking at baby items online, compiling a list that Sarah's insisted I needed to make for some sort of gift registry. I was dreading it, honestly, but I sort of got sucked into it the moment I realised how *real* it made it all feel. Looking at all the things our baby could be clothed, held, or wrapped in. It became more about August and less about me.

"Sorry. I disappeared into my own world. Are you ready for bed?" I ask.

"Those are cute," Bo says, pointing to the little pair of crocheted shoes. I was debating whether I could make them myself before remembering the blanket I have to keep up with.

"Olive green or sage? I can't decide."

"Olive, I think."

I add them to the list. "I sent you a link so you can add stuff on here too. You don't have to but—"

"How do we stop ourselves from just buying all of this?" Bo asks, plucking my phone out of my hand. "Look at this bear! Gus *needs* this bear." He taps *add to wish list*.

"Oh, wait! I have to show you what I found..." I say, taking the phone back and scrolling up the list before turning it back toward him.

"The ABCs of D&D," Bo reads, his smile growing. "Did you add this already?"

"*Obviously.*"

He looks at me, his eyes twinkling even in the dimly lit room. "Thank you."

I lock my phone and hold it out to him. "Could you plug that in for me?"

"Sure," he says, doing just that.

I sit up, fix my pillows, and turn away from him to face the wall, curling myself around the body pillow pressed against it.

Maybe Bo's body will just instinctively find mine in the middle of the night. One body seeking out warmth in another. Or I'll get the courage to push my ass against his lap and call it an accident. We're good at those.

Bo switches off the lamp, then lowers himself down the mattress, tucking himself under the blanket he brought with him. The room falls to a hushed, dull quiet. No crickets outside or nearby traffic. Only the sound of heads falling against feather-filled pillows and shifting blankets as we both settle into bed.

"Hey..." Bo whispers into the pitch-black room. "We didn't ask a question today."

I roll over, tucking a hand under my cheek. My eyes adjust to the dark enough to see that our faces are lined up. Bo's scruffy hair and softened, sleepy expression look back at me. "No, I guess not," I whisper back. "Do you have one?"

"I'll think of something." He shuffles a hand under his pillow, propping himself up slightly as he yawns. "It's funny that we haven't done this, right? Slept next to each other? We're having a baby, and we live together, but I don't even know if you snore."

"I do *not* snore." *And I wouldn't describe this situation as* funny *either.*

"Or maybe you talk in your sleep," he says.

"Do you?" I ask, looking between our bodies, the thin amount of space and bedding separating us.

"Guess you'll have to find out," he taunts. "How are you feeling? About tomorrow?" he asks.

"The ultrasound?" I clarify. Bo nods. "Mostly excited but a little nervous that something could be wrong, as always. You?"

"Me too." He lets out a deep, woeful breath. "I'm sure everything will be fine, though."

Just then, a fluttering sensation happens in my abdomen. A bit like when my stomach signals that it's hungry, but less of a rumbling and more like a weaker type of muscle spasm. It happens again when I place my hand down to feel. It's not until the third time that I realise it's not *my* body doing anything. "I think... I think maybe the baby kicked."

"Wait, seriously?" Bo speaks as if he's whispering but does so *very* loudly.

I bite down on an embarrassingly large grin. "Yeah, I think so. But I'm not sure." I roll onto my back, placing both hands on either side of my belly.

Do it again, I call through that channel I can't name inside me that feels connected to the baby, like two cans on either end of a string. When it happens again, I gasp. "Yeah, they're definitely kicking."

"Does it hurt?"

"No, not at all. It's like... bubbles popping under my skin." I press my hand to another spot, following the sensation as it moves. "Do you want to feel?" I ask.

"Can I?" He immediately sits up, his blankets thrown away. I pluck his hand out of the air and bring it down to feel. Bo's hand is warm and heavy against me. And *achingly* nice. His face appears cautious, as if he's trying not to startle the baby by moving or speaking. An anticipatory, wide-eyed excitement across his features that has my heart wishing for it to happen again.

After a minute of waiting silently, I remove my hand from his, but he doesn't follow.

"I think maybe they're done for now. I'm sorry."

"One more minute?" he asks, his voice awfully small. "Just in case..."

And his desperation does something to my heart. A tiny twist, like wringing out a wet cloth. I love him so much it's *truly* painful. As if every time I resist telling him how I feel when the truth boils up *so* close to the surface, a tiny piece of myself withers and dies.

"Of course," I say softly.

A few moments later, August decides to give the performance of their life—kicking far harder than before, right under Bo's palm.

And I decide to order the stuffed bear first thing tomorrow.

"Was—was that it?" he asks, looking between me and his hand.

"That was it," I say brightly.

"Holy shit... Hi! Hey there!" he yells to my stomach. I shush him, giggling. "Sorry, sorry." He falls back, laughing as he swipes both hands through his hair. "That was insane. I can't believe that."

"There's a whole person in there," I say.

"I kind of forget how wild this all is. What your body is doing. What *you* are doing. It's amazing..."

"You know what I found out the other day?" I ask, turning back onto my side to face him as he does the same. "If the baby has ovaries, that means I'm carrying all of *their* future kids too. I'd be like a Russian nesting doll of people right now."

"I never even thought of that," Bo says, in awe. "We've created a whole new *line* of people, potentially. A family tree. We could have *descendants*."

I laugh, tucking my hands between pillows. "See what you'd be missing if you were out there on the couch? Baby kicks, fun facts..."

"I do," Bo answers, his voice far more earnest than my little jest was. "I don't take it for granted, Win. I feel very honoured to get to do this with you."

"What, sleep in my bed?" I tease, feeling awfully shy.

I can *hear* his eyes roll. "No," he says. "Being here with you. Not having to miss out on this stuff. You didn't have to tell me about the baby at all, let alone uproot your life to move in here. I'm grateful you did. I'll *always* be grateful that you did."

"I'm grateful I did too... and for you."

"Your friendship means a lot to me, Win," he breathes out. "*You* mean a lot to me."

I squeeze my eyes shut. *Now. Be brave. Tell him how you feel.* "I—"

"That's the question I was going to ask tonight," Bo interrupts. "Who in this world matters the most to you?"

"You," I answer simply, pleading with him to *hear* me. What I said and all that it means.

"You," he repeats. "It's you for me too. With a *very* close second," he says, his eyes on my belly.

I want to be braver than I am. I want to ask what that means to him. What it means for us. Whether he feels this longing between us so deep inside him, so full and abundant, that he's also started to believe that we have souls after all.

Simply because *something* inside me is entirely *his*. Something I know would follow me into the next life, or beyond that, even if I left this body behind.

But I don't. Because my heart's just taken off like it has wings at his small admission alone, and I'd rather not risk shooting it back down.

For tonight, knowing I matter most to him is enough. Well, *almost* enough.

I shuffle closer, lining up my bent knee with his thigh, looking up at him with silent permission. Bo moves too, until our chests are touching through our blankets. I push my duvet down past my hips, and Bo lifts the corner of his blanket up like a wing, enveloping me in it with his arm behind my back.

The warmth of his body radiates through the cotton of his T-shirt and the silk of my nightgown. I nuzzle into him until my forehead rests on his pillow alongside him, our noses inches from touching. And I take a deep inhale, breathing in his scent—the cinnamon and musk mixed with the freshly cleaned scent of his T-shirt. I shamelessly do it again, breathing him in like another hit of something far better than oxygen.

His arm curls around my back, his elbow at my waist and his hand between my shoulder blades. The tips of his fingers burn into my skin with a delicate, callused touch, while his palm is mostly pressed against the silk between my shoulder blades.

"This okay?" he asks, his voice barely audible.

I mumble a sleepy, quiet agreement in place of the word *perfect*.

And so he holds me.

His thumb moves in slow circles, as if he's in no hurry. As if he has zero expectations for more.

With no words needing to be said. With no promises yet to be made.

And I let it be.

I let myself feel content. I let myself feel less lonely. I let myself feel safe. Because I *am*.

"I love you," I whisper once I'm absolutely sure he's asleep—his steady breathing loud and throaty.

And I feel lighter for it as I drift off to sleep.

CHAPTER 28

I woke up alone, with no proof of last night other than Bo's glasses on the nightstand and his prosthesis still laid up against the wall.

He'll be coming back for those, I think to myself. So I stretch with a yawn and let my eyes drift shut once again.

But they don't stay closed for long. I wake to pots and pans clattering from down the hall, alerting the rest of my senses to the light coming in through the window and the smell of vanilla wafting through the house.

The faint sound of water running also tells me that someone is in the shower. I contemplate which of the Durand men might be showering and which one could be cooking and decide it's most likely Bo in the shower, with all he's left behind.

I curl myself back against my pillow, wrapped in my warm cocoon, deciding to wait for Bo to return before going to greet his dad. But once a few minutes pass, my stomach and curiosity overrule my comfort.

I throw on some sweats and a hoodie before making my way toward the kitchen, where I find Bo pouring batter into the waffle maker.

"Morning," I say, rubbing my eyes. "I thought you were in the shower."

Bo holds on to the counter, steadying himself. "Morning," he says, closing the waffle maker with his tongue poking out in concentration. "I wanted to get up before Dad to avoid any sort of... questions." He gestures to my bedroom with his tilted chin, wearing a bashful smile. "He's not subtle, as you may have noticed."

"Got it."

"Bonjour!" Robert says, walking through the kitchen in an all-black ensemble, running a towel through his hair as he heads toward the living room.

"Bonjour," I say, smiling at Bo shyly, as if we have a much more interesting secret than having spent the night cuddling.

I cut up some fruit as Bo finishes the waffles and brews a pot of coffee. We all eat breakfast together on the couch as Robert continues to berate Bo over his lack of dining table. Bo insists there's not enough room in there between his record player and desk.

They bicker back and forth as I swallow bite after bite of delicious breakfast, only jumping in occasionally to agree with Robert, hoping to earn his favour.

Afterward, we all get ready to leave the house. Then, per his request, we drop Robert off at the local farmers' market before Bo and I drive to the hospital for our ultrasound.

Bo holds every door open between the parking garage and the clinic. I wonder, if I pretended to be nervous, would he hold my hand too?

Not that I'd *really* have to pretend.

"You okay?" he asks, opening the clinic's door.

"Yeah," I answer reflexively, blowing my chance. We walk inside and walk up to the receptionist behind a glass partition.

"Ultrasound for two please," I say to her, sliding my paperwork through the narrow slot. She blinks at me, her blank expression saying a whole lot as she sighs through her nose. "Fair," I mumble, pulling out my ID. "I'm here for my twenty-week scan," I say, placing my card down.

She takes it and begins typing silently.

"Tough crowd," Bo whispers next to my ear. "You'll get 'em next time." He nods sarcastically, giving me a thumbs-up.

I whack him with the back of my hand.

"Waiting room is the third door on your left. Someone will come grab you from there. You'll go in by yourself, and then they'll bring your husband in when they're done with the measurements."

"Thank you," I say, taking back my ID.

I turn over my shoulder and see Bo smiling broadly. "After you, *wife*." He extends his arm out toward the waiting room.

I roll my eyes and lead the way.

We sit in the last two available seats next to one another in the otherwise crowded room. Bo plays peek-a-boo with a little girl standing on the chair across from us. Her mom thanks him with ogling, overly appreciative eyes.

In an attempt to thwart her, I place my hand on Bo's arm, leaning in to speak to him. Except I did it without thinking of something to say first, and now he's stuck still, waiting for me to speak with his head tilted toward me.

"I'm nervous," I say. Partially because it's true, and also because I'm not that quick on my feet.

"What can I do?" he asks. "Peek-a-boo?"

I smirk, shaking my head. "Tell me something. A story about you. A distracting one."

He nods, crossing one leg over the other. "Okay..." he says, bending toward me. "Want to hear about my first kiss?"

"Was it embarrassing?"

"A little."

"Then *yes*, definitely."

He laughs, then licks his lips before he speaks. "I was sixteen and the only one out of my friends who hadn't had their first kiss yet. I didn't think to lie about it, but in hindsight I should have, because they teased me *relentlessly*. Anyway, a few months into grade eleven, there was a school fundraiser where all the juniors and seniors slept at the school overnight."

I huff. *Who would possibly think that's a good idea?*

"I know," Bo says, "who could have possibly thought *that* was a good idea?"

Hey, that's what I said.

"So I'm at the fundraiser, alone in the band room, because all my friends are drunk and wandering around elsewhere, and I didn't know what else to do. Eventually, I started messing around with the instruments. I was hoping a nice young lady would wander past and be lulled in by my saxophone skills."

"Naturally," I interject.

He scoffs, brushing a hand over his face. "And a group of girls *did* come in. One of them I recognised from the senior band. But we'd never talked before. She sat in the corner with her friends, and they were pretty much ignoring me, but *she* kept looking over. So I kept playing. About an hour later, her friends left, and she stayed behind. She broke the silence by complimenting my technique. Sweet, right?" he asks, his obvious embarrassment as to whatever comes next causing a nervous laugh to break free.

"Yes..." I say cautiously. "Oh god, what did you say?"

Bo looks up to the sky, wincing. "I said... want to see what else these lips can do?"

I gasp. "No!"

"Yep," he says, his eyes closed and nodding.

"And that... *worked*?"

"It did." He leans back, crossing his arms in front of his chest. "Before Halloween, *that* was my quickest close."

"Oh, you *closed* me, huh?"

His eyes drift around the room, to my tilted smirk, then to my stomach with a quirked brow. "Sure as hell seems like it."

"Well, you better rein it in, lover boy. No more unexpected pregnancies for you."

He snorts from the back of his throat. "How about you? What was your first kiss like?"

"Well, his name was Trent, and it was at a skate park."

"So he was a skater boy?"

"Yes."

"Did you say *see you later, boy*?"

I groan into my palm, smiling. "Avril Lavigne would be so disappointed, but no, I did not."

"So how'd it happen?"

"I asked him to show me some tricks after school. I was better than him, actually. I pretended I wasn't, though, which was dumb of me *but* a classic move of the time. He told me I could thank him for the lesson with a kiss, and I did. We never really hung out again. I can't remember why. Other than the kiss being nothing to write home about."

"How old were you?"

"Fourteen."

"Do you think we would have been friends? In high school?" he asks.

"I think so. You probably would have joined Caleb's nerd legion, and Sarah and I would have met you through him."

"I would have been in the grade above you all, though."

"Yeah, but then I could have said I was dating an older guy. It would've given me major cool points."

Bo's face lights up as he pouts his lips in an effort to not smirk, nodding like a bobblehead. "Oh, *really*?" he says, elongating each syllable. "So we would have dated, huh?"

Shit, did I say that? "What?"

"You said dating."

"Nope, don't think I did." I close my eyes and look away from him as I feel a blush creep over my skin.

"You definitely did," Bo singsongs. "You would have dated me in high school."

"With those saxophone moves? Of course," I say, flipping the attention back onto him. It doesn't work. Bo's smiling brighter than the damned sun, and it's fucking contagious.

The embarrassment washes away with the sight of his hopeful, giddy expression. It seems as if my little slip-up could lead to an admission from Bo, like a neon arrow pointing to an opened door.

Suddenly, it feels like I'm on the edge of a cliff, about to be handed either a parachute or an anvil. And based on the look on Bo's face, it feels like he's got a parachute with my name on it. One of his own, too.

You jump, I jump.

One of us just needs to fucking jump.

"You know... I still have my sax—"

"Winnifred McNulty?" a technician calls from the entrance.

Bo clears his throat, his smile faltering as he hangs his head for a second.

I stand, one had extended into a wave toward the technician, and turn back over my shoulder and smile at Bo. He watches me walk away with a bouncing knee and a steadfast, encouraging smile.

"Follow me," the technician says sweetly as I approach the doorway.

Thirty minutes later, the tech finishes taking all the required measurements and images and excuses herself to fetch Bo from the waiting room.

I haven't seen the baby yet or heard the heartbeat, since the screen has remained pointed toward the technician throughout. We've been making polite, infrequent conversation, but this ultrasound has been far more clinical than our last. It definitely feels as if the baby is the patient this time around, and I'm more of a walking incubator. It's an unnerving feeling, honestly.

I'm twiddling my thumbs, looking up at the square-tiled ceiling, when I hear the curtain at the front of the room rustle as it's pushed aside.

Bo comically towers over the technician as they walk in.

"All right, Dad, you can take that stool there," she says, pointing next to the right side of my bed as she walks around the left.

Bo nods his thanks, lowering onto the stool.

"All okay?" he asks with a stiff smile.

"I think so," I whisper. "I've just been lying here while she did her thing. She hasn't said anything."

Bo nods, rubbing his lips together anxiously.

"Hey," I say, capturing his attention. "It's okay," I reassure him, smiling. "I'm sure everything is fine."

"That's supposed to be my line," he says with a weak, crooked grin.

"All right," the tech says, rotating the screen toward us. "Here we go." She picks up her probe, untangles the wire from around her desk, and places it back on my swollen belly, pressing against the cool gel. With a click of a button, the baby is immediately projected onto the screen. A near perfect silhouette, just as you'd expect. Not a bean or alien-shaped thing anymore, but a full, tiny person with a disproportionately large head.

And I swear that nothing has ever been more beautiful.

I press my cheek into the bed, trying to not block Bo's view. "There they are," Bo says, breathing out a sigh of relief. I reach out to him blindly, refusing to take my eyes off the screen, and he wraps my smaller hand with both of his.

"Did you want to know the sex today?"

"No, we want to be surprised," Bo answers for us both.

She nods, moving the probe again. "Baby has everything we'd like to see at this stage," the tech says, pointing to the screen. "Spine is looking great." She twists her wrist at an angle and clicks a button, and then suddenly, we're looking at every intricate detail of a spinal cord.

It's honestly kind of gross.

With every button pressed and movement of the probe, we're shown each of the baby's organs. Bo asks some questions, but I fail to fully focus my attention on them, enraptured by every little movement on the screen.

I doubt I'll ever be fully able to conceptualise that this is all happening *inside* my body, but *damn* does it make me feel powerful to even consider it.

The camera zooms back out and onto the baby's face, a white silhouette against a dark background.

"Baby is showing off and sucking their thumb," the tech says, pointing to the screen. "It's so cute when they do that," she coos.

I unconsciously sit up, leaning closer to the screen. The pillow that had been supporting my shoulders falls out of place and onto the ground. Bo lets go of my hand to pick it up before placing it next to me on the mattress.

"You okay?" he asks, resting his hand on my knee.

"I can't see... I can't make out the shape of their hand."

"Ms. McNulty?" the tech says, her eyes held on me. She removes the probe and places it in its holster attached to the monitor.

I shake myself, lowering against the mattress. "Sorry..."

"Is everything okay?"

I feel a rolling of my stomach, like nausea but far worse. That anxiety spreads across my abdomen, tightening my chest and pooling at the base of my throat, making my next words come out like an apology. "Do they have fingers? On... on both hands?"

"Oh," the tech says, her upbeat tone remarkably still intact. "Yes. All ten fingers and toes." She types something into the computer before shutting it off. Then reaches for the chart on the side of her desk, tucking it under her arm.

I swallow an apology over and over, my face burning red. *Why would I ask that?*

"We'll get you some pictures on your way out, and you'll hear from your doctor in the next few days if anything needs going over, but"—she tilts her head, attempting to catch my eye—"the baby is growing well," she says, nodding as she looks between Bo and me. "There's no reason for concern."

"Thank you," Bo says from beside me.

I watch as she walks over to the wall, presses the dispenser for hand sanitizer, and then turns to face me, rubbing her hands together. "Best of luck," she says before stepping around the curtain and leaving the room.

I shut my eyes tight, attempting to strengthen my shaking breaths.

I thought, before today, that I knew what the phrase *bittersweet* meant. So much of these past few months has been just that. Wonderful with a painful layer hidden underneath.

But this... *this* is what bittersweet means.

All ten fingers and toes.

Every sense of relief is sharply followed by shame.

Every wave of shame is met with confusion.

Confusion gives way to guilt.

I immediately want to reassure myself that I wouldn't have loved the baby less if they'd had my hand. That I don't love *myself* any less than I would have if I had two fully formed hands. Even if I already know those things to be true, I still feel the need to repeat it, over and over.

But my initial reaction *was* relief.

I'm glad that the baby won't struggle in the ways I have.

I feel happy for them. Then consider if I shouldn't.

Afterward, I'm sad for the life experience they'll miss out on.

That they'll never know how existing in a body that the world is not designed to accommodate can create so many avenues of empathy for others, experiencing the same thing for a variety of reasons. The determination and the resilience that come from that. The community it cultivates.

The unique bond we could have shared.

With that thought comes another pang of guilt. For mourning, even for a split second, the loss of similarity. The inherent narcissism of wanting my kid to be *like* me. Because that's what parents should do, right? Separate their kids from themselves and their own experiences so that they have room to grow into their own people. Accept them and offer unconditional love along the way.

I now realise it's up to Bo and me to do the rest. Without a crash course from first-hand experience, we'll need to be the ones to teach our kid how to navigate the world with that empathy. To see their privilege as a tool to use on behalf of others.

But also, to not let our burdens overtake them.

A delicate balance.

And once the thoughts and the confusion and the guilt settle alongside my breaths, I decide to trust that we're up for the challenge.

Opening my eyes, I reach for the towel left beside me and wipe my stomach clean from the ultrasound gel. Then I turn to face Bo, offering him a timid, bashful smile.

"Well..." Bo sighs out, his tone deceptively serious, in juxtaposition with the twitch of his lips. "We'll still love them, of course. Even if they're, you know"—he grimaces—"four-limbed."

I huff out a long breath, grateful for his deflection. "Disappointed?" I ask, slowly lowering my shirt and sitting up on the bed.

Bo's lips shift into a wistful smile as he picks up my right hand from the mattress and squeezes it once. "No... but I'm not relieved either."

"That's how I feel too," I say, blinking back the threat of tears.

"It wouldn't have made a difference to me," he says, rubbing a thumb against my wrist. "You know that, right?"

I nod, sniffling as a sob breaks free. "I feel stupid for asking."

Bo stands and lowers himself onto the edge of the hospital bed, facing me. "Hey..." he says softly. "It's okay that you wanted to know. You're just trying to be prepared." Bo holds my little hand by the wrist and stares at it. He brushes his thumb across my palm, his eyes held in concentration. "I lied," he says, breathing out a bitter laugh. His face softens as his eyes trace the pattern of his thumb as he swipes it again. "I think I might be a *bit* disappointed."

I sniffle, shaking myself as a smile breaks through. "C'mon, you don't mean that."

"You're perfect, Win," Bo says, as easily as breathing. "Of course I'd want them to have every part of you."

It's shocking how forcefully his words hit me in the chest. I could keel over if I wasn't so intent on keeping his eyes held on mine.

The moment feels like a precipice. It seems obvious that he's going to kiss me. It's in his eyes. That narrowed, glazed expression I've seen before. The brief second in which he glances at my mouth. I prepare for it, wetting my lips and swallowing. But it doesn't come.

With every passing, lingering second, it seems less and less likely. Eventually, he tightens his jaw and stands, gently placing my hand on the side of the mattress as he does.

I miss him, even though he's right in front of me.

"We should probably get out of here," he says, looking at the curtain and the door beyond it. "Dad's been texting me updates," he says, scratching his chin, looking wayward. "We'll be eating like kings for the next few days. He's bought half the market."

Bo grabs my jacket and bag from the hook on the wall and places them next to me, not looking *at* me but around me. "I think he might be wandering around downtown with live lobster in his bag..."

I nod, laughing faintly as I hop down and stand at the edge of the bed, holding on to it tightly for balance as my head spins.

"You okay?" he asks, his hand on my forearm to steady me.

I nod, moving away from his hold to put on my jacket. I pull my hair out of the back of it when it gets caught and look around cluelessly for my bag before realising Bo's holding it out to me. I force a smile, taking it as he looks at me with growing concern.

"I'm fine. It's just... I feel..." I laugh, rubbing my face. "I don't know. I think I'm just hungry, maybe," I lie. Well, it's not a lie. I am hungry. That's always true these days.

He nods, running his teeth across his bottom lip. "Okay. We'll grab something on our way home."

Shit.

"Oh, actually..."

I had completely forgotten to tell him that I needed to be dropped off at Sarah's after our appointment. She's taking me to the store to grab everything for Bo's party tomorrow, and then we're going back to hers to bake a cake. "I have plans with Sarah this afternoon. Do you think you could drop me off there? After we grab your dad and his new pet lobsters?"

"Oh, uh, sure." Bo's face falls, his lips curling inward.

It pulls like a weight in my stomach, watching his frown twitch as his eyes look at the floor between us.

But some space might do us both good. I know I could use a bath and a long chat with Sarah, at least. "Also..." I say, swallowing. "I might sleep over there tonight."

Bo opens his mouth and shuts it just as quickly. He swallows tightly as his eyebrows press together. "So I'll see you tomorrow? For my, uh—" He hesitates, looking up at the ceiling as if he can't believe he has to say this next part out loud. "For my birthday?"

The point of a surprise party is, *of course*, to make it a surprise. But it takes *everything* in me not to ruin it when I see the flat expression he's forcing to replace his obvious disappointment.

"I've been sworn to secrecy, but your dad has a plan for you both tomorrow." *The one I asked him to make.* "I'll be home when you get back." *And so will six other people.*

"Promise?" he asks, far too quickly for it to have been intentional.

My brows knit together as I nod. "Yeah, of course..."

"Okay," he says, smiling weakly, his eyes still on the floor. "Sounds good," he says, tilting his head upward and looking over his shoulder to the door. "Ready?"

"Yeah," I agree, my voice far more defeated than I'd like it to be.

CHAPTER 29

"Caleb, I swear to god if you eat another pinwheel before Bo gets here, I'll give you and Win matching fingers," Sarah says, setting a pitcher of lemonade on the table.

Caleb shoves his hand into his pocket and slowly backs away from the table of food.

"They're two minutes away," I announce to the room of guests, putting my phone on the counter next to the cake that Sarah and I decorated to look like a Hobbit door, complete with a large *30* in the centre.

Bo has been out with his dad since this morning. I know they started by getting lunch and ended at a brewery, but I'm not sure where they've gone in between. The only hint I have is the photo Bo sent of himself in a barber's chair, covered in white towels and with a caption that read: *I'm the mummy now.*

I looked at the photo for way too long, even amongst the chaos that was throwing this party together.

I *love* that dork.

And I'm going to tell him. Tonight.

Sarah and I talked about *everything* last night, and one thing became clear. I physically cannot handle living here with him another second without telling him. I just have to leap blindly and hope he feels the same.

And even if Bo's not fully moved on from his past relationship, I think he'd be willing to try starting something new. There were so many instances yesterday where I just *knew* he could feel the same way about me as I do about him. The waiting room, his disappointment when I asked him to take me to Sarah's, the look in his eye when he said I was *perfect.*

I think I could be content, even if Bo's heart is in two places. Honestly, at this point, I think I'd happily settle for half of his affections. I have a feeling Bo would love me better at half capacity than anyone else ever could.

Kevin and Jeremiah burst through the door, apologising for being late as they become a flurry of scarves and jackets being removed. "We saw them pull onto the street, but they didn't spot us. We parked around the corner like instructed," Kevin says, handing a plate of food to Jeremiah as he dramatically rips off his shoes, tosses them into the closet, and barrels toward me.

"Where do you want these?" Jer asks as his husband wraps me up in a hug.

"Just on the table please," I squeak from the inside of Kevin's tight hug.

"How ya doing?" Kevin asks, releasing me.

"Fine!"

He studies me with a knowing smile. "You seem nervous."

"I want Bo to love his party..."

"The party... *sure*," Kevin says, patting my shoulder. "Sarah!" he shouts, walking over to her. "I made the bacon-wrapped scallops I was telling you about..." I lose focus of their conversation behind me when Walter raises his hand, pointing outside the window.

"They're here," he says, dropping the curtain. Adamir shuts off the lights as I pause the music, and everyone else crouches behind furniture or walls.

I move to the centre of the archway, between the dining and living room, and wait, my heartbeat thumping in my ears.

Bo's dad opens the front door and quickly jogs inside, hiding on the other side of the archway, tucked inside the living room. He smiles widely at me with anticipatory excitement across his features.

I wink at him, my giddy smile growing by the second.

"Dad?" Bo calls out from the front steps. He's nearly laughing but mostly confused as he steps into the front hall.

Then he sees me, wearing my dorky cone-shaped party hat and my purple linen dress, and his shoulders fall with a contented smile.

The seconds pass like minutes as we stare at each other from across the room.

But chaos explodes all around us soon enough, once Sarah restarts the music and everyone shouts "Surprise!" as they pop out from their hiding places.

Bo jumps backward, nearly falling on his ass. He clutches his chest, laughing as he regains his balance with one hand on the wall. "Oh my god," he says, breathing heavily, half bent over. "Hi, everyone..." he says, straightening, his eyes on me.

"Happy birthday?" I say, wincing.

He shakes his head, smiling broadly as he beelines across the room toward me, dodging furniture and people in his path. Without warning, Bo picks me up off the ground and into his arms, crushing me against him in a tight hug as my feet dangle underneath me.

"I'm so glad you're here," he whispers, his mouth tilted into the crook of my neck.

I wrap my arms around his shoulders and hold him too. "I said I would be," I whisper back.

"Did you do all of this?" he asks, his voice less strained but not quite right.

"Yeah."

He sighs out, his breath warm against my throat. "Thank you."

"So *this* is what it's like up here," I say, admiring my new viewpoint from over Bo's shoulder. "I like it."

"I missed you," he says, lowering me back to stand on my own two feet.

I reach beside me for a party hat and hold it up to him. "It was just one night," I say.

Bo bends at the waist, allowing me to fasten it to his head.

"Happy birthday," I repeat, just for him this time.

"You didn't text me back," he says, his lips twitching into an uneasy grin. "I thought you were..."

I narrow my eyes on him, noticing the unusual mopiness across his face and the wildly tousled hair that usually signals his unease. His beard got tidied up and trimmed, but I'm glad he didn't let the barber take off any of his hair. I love it longer.

"I'm sorry. I was busy doing this, and I forgot to reply."

"No, don't be sorry. This is amazing. I'm..." He shakes himself, reaching out for me. "Hi," he says, pulling me against his chest again.

I laugh, hugging him. "Bo, are you okay? There are other people here who—"

"I'm a little drunk." He straightens, wiping his brow with the sleeve of his grey sweater. "I haven't had a drink since you told me about the baby. Solidarity, you know? But I think I'm a lightweight now?" He swallows, dropping his chin. "I had two sampler flights, and Dad ended up having to drive us home." He scratches his jaw, looking around with a polite smile. "Everyone's *looking* over here..." he whispers.

I nod thoughtfully, trying not to smirk. "You gonna be okay, big guy?"

He nods, licking his lips. "I'm gonna get some food. That'll help."

"Great idea." I pat his back as he wanders over to the food table, greeting more of his friends as he forgoes a plate and shoves a few different things into his mouth at once.

Sarah widens her eyes at me, her lips pulled inward as I walk toward her in the kitchen. "That was *quite* the entrance."

"He's a little tipsy, turns out." I grimace, laughing.

"I thought he was going to carry you around the whole party like a favourite toy." She hands me a wineglass filled with lemonade. "He looked a little tortured when he saw you. You should probably put him out of his misery. Or not, if you're *into* that sort of thing."

"He thought I was mad at him," I explain. "I didn't text him back, and... after yesterday, I think he probably feels as uneasy as I do."

"Well, you should definitely show him how *not* mad you are," Sarah says, smirking into her glass of merlot.

"He'll have to sober up first," I laugh.

Kevin joins us, sipping on his drink as all three of us watch Bo introduce his dad to Walter, Jeremiah, and Adamir.

"Bo's dad is *insanely* hot, right?" Kevin whispers.

"It's a little jarring, honestly," I reply, the hand on my neck slipping down to my chest.

"Would it be weird for you if I invited him to be our third?" Sarah asks, turning her smirk toward me. "I think Caleb could be persuaded."

"Shut up," I say, sputtering my drink.

"I think I'd risk our friendship for him," she whispers.

"Oh, you would, huh?"

"*Oui, oui,*" Sarah says, giggling into her wine.

The party was a *huge* success.

Bo bounced around between his friends all evening, all the while devouring a truly startling amount of food. Sarah challenged Walter to a lip-sync battle and got her ass handed to her with a vote of six to one. Caleb, of course, voted with his heart.

Robert held court with Jeremiah and Kevin most of the evening, discussing French cuisine. Adamir and I bonded over our love of plants, and I sent him home with a dozen cuttings to propagate when he cut out early.

Then, after a truly wonderful evening, the party died down a little after midnight. Walter caught a ride home with Jeremiah and Kevin. Caleb and Sarah stayed to help clean up. Not that Sarah is *any* help in her current state.

"This was great, Win," Caleb says, tying a garbage bag.

"I had fun," I say, smiling into the sink as I wash wineglasses. "I hope Bo did too."

"Sure seems like it," Caleb says, peeking out into the living room. "I think we should get going, though. Have you got this?"

"Yeah, of course. I'll just do the rest tomorrow," I say, drying my hands on a tea towel. "Thanks for helping."

"Any time," he says, putting his arm around me as we turn the corner into the living room. I fall next to Sarah on the couch and begin petting her hair away from her face. "Time to go, babe," I whisper. "You can sleep in your nice, warm bed."

Sarah sits up, groaning.

"Ready, love?" Caleb says, bending over the back of the couch. Sarah stumbles over to him, then pets his face as he shakes his head affectionately. "Yeah, you're ready. Okay, here we go." He guides her to the front hall with a hand on the small of her back and helps her into her shoes and coat.

"Byeee," Sarah whines out, waving from the door with her eyes mostly shut. "Robert, it was *so* good to meet you. Bo, happy birthday. You're great. Win..." Sarah opens one eye, looking at me with a soft, hazy smile. "Best of luck with all your future endeavours," she hiccups.

"Nailed it," Caleb says gently, rubbing her back. "Bye, guys. Happy birthday, man!"

"Thank you," Bo says to them both. "Thanks for coming," he repeats.

"Love you!" I shout after them as Caleb shuts the door.

"You've got a good group of friends, Robbie," Bo's dad says, sighing. "It's nice to see."

I glance between the men, but they both slowly turn toward me, smiling appreciatively.

"I'm very lucky," Bo says softly—eyes held on mine.

I blush, but the dimly lit room is hopefully dark enough to disguise it well.

"I'm going to go take a shower before bed," Bo says. "You okay?" he asks me.

"Of course," I say, smiling up at him.

As soon as Bo's out of the room, Robert stands and moves to the opposite end of the couch from me. "Thank you," he says earnestly. "I like knowing my son is well looked-after."

"Ah, well, it's just a party."

"No, it isn't. He's happy now. He was *not* happy last year. Who could blame him?"

"Sometimes I wish I'd known him then," I admit. "I hate thinking that he felt so alone."

Robert tilts his head into his palm, listening to me with a warm grin—an almost proud expression. "Joanna would have loved you, you know. You have her same... care. I can tell life has not been easy or always kind to you, but you haven't let it turn you hard. Not like a stone. You became like water. You move with it all. You're soft... but powerful."

I immediately have to blink away tears, shaking my head. "Oh," I say, sniffling. "That's, um..."

"The odd musings of a drunk Frenchman, *oui*."

"No, I mean... That's very kind. Thank you. From what Bo has said, Joanna was a fantastic person. I certainly admire her taste in music," I say, offering a piece of levity.

"What *has* Bo said about his mother?"

I wince, hoping I don't make Bo sound cold or uncaring. But I don't want to lie either. "Not a lot, honestly. Just... how you two met. How much you both miss her. The music, and—"

"How she passed?" Robert interrupts.

No, I say silently, shaking my head.

He hums, nodding softly. "Joanna struggled the way a lot of artists do. Her feelings often felt too big to hold on to. Too out of control. But it made her *great*. Passionate about her music." He licks his lips, leaning back on the couch. "When we decided to have children, we'd already been together for eight years. We had this nice little apartment in Toronto. We played music together every day, and we had so much happiness. Joy and laughter and... I thought the best was yet to come."

Robert chokes up and immediately reaches for his throat. I do the same without thinking. My heart starts pounding in my chest, waiting on every word.

"Back then, there was no real word for the way Joanna seemed to lose herself during pregnancy. She became... like a ghost. I tried to help. I tried to *get* her help, but..." Robert sighs, shaking his head at the ceiling. "It was all too much for her. She left a note, saying that she was sorry. That she loved us. That she couldn't explain why she couldn't stay, and... she took her own life. Bo was only twelve weeks old."

I inhale sharply, covering my mouth as my lips quiver. "I'm so sorry," I whisper. "I... I had no idea. I'm so—"

"I wish every day that I could have helped her more."

"I'm sure you did everything you possibly could have." I rest my hand on his knee.

He pats my hand twice with his, and I notice it's shaking. He then brings it to his chin, rubbing it back and forth. "A few summers after she passed, Robbie was still small—just turned five—and I left him with Joanna's sister for a week. I had a show to play outside of Canada, and I thought..." His voice trails off as he takes a deep breath in. "The horrid woman told him what happened. Told him the truth about how Joanna passed. And... I've felt that, ever since then, Robbie's held on to a responsibility. That he feels partially to blame. I regret that too."

My jaw shakes, then loosens as my tears threaten to pour, thinking of that little boy who's grown into the man I know. The realisation as to why *every* step of this pregnancy has held such weight to Bo. My feelings, my housing, my finances, my health. All because of what happened to his mother. Because of that guilt he feels.

I wish he'd told me, but I understand why he didn't, or *couldn't*. It's unimaginable, that level of pain.

"When he called to tell me about the baby... about *you*... I think he felt like he'd been given another chance, almost. I tried to talk to him about it. Tried to tell him that it was not his burden, but mine. But it's hard to do. Robbie would always rather worry about someone else than himself. He's always been that way."

"I... I'm okay, though," I say, because part of me thinks Robert needs to hear it too. "I didn't need him to—"

"Yes," he agrees. "I think he thought at first that he had to keep you close for your sake. To not have history repeat itself. But now? Now is different. I think *he* needs *you*."

"Bo's... Bo is... He's wonderful."

"He is," Robert agrees. "But he has a *soft* heart, like his mother. Like you. You must be gentle with each other, okay?"

A soft heart like his father, it seems, as well.

"Yes," I agree, my voice barely audible.

"Good..." Robert sighs, standing up slowly. "I fear I've ruined the evening now, with all my sad ramblings."

"Oh, no... No, you—"

"I miss her today, especially. Thirty birthdays for our boy. She should be here."

"Maybe she is? In a way we can't see?"

"Perhaps," Robert says, swaying as he places a hand on the back of the couch to steady himself. "Thank you for tonight, Win. But more importantly, for giving Robbie a reason to celebrate again."

"Good night," I say, looking over my shoulder as Robert walks around the back of the couch toward Bo's bedroom.

And I wipe my eyes, determined to go find Bo and hold him for as long as he'll let me.

CHAPTER 30

When Bo comes in after his shower, he's wearing his usual beige hoodie and black shorts combination, as well as his glasses under freshly washed, towel-dried hair. He finds me sitting up in bed, waiting for him, wearing a white crewneck sweater and black bicycle shorts.

"Hey," he whispers, looking over at me as he places his prosthesis next to my dresser. "I thought you might be asleep by now."

"Hi," I say, "I wanted to talk to you first..."

"Everything okay?" he asks, lowering to the edge of the bed, his back facing me. I watch as he takes off his glasses and places them on the bedside table next to his phone.

I take a trembling breath in and dive toward him, wrapping my arms around his waist and pressing my head between his shoulder blades.

"Hey," he says gently, his neck turned as far as he can over his shoulder. "What's going on?"

"Nothing," I answer, my voice muffled by his sweater. "I just needed to hug you."

"Okay," he says, placing his hand on mine over his ribs. "Let me lie down, and then we can both get in on this."

I nod, pulling away.

Bo twists and lowers himself until he's flat on his back, then gestures for me to come snuggle into his side with an outstretched arm. Instead, I crawl over top of him, straddling his hips and burrowing my face into his chest.

"Win..." Bo says as his large hands spread across my shoulders, rubbing up and down my back. "Talk to me, honey. What's going on? Did something happen?"

"When you went to shower, your dad and I talked for a little bit."

"Did he say something to upset you?"

"No..." I say, turning my head out to the side. I wipe my face with the sleeve of my sweater and sniff back tears. "But he told me about your mom." My voice pitches up, near breaking. "About how she passed, and... Bo, I'm so sorry."

"Oh," he breathes out, his hands stilling on my back. "I was going to tell you, Win. I just—"

"No, no." I sit up, teary-eyed, and look down at him. When I do, his expression isn't what I expected. He looks scared, almost. Not sad. Not mournful. But scared. His jaw hardened and his eyes soft and held on me with a concern that has me wanting to smooth out the line between his brows with my thumb. More than that, actually. I wish I could take out his soul and smooth it out too, remove every wrinkle and crease and stain and give it back to him as good as new. "I'm not upset you didn't tell me. I'm just... I wish I'd known," I say. "So I could help somehow."

Bo lifts up, forcing me to shift off his lower abdomen as he moves to sit with his back against the headboard. I go to move to the mattress next to him, but he pulls me back onto his lap with his hands on my hips.

With our faces just a few inches apart, Bo moves his hand to my neck, his thumb tracing my jaw tenderly next to my ear as his eyes delicately track the pattern.

Let me in, I want to say amidst the silence. *Love me. Trust me. I won't let you down. I swear it.*

"I was scared that if I told you how my mom died, you'd think I was doing this for all the wrong reasons," he says, his chest rising and his tear-brimmed eyes held tentatively on my jaw. "I didn't want you to think that I asked you to move in just so I could *monitor* you or something. And..." He sighs, letting his forehead fall against my chin as he sniffs back tears.

"It's okay..." I say, wrapping my hand around his neck, brushing over his hair. "You don't have to explain. It's okay..."

"I convinced myself that you wouldn't be honest with me about how you're feeling if you knew what had happened. I never wanted to risk your safety because you were more worried about my feelings than your own." I feel his hands move to my hips, the tension pulling on my sweater as he balls up the material in his fists on either side. "But I did want to tell you, Win. I don't want any secrets between us. Not anymore."

I nod, my lips quivering against his hairline. He shakes with a soft sob, his shoulders falling forward. "It's okay..." I say, over and over. "What happened is not at all your fault. It's no one's fault. You were just a baby. You're not to blame."

"I think..." He clears his throat, sitting up, his face level with mine. "I think having August is helping me realise that." His nostrils flare on a deep inhale, and a tear drips down the left side of his cheek that he quickly wipes against his shoulder.

"Good." I put my hand on his cheek, forcing him to look at me, to hear me. "Because we'd *never* blame them, would we?"

He shakes his head, his eyes locked on mine.

"You've given me so much, Win."

"No..."

"Ever since I met you, it's like every part of me has healed a little bit. Do you know that? Do you know that you do that for people?"

I nod. Not because I agree, but because I understand. "I think we both needed a fresh start. I think we gave that to each other."

Bo's hands begin shifting against my hips, his thumbs brushing the front of my stomach as he looks down between us. "It's more than that, Win." He tilts up to face me, his gaze pleading. "At least, it is for me."

I swallow tightly, my hands still on the back of his neck.

"I'm not sure how to pace myself here. How to slow down so you can catch up," he whispers.

"Catch up?" I ask, trembling.

"I think we both know how this is going to end," he says, his voice gruff. "I'm just trying to figure out how to get us both there at the same time."

"But... what about Cora?" I stutter out.

Bo leans back, studying my face intently with pouted lips and a raised brow. "What *about* Cora?"

I look down between us, dropping my hands from his neck. "That day, on the beach... you said you *love* her. You said you hadn't gotten closure. It *sounded* like you were still—"

"I called her as soon as we got home, Win," he interrupts.

"What?" I stammer.

"We got home from the beach, and all I could think was, here I am at the start of something new and beautiful, and I'm still stuck in the past. I realised I couldn't keep making excuses for her. That I couldn't leave things unresolved for the sake of peace. You deserved better than that. The baby deserved better than that. You made me realise that *I* deserved better than that. So I called her."

"I... I didn't know."

Bo licks his lips, his eyes focused on something off to the side. "We talked for a few hours. I apologised for clinging to something long-over out of fear, and she apologised for... well, everything else. I think she'd been expecting me to call. She seemed ready for it. We both said our piece, and then she asked how I was. And then... I talked about you."

"Me?"

Bo shakes his head, smiling. "I've been talking about you to pretty much anyone who would listen for months," he laughs out softly. "I thought you knew, Win. I thought it was so painfully obvious how I feel about you. What I want here. I thought that's why you set such clear boundaries. I thought you didn't feel the same."

I bring a hand to my mouth, covering a wavering smile. *He wants me.*

"I've been hanging on your every word, hoping you'll give me a green light. I don't want to push you. I don't want you to *ever* feel uncomfortable, but... I don't think I can pretend any—"

I kiss him. Because I *have* to. Because I can. Because it's right.

And he kisses me back, fierce yet gentle, and it's like a thousand hours spent *wanting* each other spilling between us. His hands go from my hips to my hair, clinging to me.

"You're sure?" he asks, pulling back.

I giggle against his lips. "I'm sure, Bo. I've wanted this for so long."

"Okay... we'll talk after?"

"After," I agree, laughing still, giddy and relieved and so effervescently happy.

Our kiss quickly turns feverish, with an intensity I've never felt before.

I don't question if he wants this, because he's told me he does. I don't question if it's a good choice or a bad one or worry about all it could ruin. Because when you love someone *this* much, when you've seen their hurt and their heart and you recognise them as your own—you're left with no choice but to give yourself over to it. And I'm tired of being scared. I long to be loved by a man like Bo. I long to love him, the way he deserves.

Our souls were tied a long time ago, I think. We're just finally admitting it to each other.

Bo twists and lies down lengthways across the headboard, keeping me on top of him with a steady hold. We're both smiling when our lips meet again, but that ends when Bo's hand curls around the back of my neck, pulling me farther against him than it seems I can go.

I feel it too, wanting to fuse our bodies together—the need to become one living *thing*.

I sit up, reaching for the hem of my sweater, but he takes it off for me, throwing it across the room. I fumble with his hoodie as he struggles to lift enough for me to get a good grip. We both laugh softly, tugging and pulling and shifting until we're both topless and pressed against each other again. Bo rolls us so I'm on my back and he's between my legs.

"They're *really* sensitive now," I whisper, holding my tits as he pulls my shorts and underwear off.

Bo lifts my foot onto his shoulder and begins kissing his way down the inside of my leg. "In a good way?" he asks, nibbling at the side of my knee, watching my hands eagerly.

"In a *great* way," I say, plucking my nipples. "In a way where I've been imagining *you* touching them every night."

Bo's smile turns heated, his eyes locked in on my tits as he wets his lips. He continues kissing the inside of my thigh, holding my leg over his shoulder as he makes his way down to my centre. He brings his other hand to my breast, his palm covering the peaked flesh and squeezing indelicately.

He pulls away, holding my calf with both hands as he shakes his head, his eyes skimming over every part of my body. "God, I can't decide where to start. I've missed your body so much. I wish I had more hands."

I raise a brow, and he nods, his lips tight. "Heard it."

"We've got time," I reply breathlessly. "But touch me *some-where.*"

Bo nods, lowering himself to the floor at the side of the bed.

He reaches across the mattress, the tendons in his arms flaring as he grabs the extra flesh of my hips and uses it to pull me to the edge.

I yelp, biting my lip as I smile down at him, grateful for his roughness.

"I've decided," he whispers, biting the opposite thigh as he parts my legs with his hands.

"Yes," I whisper. "Good decision..."

He laughs darkly with his mouth against my core. Then he swipes his tongue expertly from my wet entrance to my clit.

I cry out, covering my mouth with my forearm. "Yes," I say. "Right there."

He sucks and flicks his tongue against that same spot until I'm panting, gripping the sheets and his hair. Unwinding into a complete, utter mess.

Removing his mouth, he presses two fingers inside me and curls them, tapping in an achingly perfect rhythm. I match each motion with uncontrollable gasps and squeaks and moans. "Oh my *god,*" I moan, baring my teeth as pressure builds.

"Fuck yes..." Bo's voice is low and steady, in complete contrast to how I feel, floating above it all. "Do you have any clue how sexy you are? How sweet you taste? How much I've been thinking about you like this?"

I whine, biting my bottom lip as I try to will myself closer to that sweet oblivion.

"I've thought about hearing my name come out of those perfect lips *every* fucking night since I heard you from down the hall. Please, Win. *Please.* Say my name."

"Bo," I say like a promise. "Bo," I force out from the hollow of my chest. "Fuck me," I beg. "Please," I whine, thrashing backward.

"Not yet, honey. Not until you come on my fingers first. I'm fucking *dying* to. Trust me. But I need this from you first. Need to watch you." He places a hand on the swell of my stomach as his eyes grow hooded. "I was obsessed with your body before, but now, I think... I think I'm a goner. Look at you. Fucking *perfect.*"

"I'm... I'm close," I say, my jaw clenching as my legs fight to close. Bo pins my knee down with his shoulder, keeping me open for him as I begin to shake.

"That's right, honey. Come for me. Please."

I come so hard I hear a ringing in my ears, my body taught and contracted and spasming all over. I scream around my wrist, silencing myself as best as I can.

Once my body stills and my breaths slow, Bo starts tenderly kissing my throbbing sex. It's *almost* too much, but I press my lips together and force myself to relax into it.

Bo whimpers alongside little throaty sounds of greed as he laps up every single bit of my release. "God, you taste so fucking good," he grinds out before gently kissing my clit one last time, sending a shock of overstimulation through my system.

"Show me," I offer, rolling my neck to see him. "Kiss me," I say, wearing a satisfied smile.

"Gladly," Bo says, using his arms to help lift himself off the ground.

I rotate myself, lying lengthways on the bed, and make room for him to lie down next to me. Once he's settled, I drape myself across his chest and kiss him leisurely.

"My favourite thing in the world," he says against my lips, swiping his thumb across my cheek, then trailing a lazy finger down my neck to my chest, where he taps the space between my breasts, coloured pink. "I was scared I'd never get to see this type of blush from you again."

I lean down to kiss him again. He grips the side of my face as I nibble his bottom lip, pulling it between my teeth and releasing only when I lift away, pressing my forehead into his. I groan in frustration, angry that I can't be *nearer* than this.

"I wish I could..." I say, not knowing where I want that sentence to end. What I mean is I want him *inside* me. But not only in the way he will inevitably be soon. But burned inside of me. Like lightning hitting a tree and starting a fire from within. I want him, his life, his lessons, his soul and its impressions to be branded under my skin. "Eat you" are the closest words I can find.

"That's frowned upon, honey." Bo says as I lift a leg over his lap to straddle him.

"Would you let me?" I ask as he grips my lower back, then lowers his hands to the globes of my ass, his fingers digging into my flesh. "If I asked nicely?"

"You know I would," he says, laughing.

I bend down and kiss him some more, my nipples grazing against his chest in the most incredible way.

"Turn around for me," Bo says, his teeth against my jaw. "I want you to lower yourself onto me, then lean back against me, okay?"

I nod, repositioning myself. Bo's hand wraps around my waist as he sits up underneath me. He kisses across my shoulder, pushing his forehead into the back of my head as I raise up onto my knees and sink onto the length of him.

"*Fuck,*" I whisper, my lips parting on a ragged inhale. No matter how many times I replayed the memory of our night together, I knew, deep down, it was never close to the real thing. Nothing could have prepared me for how incredible it would feel again.

"Win..." Bo moans, his voice breathless. "How is it even better this time?"

"Because now we're *us,*" I reply, whispering through a thick fog of desire.

I do as I'm told and lean back against his chest. Bo's arms wrap me in a tight embrace, one hand reaching across my abdomen, holding me there. The other has a tight grip on my breast. I use my shins and knees pressed into the mattress to roll against him. "Like this?"

Bo hisses, his teeth on my ear. "Yes," he says sharply. "Fucking hell..." He slowly lowers his hand from my stomach to between my legs, spreading goose bumps in his wake.

"Too much," I say as he begins playing with my clit, my movements jittery. "I can't move while you're doing that. It's too good."

"Then don't move," he commands sternly. "I need to feel you come around my dick before I lose my fucking mind."

"Bo," I hiccup, bringing my hand up to play with my breast. "I'm so *full*..." I say, feeling myself twitch and tighten around him. I roll my neck back, letting the back of my head fall against his collarbone.

"That's it, honey. Relax. I've got you," he says, the corner of his lips against my forehead.

I begin rotating my hips in small, circular motions, my ass pressing into Bo's abdomen.

Bo moans, broken and gruff with warm breath across my hairline.

"Can you come with me?" I ask, swallowing tightly, feeling a bead of sweat trickle down past my shoulder blades.

Bo laughs once, without much humour to it at all. "Win, that's all I've been trying *not* to do."

"Please," I beg. "Please, I'm close. I want to. Together."

Bo applies more pressure to my clit, keeping his movement consistent as I continue rotating my hips. He presses his nose into my hair, breathing me in deeply as he whimpers again.

"It's *so* good," he says, his voice in a near whine.

"Almost..." I say, gasping.

"Almost," he repeats raggedly.

"Yes," I gasp.

Bo grunts, pumping into me from below.

My stomach tenses as I feel the anticipatory *drop*, my heart skipping a beat before my body's overcome with pleasure. "Now," I cry out around shaky breaths.

"Win," Bo says, parting my name into two syllables. Then I feel his warmth spill into me, sending me further into bliss.

I tremble against him, and his hold tightens all around me.

"*Shit*," he groans out before collapsing backward, taking me with him. His back falls onto the mattress as I fall onto him. The sweat that has been dripping down my back meets the hot flesh of his abdomen underneath me.

"Wow," I say, catching my breath, pressing my ear to his neck. His heart's beating almost as fast as mine.

Bo laughs, just once. "*Damn*."

"Yeah," I agree, smiling to myself, my eyes drifting closed with every exhale.

I feel his heavy breaths under my back and bring my hands up over my head to touch his face. "Amazing work, *honey*." I throw the nickname back to him as I pat his cheek.

"Who said I was done?" he asks mockingly, lifting his hips and reminding me that he's still *very much* inside me and growing harder by the second. "I've been waiting for this... *honey*."

CHAPTER 31

e went for two more rounds before I demanded a shower and some rest. Bo gave in, under the condition that I'd sleep naked and on top of him. It was without a doubt the best sleep of my life. When we woke up this morning, the room was still dark as rain poured outside.

But I've never felt brighter.

Bo stirs next to me, his nose tucked against his pillow as he blinks awake, then lets his eyes flutter closed again. I watch him sleep shamelessly, noticing the delicate twitch of his eyebrows, the startled and settled breaths in between, the rising and falling of his chest. I memorise every detail of his face. His cupid's bow tucked under a soft spray of golden facial hair, the twenty-one freckles across his forehead, cheeks, and nose. The small few on his eyelids that are my favourites.

Then, once I've had my fill, I sit up next to him, my back against the headboard and my blanket wrapped around my torso. I wake him with a gentle brush of my hand across his beard. He cracks one eye open, his smile sleepily searching as he looks up to find me.

"Good morning, gorgeous," he whispers, his voice rough. He wraps one arm around my lap, holding my hip, then pulls himself over me, his head landing across my thighs. "Five more minutes," he yawns, curling into my legs.

I'm not sure if it's the proximity of his voice to my belly or the way my heart started beating that got the baby's attention, but they're awake now too. Greeting me with fluttering little kicks on my left side. I place one hand where the baby seems to be and one hand on the side of Bo's head, using my little fingers to stroke his hair.

And I think to myself: life has *never* been so good as it is at this exact moment. The only thing left to do is tell him how much I love him... and I'm unprepared to wait five more minutes.

"Bo?" I say his name like I haven't ever said it before. Like it's foreign on my tongue with all of these new feelings and depth that it holds. "Bo... I need to tell you something."

"You have to wait," he says, grumbling, talking out the side of his mouth squished against my lap. "I want to say it first, but I'm too tired to do it properly right now. Later."

I smile so wide that it tilts my head back, pointing my face up to the ceiling. "Say *what* first?" I ask, brushing his hair back and trailing my thumb from the top of his ear down his neck.

"Three big, important words. You know them, yes?"

"No, sorry, I'm unfamiliar. You better wake up and tell me."

"You deserve better than a bedroom confession. There should be spectacle," he says, smiling to himself, his eyes still shut tight. "*Pizzaz*," he adds, sighing.

"I don't *need* spectacle." I just need *you.*

Bo groans as he sits up, his head hanging between us until he rolls his neck and gives me that classic mischievous schoolboy grin that kills me every time.

"Morning," he says, pulling his blanket farther up his lap to cover his bottom half.

"Oh, good morning," I whisper, leaning forward to capture his lips in a single lazy kiss. "Something wake you?"

"Hmm," he moans, rubbing his eye with the heel of his palm. "I didn't think I'd feel hungover. I felt sober when I got to bed."

"Ah, but love, you're thirty now."

He tilts his head slowly, his hair flopping to one side. "I like that," he says, smiling.

"What?"

"My dream girl is in bed with me, calling me *love*."

"Dream girl, huh?" I say, pulling the blanket farther up my chest when I notice his eyes dip lower. I need him to focus.

"How are you so awake?" he asks, widening his eyes and blinking slowly. "I feel like I swallowed rocks."

"I'm *actually* sober, remember? The whole baby thing?" I tease, rubbing my hand from his shoulder to his neck, tilting his drooping head back up to look at me. "Wake up." I *need* him to tell me how he feels. Because I truly feel like I'm about to burst. "If you're not going to say it first, I will."

He chuckles, letting his head fall between us again. "You know, you've got a really interesting way of keeping me on my toes. I've been fighting every impulse around you because *you* said we had to be nothing more than friends. Then, after one night together, you want all the cards on the table. Do you know how hard it's been to not tell you every day? Maybe I should make *you* wait," he says, narrowing his eyes at me playfully.

He's got a point. I've led the way this entire time. My boundaries and my rules. He's kindly and respectfully followed me every step of the way. That's probably one of the many reasons I'm so in love with him. And I *could* let him torture me a little—since I've been unknowingly keeping him on ice all this time.

But he's a better person than I am.

I reach across and take Bo's hand in mine, wrapping my palm around his fingers and squeezing. His smile is still hazy, but his eyes are clearer now. I wait for a small look of permission, a little softened corner of his eye that says *go ahead...*

"I love you," I say, squeezing his fingers again. "I'm fully, madly, deeply, and unquestionably in love with you."

Bo's shoulders fall on a deep breath in, like he's taking my words inward. His face contented and patient and so, *so* happy.

"I've been *so* scared of letting myself feel that way again. I have questioned my judgement, my intentions, and my reasoning since we met, but all along, you've been showing me that I can rely on you with little acts every day. And those small doses of kindness and generosity and support and gentleness have chipped away at the hard wall I built around my heart. You never asked for more. You never rushed me. You..."

I swallow, clearing my throat from the emotions clogging it as best I can. "You've seen me. Understood me like I've never been understood. And I see you now too. I see how truly lovely you are.

More importantly, I believe it. With everything inside me, I believe you're going to be gentle with my heart."

Bo blinks rapidly, his eyes fluttering as he looks down between us and pulls my hand to his mouth before kissing each knuckle. He leans against my palm, so I cradle his face, and I feel his jaw trembling. "I love you, Win. I love you so much it makes me feel like I've hated everything else in my life up until now. Nothing compares to what I feel for you. Not even close."

"Thank you," I whisper, pressing my forehead to his.

"Thank *you*," he replies.

I want to scream. I want to dance. I want to stay in his arms all day, all year. Mostly, I want to kiss every inch of his body and show him how much I love him over and *over* again.

"Kiss me," I say.

His sweet, post-confessional kiss is met with *my* heated, voracious hunger. He laughs against my mouth, breathless, as I begin trailing kisses down the column of his throat.

"Already, honey?"

"Get used to it, *honey*."

Bo pulls the blankets away from my chest and off his lap before tugging me toward him with such force I giggle on impact.

"All right," he says, lifting me with two strong hands on my hips and dropping me onto his lap. "Let's see how many times we can do *this* before breakfast."

Bo slides his arms under my thighs, lifting me up as he links his hands behind my back, supporting my weight.

"Have I mentioned how much I love you?" I say teasingly as he lines himself up at my entrance, my head rolling back with anticipation.

"You'll be chanting it soon if I do this right."

I dart across the hall to the bathroom, covered in only a towel, while Bo goes to check if his father is awake yet. If he is, Bo will also have to do some explaining. *And* apologising, perhaps. Old house, thin walls, and whatever else.

Either way, not my conversation to have. But I *do* text Sarah an update about our night and morning together before getting into the steam-filled shower. I watch with glee as my phone buzzes and lights up so many times on the bathroom counter that it slips and falls into the empty sink.

Once finished, I dry my hair, rub lotion on my slowly growing belly, brush my teeth, and tiptoe back across the hall. Once there, I find a freshly brewed cup of coffee from Bo on my dresser. He even made the bed. I don't think I've *ever* made my bed, but I appreciate the sentiment.

I dress in thick, black leggings, my favourite emerald green West-cliff sweatshirt, and a pair of woolly socks. I tie my hair up in a messy bun and make my way toward the scent of something delicious from down the hall, coffee in hand.

"Morning," I say, slipping into the kitchen.

"Just me," Bo says, flipping a pancake on the stove. "Dad really must have had too much to drink."

"Should we wake him? When is his flight?"

"I'm dropping him off at nine. It's an overnight. Let's let him sleep."

"Have you talked to him about coming to visit once the baby's born?" I ask, filling a glass with ice from the fridge.

"No. Actually, I was thinking... Maybe we could go there. A little family vacation... you ever been to Paris?"

I beam, shaking my head. *Family*. That's exactly what we are. "I've always wanted to, but no. Maybe we could do a little world tour? Stop by my mom's too?"

"She's still not sure about coming up in August?"

"No... something about having to pay an entrance fee to this new business she's doing—she swears she's going to earn it back soon but," I say, shrugging, "who knows?"

"Does your mom know... about..." Bo gestures between the two of us with the spatula.

I smirk into my coffee, taking a long sip. "She knew before you did, actually. I sort of just lied from the start when I didn't clarify in what *nature* we were living together. But now, I guess I can call it manifesting," I say, going up onto the tips of my toes to kiss his cheek.

Bo flips a pancake, nodding to himself. "So, I've been thinking..."

Sarcastically, I look between the bathroom down the hall and him. "In the last ten minutes? Did I leave you alone for too long?"

"I'd like you to quit the café."

"Bo." I roll my eyes with affection. "I like being home too, but I still have to save money for the camp and pay my fair share around here." I drape my hand around his neck, rubbing his shoulder. I love that I can just *touch* him now. I love that it feels like maybe I always could have. "And I'd get you fired..." I say in a low hum. "Those sweaters you wear for work and your glasses? They do it for me."

Bo laughs, his throat working as he lifts a pancake from the pan to an already full plate, then turns off the burner. "You'd still be working. Just not at the café."

"I *also* consider sex work to be an honest living, but gorgeous, that's not happening."

Bo leans on the counter, his hand flat on top of it. "I got an email from James Burrough—the investor—this morning. Well, last night. But I was *busy* then." He winks. "I saw it this morning."

I place my mug on the counter, nearly chipping the thing with the speed I do it. "And..." I wave him on with both hands.

"And he wants to invest. He's offering 78 percent of what we need."

I bring both hands to my face, covering my gasp. "That's amazing!" I throw my arms around Bo's shoulders and hug him. He stays unmoving, other than bending to tuck his chin into my neck. "But wait. That still means I—"

"I want to invest the rest, Win. But..." he says, tapping his fingers on the countertop. "I want to know my *investment* won't be burning themselves out running between two jobs. You've got four more months before the baby shows up, and I think if you were able to focus on the camp, you could make some serious progress."

"Bo, that's…" I try to do the calculations in my head and come up empty. "That is…"

"One hundred, thirty-eight thousand and six hundred dollars."

"You don't have that!" I exclaim, my mouth open.

"No?" He pouts his lips. "Huh… could have sworn I did."

"Bo…" I whisper, side-eyeing him. "Are you rich?"

"I do well."

"*I do well* sounds like something a rich person would say. I know you have a really great job, but that is some *serious* money."

"I've been lucky with some investments. Adamir approached me for some advice when he finished school, and I ended up partnering with him on an app he built. It sold over a year ago for just under three million."

"And when you say *partnered*, you mean…?"

"I got about 30 percent of that."

I grip my forehead, laughing without sound. "There is so much math going on this morning."

Bo drops his hand from the counter and wraps it around my back, tugging me to him. "There have been a lot of things I wanted to do *and* say these last few months, and I've been waiting *not* so patiently. This is one of those things. Now that you trust me," he tilts my chin up toward him when I look down between us, "I want you to let me help, okay?" He nods, his eyes locked on mine, as if he's trying to get me to do the same. "It's your turn now, Win."

"My turn?" I ask, my voice distant.

"Everything you poured into your relationship with that..." Bo's eyes flare, and he takes a breath, steadying himself. "I don't know everything yet—and I'd really like to talk about it more when you're ready—but when you said you supported that asshole through school just to get nothing in return, it destroyed me. So yeah, it's your turn now, Win. To get back that time. To get to where you want to be. Where you deserve to be. And not just because you deserve it. But also because kids like Henry do. Kids like *us* who need this camp. So, please, let me be a part of it."

"It's not up to you to fix Jack's mistakes..."

"No," Bo says, leaning down to kiss me just once, brushing his nose against mine. "But it *is* my job to love you the way you deserve to be loved from now on." He presses his forehead against mine, breathing out slowly. "Let me do that, honey."

"Okay," I whisper, breathing him in. Bo straightens, his face still pointed toward me. "You promise you're not just doing this because we've finally had sex?" I say, wincing.

Bo laughs, playing with the hair over my shoulder, twiddling it mindlessly. "As good as the sex is, no. It's so much more than that."

"So... just like that? I quit my job?" I ask, wrapping my arms around his middle and placing my chin on his chest, looking up at him adoringly. "You really did want a kept woman. I was right."

"The sooner you quit, the sooner you can focus your attention on the camp," Bo says. "Plus, we're not going to be *just us* for much longer. As excited as I am to have August, I'd like some more one-on-one time before then."

"Hmm. And sleep," I agree.

"That too."

"So... do we email James? Tell him the plan?"

"Well, we're going to have to do a lot more math, because *none* of those plans we made matter anymore. But then, yes."

"I *love* when you talk dirty to me," I say, wiggling my eyebrows.

"First, breakfast." Bo twists within my hold and hands me a plate with a sly wink. "I've gotta keep you fed," he says, brushing his nose across my temple. "For later."

I have a feeling I'm going to enjoy *later* very much. "Yes, for all that math."

"Exactly."

CHAPTER 32

Twenty-Six Weeks Pregnant. Baby is the size of an eggplant.

"Y ou're being ridiculous!" I shout, storming down the hall after Bo. "April fool's day was *two* weeks ago, so if this is some sort of prank, it is not funny *or* well-timed!"

Bo turns sharply into his room. Sorry, *our* room. I keep having to remind myself of that.

I follow in after him, watching as he backs away from me. He's audacious enough to be *laughing*.

"If you want to fight with me, that's fine, but can it wait until *after* the installation guys leave? That way we can at least have make-up sex when you're done being angry." He stops when he hits the wall. I corner him, my finger prodding his chest on impact.

"You. Said. No. More. Gifts," I say, announcing every word with a poke of my finger against his muscle.

He swipes my hand away, keeping it tightly in his grasp, and kisses my palm, smiling into it. "I never said that. *You* said that."

"Robert!" I snap my hand back, momentarily falling into his soft, lulling trap of tender kisses.

"Winnifred!" he laughs out, his eyes creasing on either side.

The *nerve* of this man. "Don't," I say, crossing my arms over my chest.

He admonishes me with a gentle exhale, his face falling into something a touch more serious, but still not as sincere as I'd like him to be. He runs a hand through his hair, letting it flop back onto his face.

He hasn't gotten it cut since I've known him, and I have to admit I *really* love it longer. More to grip on to in bed or play with when he lies across my lap on the couch, watching another movie I'll inevitably fall asleep during.

"Honey, it's a bathtub. We need one eventually. Were we seriously going to bathe August in the sink for the next four years? A bucket? You want it, I want it. What's the big deal?"

"The big deal is that you didn't tell me beforehand so I could have had the option to say *no*. Every time you do something like this, I feel one step closer to becoming some spoiled princess with no job who—"

"You have a job," he interjects, placing a hand on my stomach. He knows when I get riled like this, August kicks, and dammit, it's so much harder to continue being mad when he's smiling at my belly, listening to me absently as he awaits the baby's movement.

"With *no* income," I correct myself, moving his hand lower to the spot where the baby was *already* kicking. "Who is waited on hand and foot and contributes nothing. You keep doing all these extravagant things for me, and I'm uncomfortable with it. I've *told* you that. First, it was the camp loan—"

"Not a loan. An investment," Bo argues, spreading his fingers wider on my bump.

"Then it was the *shed*." I use air-quotes aggressively around the word *shed*, comically attempting to do them with my small fingers as well.

When Bo announced he was getting a shed for the backyard for gardening and storage, I didn't think much of it. Though I did have a sneaking suspicion it was related to all my questions about what the garden would bloom into in spring. I made plans to start a *small* vegetable garden, and suddenly, I was the proud owner of a greenhouse. *Not* a shed. A *beautiful* glass greenhouse with running water and electricity.

Because this man is *ridiculous*.

"In my defence, that had selfish motivations. *Some* of the living room plants did move outside, which—"

"Now a friggin' bathtub!" I shriek, then take a deep, centring breath as he annoyingly tries not to laugh at my outburst. "Bo, you had a nice shower. A walk-in shower. One that was designed to suit your needs. This is absurd. It's unsafe," I say, my eyes falling to my belly, where Bo's hands rest comfortably.

"Fred..." Bo says, bringing a hand to cup my jaw and tilting my face up toward him. Him and his stupidly cute, albeit condescending, grin. "It's a *walk-in* tub with a door. Emphasis on the *walk-in* part. Best of both worlds. You need your baths, honey. Sarah and I—"

"And that's another fucking thing!" I say, poking his chin. He looks down at my finger with knotted brows and releases one sharp, shocked laugh. "Stop talking with Sarah about all these

OUT ON A LIMB

things *before* you talk to me. She *likes* being spoiled. That's her and Caleb's dynamic—not ours."

"It. Is. Not. A. Gift," Bo says, bending to kiss my forehead like a woodpecker between each word. "A gift would be something you want, not something you *need*," he says, moving toward the corner of the room where I've put a palm plant. "Is this new?"

I growl, turning away from him as I flop onto our bed like a dramatic starfish.

Bo silently moves to shut the door. Then he walks over and sits next to my hip on the edge of the bed. He says nothing, no doubt waiting for me to look at him. But I refuse. "If you *really* need me to, I'll send them home. But there's a chance by now it's too late. I'm pretty sure I saw our old shower door being carried outside."

I cover my face, groaning into my palms.

I love baths. I miss baths. Admittedly, I can't wait to take a bath *here,* in *my* home. I want Bo to sit in there with me and do his sudoku puzzle while I soak and prune, listening to music and telling each other about our days. I want him to look over at me and pray the bubbles will turn to white, silky film so he can see more of my body through the water. I want him to pull me out of there just to dry me off with his tongue. I want to soak in warm water when I go into labour, waiting out the early contractions in the place where I feel the most at peace.

I just don't want this tilted scale.

This uneven score. This tally I'm still unconvinced isn't being counted. Bo's gifts, kind acts, and generosity weighed against mine. The competition it feels like I'm losing.

"I don't want you to send them home," I say, my voice muffled by the hands across my face.

"So what *do* you want? A snack, maybe?"

"I'm not being cranky because I'm hungry," I say, removing my hands to glare at him.

He purses his lips and nods sarcastically. "No, you? Never."

"Tell me how to spoil you back," I say, pouting. "And do not say blowjobs—"

Bo shuts his mouth as quickly as he opened it, smiling coyly as he scratches above his eyebrow.

"I just want this to feel fair, Bo. That's all I've ever wanted."

He places his palm back on my belly and sighs out a long, heavy breath. He swipes his thumb back and forth, bunching and stretching my T-shirt in its path. Well, actually, *his* T-shirt. Most of my clothes don't fit comfortably ever since my bump popped. I refuse to buy anything new. I like wearing Bo's clothes because he gets all worked up over it. I think it's because it's almost like announcing to the world that I'm *his*. *His* woman carrying *his* baby in *his* clothing.

And I like that they smell like him.

"I know, Win. But, to me, it will *never* be fair. No matter how much I do, you're the one carrying—"

"The camp is going to take years, Bo. *Years*. If it even *does* happen—because who knows? Things could go wrong. Maybe we can't find a property. Maybe we open it, and no one comes. Maybe it will fail. Then what?"

"I believe in you *and* this idea," Bo says, shifting closer to me. "But if it didn't happen, I would *never* hold that against you. I want this for *us*. And I bet, someday soon, you'll be earning more than me doing what you've always wanted to do."

"But that doesn't mean you need to spoil me."

"I want you to love it here just as much as I love having you here."

"And I appreciate that, but these things all feel like not-so-subtle reminders of how little I have to give."

"Honey." Bo laughs without humour, his eyes pleading. "You're giving me *everything*."

"Just... talk to me first before you decide to do anything else this grand, okay? Not Sarah, not your dad, not Caleb or the other guys, but *me*. I don't find surprises fun."

"This one was"—Bo says, dropping his chin onto my belly and looking up at me with soft, puppy dog eyes as he tilts his cheek against me—"wasn't it?"

I roll my eyes, fighting a smile. "Yes," I agree stubbornly.

"And... the other night... *that* was a surprise," Bo says, wetting his lips as he lifts himself overtop of me, kissing his way up my body through my clothes.

He's talking, of course, about the new toy he got me. Well, *us*. After Bo told me he heard me from down the hall, I was never able to look at my vibrator the same. Eventually, I just tossed it. But, as it turns out, Bo wanted to play out that fantasy and got me a brand-new one he could watch me use. He wanted to see if his imagination lived up to the real thing.

Based on the crazed way in which he behaved afterward, I think it did.

Then it was my turn to live out the fantasy I'd been denying myself, using the silky black rope Bo had stored away in his closet. Turns out, he'd bought it for a cosplay of some kind, but that's beside the point. It did the job *well*.

"A compromise," I say, playing with his hair as he kisses across my belly. "Surprises under fifty dollars are allowed."

"How about five hundred?"

"What did you do?" I sit up, forcing him so far back he nearly falls off the bed.

"Nothing!" he says defensively. I raise a brow. "Nothing that I can return..."

"New rule. Starting today," I say, flopping back down to the mattress. "Fifty."

He smiles mischievously as he crawls his way up my body, then he lowers his mouth onto mine. "Agreed," he whispers against my lips. "I *do* love seeing how long it takes you to break your own rules," he says, dropping his sweet kisses down my neck and onto my chest.

Immediately, my nipples harden and beg for his attention through the thin layers of my cotton bra and T-shirt. Damn these hormones. I'm constantly fluctuating between agitated and horny these days, with not much else in between.

Meanwhile, my body feels achy and swollen all over. Still, Bo makes it obvious he couldn't be more attracted to me. I think the guy might actually prefer me knocked up.

"They'll hear us..." I say, panting as Bo brings one hand up to palm my breast and licks his way around my nipple on the other, wetting the material with his tongue. I squeeze my thighs together, trying to subdue the overwhelming urge to have him *right* now.

"Well, then, make sure you say my name clearly, honey. I want them to know who makes all those pretty noises come out of your mouth." He stands up, pulling my leggings off in one swoop. He then throws my legs over his shoulders as he drops to his knees at the end of the bed.

"No, get up here," I beg. "I need you. Hard and fast."

"Got somewhere to be?" Bo says, his mouth hovering above my clit, his proximity teasing me. His eyes flick up to me, darkened and full of lust. I subconsciously twist my hips, rising to meet him. But then I remember I actually do have somewhere to be.

"Yeah," I reply breathlessly. "The appointment *you* made..."

"Oh, the stroller testing?" he asks, kissing the inside of my thigh.

"Yeah," I say, giggling as he tickles my leg with his beard. "Stop," I whine.

"You could be a little late," he argues before swiping his tongue up my slit. He hums as he presses his mouth against me, sending a shudder up my spine.

I sit up and watch as his eyes roll back into his skull before they close tight.

"And you're supposed to be working right now," I say, running my hand through his hair.

He flicks me with his tongue, flashing his teeth as he smiles up at me. "I am *trying* to do some of my best work."

I move myself farther up the bed, away from him. "Please," I ask nicely. "I want you inside me. I want to feel you. I want... I want it rough." I move onto my knees in the centre of the bed, removing my T-shirt.

Bo stands, unfastening the buttons of his jeans before pulling them off and tossing them aside. "Fine, have it your way." He takes a step toward me, his smirk crooked and his eyes deadly as he holds out his arms. "C'mere, honey," he says, his voice arrogant as he crooks his fingers for me to follow.

"Can—Can we?" I ask, biting my bottom lip. I know that Bo's a lot more comfortable on his feet since he got his new prosthesis, but we haven't tried to have sex standing up yet. Plus, I'm not exactly as light as I once was now that I'm in my third trimester.

"Let's find out," he says, shrugging a shoulder as he leans over the bed, attempting to pull me to him.

"Don't drop me," I say, crawling toward him enthusiastically. Bo picks me up effortlessly, and I curl myself around him, my legs hooked over his hips and my arms around his neck. He then takes a few steps backward as we kiss, turning us as we go so my back hits the wall with a perfect amount of force.

Once balanced, he grinds into me, and I gasp, overcome with a heady need for him. I reach between us, tugging my panties aside, then cup him through his boxers. I work him over with my hand, feeling him harden and twitch underneath me. All the while, his kisses are on my face, neck, and shoulder. I'm growing impatient and damn near furious at the thin layer of cotton separating me from what I want.

I throw my arm back around Bo's shoulder and tighten my grip to hold myself up. "Take it off *now*."

Bo nods, removing his face from my neck for half a second before his boxers hit the floor and his hands are back on my thighs, lifting me back up his body and into position.

"Are you ready for me, honey?" he asks, holding my pussy so close above him that I literally begin shuddering with anticipation.

He tilts his hips, notching himself against my entrance. I whimper pathetically, begging for him.

"I said, are you ready for me? Because I don't plan on being gentle with you."

"Yes, yes, I'm ready. Please," I reply, my eyes screwed tight, waiting for him.

"Look at me," he commands. "Eyes open."

I open my eyes, but they're heavy, just like my breathing. "Please," I whisper, licking my lips. "Stop it," I whine when he teases me again.

"Tell me you want the bathtub," he says, his face hardened. "Tell me you *love* it."

I open my mouth to speak, but only a gasp escapes as he lowers me, angled so I press up against his hardness. Blissful in and of itself, but *not* what I want. Not him inside me.

"Bo..." I whisper, rubbing myself against him.

"I know you're not used to it, but so long as I'm around, I'll be looking after you," he says, voice low and gruff. "I consider it my job and my privilege from now on. You want things to be fair? So do I. Trust me that I know what's fair. Trust me to look after you, Win. Trust me to take care of you the way I need to."

He lifts me up, then tilts into me, filling me so completely it takes my breath away.

"Tell me." He groans into my neck as my head falls back against the wall. "Tell me who's going to take care of you," he says, his mouth pressed to the side of my cheek.

"You," I say through heavy breaths. "You are." I move my hand to his face, turning his cheek to kiss me. Bo pulls out of me, hoists me up, then hooks his arms under the backs of my knees, spreading my thighs wider for his hips to slot between.

"Hold on to me, honey," he says, pushing himself into me slowly.

"Fuck..." I groan, my teeth finding my bottom lip. "Yes," I whimper with every delicious inch of him sliding in.

"Remember," Bo says between grunts of effort, or maybe restraint, "if they're going to hear us, let them hear my name. Tell them"—he groans, his teeth at my jaw—"who's taking care of you."

I bite my lip to the point where I'm sure I could draw blood as Bo begins relentlessly pounding into me, hitting the spot deep inside that feels almost *too* good.

"Fuck," I cry out, the sound muffled by his neck. My skin is heating and blushing all over. I'm embarrassed but equally exhilarated to know we might just be heard. I bite into his shoulder, using him to mute the sounds of pleasure threatening to pour out.

Bo grunts, holding me to him and stepping to the right. With one hand wrapped around my thigh, he uses the other arm to swipe off the dresser. A dozen items clatter to the floor, but neither of us cares.

Bo drops me onto the hard surface, my back falling against the wall on impact. He tilts his hips up and away, agonisingly slow, his eyes darkened and held on where we're joined, with one hand under my knee, holding me open for him.

Then he surprises me.

Bo covers my mouth with his free hand forcefully, pushing the back of my head into the wall. His hooded eyes find my shocked ones, and he waits for my signal.

I nod. Saying, silently: *yes, sir.*

"You don't want them to hear?" he asks, leaning in so close my eyes have to widen to see him. I shake my head *no.* "Okay," he says, his hand flexing over my face. "I've got you," he says, removing himself fully. "Hold on, *princess.*"

Bo starts fucking me so hard that even more items clatter to the floor, the dresser hitting the wall in time with each thrust. His voice is strained next to my ear as he praises me. A soliloquy filled with the filthiest phrases. *Good girl. You take me so well. Your pussy is perfect. You're so fucking perfect. I love you.*

From Bo's lips, I consider it all to be poetry. Praises so beautiful and genuine and earnest that I collect each of them and lock them away inside my chest.

My toes curl as my pleasure builds like a windstorm inside my belly. The look of intensity on Bo's face as he uses my body fills me with deep, aching lust. Without warning, he removes his hand from my mouth and moves it to my hip, gripping my flesh as he pistons into me.

"Please," he begs. I know what he wants. Perhaps he's fucked all the shame out of me, but I don't care anymore. I nod for him, and he smiles as he tugs me to the edge of the dresser, angling me just right.

I whimper, throwing my head back as I feel an orgasm wash over me like a warm breeze—subtle but so damn *perfect*. The kind of release you feel in your bones all the way to the ends of your hair, possessing your body and mind.

"Bo," I cry out, gasping at the immediate feel of his release as he trembles and stills between my legs before removing himself.

I watch, my head hanging between us, as Bo pushes his cum back in with two fingers.

I'm not sure *why* I find it so hot, but I do. There's something so primal about it. Him wanting to fill me, even though I'm already pregnant. Like he's saying, not-so-subtly, he'd do it again if he could. That he's glad for it all.

He removes his fingers, and I open my mouth, smiling wickedly as he pushes them between my lips, and I suck them clean.

He laughs in a bittersweet way. In an *I cannot believe my life* kind of way that has my shoulders lifting with pride.

"So..." I say through panted breaths, smiling at the ceiling as my chest heaves. "We *can* do it standing, then."

Bo's own chest is working overtime with each quickened breath, but he still breaks into a beaming smile, his face pointed up to the ceiling. "Seems like it..." he whispers, more from exhaustion than a need to be quiet. That is *long* gone.

When he tilts his face down toward mine, looking all too pleased with a boyish grin and an arrogant satisfaction behind his eyes, I kiss him.

I kiss him because I'm grateful, even though I'm often terrible at showing it.

I kiss him because he truly does want to take care of me.

I kiss him because I think I'm going to let him.

I kiss him because I love him.

More and more each day.

CHAPTER 33

Thirty-Three Weeks Pregnant. Baby is the size of a pineapple.

I take a deep breath, cooling my frustrations, as I stare deep into the mirror at my own reflection.

I've got the cute dress on, the one Sarah insisted I buy from the maternity section that *actually* fits my growing frame. It's a sage green floor-length wrap dress with white hand-sewn flowers all over it. It ties in the back, creating the illusion of a small waist above my now prominent bump. And it showcases my new boobs—two sizes larger than they used to be.

Both Bo and I are *big* fans.

I've also got the makeup on. Though, pathetically, bending over the sink to apply mascara was causing me to get winded.

What's making me frustrated is my hair.

I had this whole vision that I'd braid it, keeping it off my face in this wispy sort of way that matches the bohemian vibe of the dress, but it's just not happening.

I've twisted and contorted myself in every which way, trying to see it in the mirror as I reach over my shoulder. But no matter what I do, my right hand will not cooperate, and I drop the third strand every time.

Once I told Bo I didn't want any more surprises, he confessed about one that he and Sarah had been cooking up ever since *his* birthday. A birthday party for me. Except, knowing me the way they do, they decided I'd rather kill two birds with one stone and have a combined baby shower *and* birthday party.

Bo insisted *this* way I could tell myself the party was for August, and sort of him too—so I caved.

But now I'm probably already late, and I look like I've never held a hairbrush in my twenty-nine years of life. I'm about to throw it into a low ponytail, curse my rectangular-shaped forehead, and call it a day when Bo knocks softly on the half-open bathroom door.

"Need a hand?" he teases, leaning on the doorframe.

I roll my eyes, smiling at his reflection as he moves to stand behind me. He's wearing a long-sleeve grey waffle-knit shirt over black jeans, looking as gorgeous as ever.

"Classic." I shake my head.

"Never gets old," he says, kissing my cheek.

"I was trying to braid my hair, and now I look like this," I say, gesturing to the mess I've made. "I've never been able to braid. I'm not sure why I thought today would be any different."

Bo rests his chin on the top of my head, curling both arms across my chest as he holds me to him. "You look beautiful, *Fred*."

"You had to ruin that compliment, huh?" I say, letting my hands roam over his forearms. "I *will* start calling you Bob."

"You look beautiful, stunning, and downright ethereal... Fred."

"I might shave my head," I whine, pouting. "Would you still love me if I shaved my head?"

"Is this like that worm question you asked me last week? Is there also a correct answer I should know about? Yes, I'd still love you if you were a worm, or bald, or—"

"When do we have to leave?" I ask, interrupting.

"About now."

"About?"

"Ten minutes ago, probably. But you're allowed to be late." He presses his lips to the top of my head, then releases both arms from around me, bringing his hands up to my hair and pulling it all back over my shoulders. "Mind if I give it a go?"

I nod shyly.

Bo separates my hair into three pieces, combing through them with his long fingers, untangling. Then he *actually* begins to braid it. I open my mouth to ask how, but he intercepts. "In middle school, I learned how to make friendship bracelets because there was a cute girl in my class who was really good at them. I guess I never forgot."

"The things we do for love..." I sigh out, admiring myself in the mirror as Bo reaches over my shoulder for the hair-tie on the counter.

"There," Bo says, letting the braid fall down my back. "I think that's good?"

He did a perfect job. He's even left all the loose, wispy parts in all the right places. I could cry.

Actually, I'm *very* pregnant and *very* in love with the guy, so I *do* cry.

"One more thing," he says, leaving me in the bathroom all alone with my watery eyes. I gather myself, fluffing my bangs in the mirror before turning to the side to get a full view of my bump. I place two hands on it and rub back and forth, soothing for both me, and I hope, August. Every day, I feel bigger than the last, and more and more ready to meet them. And with every little addition, Bo and I become more prepared.

After I moved some of my things into the master bedroom—and some of Bo's items elsewhere to make room—we found a happy medium with the rest of the house. Decorating to suit both of us and merging our styles into one. Afterward, we started on the nursery.

Bo built a crib we'd ordered offline that is made from sustainable bamboo, and I painted the walls a soft green. We put my trusted old lavender dresser in there and bought the comfiest grey rocking chair that we both now like to nap in. Plus, of course, some of my plants got moved in there too. Bo hung up shelves for books, and I've been thrifting little decor art pieces slowly over time. It's really coming together.

Bo calls it a little Hobbit's den, whereas I think of it as more of a nature-inspired cottage. Either way, we both win.

And I suppose, after today, we'll have a lot more things to fill it with.

I trace one finger from the largest point of my belly to my chest, smiling to myself as I go. When I look up, I find Bo leaned against the doorway, holding a massive bouquet of wildflowers.

"I was supposed to give these to you later, but"—he plucks out a stem of baby's breath, breaks off four small branches and then moves to stand behind me—"I think these would suit your hair." One by one, he slots tiny bunches of white flowers between the strands of my braid, his eyes concentrated as he fixes them to be precisely right.

"Perfect," he says, straightening and shoving his hands into his pockets.

"I love it," I say, twisting to admire it as best I can in the mirror, seeing Bo doing the same. "But you need something too." I pick up a purple ranunculus flower from the bunch, break its stem shorter, and reach up to tuck it over Bo's ear. "There." I kiss him, just once. "Now we match."

He smiles, his eyes sparkling down at me. "Ready to go?"

"Ready."

We make our way outside, hand in hand, out into a beautiful May day. The birds are singing, the sky is blue with the perfect splattering of clouds and the breeze smells fresh. Like newly cut grass and sunshine filtered through blossoming trees. After what has felt like a long winter, I'm so grateful to see spring every time we step outside.

Still, I'm so grateful for what *this* winter brought me.

Bo drives with the radio on, but we talk above it like always. Everyday we seem to talk about nothing and everything all at once. Every thought, every feeling, every memory recounted until we run dry. We continue to pour all of ourselves out to each other. Until our histories and stories started becoming more of a woven tapestry than a blank slate. And the *nothing* too. The insignificant observations and the silly anecdotes that no one else would care to hear. Those are just as important.

When we pull up into the driveway of Sarah and Caleb's home, I brush my hand over Bo's hair and onto his cheek. Revelling in the simple notion that he *is* real. That someone could love me *this* much. Choose to fill me up instead of pour me out. Build a fire to keep me warm instead of burn me out.

Sometimes, it feels like saying I love you isn't enough. Not when my whole life has changed because of this man.

Bo loves me for free.

No expectations. No demands. Not a single ounce of selfishness.

I love you, I think, rubbing my thumb across his cheek as he smiles shyly at me.

I love you too, he says, silently, when he winks back at me before pushing open his door and rushing to open mine before I get the chance.

"Sarah doesn't know that I know, right?" I whisper as we walk up their driveway.

"No, she really did want it to be a surprise."

"Okay," I say, stopping just short of their porch steps. "How's this then?" I ask before putting on my best shocked face, a hand gently in front of my parted lips.

Bo laughs, his throat bobbing as he takes the front steps two at a time. "Great. Very convincing." He presses the doorbell, and we wait for what feels like a *long* while before it eventually opens.

But it's not Sarah on the other side.

"Mom?" I choke out, covering my parted lips with a shaky hand.

"Yep, looked just like that," Bo whispers to himself.

My mother, who recently told me she couldn't come down until Christmas, stands in front of me. With her bleached-blond hair in long barrel curls, orange tan, and lacey, tight off-white dress. With the same familiar warmth in her smile that I wonder if I'll ever not miss.

"Hi, baby," she says, opening her arms as I rush into them.

"What—how—when?"

"Ask your man!" she laughs out, tightening her hold around me and swaying us from side to side. I look over her shoulder to see a very smug, proud Bo taking our photo before placing his phone back into his pocket.

"When?" I ask him.

"Remember that purchase I told you about the day we had the new bathtub put in? The one that I said I couldn't return *prior* to our agreement about surprises?"

I step back, my hands stuck on my mother's shoulders. She's a little shorter than me, but her heels make it so we're almost the same height. I find myself glancing over her from head to toe. "You look beautiful, Mom," I say, admiring her.

"Ah, well, I had to make a good first impression." She tilts her head towards Bo.

"Oh, right, I'm so sorry! Bo, this is my mother, June. Mom..." I say, sidestepping to wrap my arm around Bo's back. This is... *my* Bo."

"Very good to meet you, Ms. McNulty," Bo says, extending his hand.

"Anyone ever told you that you're *stupidly* tall?" my mother asks, laughing as she shakes his hand with both of hers.

"Your daughter, a few times a day."

"And, please, you can call me June. We're family now." My mother curls her lips in, smiling as she admires Bo a little *too* intently. I notice she's yet to let go of his hand and smirk at my feet. "You know, Win didn't mention how gorgeous—"

"It's really good to see you, Mom." I say, pulling her arm away and wrapping it around mine. "I've missed you," I sigh out, meaning every word more than I thought I would.

My mom stops, her eyes tracing my face with a soft smile I haven't seen much of before. Pride, I think. "You look so well, sweet girl. So... *glowy*." She boops my nose with her finger.

"Thank you for coming," I say, twitching my nose as I fight back tears. "Sorry, this happens now," I say, fanning my face and blowing out a long breath. "I've been crying a lot more these days."

"Don't cry, baby. You'll ruin your makeup."

I laugh, a touch sad but mostly amused. Same old Mom.

"How are you feeling?" she asks, her eyes held on my belly.

"Very, very pregnant," I answer truthfully, getting a chuckle from Bo. He's been amazing, but the third trimester has been no joke. I'm tender and sore all over. Cranky and swollen and constantly hungry and irritable. Still, he takes it all in stride. Every mood change and craving.

She nods knowingly. "Let's get you in a chair."

"Wait," I say abruptly, making my mom and Bo freeze on the spot. "How intense is it in there?"

My mom's smile twitches. "Sarah did what Sarah does, but you're still early. I think she wanted you here before everyone else so you could settle in before they arrive. And we're set up in the backyard. She thought you'd like that."

I choke back tears *again*. Because Sarah's a whore for spectacle. The *surprise* moment of a surprise party. Yet she let me have a subtle entrance with my mom at the door and time to settle in.

I nod, standing straighter. "I'm ready."

CHAPTER 34

S tunned, I look around Sarah's backyard.

"Win!" Sarah says, bounding over in her bright pink dress. "Surprise!"

I don't respond. *Can't* respond just yet. Bo's got his hand on the small of my back, but other than that, I feel completely untethered to the earth as I take in the view. It's *so* beautiful.

There's one long table for no more than twenty people that's covered with wildflowers and light green tablecloths. There's a clothing line of linen baby onesies and a pale green balloon arch over a table of food and drinks. A mostly empty table with one wrapped gift placed on top.

"Sarah, I—"

"Before you say anything, you should know I wanted to go *way* bigger than this and dialled it back. So if you say it's too much, I will pounce on you."

"I love it," I say, admiring my best friend with tear-filled eyes. "I was going to say that I love it. Thank you. It's perfect."

"Really?" Her smile is proud, if a little uncertain. "That easy?"

I nod, smiling wide. "It's beautiful, Sar," I say, pulling her into a hug. "Thank you," I whisper over her shoulder.

"It wasn't just me, you know," Sarah says before we step away. She looks at Bo with one raised brow, then back to me.

I play along, looking up at him with narrowed eyes. "Did you know about this?" I ask, trying not to break a smile.

"Guilty," Bo says, raising his hands up in the air, looking sheepishly at Sarah.

"He did the party favours," Sarah says, picking one up and handing it to me.

Fred's Flowers, Bo's handwriting reads on a small white box. I turn it over in my hand. "You made these?" I ask him, *actually* surprised.

He shrugs, smiling coyly. "I wanted a pirate theme, but Sarah said no."

"I didn't think you'd want to explain *that* particular inside joke over and over," she says, smirking. "Plus, I gave him *one* pirate thing," Sarah says, pointing toward the gift table with letter blocks that spell out "*ahoy there, baby.*"

"It's amazing." I say, smiling between them. "Seriously, it is exactly what I would have chosen. Thank you."

"We make a good team," Sarah says, pushing Bo's shoulder.

"It's because I do as I'm told," Bo whispers into my ear.

"Yeah, you're a very good boy," I whisper back, patting his cheek.

The afternoon passed in a sweet, bustling, tender blur.

The guests arrived slowly a little after twelve. My mother took charge of greeting them and guiding them toward the backyard, proudly introducing herself as Grandma June time and time again. All of Bo's friends, who I hope have also become mine, mingled nicely with a few friends of mine from Westcliff and my ex-coworkers from the café that Sarah and Bo managed to track down. Henry and his parents, Tonya and James, came too—and Henry got a big kick out of being the only kid at the party. Sarah made beautiful cupcakes, each decorated to look like a different flower. And Caleb did what Caleb does best, helping wherever needed most. Which was conveniently near the food table, alongside Bo, most of the afternoon.

I managed to only blush half a dozen times while Bo and I opened gifts. And it was truly, genuinely lovely. To feel all the love for a baby they've yet to meet. Who, as Bo said during his speech, was *such* a welcome and needed surprise.

As the afternoon sun faded to a chilly spring evening, the few of us left standing took the party inside, not wanting the day to end. We called Bo's dad to show him how much he was missed and introduce him to my mom. My mother hogged the phone for a while as she sat cosied up on the couch with Sarah. Naturally, she made one too many jokes about them both being hot, single grandparents. Or GILFs, as she called them, much to Sarah's amusement.

Eventually, Bo and I said our goodbyes, packed up our car with an absolutely *absurd* number of presents, and drove home alone—my mother insisting she'd rather stay at Sarah's. I, admittedly, was relieved. I'm so glad my mom is here, but I'm learning that she and I do best in little doses.

"Did you have a good time?" Bo asks, his hand on my thigh as we turn onto our street.

"I *really*, really did," I say, turning to smile at him. "Did you?"

"Yeah," he says, pulling the car into the driveway. "I did."

"I have a present for you," I say proudly. "I thought it would blow my cover if I brought it with us, but I wanted you to have something too."

"I actually have something for you too," Bo says, turning off the car.

"I bet mine is better," I tease, taking off my seatbelt.

Bo smirks, shaking his head as he gets out of the car and walks over to my door, helping me out. We walk hand in hand up the driveway and into the house.

Bo watches me, soft eyes but serious smile, as I take off my shoes and drop onto the couch.

"What?" I ask, my eyes narrowing on him.

"You," he says, admiring me thoughtfully. "Will it *ever* stop?" he asks slowly.

"What?" I say, placing my hands on my belly. "Growing?" I laugh, falling backward. "I don't see how I *could* get any bigger."

"No," he says, stopping next to the couch. He lifts my feet, sits down, then drops them onto his lap. "Not that."

"Then what?" I ask.

"Wanting you this much."

I raise a brow. "Do you *want* it to stop?"

He shakes his head before pressing his ear to my belly. I bring one hand up and brush over his hair lovingly. "Then I don't think it will."

"It's tiring," he says, lips squished against my bump.

"Ah, well, so sorry," I laugh out.

"No, I don't mean it like that. I mean that it feels like my heart is on the outside of my body," he says, his voice low. "And I miss you so much, even when you're just a few feet away. I think about you every second of the day and struggle to think of much else. I meant what I said that first night. You *are* maddening."

I run my fingers through his hair, letting it fall against the back of my knuckles. "I know. I feel it too. But it's also kind of wonderful, right?"

He sits up after pressing a kiss to my belly, then reaches under the coffee table for a box. It's the size of a shoebox but wooden with a dark grain and golden clasp.

"What's this?" I ask, sitting up eagerly, twisting to place my feet on the floor.

"It's... well, I suppose, it's us," he says, handing it to me. "So far."

I hold it in my lap, tracing the wood with my eyes and palm.

"When you first told me about the baby, I started thinking a lot more about my mom. Though I didn't have much in terms of memories, my dad had all these... remnants of her. He kept everything. So every time I needed a piece of my mom, I knew I could go to him, and he'd show me something new." Bo turns, placing his knee on the couch to face me. "He had this box under his bed filled with photos, jewellery. Things as insignificant as buttons that had fallen off her coat or pennies she'd picked up off the street. All of Mom's notebooks filled with music she'd written...journals, notes, letters..." Bo says, looking toward the dining room over my shoulder.

I reach out my right hand, putting it on his knee and squeezing as best I can.

Bo smiles wistfully, taking a deep inhale, his eyes turning back toward me. "And through those things, through those little pieces of her, I learned that her story wasn't just how it ended. I learned about her life. I saw all those scraps of her Dad kept and realised how deeply they had loved each other." He swallows, licking his lips. "I wanted our baby to have that too. Even if *we* weren't in love. Even if the baby was unexpected... I wanted them to have something they could hold on to. Tangible memories. Something that meant if *one* of us..." he says, his chin folding down and his voice wobbling. "If *I* got sick again and..."

I put my hand on his cheek, brushing gently along the line of his beard with my thumb. "You're not going anywhere," I say adamantly, nodding my head so he does the same.

He smiles, tilting his lips toward my hand. "I know. I'm not allowed."

"Damn right," I whisper, my voice wavering.

"Anyway, I wanted them to have this," Bo says, pointing to the fastener of the box. "But now, I think I want you to see it too. Because... I always wondered if my mom *knew* Dad'd kept these things. That he'd been so madly in love with her, that she was memorialized before she was even gone."

I unhook the latch and open the box, revealing the treasure trove of items inside.

"It's mostly just junk..." Bo says, rubbing the back of his neck as I pull out a receipt and read it over.

"From... from the café on Cosgrove?" I ask.

"The day you told me about them."

I reach in, pulling out a mason jar of stones and turquoise sea glass.

"From our walks to the beach," Bo says.

I laugh, tears springing free as I pull out the photo of us from that first ultrasound—my dazed, confused smile in hilarious contrast next to Bo's bright enthusiasm in the lobby of the medical building. Underneath it is a photo of me, one that I didn't know he'd taken. I'm gardening in the backyard, dirt across my face and tummy sticking out from under my T-shirt. It had to have been less than a week ago.

"And this?" I say, laughing as I hold up a small, rectangular piece of plastic.

"I may have taken some *Catan* pieces... from that first game night," Bo says, shrugging one shoulder. "Don't tell Sarah."

I pull out the *father-to-be* book Sarah gave him, now annotated with notes in the margins and flagged pages with bright pink tabs. I flick through it, realising that he's left notes to the baby amongst the pages. Telling them how excited he is for every stage. How much he can't wait to meet them. *Your mom is doing such a good job at growing you*, I read. *She's going to be an incredible mom.*

Every little item I pull out next fills my heart more and more. The pack of twenty questions, with short forms of our answers written on the back of each card. His copies of the ultrasound photos, scrap pieces of paper, more candid photos of me—my bump going from unnoticeable to overflowing.

"This is a beautiful gift, Bo," I say, wiping my tears. I move the box to the couch beside me and wrap my arms around him. "I'm sorry," I whisper, crying. "I only made you socks."

"I love socks."

"I love you," I say.

"There's one more thing that I took out."

"Hmm?" I ask, leaning back as I wipe my tears away.

"Remember on the first day, I told you I hid something so that you wouldn't find it while snooping?" He reaches into the side of the couch. "I stashed it here earlier, for the record. This isn't where I hid it."

"So mysterious..." I say, my smile faltering into confusion as he pulls out... *oh.*

"This I can't explain," he says, holding out the red bandanna I lost on Halloween. "This I kept before I knew *anything* about the baby. Before I knew how much I was going to love you. Because, clearly, some part of me already did."

I cover my mouth, looking down at his hand, clasped tightly around the bandanna as my brain catches up with my soaring heart.

"I think I knew that I needed a piece of *you* to hold on to. I was walking out of that room and I saw this on the chair next to the door and... I don't know. I just needed to take a part of that night with me."

"But... but you left."

"You said you wanted *casual*, Win."

"You really need to stop listening to me," I say, tears springing free *again*.

"Noted," Bo says, smirking. He takes a long breath, steadier this time, as he searches my eyes. "Every day for *weeks* afterward, I thought about you. I thought about your smile. Your laugh. Your eyes... your mouth. I came close to asking Caleb for your number, but I was scared. I was scared after everything with Cora, with my cancer... with all of it, that I wasn't enough. That I wouldn't be enough to get you from casual to more."

I shake my head, *refusing* to accept that he ever felt that way, wishing I'd known, and place my hand in his, squeezing tightly.

"Then, on one random day in December, you texted me. I felt like I'd won the lottery."

I laugh, rolling my eyes, as Bo brings my hand to his mouth and kisses my wrist.

"Ever since then, I've fallen deeper and deeper in love with you. Your heart, your kindness, your strength, your joy, your selfless-ness." He reaches around me, dropping the bandanna back into the box along with the rest of our beautiful, if unconventional story.

"Bo, I..."

He turns, reaching into the couch again, smiling mischievously. "One more thing..."

"I'm searching the couch from now on," I say, wiping a tear off my cheek. "You'll have to find a new hiding spot."

He turns back around, his palm covering something he's placed in his lap. Something, I suspect, that's shiny and in a smaller box than the one sitting next to me. I put a hand on my stomach involuntarily, feeling the baby kick with the quickened rhythm of my heart.

"Bo," I choke out.

"You are my soul's purpose, Win. To know you, to love you, to build a family with you, to spend every day taking care of you, to watch you shine and get all the good things you deserve out of this life." Bo ducks his head and reveals the small leather box in his hands, opening it to show me the most stunning, simple gold band.

"Yes," I say involuntarily, looking up to him. "Yes," I repeat.

He chuckles lightly, shaking his head. "Can I ask first?"

"Oh, yes. Sorry." I wave him on, smiling as tears roll over the corners of my upturned lips.

"Winnifred June McNulty, love of my life and mother of my child, will you *please* marry me?"

"I will," I say, throwing myself at him. "I will, and I *will* be proposing back to you."

"It's only fair," Bo says, his lips trembling against my own.

"It's beautiful," I say, kissing him sloppily as he attempts to slip the ring on my finger. "But it's far too small, honey. I'm *very* pregnant."

"We'll get it resized when we put a stone on it," he says, holding it out to me.

I slide the ring onto the ring finger on my right hand, which it's *far* too big for.

"It was my mom's," Bo says, bringing my right hand between us, twiddling it with his thumb. "I hope that's okay."

"Absolutely," I say, punctuated by a kiss. "I wouldn't want it any other way."

For the rest of the night, I wear the ring on my smaller thumb, refusing to take it off. We eat leftover food from the baby shower in our pyjamas and dance to Frank Sinatra in the dining room afterward, my belly poking out between us.

All evening I look around the house, look at my fiancé, look at my belly, smiling with so much gratitude it's quite nearly painful. Thinking that I cannot wait for whatever comes next. How *capable* I feel to face it all with Bo at my side.

August Durand was born at 11:56pm on July thirty-first, only four minutes shy of her namesake. Her mother decided on the middle name Sarah, and her father decided that he'd never witnessed anything as formidable as his wife-to-be during labour. It was a short but intense delivery—having barely made it to the hospital in time—but they held hands through it all and welcomed their daughter with tears streaking down their smile-risen cheeks. As a matter of fact, the new parents cried far more than little August as the nurses placed her across her mother's chest for the very first time. They lay side by side, curled around one another inside the narrow hospital bed, and looked down at their daughter with awe—completely enraptured by every perfect piece of her. Her cute, if a little purple, feet. Her tiny, adorable hands that they couldn't stop reaching for. Her bald head and dark eyes, leaving them guessing at who she'll most resemble. They speculated aloud to one another in those first few moments that no baby had been or will ever be as wise as August. They watched her as she seemingly took in her surroundings, her eyes opened wide and surprisingly aware as she lifted her head with muscles that shocked even the nurses. *She's smart like her father*, her mother said quietly. *She's strong like her mother*, her father said loudly to anyone who would listen. *We love you*, they whispered to her over and over and over again. *Thank you*, her father added, kissing her mother. *I did it*, her mother whispered, kissing him back.

EPILOGUE

Ten Years Later

"Gus!" I shout, tripping over her purple Converse on my way through the door. "Your shoes... again!"

Charlie, our five-year-old, comes bounding over as soon as I step inside. I kick the shoes out of the way to shut the door with my hip and drop my suitcase.

"Want some help?" she asks, holding out two hands. I smile at her, scrunching my nose as she does the same. She's got freckles just like her father and older sister do. Sometimes I want to paint them on myself before I leave the house just so I can match them all. Joey, our two-year-old, looks more like me with her black hair and blue eyes and no freckles yet. And her drooling and affinity for poop jokes, as Bo likes to point out.

"Hi, baby. Thank you." I drop the brown paper bag filled with groceries into Charlie's arms, and she nearly collapses under the weight of it. "You sure you got that? Is Dad—"

"Here!" Bo says, appearing in the living room with Joey glued to his hip as always. She's got a wide-spread smile slathered with chocolate icing, and Bo's got flour all over his navy sweater and trousers. "We got a bit delayed. The girls wanted to help me make you a welcome home cake, but then Joey was the only one who stuck it out. None of them are in their costumes yet, and August, apparently, doesn't want to be a pirate this year. So now the cake is still baking, and no one is dressed on time to leave, and I'm not even sure where—"

I go on my toes to kiss him, cupping his face with my hand to pull him the rest of the way down toward me. "Happy anniversary, darling." I pat his cheek, searching his eyes until he takes a much-needed breath. "I missed you."

Bo settles, his chest falling. "Hi, honey. Sorry." He bends down, kissing me again. "How was your trip? We missed you too. *I* missed you."

"Mama home!" Joey says, her messy hands reaching for me. I take her, kissing all over her face as she squeals. Bo comes behind me and tucks my hair out of the way so she at least doesn't get that part of me covered in chocolate icing. We don't have time for showers before Sarah's Halloween party.

"I grabbed extra candy to leave out on the porch." I point to the bag that Charlie is struggling to drag across the floor toward the kitchen. "Someone should probably help her..." I mumble, following after Bo to the kitchen. He swoops down and picks up both Charlie and the bag of groceries on his way. She giggles, flopping like a fish in his arms.

"So, your trip?" he asks over his shoulder, dropping the bag onto the counter but snuggling Charlie closer. We don't have favourites, of course. But Charlie is Bo's twin in every way. While they share the same golden hair, hazel eyes, and freckles as August—Charlie's temperament is *all* Bo. August has *strong* firstborn energy. Since birth, that girl has been ruling our house. Hell, she was ruling our lives *before* birth.

But Charlie is our peaceful, helpful, curious girl. She asks a million questions every single day, especially before bed. It's a tactic to delay bedtime, of course, but they're all such interesting questions, so we can't help but give in. Bo especially. He lies next to her, his long body crammed into her small twin bed, and they ponder existence together.

Why does the Earth have so many people? Will there ever be too many people? Are there people on other planets? Galaxies? Do they have chocolate too?

She *also* has his sweet tooth.

But they *all* have that.

"Honey?" Bo asks, smiling softly. "Your trip?"

I shake myself from my wandering thoughts. "Sorry, yes. It was great. Camp Piyette was *stunning*. I took pictures of a few things I think we should try to fit into the budget next summer. Also, they've just upgraded to be all-season, and I *do* think we should seriously consider—"

"Mom?" August says, pulling her headphones off, halfway from the bathroom back to her bedroom. "When did you get home?" She takes off running toward me.

"Hi!" I say as she crashes into my side, the opposite hip from her baby sister. August circles her arms around my waist and squeezes. Because, suddenly, she's big enough to reach all the way around her mama and do such a thing.

I blinked, maybe three times too many, and now she's this big, strong girl with so many clever thoughts and strong opinions.

"I missed you too, kid," I say, my chin resting on the top of her head. "It was four days too many."

"Wait! Me too!" Charlie says, tugging Bo by the collar. He walks over to us, laughing as he drops Charlie onto my shoulders.

"Happy Halloween, my little gremlins!" I say, giggling as I juggle all three of them. "Were you good for Dad? Do we still get to go to Auntie Sarah's party tonight?" I look to Bo for an answer.

He smiles proudly, a tilt of his chin as he admires all of his girls. "It was touch and go for a minute there. There was a biting incident," he points to Joey, wearing an insincere scowl, "and someone *else* failed to tell me about her math homework until the night before it was due."

"August Sarah Durand, you *know* it hurts your father when we keep math from him."

August rolls her eyes. "I just forgot. I got an A on it, though."

"Course you did, smartie pants. And what about Miss Charlie?" I say, shrugging my shoulders so she bounces. "What did she get up to?"

"Charlie was Charlie," Bo says, grinning from ear to ear. "She kept everyone in line."

"I also found a bird's nest in the backyard. It's empty... for now," Charlie tells me over top of my head.

"A bird's nest? That's amazing!"

"Can I get down now?" she asks Bo, who nods and walks over, lifting her off and placing her onto the floor. She takes off skipping toward her bedroom. I shuffle Joey up my hip, but she reaches for Bo, who's got a washcloth ready and waiting to clean her up.

"So..." I say, turning my full attention to August. "What's this I hear about you not wanting to be a pirate this year?" I ask, brushing her hair away from her face. I trace the line of the teeny, faded scar on her forehead with my thumb. She ran head-first into our coffee table a little after her first birthday. Bo broke it down into firewood the very next day. We were so new to parenting, then. So sensitive to every cut, bump, and bruise. That one, though, *was* awful. "Have we finally outgrown our little tradition?"

"Will you be upset?" August asks, looking cautiously between Bo and me.

"No, of course not, sweetie. Just, what will you dress as? It's a bit late to go shopping."

"I was thinking a ghost. If you're cool with me cutting up a sheet..."

I immediately sense her hesitancy. The *do it first, then ask for forgiveness afterward* attitude I swear she somehow inherited from her Aunt Sarah. Bo and I make eye contact from his crouched position on the floor as he wipes Joey clean. He grimaces, and I immediately spot the missing scissors from the knife block on the counter.

"Well, that depends, sweetie. Did you *already* cut the sheet?"

"Maybe." She smiles mischievously, twisting from side to side. It's so similar to her dad's guilty face that it's *very* hard to be as annoyed as I probably should be. But I just got home. I can't be the bad cop *right* away. And I would have said yes *if* she'd asked first.

I close my eyes, nodding as I take a deep inhale.

"Sorry," she says softly. "It *was* an old one, from the closet."

"Ask first next time, kid. Go get ready. We're supposed to be out of here in ten minutes." I kiss her forehead, then bend down to pick up a now naked and clean Joey off the floor. "And let's get *you* ready, parsnip."

Bo pulls the delicious smelling cake out of the oven as I carry Joey down the hall toward the bedroom that she and Charlie share. Inside their orange and floral explosion of a room, I find Charlie already half-changed into her black and white striped leggings and pulling her pirate dress over her head.

"Aye, aye, Captain Charlie!"

"Aye, aye, Mommy!" she says, giggling as she unsheathes an imaginary sword from her belt loop.

"Your sword is in the closet," I tell her.

"Win?" Bo calls out, shouting from the kitchen. "Your mom is calling. She wants to see the girls' costumes."

"I'm dressing Joey!" I say, forcing Joanna to remain still by pinning her between my knees. She's so much more active than the other girls were at her age—I swear she'd scale a wall if given the chance. "Tell her we'll call when they're all dressed!"

Bo appears at the door, holding a phone in his hand, pointed outward toward us, apologising silently with a tilted grin.

"Oh, hey, Mom! Sorry, it's a little *busy* at the moment," I say, looking at Bo with a deadly smile.

"Charlie June, are you going as a pirate *again*?" Mom asks. She *always* calls her Charlie June. The moment we told her June was her middle name, Grandma June decided Charlie had two *first* names.

"Yes, Grandma," Charlie says, running over to the phone. "But not August. She's a ghost this time."

"And Joey?"

"A parrot," I say, holding her up to the screen. The beloved costume that each of our girls has worn their first few Halloweens. "It's definitely the last year it's going to fit any of them." I pout toward Bo, off screen. "I could barely do up the zipper."

"I guess we'll just have to have another," Bo says, giving the phone to August as she passes behind him in the hallway. With two eyeholes cut in not exactly the right place, Gus takes the phone and walks away, chatting busily to her grandmother.

"And put them *where*, exactly?" I ask, looping my arms around Bo's neck. We've already filled this little house with as much furniture, children, and love as it can probably hold. But we're sentimental people. Neither of us wants to leave the home where we fell in love or brought our girls home to. We've marked the girls' heights against the bedroom door since they could stand. We've planted an apple tree in the backyard, above their makeshift treehouse, that is just starting to harvest fruit. The greenhouse has grown over with ivy, the earth claiming it back. And I feel the same—claimed by this house.

He hums, tucking his face against my neck and breathing me in. "I missed you."

"Don't dodge the question," I say as he trails kisses along my jaw. "And don't distract me either." I giggle.

"Haven't you heard? I have a hotshot wife. She could buy us a fancy new house," he says, his hands drifting low on my back.

"Oh, could she, now?" I ask, tilting up to kiss him.

"Maybe if I ask nicely..." he says, tugging my lip between his teeth. "Or *not* so nicely?"

"I missed you too," I say, brushing his hair out of his face. He's continued to grow his hair and beard over the years, and I *really* like it this long. It suits him. He also ditched the contact lenses for glasses permanently—after I begged for a few years.

"But no new house. I'm staying put here. This is *our* home. How could we possibly leave? It's bad enough when we're up at the camp all summer."

"Fine, we'll dig out the basement."

"Yes. And have *cellar* children."

"They'll age like fine wine," he says, smiling. "Don't you want another?" he asks, his hands gripping the fullness of my hips as if he's ready to get started.

"Do you really think we could handle another? You just spent four days alone with them—you seriously want more?"

"You know I do, honey." He brushes his nose against mine, then his lips. "Want to play worst-case scenario?" he asks, his mouth gently brushing across mine. "Or... best case?"

After the camp was a roaring success for the fifth year in a row—and Bo couldn't resist knocking me up for a third time—he decided to quit corporate life and become a full-time dad. He's never been happier. Still, three children is already a *lot* of children.

I check my watch and groan, kissing him one last time. But he doesn't get the memo. "Bo, hey," I say between kisses, smiling against his mouth. "Quit it. We're gonna be late."

"Let me help you get dressed, then," he says, scooping me up and hauling me over his shoulder as I laugh ferociously. "I seem to recall there being fishnets one year. Can we bring those back?" he asks, turning the corner into the hallway.

"Dada!" Joey says, standing next to Charlie, who narrows her eyes at me. "No!"

"We've been spotted," I whisper, holding on to Bo for dear life as he takes off jogging.

"Put Mommy down!" Charlie says, giggling as she swipes at Bo's calves with her foam sword.

"Never!" he shouts.

Yes, it's chaos. And yes, we have our hands full. But it's a perfect little life. A beautiful, contented life. Hours spent by the water when we can. Cosy days on the couch when we need them. Dancing in the dining room whenever we want.

And as August turns the corner, leaning against the wall as she shakes her head at just how *ridiculous* her parents and siblings are behaving. I thank her, silently, for all she's given me.

For all she's taught me. For bringing her dad and me together. For making me realise just *how* capable I am. For every single wonderful thing that's happened since she entered our lives and flipped them upside down.

And I know for certain that I'd do it all again.

Acknowledgements

Thank you so much for reading Out On a Limb! I poured so much of myself into writing this one, and I'm so grateful you gave it your time. If you skipped over the author's note at the beginning, I'd encourage you to read it, as that explains just how important this story was for me to write.

I've never relied on my friends, family, and online community more than while I was writing this book. I think it's partially because of the busy season of life my husband, kids, and I were in, but also because of how *deeply* personal this book is. Often, I felt as if I was leaving too much of myself on the page—unsure if it was at all entertaining or worthwhile for the reader. So this time around, my process included a *lot* of friends and members of the romance community who were willing to lend me their eyes, ears, and opinions.

A.k.a. I made this book *everyone's* problem.

So thank you to my incredible support system, family, friends, alpha and beta readers, and everyone who let me voice-note incessantly about these characters. Specifically, Sophie, who spent *hours* on the phone with me planning, plotting, and de-esca-lating my anxiety—this book wouldn't exist without you. Tabitha and Tarah, for their friendship, support, and guidance—I adore you both endlessly. Millie, for her kindness, enthusiasm, and friendship throughout this process (and for inviting me to see Taylor Swift with you, because that was the best night of my life). Esther and Laura for being willing to put up with my nonsense and love me despite it all. Natasha, Meg, Marianne, Taylor Smith, Kelsey, Janni, Gracie, and Zarin (a.k.a. Doctor Salim), for being such incredible champions of me and my work and reading each and every stage of this book. Christina, for being my first writer-friend and one of the kindest people I know. Taylor Torres, Julie Olivia, R.M. Derrick, and Lindsey Lanza, for making the indie author community a more beautiful place and supporting me through this project! And Abi, who is the Sarah to my Win (though we're not all that similar to them in real life).

Thank you to my editor (saviour) Beth, my cover designer Mary Scarlett, and the incredible Kelsey, who designed the artwork for the title page. I'm very, very lucky to be able to work with you all.

To the *Bookstagram* and *Booktok* communities, who embraced the *Next* series and allowed me to pursue this authoring *thing* full time—I have endless gratitude for you all. You've changed my life, and more importantly, my kids' lives too. The internet can be an incredible, safe, welcoming, and encouraging place when *good* people make it so—and the *bookish* corner of the internet is the best of the best.

Then, the man of the hour, Ben. I dedicated this book (my favourite yet) to you for a reason. I love you so much it's honestly a bit gross. I think you're the funniest, kindest, hottest, most dedicated person to ever exist. When my brain was being mean to me during this process, you took it all in stride and continued to love me the way I needed—as you have for twelve years now. Thank you for never making me feel anything but capable, strong, and beautiful. I'm sorry I borrowed some (all) of your nerdiness for Bo. I meant it with only the highest praise. Thank you for tying my shoelaces, braiding my hair, helping with buttons, and all the things you do to help me feel less frustrated.

If you made it this far, thank *you*, dear reader. Whether you're new to my books or whether you've been here since my debut, thank you for spending your time with my characters. It's a true joy to write them for you.

Lastly, to my fellow disabled folks of all shapes, sizes, abilities, and understandings—we deserve love too. Most of all, we are worthy of it. But be sure to give it to yourself first.

About Author

Hannah Bonam-Young is an Amazon bestselling author from Ontario, Canada. She lives with her childhood-friend-turned-husband Ben, two kids, and bulldog near Niagara Falls on the traditional territory of the Haudenosaunee and Anishinaabe peoples. Hannah  writes romances featuring a cast of diverse, disabled, marginalized, and LGBTQIA+ folks wherein swoon-worthy storylines blend with the beautiful, messy, and challenging realities of life. When not reading or writing romance you can find her having living-room dance parties with her kids or planning any occasion that warrants a cheese board. You can keep in touch with her at @authorhannahby on Instagram.

Made in the USA
Coppell, TX
16 October 2023